OF ICE AND VILLAINS

A DARK FANTASY ROMANCE

HOUSE OF CRYOS
BOOK 1

VERONICA LANCET

Copyright © 2024-2025 by Veronica Lancet

Editing by Emily Lawrence Editing

Cover by: Addictive Covers

All rights reserved.

No part of this book may be reproduced in any form or by any electronic or mechanical means, including information storage and retrieval systems, without written permission from the author, except for the use of brief quotations in a book review.

No AI has been used in the making of this book.

The contents of this book may *not* be used in training any AI.

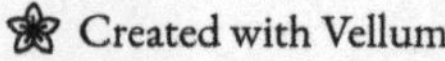 Created with Vellum

OF ICE AND VILLAINS

PREFACE

Of Ice and Villains is a dark fantasy romance. It is part of a trilogy and ends on a cliffhanger. While this is not very dark, reader discretion is advised. Previously known as Mayhem and Minnie.

Trigger Warnings:
Attempted SA
Blood
Desecration of a corpse
Gore
Murder
Mentions of DV (not between the main characters)
Torture

ONE

IT'S BEEN one hundred and seventy-four days since my last kill.

One hundred and seventy-four days since I last felt the thrill of the hunt.

My heart beats faster in my chest as the images flash in my brain. The sight and smell of blood fill my senses until I'm almost drunk on it. But memories are a paltry substitute for the real thing.

I tap my foot uncontrollably against the hardwood floor. Biting on my nail, I move my finger a bit farther into my mouth until I bite down on flesh.

The pain makes it a little more bearable.

"Mr. Spencer-Astor, I asked you a question."

My gaze shoots up.

I blink.

"You did?"

"Yes. I did," Dr. Leonard, my therapist, says with a roll of her eyes.

I'm pretty sure she shouldn't be rolling her eyes at a patient. But I'm a rather aggravating case, if I do say so myself. We've been meeting twice a week for three months now, and we've barely made any progress. Not that I don't want to. I really do. Otherwise, I wouldn't have sought her help. But I have a very limited attention span thanks to my ADHD, and she speaks far too much for me to be able to focus on everything she's saying.

Like now.

She's been asking too many questions.

Shouldn't a patient speak more than a therapist?

But I suppose she just loves hearing the sound of her own voice—not the best quality in someone whose job is to listen.

Perhaps I should kill *her*. But that would go against my moral code—I do have one, albeit it's rather skewed. I don't kill women. And no matter how annoying Dr. Leonard is, the sessions have helped temper my urges.

A little.

I bite harder on my finger.

"Can you repeat the question?" I ask, letting my lips curve into an amiable smile.

She presses her lips together in annoyance. She does that quite often.

"I asked when the last time you've seen your family was," she repeats.

I blink again.

"A year ago," I answer with a shrug.

The tapping on the floor intensifies.

"When will you see them again?"

I tilt my head to the side and narrow my eyes at her.

What's she trying to get at?

"I'm here to talk about my urges, Doctor, not my family," I say in an even voice.

Not that she knows exactly *what* urges I'm talking about. That would be criminal, and she'd be forced to report me to the police.

As far as Dr. Leonard knows, she's treating me for my obsessive tendencies, or as she calls it in her medical terms, obsessive-compulsive disorder. It's not too far from the truth. I'm obsessive. One might say fanatical. But not about mundane stuff like the matching color of my socks and underwear, though they're all black—see, problem solved. No, my obsession runs far deeper than that.

I'm obsessed with watching the light go out of people's eyes. Slowly.

I'm obsessed with seeing their blood paint the walls red.

I'm obsessed with...well, death.

I clear my throat.

"My mother's birthday party is soon," I mention.

Unfortunately for me, it's an invitation I cannot refuse. My mother would get sad. And I hate it when my mother gets sad.

Dr. Leonard nods.

"Good. That will be a good opportunity to be among loved ones. You spend too much time on your own."

"I like it on my own," I clip out.

I don't like *not* being on my own. I started living on my own the moment I turned eighteen, and although I see my family once a year or so, I've lived alone for the last ten years.

It's better that way. I can be myself without sending someone screaming for the hills.

"Do you?" She raises a brow. "You're almost twenty-nine. Haven't you ever thought about settling down? Meeting someone?"

My lip twitches. We've talked about this before, and the answer is no. Why does she think a few months would have changed my outlook on things?

"No," I state harshly.

"I think it would do you some good, Mr. Spencer-Astor. You have never been in a relationship before. You have not even dated. Isn't that right?"

"I don't have an interest in it."

"Human beings are not supposed to be alone. We are social creatures, Mr. Spencer-Astor."

Little does she know that at times I'm more animal than human being.

"I don't require anyone in my life, Doctor. May we change the topic?"

She clicks her tongue against her teeth. The sound rakes on my brain, and a vision of snapping her neck appears before me.

Calm down, I chant to myself. *You do not kill women.*

I wouldn't even enjoy killing Dr. Leonard. She'd probably bitch at me while I was killing her as she does during our sessions. But at least then she'd shut up.

Hmm, appealing...

"This is your homework for the month, Mr. Spencer-Astor. I'd like you to meet someone, put yourself out there."

"No," I grit my teeth.

"Yes," she counters. She waves her finger at me as if I were a little boy in need of chastising. Although I suppose considering her advanced age, she does see me as such.

My tapping becomes more erratic.

"I think we're done with this session, Doctor." I stand up and turn my back to her.

"Mr. Spencer-Astor? Mr. Spencer-Astor?" she calls out after me as I exit her office.

I leave a hundred-dollar bill at the receptionist's office and stride out of the building without a backward glance.

Pity. I thought we were making some progress. But it seems it might be time to seek out another therapist.

Grabbing my car keys out of my pocket, I head to the parking lot and get in my car.

The therapy session lasted exactly fifteen minutes. And in those fifteen minutes, my car was entirely covered in snow.

I hate snow.

While I wait for the obnoxious substance to melt from my hood, I check my phone.

Six missed calls. From my mother.

I groan aloud.

I know better than not to return her calls.

Clearing my voice, I dial her number.

"Marlowe, dear. Why did you not answer when I called?"

"I was busy, Mom," I add drily.

"Doing what? We all know you're not doing much with your life," she chides in that motherly tone of hers.

"Thanks for the vote of confidence, Mom. What would I do without your precious advice?"

"I'm serious, dear. You're always cooped up in that house of yours. When is the last time you've had fun?"

"It's a very nice house," I mumble.

"I didn't ask whether your house is nice or not. Although that's good to know since you won't allow any of us to visit you—"

"Mom, you get one visit from me a year. Be thankful."

"But it's not enough," she whines.

I can imagine her pout. She always pouts.

"It's enough for me."

She tsks.

"Why can't you be more like your older brother? He loves coming over, and *not* only once a year."

"Because my brother is a wimp who needs your constant supervision to do anything. I do not."

"Yes, yes. I know you've always been so independent. But would it cost you much to come visit more than once a year? I do miss you a lot."

"We talk daily," I remind her.

"But it's been a year since I've last hugged you!" she exclaims. "Talking is not a substitute for physical interaction. Or is it that you've found someone?" Her tone becomes excited. "You'll finally give me grandkids?"

I hate hugs. And physical interaction.

"Mom," I groan. "Can we not do this right now?"

"If not now then when? I was hoping you'd bring someone special to the party and—"

"It's enough that I'm coming. Don't push your luck," I tell her sternly.

"I don't know what I did wrong, Marlowe. All your other siblings turned out fine except for you. Why can't you be a team player too?"

"Because I'm not," I grit my teeth. "Now if that's all you wanted to talk about, I'm going to hang up," I say, checking my watch. It will take me about an hour to get home. Since I always go to bed at eleven on the dot, that means I'll have time to watch five episodes of *Supernatural*.

"Wait!"

"What?" I ask and roll my eyes.

"What about the job I asked you to do?"

"It's done. But it's high time Cristopher dealt with his own shit."

"Marlowe! Language."

"Sorry," I mutter. "But he needs to learn to stand on his own feet. What is he going to do on his own?"

"Your brother is the artistic type," my mother interjects. "He doesn't have your affinity with computers. We're a family and we need to help each other out."

"Yeah, well, he fucking needs to learn that everything you post on the internet *stays* on the internet."

"Marlowe!" Her scandalized voice makes me grimace.

"*Fricking*," I amend.

Mother hates swearing. When I used to live with my parents, whenever I swore, she'd wash my mouth with soap. Old-fashioned, and it still didn't work. It only made me want to swear more.

Fucking hell.

There. Better.

"You're a good brother, even if you're a bit surly sometimes. Cristopher appreciates your help."

"Then he can say so himself. Why does he always need *you* to speak for him?"

"Marlowe! You know why!"

I take a deep breath and look at my watch again. The minutes are going by and that will mean one less episode of *Supernatural* when I get home.

I can't do quarters or halves. It's everything or nothing. But that will free up a small window of time before I go to bed. What should I do?

The noise of my foot tapping against the car floor interrupts my thoughts. I should stop doing this—but that's what I've been saying for years and I'm still here.

Still, an episode is forty-five minutes on average. A quick calculation reveals that with my current delay, I'll have about thirty minutes to spare before bed.

Anxiety rushes through my limbs.

What can I do in that time? What takes *exactly* thirty minutes and not one second more or less?

I bite my lip as I debate.

"Marlowe? Are you still there?" My mother's voice startles me.

"Yes," I reply.

Did she say something? I lost the thread again, damn it.

"About my birthday party," she starts, her voice already dropping an octave. "Are you bringing anyone?"

"No. I'm not," I add slowly.

"Well, Julius is bringing his fiancée, and it will be our first time meeting her. I want everything to go well. I think she might feel better if there's another woman around—"

"He's bringing her to the party?" I cut her off. The last thing I need is for my mother to talk to me about women—again.

"Yes, of course. Julius is excited to introduce her to us. He proposed, too."

"That's news to me." I narrow my eyes.

I don't speak with my brothers unless it's through Mother.

We've never been close. Each of us has different personalities that have never meshed well. But to hear that he has a serious girlfriend that he actually proposed to? That's quite...interesting.

But not surprising.

At thirty-five, Julien is an accomplished heart surgeon and the face of his hospital. He's the charming one, all smiles and fake platitudes.

He only cares about his reputation. Since the expectation was for him to get married soon, he of course decided to do what's right. Never mind that he probably has a slew of other women on the side.

He's a fucking selfish prick.

"Marlowe, why would you call me if you cannot be bothered to talk? You're worrying me, you know."

Another glance at my watch has my anxiety spiking again. The time is dwindling.

Damn it.

"I have to go, Mom. Have a good day," I say as I hang up.

Immediately, I pull onto the road and start the long drive home. With the icy roads, I have to drive carefully, which means I'll lose even more time.

Double damn it.

This snow annoys me, as does the white background it creates.

I hate white.

A tired sigh slips past my lips.

Fifty-two days until I have to go to the family gathering. Fifty-two days until I have to bear the presence of other humans in my proximity for an entire day.

Fuck.

I hate people.

TWO

IT'S ALMOST dark by the time I make it onto the highway.

Twenty-five minutes until I arrive home, and the minutes cannot go by fast enough.

My house is located in Upstate New York, an intentional choice on my part since it's in a secluded area, with my nearest neighbor a few miles over.

From the moment I moved out of my parents' house, I knew I wanted to move somewhere remote, where no one would bother me. My family knows the general location of the house, but they don't have the address. No one does. By all intents and purposes, no one, not even the government knows who resides there. My mailing address is in the city, and I drop by a few times weekly to pick up my mail.

This is both for my peace of mind, since I don't want anyone to drop by unannounced.

I hate guests.

But it's also because at times, I might engage in some...questionable activities. And it wouldn't do for my neighbors to hear people's screams coming from my house, would it?

Or I used to, anyway. I'm supposed to turn a new leaf and all that, no?

When I turned eighteen, I got access to the trust fund my grandfather set, and I was able to buy the house with cash. It's a five-bedroom Victorian house with a sprawling basement—or, better said, dungeon. It is, of course, my favorite place and why I bought the house in the first place.

Even better, the basement is split in two. A small section is directly underneath the house. But there's another, secret section, of nearly three thousand feet that's underneath the land, which ensures that even if by some stroke of misfortune the police got wind of my activities, that room is well hidden away. But of course I'm not one to trust that alone, so there's a mechanism in place that should the police come with a warrant to search my place, the entire secret basement will explode at the touch of a button.

A scowl pulls at my lips.

I shouldn't be thinking about my dungeon. Not when it hasn't been used in one hundred and seventy-four days.

Soon-to-be one hundred and seventy-five days. An odd number.

I hate odd numbers.

I have purposefully kept myself from even going inside for fear I may give in to my urges and fall back into old habits.

See, I try to be a good boy. It just doesn't always work.

And since my therapy isn't going as well as I planned, maybe it's time to reassess.

You may be wondering *why* I went to therapy since I crave murder so badly.

Even *I* wonder about that and whether it was a good idea to change in the first place. I was doing *fine* before. The only downside was that I was slowly getting out of control.

I was feeling myself slip and didn't like what I was becoming.

From my first kill, I prided myself on being the picture of calm.

Murder was not a spur-of-the-moment thing. It was a methodical process. It was a puzzle to be worked out.

Who? When? Where? Why?

I had to find an answer to all those questions before I even made the first step. After that, it was all a matter of *how*. Every piece had to fit together. From the method, timing and precision of the kill to the disposal of the body. There was no room for error.

And I've been so successful at it for so long *because* I did everything by the book.

I chose my victims carefully so I had no connection to them; most usually by using a back door into the police's database. It was always people who would not be missed, people society would be far better off without.

But it all changed two years ago.

Something set me off, making me go off my script and throw caution to the wind.

That's not who I am. That's not how I operate.

That failed incident has haunted me ever since.

And for a perfectionist, failure is inadmissible.

Somehow, that one faux pas has stained all my subsequent attempts, and despite trying to put it out of my mind, it has turned killing into something...I'm no longer confident in.

It pains me to admit to it. It's even more painful because killing comes to me as naturally as breathing. And to wake up one day and realize I can no longer breathe as smoothly as before was akin to a death sentence.

My last attempt ended up with a botched kill. One that stained the walls of my basement—something I didn't intend to do.

And that lack of intention is the problem.

How can I trust myself to toe that line of danger without confidence?

It's better to abstain from it altogether than do a poor job.

For a while, I simply locked myself in my room, sequestering myself from the world even more. I knew that if I got out, I'd seek to quench my blood thirst, and in return, become even more disappointed in myself when my kill turned out anything less than perfect.

I went to such extreme lengths that I locked the door and flushed the key down the toilet.

Of course, that didn't stop me from breaking the door—maybe I should think about replacing all doors in my house with steel ones, perhaps even titanium.

As soon as I was out, I was on the prowl once more.

When I made yet another mistake while stalking my would-be victim, I decided that if I cannot fix myself, perhaps someone else can.

But now I see that was a useless idea.

Mrs. Leonard didn't understand. Meeting new people is not the solution. It's a mere catalyst that would make me fall back into old habits.

I release a frustrated sigh as I bang my fist against the steering wheel.

Maybe I should just call in an anonymous tip at the police so they can lock me away. Maybe behave badly and they can put me into solitary. Then I will not kill, nor will I have to entertain other useless humans.

The idea is appealing.

Alas, I'm far too attached to my comforts to give them up. And though appearances might be deceiving, I do have a job in IT that I surprisingly enjoy—remotely, of course.

I continue to contemplate the sorry state of my life when something on the sidelines catches my attention. My brows go up as I slow down, keeping my gaze on the couple seemingly having a tiff by the side of the highway.

My focus is on the woman, though—if she can be called that. She's a tidbit of a girl. Doubtful she's taller than five-two. But it's not her diminutive size that demands my attention. It's the way she's dressed in a shirt and a pair of jeans.

In this goddamn weather.

My eyes rake down her body.

She doesn't even have proper shoes. She's wearing a pair of slides. No socks. At this rate, she'll get frostbite in no time.

A shudder goes down my back.

Who the hell goes out dressed like that?

I fucking *hate* the cold.

Yet there she is, brazenly standing in the cold, letting the icy snow slide down her body. White snowflakes have created a crown atop her dark hair.

Another tremor grips me, and I reach for the heat controller to make it warmer in the car.

The man is much older than her, and he's dressed appropriately for the weather.

He's no gentleman, that's for sure.

He sees that little thing barely clothed and doesn't even offer to give her his coat.

I shake my head in disapproval.

Even *I* would offer. If only to get her to stop looking so cold, which in turn makes *me* feel cold.

Self-serving?

Perhaps.

My car has come to a halt at this point. I'm so enraptured by what's happening between the two that I absentmindedly must have stopped by the side of the road.

Now, seeing them up close, I realize they're no couple. At least not based on the girl's body language as she's all but baring her teeth at him.

The man, on the other hand, continues to walk toward her and invade her personal space.

My jaw clenches.

Personal space is something that should *not* be invaded. Just thinking of someone trying to come *that* close to me gives me a headache—and the urge to drive off and lock myself in my house where no other soul lives.

Yet despite everything that would normally compel me to leave, I can't find it in myself to do so.

The man takes another step toward her and she puts her hands up in a gesture for him to stop.

And as the wind blows her hair out of her face, I get my first glance at her features. She has big, doe-like eyes that are almost too big for her face. Her small nose and dainty lips make her look as if she's all eyes.

Big, soulful eyes.

Big, terrified eyes.

I gulp down.

She's slender, bordering on malnourished. Suddenly, the state of her clothes doesn't seem so strange after all.

"Don't be shy, dove." The man's lascivious voice reaches my ears—he's not even trying to mask it.

"Go away," the girl responds. She takes a step back, and her flimsy slippers do as their name implies—they slip. Her eyes widen and her mouth forms a big O as she falls to the ground.

I wince.

The ice is newly formed, but with recent temperatures, it's hard as fuck.

That fall must have hurt.

A nasty grin appears on the man's face as he approaches her. He knows he has her trapped, and he's about to act on it.

I should drive off and mind my own business. I'm never one to get involved in things that don't concern me. Hell, I'm not one to get involved with people, period.

Yet a strange impulse has me sliding down my window and poking my head out.

"Is there an issue here?" I ask in a hard, steady voice.

That's enough to give the man pause as he turns to glare at me. His nostrils flare and his body tenses.

"No issues," he mentions. Threading a hand through his slimy hair, he forces a smile on his face. "I'm just trying to get my daughter back home. She ran off without her clothes, as you can see," he adds nervously.

I narrow my eyes at them.

He's old enough to be her father now that I take a better look at them.

That should be my cue. She's his problem, not mine.

But then the girl's eyes meet mine. On the ground like that she looks even smaller. More frail.

She looks like a deer caught in the headlights. And for some reason, that one look from her gives me pause.

I tap my foot against the floor as my mind tries to make sense of what I'm seeing. If there's anything I hate more than the cold—and the snow—it's when things don't make sense.

And though this man claims to be her father, there's something off about the situation.

"Is that true, miss?" I address her.

"Of course it's true," the man interjects. He steps closer to my car. "It's none of your business what happens with my daughter," he adds ominously. He plants himself right by my window, his burly body covering my view of the girl. His hands are on his hips as he undoubtedly tries to intimidate me into dropping the matter.

Ah, but that makes me want to poke at it even more.

"Is that so?" I tilt my head to the side.

I stare right into his eyes, and though for a moment he returns the stare, he soon becomes flustered, fidgeting on his feet.

"What the fuck do you want?" he suddenly shouts, placing his meaty hands on my car door. My gaze drops to where his hands are touching my car, no doubt his sweat, odor, and bodily fluids getting onto my vehicle.

A twitch pulls at my lip.

"You better run, boy," he starts. But before he can finish with his not so intimidating threat, I push the button for the window to slide up.

It catches him by surprise, and he doesn't manage to pull his hands away before they're caught between the window and the door.

He yelps in pain, shouting more obscenities.

"What the fuck is your deal? Let me go! I'm calling the cops. Fucking asshole. I'm going to—"

I push the door open and slam it against him.

Another yelp of pain slips past his lips as he falls to his knees. His hands are still trapped in the window, and I shake my head at the pitiful sight.

He struggles, but he's only hurting himself.

Leaving him to tear his fingers off if he dares, I make a beeline for the girl in the snow.

The cold wind brushes against my skin and briefly reminds me why I should *not* have gotten involved in this. Now I'm cold. And I get cranky when I'm cold.

But as I approach the girl, I forget all about my physiological needs.

"Are you all right?" I ask as I stop in front of her.

She plants her hands in the snow to help herself up. She wobbles on her feet, but I don't offer to help. I don't like to touch people unless I absolutely have to. Besides, her hands must be freezing, and they'd make me freeze too.

Slowly, she manages to get herself to her feet.

The man continues shouting in the background, threatening to call the police, but at this point, it's just white noise.

"T-thank you," the girl murmurs as she drops her gaze to the ground, almost as if she doesn't dare meet my eyes again.

Odd.

"Is that man your father?"

She immediately shakes her head.

"Is he bothering you?"

She nods.

"I see."

Taking my jacket off, I wrap it around my hand and turn back to the bemoaning man. I grab him by his slimy hair with my covered hand and slam his face against the car door, aiming with precision so I don't break my window—that would be a pain in the ass.

"Agh!" he yells.

I slam his face again.

And again.

And again.

Blood pours down his face, and something drops to the ground. I assume it's a tooth.

Good.

"She says you're not her father."

"Lying whore!"

I slam his face again.

My urges are right beneath the surface as I see the blood pool down. His features are contorted in pain, and glee erupts inside of me at the sight.

Ah, how I've missed this.

I slam his face again.

Another tooth falls.

I smile.

It's dark, and I cannot see too well, but I assume it's an incisor, maybe a canine.

Maybe next I can get a molar out of him. Then he'll remember me whenever he tries to chew something.

Yet just as the darkness inside of me rises, my sense returns with a vengeance, stamping down on it.

This won't work. I need to stop.

It's too public. I'm basically assaulting a man in the middle of a highway.

I don't do that—or at least, I didn't.

Until now.

I release an annoyed sigh.

With great disappointment, I let go of the man and step back.

Glancing back, I note the girl is watching me with an odd look on her face.

She's shivering. Her slight body is almost blue from the cold.

It's not your business to care, my inner voice reminds me.

Yet I did stop my car. I did assault a stranger for her.

I might as well fulfill my Good Samaritan role to the end. God knows it might be the one and only time in my life I decide to do something noble instead.

Hurling the coat at the girl, I grind out a, "Cover yourself," before I slide into the driver's seat and lower the window.

The man crashes to the floor. The only sounds coming from his mouth are a few feeble moans. He curls into a fetal position and stays there.

Good.

The girl hasn't moved from her spot.

She's still staring at me with those big, soulful eyes of hers. My coat is now hanging around her shoulders, looking more like a robe considering how tiny she is.

The passenger door to the car unlocks with a loud beep.

She doesn't move.

I look at her. She looks back.

And she doesn't fucking move.

Goddamn, does this girl have no self-preservation? She's going to freeze to death.

"What are you doing?" I call out.

My voice wakes her up from her reverie, and alertness enters her gaze.

"Get in," I say as I push the door open.

She takes a step forward but then hesitates.

"Get the fuck in before the cops come," I grind out.

Though there's still indecision written all over her face, she comes forward and reluctantly slides inside the passenger seat. I close the door and turn the heat on to the maximum before I steer the car back on the highway, leaving that creep writhing on the floor behind us.

Silence ensues.

She says nothing. I say nothing.

I continue driving for half an hour, far past the location of my home.

I just keep driving. Aimlessly. Angrily.

My jaw clenches as I realize what I got myself into.

There's a stranger in my car. A *female*.

I just beat a man close to his death in a very public place, and that shit might get back to me.

Fuck. I'll need to scrub the CCTV on the highway and maybe replace my registration numbers. Who knows how much the creep will remember.

Goddamn it!

At some point, as I reach the outskirts of a small town, I stop the car to think.

I scrub my hands over my face in an attempt to calm myself and ignore the fact that there's another person next to me.

Too close to me.

That's a first. And I don't think I like it.

But I took her with me, and now I need to do something about her. I suppose I could always throw her out somewhere and leave her on her own. Yet as soon as that thought crosses my mind, I scowl.

No, that wouldn't do. I don't kill women, and I don't harm them.

I don't save them either, yet here we are.

Fuck.

I bang my fist against my steering wheel.

Fuck. Fuck. Fuck.

But as my mind races to figure out how to get myself out of this mess, the girl finally finds her voice.

THREE

"UHM, WHERE ARE WE GOING?" she asks in a small, soft voice.

I stare at her.

Her accent is odd. Not local. A little affectated.

"Where do you think we're going?"

She swallows.

"I don't know. Are you going to do something to me?" Instinctively, she shrinks against her seat, putting distance between us.

"No," I grind out. "I will not do anything to you."

Her eyes widen. She looks at me as if she couldn't believe such a thing.

"Where's your home? I'll take you there."

She blinks. Biting her lower lip, she seems deep in thought. Meanwhile, the minutes go by and I'm wasting more time.

Goddamn it! Why did I do this to myself?

Instead of minding my own business, driving home and getting there in a timely fashion to watch my show, I'm now left babysitting this girl.

I scowl at the thought. Then I scowl at myself.

I've never had an altruistic bone in my body. So what the hell was I thinking tonight? My own behavior puzzles me, which in turn fuels my annoyance until I'm tapping my foot so aggressively against the car floor that I might break a hole through it.

"Sir?"

I snap my gaze to her.

Did she say anything? Doesn't matter.

"Your home. Where is it?" I repeat.

She wets her lips. Her big eyes are watching me warily.

"Are you sure you don't want to do anything to me?"

"Damn sure." I roll my eyes. "Sorry, kiddo, but underage girls don't do it for me."

"I'm not underage," she mumbles under her breath.

I raise a brow.

"I'm twenty-five."

Surprise flickers across my features, and I let my gaze roam over her.

She doesn't look it.

She's so small and frail, especially with my coat swallowing her up. Her face is devoid of makeup, her lashes long and incredibly dark. She has an innocent look about her. I suppose the more I look at her, I can see that she's not *that* young.

It's her eyes.

It's those damn big eyes of hers.

There's something unsettling about them.

"Doesn't make one damn difference." I roll my eyes.

Now it's her turn to study me with an inscrutable expression.

She shrugs the coat off her shoulders and leans closer to me.

"Really?" she asks, blinking repeatedly.

I take hold of her shoulders and push her back in her seat.

"Really. Now tell me where your home is so I can take you." *And wash my hands of you.* But I don't say that.

"You don't find me irresistible?" She frowns.

"What the hell is with these questions? Did you hit your head when you fell?"

She shakes her head.

"I thought that's why you saved me. So you can..." She swallows. "So you can have your way with me."

I tilt my head to the side, staring at her.

This girl. She's testing my patience.

"Why the hell would I save you to take advantage of you myself? That makes no fucking sense," I tell her.

"You swear a lot," she murmurs.

"Yeah, so?"

"I don't like it."

"Well, I don't fucking care what you like."

"But it's crass," she goes on.

"Don't care. My car, my rules. If you don't like it, see yourself out," I say and click the button to unlock the passenger door. Stretching over her seat, I push the door open.

Immediately, the chilly wind makes its way inside.

She purses her lips as she stares at me, a hint of mutiny in her gaze. She grabs the handle of the door and closes it.

Oh, so the little rabbit has some spunk after all.

"Why did you save me then?" she eventually asks.

"Fucking hell," I groan as I scrub a hand over my face. "Now I'm wondering the same thing. Why the hell did I have to save you?" I mumble under my breath.

"No one else did," she continues, turning fully toward me. "No one else stopped to ask what was going on."

"Yeah, well, don't make it into something more," I mutter, heat traveling up my face.

"You really don't want me?" she asks incredulously. "You don't find me irresistible at all?"

"What, are you offering?"

"Uhm, no?" she stutters, averting her gaze.

Another thought suddenly crosses my mind.

Fuck.

Why did I not think about this earlier?

She's scantily clad, by the side of the highway. There's one other explanation as to why she would do that.

She was there to ply her trade. And that man must have been a potential customer who was getting a little more rowdy after she rejected him.

I sneak another glance at her.

How the fuck would someone like her be a prostitute? Aside from her lack of clothes in this nasty weather, there's nothing else that screams sex worker. Her clothes are normal, not sexy. She's not wearing any makeup. But maybe that's her style.

I already assumed she was underage. I have no doubt others would, too.

My lips pull back in disgust.

Fucking hell. Don't tell me she's *trying* to appeal to fucking pedos!

The urge to get names out of her so I can hunt them down is overwhelming. Now *those* make the best kill. They're fucking cowards who prey on those weaker than them and deserve nothing but a slow and painful death.

I've killed my fair share of them. But the sad reality is that no matter how many I kill, there are still many more out there, most of the time hiding behind a mask of normalcy and living their lives without ever being found out.

There's nothing more that I hate in this world than fucking cowards—those pieces of shit who abuse and exploit helpless people and animals—although I'm rather partial to animals. Children, women, and animals should be protected at all costs. They should *never* be hurt.

A flash of white dances in front of my eyes.

Once more, I find myself lost in my musings. And as I blink, it's to find the girl nearly on my lap. Her face is inches away from mine—so much so that I can feel her breath on my lips.

My eyes widen in alarm and I freeze.

What the hell is wrong with her?

I stare at those haunting eyes of hers, and a sweet, musky scent invades my nostrils.

She smells good, my brain tells me as it processes that stimulus. She smells better than one hundred percent of the people I've met, and I can't stop myself from breathing her in.

It's not a perfume. There's nothing chemical about the scent —and I'm *very* familiar with all types of chemicals.

No, it's something natural. The scent clings to her skin, made more potent by the warmth surrounding us. She's left my coat behind, so she's once more scantily clad. Her bare arms cage me in, and if I were to turn my face, I could brush my lips against her skin.

Goddamn it, Marlowe. There will be no lip brushing of any sort!

Her eyes are even bigger up close. They're a warm shade of brown, that on any other day, I would have called woody. But in this moment, the color is like a magical swirling amber that's trying to hypnotize me.

And I almost fall for it.

Almost.

"What about now?" she asks huskily. With every word she speaks, her hot breath brushes against my face. It makes me... uncomfortable. "Do you find me irresistible now?" She bats her lashes slowly at me—she probably thinks she's coming across as flirtatious.

"How much do you want?" I ask.

Her brows go up and a smile slowly curves at her lips.

"A thousand dollars? Two?"

"So you do want me," she murmurs, her voice dropping an octave.

"To leave me alone," I add. Grabbing her by the arms carefully so I don't touch her skin, I deposit her back in her seat.

She gasps, her eyes wide with shock.

I shake my head at her.

"You're a hooker, aren't you? I get you need to make money and whatever, but you're doing it all wrong," I tell her. "You can't go out dressed like this or you'll freeze to death, and then you won't make any money at all. And you should probably change your stakeout area. There are all sorts of creeps on the highway, truck drivers and the like. They're not known to be the most hygienic. But there's also the danger of running into a serial killer and the next thing you know, you're all chopped up and dumped somewhere," I add seriously.

I mean, I should know. I am one. But she's lucky she came across *this* particular serial killer, since I do have my standards. I'm also not a fan of chopping. I like to incinerate my victims after they've endured the most grotesque pain imaginable.

She gawks at me, her mouth wide open.

"W-what?" she stammers.

"I'm not judging you. Hell, in this economy, anything's fair game. But you're too vulnerable. You're smaller than the average woman, and"—I pause as I peruse her—"you don't seem to have any weapon. You should get one."

"What are you—"

"In fact, I'll help you. I'm sure I can find you a workhouse or something—by that I mean a brothel—where you can continue to ply your trade sans the danger."

I nod, satisfied.

Who knew I was so magnanimous?

My mother would be beside herself with glee if she heard about this.

Alas, I don't plan to tell her. The moment she realizes I've been in the vicinity of a prostitute, she'll start making assumptions and I'll never hear the end of it. Just the fact that I hung out with a female once would be enough to give her something to talk about for years to come, always ending with the same question—when will I give her grandchildren.

Right about fucking never.

But I don't tell her that. It would break her heart. Both the swearing and the fact that I have no plans of having kids. Ever. It's better if she still has some hope that her dream will one day come true. She's certainly become more insistent about it since I'm nearing my thirties.

"You think I'm a...hooker?" she speaks slowly, her tone implying shock.

"You don't have to sound offended. I told you, I'm not judging you," I say with a wave of my hand.

"But I'm not!" she cries out. "How could you even think that?" she demands, covering her chest with her arms.

"How could I not?" I ask with a raised brow.

"You... You..." She blinks rapidly as she sputters. "You're an asshole!" she exclaims loudly, pointing a finger at me.

I smile, now entirely more comfortable with that exchange.

"Oh, thank you. I do try," I reply drily.

She stares at me for a few moments before she releases a deep breath. She reclines back in her seat, pulling the coat around her shoulders and pressing her knees to her chest.

It's on the tip of my tongue to tell her to get her dirty slippers off my leather seat. But I hold it in.

Ah, yes. I'm beyond magnanimous now.

"I'm not a hooker," she continues. She doesn't look at me, merely staring forward. All the confidence from before is gone, leaving behind a vulnerability that makes me uncomfortable.

"All right."

"I'm not!" she repeats.

"Fine. I believe you."

"I just wanted to test you," she adds. My curiosity is piqued. "To see if you would take advantage of me."

"I assume I've passed?" I chuckle.

She just gives me a sharp nod.

"Don't take it personally, pet. I'm sure you're a lovely girl and all that, but as I said—"

"I don't do it for you?" She cuts me off, her tone defiant. She raises her gaze to glare at me.

"Precisely."

She mutters something under her breath and promptly looks away.

She...puzzles me. I don't understand her or her reactions. One moment she's seemingly trying to seduce me, the next she's colder than that goddamn weather outside. But then she's *not* trying to seduce me, she's just testing me, and I'm still not sure whether she's pleased or upset I turned her down.

Fucking hell!

Women. Strange creatures.

There's little wonder I don't want to associate with them. They function on a completely different frequency than me.

A loud noise erupts in the silence of the car—something like a growl.

Frowning, I glance at her.

She's staring at her hands as she fidgets with her fingers. She audibly gulps down, which is followed by yet another noise.

"When was the last time you ate?" I ask her. My voice comes out rather sharply because she jolts up, her pale cheeks reddening.

"Uhm," she murmurs, fidgeting some more with her fingers. She wiggles uncomfortably in her seat. "A few days ago." Her answer is so soft, I barely hear it.

"A few days ago?" I repeat incredulously.

Her chin tips down in an abrupt nod. She doesn't look at me.

My lips flatten.

How the hell did she go a few days without food? But as soon as the question arises, I'm reminded of her slight frame.

She *is* malnourished.

Fuck.

I was supposed to dump her somewhere and be on my way. I've already wasted too much time as it is. Yet the more I look at her, so thin and frail, the more I can't bring myself to leave her as it is.

With an annoyed sigh, I start the car again. Checking the GPS, I see there's an open diner a few miles away.

As I drive, I note her curiosity from the corner of my eyes. Yet she doesn't say a word.

She doesn't ask where we're going or what my plans are with her. Perhaps she's already established I'm not going to do anything to her. Or, perhaps, she's just too desperate to say no to anything.

Once more, I ask myself—what the hell did I get myself into?

It takes me about ten minutes to get to the location on the GPS.

Wendy's Diner is written in neon letters on the front of the building, one of which has flickered out. I steer the car into the parking lot, pleased to see some other cars, too.

Good. Maybe this isn't such a dump after all.

"Come on," I say and get out of the car.

She's slow to react and even slower to get out of the car. But as she does, she forgets the coat inside.

Cursing under my breath, I go around the car, get the coat from her seat, and drape it around her shoulders.

She releases a gasp of surprise and directs those big eyes of hers toward me. There's something there in her gaze. Something I can't quite make sense of.

My hands are rooted on her shoulders as I stare down at her.

This close, I realize how small she is. My assessment of five-two was wrong. She's *barely* five feet tall. To my six-three frame, her head only reaches the middle of my chest.

A tightness forms in my chest the more I look at her.

Clearing my throat, I say, "Let's head inside or you'll freeze to death."

With that, I turn around and expect her to follow me.

She does.

Slowly. Almost reluctantly.

Yet there's a look of wonder on her face as she steps inside the shabby diner—as if it's the finest place she's ever seen.

A waitress greets us at the entrance, and I grunt, "A table for two."

She shows us to an empty table, but she makes no effort to disguise her interest in my barely clad little companion.

I give her a harsh stare.

She scurries away.

Now just gotta hope she won't pose any trouble. Although by the way she hurries to the other staff and immediately starts whispering, that doesn't seem to be the case.

God, I hate people. Why the hell do they have to be such busybodies?

"Sit," I order the girl as I slide into my own seat across from her.

She does as told and hugs the coat closer to her body.

It's not cold inside. But it's not warm either—not as warm as I'd like it to be anyway.

Damn it, the sacrifices I'm making for this little chit. I should be given a fucking award for it.

The waitress promptly returns with two menus that she places in front of us. Then she hovers.

She fucking hovers.

"Aren't you cold, honey?" she asks the girl with a concerned look.

She raises her eyes and meets the older woman's gaze. She gives a low shake of her head.

"She's fine," I bark out.

"I wasn't asking *you*, sir," she snaps back at me.

I raise a brow at her.

"I'm fine," the girl finally speaks, plastering a smile on her face. "He saved me from the cold."

The waitress narrows her eyes at us.

I get it. I do. She looks fucking young, and I look like...well, like a surly asshole. In one case appearances are deceiving, but in the other not so much.

"You tell me if there's anything you might need," the waitress continues, placing her hand over the girl's. Her eyes widen. "My, you're so warm. How can you be so warm dressed like this? And your feet..."

"I'm fine," the girl repeats.

It takes a few more words for the waitress to finally leave us alone to peruse the menu.

Thank God for small mercies.

The girl turns to the menu but doesn't pick it up. She simply stares at it.

"What are you getting?" I ask casually.

She bites on her lip, her entire body tense.

"I don't have any money," she whispers, her gaze still on the menu.

"I have." I shrug. "And before you ask, I won't demand anything in return. Take it as goodwill."

She slowly looks at me. She blinks. Then she swallows.

My ears pick on another noise coming from her stomach.

"Pick something. The sooner you decide, the sooner we eat," I say and look at my own menu.

My lips curl. It's all quite basic for a diner and things I wouldn't normally eat.

But as I glance around from the corner of my eye, I can't help but shudder at thinking about how sanitary this place is—or *isn't*.

Fuck.

With how reluctant the girl is, I doubt she'll eat anything if I don't, so I settle on a cream cheese bagel and an omelet.

"So?" I ask again.

She's still staring at the menu.

"I'll have what you're having," she replies slowly, her lips pulling in a half-smile.

I raise a brow at her. Really? She's fucking starving and she doesn't even dare to pick something?

Instead of arguing with her, though, I signal the waitress over.

"What can I get you?" she asks as she pulls out her notebook.

"One of everything on the menu," I say.

"What? Are you su—"

"Is that a problem?"

"No, of course not." She glances at the girl briefly before she jots down the order. "And to drink?"

"I will have a coffee. Steaming hot. No milk. No sugar."

I wait for the girl to say what she'd like, but she just stares blankly at the menu.

"Do you have tea?"

"Of course. What type would you like?"

She takes a moment to think.

"Peppermint?"

"You got it. I'll be right back."

After the waitress leaves, I turn my attention to the girl.

"What's your name?"

Not that I'm interested. But I'm tired of referring to her as *the girl*.

"M-Minnie," she answers in a soft voice.

"Minnie?" I repeat, surprised. Well, the name sure fits.

She nods. "What is yours?"

"Marlowe."

She nods again.

"What were you doing on the highway dressed like this?" I ask.

She's a curiosity, I'm not going to lie. There are so many contradictions to her that I can't make sense of. And what do I do when I encounter a problem?

I obsess over it until I solve it.

She presses her lips together. Seconds go by and she doesn't answer me.

"Where do you live?" I try with another question.

Again, silence greets me.

"Do you have anyone I can call to pick you up?"

With each question I ask, she seems even more reluctant to speak.

But just as I think of how else to formulate my questions, she finally answers.

"I don't have a home. I don't have anyone you can call. I..." She trails off.

"You?" I raise a brow.

"I sleep in a park not far from the highway. Sometimes."

I stare at her.

"You're homeless?"

She slowly raises her face to look at me, and she gives me a small nod.

Before I can help myself, I pull on her hand and fold the sleeve of the coat so I can check her arms. Given her weight, she might be a user.

But I soon realize my mistake. Her arms are flawless. Her green veins are visible through her almost translucent skin, but there's not one mark on her arms.

A wave of shame hits me at my assumption.

Yet that quickly vanishes as I feel the warmth of her skin.

The waitress was right. She *is* hot. Too damn hot.

Pulling the sleeves back down, I lean over the table and place my hand over her forehead to check the temperature.

She's running a fever. A *very* high fever.

"Fucking hell, Minnie. Why didn't you say you were burning this badly? We should go to a hospital."

She grabs my hand as I try to wrench it away and keeps it in place.

Slowly, she shakes her head.

"It's not a fever," she whispers. "It's my normal body temperature."

"The fuck you say? No one's body temperature is *this* hot."

"Mine is. Please... No hospital."

More questions swim through my mind.

Is she ill? Is she contagious?

I just touched her. I breathed in her air. What if she has some disease and she passed it to me?

"I'm not sick," she murmurs as if reading my thoughts. "I've always been this way."

"Is that why you're not dressed properly?" I frown.

She gives me a nod and a small smile. A *genuine* smile.

"I'm always hot."

And I'm never hot enough.

Fuck.

These thoughts are dangerous.

"Fine. If you say so," I grumble. "But if you get sick later on, remember I offered."

"Okay." She releases a soft giggle.

My body tenses.

She's almost...beautiful?

For fuck's sake. My mind is going to mush if that's what I'm thinking about right now.

"You shouldn't sleep outside anymore. There are shelters for women. I can get you in contact with a few."

"No."

"No?"

"They won't take me in," she admits, almost ashamed.

"Why the hell not?" I burst out.

She fidgets with her hands. Her eyes roam wildly around as she prepares a reply.

"I have a...record," she stammers. "Aggravated assault. I... I tried to go to a few, but they kicked me out after they found out about the assault. They said they didn't want any trouble."

"You? Assault?" I ask in disbelief.

Who did this five-foot-nothing little girl assault?

She forces a smile.

"I got arrested shortly after I turned eighteen. I recently got released."

Not many things surprise me. But Minnie just managed to shock the hell out of me.

Seeing my expression, she hurries to add, "It's not something one says to someone they've just met, no?" She laughs nervously. "It's fine if you want to leave."

I TILT my head to the side and study her, suddenly seeing her with new eyes.

"Who was it?"

"Huh?"

"Who did you assault?"

The waitress shows up with our beverages, giving Minnie the opportunity to evade the question. She certainly doesn't look very pleased about it.

"Everything all right?" the waitress asks with a fake smile.

"Fine," I bark out, though my gaze is still on Minnie.

She fidgets in her seat.

The waitress mutters something, but I don't really care about what she has to say. Not now. Not when I've found the most interesting thing in...forever. God, I almost forgot what it was like to feel the thrill of the chase. This time I might not be physically chasing someone, but I'm chasing information. That will have to do.

As the waitress leaves, Minnie looks left and right—no doubt thinking of how to change the subject.

Someone more delicate would let this slide. Someone with more empathy would see her distress and aim to make it better. But I'm neither. I *need* to know.

"Who did you assault, Minnie?" I ask again, more punctuated.

Give it to me, Minnie.

Tell me all your secrets.

"My foster father," she whispers.

My eyes flash at her.

"He hurt you?" I continue my interrogation.

"He...tried to," she replies uneasily.

"What did you do? How did you hurt him?"

Now we're getting to the best part. If I can't have my thirst for blood assuaged, then at least I can live vicariously through someone else. Who would have thought, though, that it would be through a mere slip of a girl who served time for it?

My heart pounds in my chest.

Tell me, Minnie. I need to know.

"I stabbed him." She pauses. Glancing up, she watches me closely to monitor my reaction. "Ten times," she adds in a low voice when she sees I'm not disgusted by it. Oh, if only she knew.

"Ten?" I repeat huskily.

My heart is about to fucking explode.

"*Only* ten?"

Her eyes widen in shock. And before she can help herself, she lets out the truth, "Twenty-seven times."

A smile spreads across my face.

"And he still lived after that?" I ask, surprised.

She purses her lips.

Her hands reach for the hot cup of tea and she brings it closer to her body, blowing in the steam. My coffee is there, somewhere on the table. But I don't have time to think about it. Not when my sole focus is this little slip of a woman with the courage of an Amazonian.

More. I need to know more.

She lifts the cup to her lips, but she doesn't drink. She merely uses it as a cover for what I note to be the twitching of her lips.

"I didn't *want* him to die," she murmurs. "Now he will remember me for the rest of his life."

God! Have I perchance gone to heaven and met an angel?

I lean closer to her, the pounding of my heart becoming an echo in my ears.

"Then you don't regret it, do you?"

She takes a sip. How, I don't know, since the liquid is scorching hot—I can tell by the amount of steam coming off it. But she makes no note of it, her features as serene as before.

"Do *you*?" she asks, her lips curving into a full smile.

I frown.

What?

FOUR

"WHAT DID YOU JUST SAY?" I ask sharply.

She wets her lips. "Would you? Regret it?"

I narrow my eyes at her.

"No. I would not," I answer slowly.

"I don't either. He was a bad man." She shrugs. "Bad things should happen to bad men."

The tension exits my body and I lean back, chuckling.

"I can't argue with you there."

She gives me another one of those smiles that illuminate her entire face, turning her into...something else.

The waitress returns with our food, and she lays five plates on the table the first round before coming back with another three.

The table is filled with dishes, and Minnie stares at them wide-eyed.

Once more, the waitress lingers, and I shoot her a questioning glance, after which she finally leaves us alone.

"Help yourself to whatever you want." I incline my head toward the food.

She licks her lips, but she doesn't reach for anything.

She's just staring at the food, particularly at a juicy cheeseburger with a side of fries.

I shuffle the items around the table and push that plate toward her.

Her gaze meets mine and she swallows.

"Eat," I tell her sternly.

"I..." She presses her lips together. "Thank you," she murmurs before she reaches for the cheeseburger with both of her hands, then brings it to her mouth and takes a big bite out of it.

The melted cheese and sauce smear around her lips, but she doesn't notice as she eats with gusto.

"Don't eat too fast. You'll get sick."

At my words, she suddenly stops. She stares at me and slowly swallows.

I chuckle.

"You like it?" I raise a brow.

She eagerly nods. "Are you not eating?"

I ASSESS the food in front of us and my nose wrinkles in disgust. "I'm good."

SHE FROWNS but then shrugs and proceeds to devour the cheeseburger before moving to the fries. When she's done with that course, she switches the plate for one containing pancakes.

For such a tiny thing, she can certainly eat a lot.

"Thank you," she speaks in between bites of food.

My lip curls.

I *hate* it when people talk with their mouths full.

But just as I'm about to reprimand her for it, she swipes her arm across her mouth, cleaning up a mix of cheeseburger sauce, powdered sugar, and maple syrup.

With the sleeve of my coat.

I cross my arms over my chest and lean back—so I don't strangle her.

Homeless—check.

Malnourished—check.

Police record—check.

Lack of manners...double check.

I shake my head. Perhaps I could talk myself into killing her. Just this once.

According to her own words, she has no one in the world. She has no job, no home, no relatives.

By all intents and purposes, she's the best candidate.

No one would miss her. In fact, she might thank me because what does she *really* have to live for?

Nothing.

She has nothing.

I click my tongue against my teeth as I continue to study her—and try to tune out her obnoxious eating sounds.

Perhaps this was fate. She fell into my lap at the perfect time—when I've been dying to get my mojo back. She would be my grand return to the game. And it's *because* she's not like the others that this has the opportunity to become my greatest kill.

Yes, Marlowe, you do need a change.

I nod to myself. I do, indeed.

Whereas I've previously fed my thirst for death with men who preyed on the innocent, this time I can take it a step further.

My mother would have my head for it if she knew.

But she doesn't have to know. No one will.

I let my eyes roam over her again.

Despite her diminutive stature and average looks, there's something about her that's rather...captivating. I don't know what it is, but something about her screams *stop and look at me.*

And by God did I stop.

Hell, I'm still looking.

She raises her gaze and gives me a tremulous smile as she licks her lips.

Now those eyes. They're her most attractive feature. There's something almost otherworldly about them. And when she bats her long lashes at me, a low tremor goes down my back.

"Are you sure you don't want to eat? This is so good," she says, once more with her mouth full.

It takes everything in me not to snap at her and tell her to eat properly.

But before I can voice my refusal, she cuts a piece of pancake, slathers it in sugar and syrup, and pushes the fork against my lips.

My eyes widen.

Hers sparkle with a hopeful glint.

I press my lips together and glare at her.

"It's so good. Try it," she continues.

I stare at her with a mutinous expression.

What the hell does she think she's doing?

I'm not eating anything from this run-down diner, much less that maddeningly sweet thing dripping in sugar.

The sweet scent assails my nostrils, and I find myself twitching.

She smiles expectantly at me.

I shake my head, flattening my lips, but she continues to push the morsel of food against my mouth.

"Come on," she encourages, leaning over the table and all but lying on top of the food.

From the corner of my eye, I note the end of my coat dipping into the oily food. The sleeves are already stained with sauce. Now the entire coat is getting dirty.

She waves the fork in front of me, moving it from side to side almost as if she were trying to hypnotize me with it.

I don't eat sugar. I don't eat processed food.

It's not a matter of diet. It's simply a matter of discipline.

Sugar is addictive.

I don't partake in addictive things, since I know that one taste would ruin me forever. With my obsessive tendencies, I'm prone to addictions of all sorts—something I learned early on in my life and which therapy later confirmed.

I don't drink alcohol. I don't do drugs.

My only vices are murder and trashy TV—the only ones I find it hard to part ways with.

The maddening sweetness coming from the pancake bite confuses my senses. It's especially potent when coupled with the way Minnie is looking at me with those beguiling eyes of hers.

I gulp down as I stare at the fork, then at *her*.

Goddamn it.

Why is her smile so wide? Why are her lips so full? And why the hell am I not *that* disgusted when there's still white powder smeared around her mouth?

She's moving the fork around like an airplane. As if I were a toddler in need of persuasion.

My features harden when I realize she's getting *too* close to being persuasive.

"No, thank you," I grit out.

But just as I open my mouth to speak, she takes advantage of it to shove the piece of pancake in my mouth.

I freeze.

A shudder racks my body.

I taste...sweetness.

My atrophied tasting buds roar back to life as the strong flavor of the pancake bathes my tongue. It's soft. Chewy. And sweet.

So fucking sweet.

No!

I must not give in. I need to retain control over myself.

Yet the more I chew, the more I find myself closer to the edge of the cliff and ready to dive off it.

I begrudgingly swallow.

"Good, isn't it?" she speaks while the wheels in my mind turn and turn, trying to find a proper excuse for *not* indulging in that sweetness—for not consuming it all.

My lips twitch in annoyance.

Now that she's no longer the scaredy cat I saved, she's effusive and warm—too bubbly.

I hate bubbly.

She speaks too much too. She *does* too much. Why can't she eat quietly and be thankful she's not starving tonight?

"Try this, too," she hurries to add, grabbing another piece of pancake, this time with some chocolate sauce on top.

A shudder goes down my back.

I despise chocolate.

It's far too sweet. Too milky. Too...delicious.

One misstep is enough.

I grab her hand and stop her, communicating with my eyes that she has overstepped her boundaries. But she doesn't notice. She thinks this is a game. So she leans farther across the table.

In her attempt to reach me, she ends up knocking a plate to the floor. Onion rings and mozzarella sticks fall to the ground. Her pouty mouth forms a small O as she stares at the food on the floor. I lift my hand to signal the waitress to come clean the mess when she suddenly drops to her knees on the ground, grabbing the plate and placing the food back on it.

She won't eat that, will she? She'll throw it away, right?

Wrong.

As she places it in front of her, she grabs a mozzarella stick, blows on it a couple of times, and stuffs it in her mouth. Then she smacks her lips together as if it were the most delicious thing in existence.

True horror grips me. I hold on to my seat so I don't explode.

That thing touched the dirty floor. Tens if not hundreds of shoes have stomped on that floor since God knows when it was last cleaned.

Hundreds of shoes that carry all types of grime, dirt, and bacteria with them.

My stomach rumbles in protest.

Acid makes its way up my throat.

Minnie pays it no mind, however, taking another stick, then an onion ring. She blows on them as before, and she eats them with gusto.

"How can you *eat* that?" I mutter, my voice full of shock.

She raises her brow at me. Her lashes flutter in confusion.

"What do you mean?" She frowns.

"It fell down. You should have thrown it away."

"Throw *food* away?" Her expression is horrified. "Are you mad?"

"I should ask you the same," I say through gritted teeth. "Have you any idea how dirty that floor is?"

She tilts her head to the side, then shrugs.

"I've had worse."

I gawk at her.

"Worse?"

"It might not be the best time to tell you about dumpster diving." She giggles.

Images suddenly assail my mind. I see this little thing happily dive into a stinky-ass dumpster to hunt for food, then eating whatever disgusting thing she found.

I cough/gag.

"There will be no more dumpster diving," I tell her sternly after I get myself under control. "There will be no more eating from the floor. Is that clear?"

She looks at me with confusion.

"Is that clear, Minnie?" I narrow my eyes at her.

She seems taken aback by my question, but she eventually nods.

Good. At least she's susceptible to training. But she'll have to undergo extensive detox and a succession of thorough baths before

I can allow her anywhere near me or my house. It's bad enough that I need to have my car disinfected and throw my coat out.

I rather liked that coat.

The more she behaves like a little heathen—a rather sweet heathen, though—the more I think that perhaps I should just give in and have her.

Though she has a tendency to drive me mad, I have to admit to myself that she is rather...entertaining. And that's what I've been missing from my life.

Always the same routine. The same shows. The same work.

Always the same type of victim.

I strive to avoid disorder.

I don't like people, much less the body parts of people.

I conduct my kills rather clinically, in a manner that ensures the most amount of pain before death. After, I simply dump the bodies in my furnace and turn them into dust—which, of course, I keep in my prized cellar.

Perhaps it's time to switch things up a little. Though I admit it would not be an easy feat to achieve, since I'm rather set in my ways. Despite that, something within me tells me that this is special—a once-in-a-lifetime opportunity.

She's everything I hate and everything I avoid.

I tilt my head to the side.

Yes, I would not torture her.

The thought of her in pain doesn't sit right with me. But I could get creative. I could kill her in a way that would satisfy my craving for control but also one that would not harm one single hair off her body—I'm rather fond of that luscious dark hair of hers. And her eyes.

The thought of this new project awakens my previously defunct excitement.

She might struggle.

My lips curl up.

Ah, I do love a good challenge.

Besides, maybe I would like her to struggle.

A little.

That familiar hum in my veins appears anew, and joy I had previously forgotten pokes its head to the surface—or, perhaps, the type I've never experienced before.

She eats the last bite of the dirty floor food before she leans back in her seat, a satisfied smile on her face. Her teeth are showing. They're white and perfectly formed. But there's also something...unseemly.

"You have something stuck between your teeth," I mention, doing my best to keep the disgust out of my voice.

Yes, another thing to add to the never-ending list of things I hate.

"Oh," she gasps, covering her mouth with her hand. "Is it bad?"

I lift a brow at her.

Her eyes widen.

"I-I'll be right back," she says as she all but jumps out of her seat and rushes toward the bathroom.

I release a sigh as I find myself alone for a moment—a well-deserved break after dealing with the little heathen. But even that's short-lived as my eyes take in the mess she left behind.

Crumbs of food litter the table, together with smeared sauce and powdered sugar everywhere—including on her seat.

She hasn't eaten in days. I suppose I could forgive her, but that doesn't mean I find her uncouth manner any less disgusting.

Shaking my head, I call the waitress over and ask her to clean the table and pack the rest of the food. She once more glares at me but does as told.

Just as my scowl becomes evident, it softens as my thoughts return to my new little project.

My thoughts once more become wrapped in her and how her demise might look like.

For the first time in my life, I'm about to break the most

important self-imposed rule I've ever had. And while I'd normally feel anxious about straying from my very well-thought-out path, the usual critters making noise in my brain are quiet for once.

There's no anxiety.

Just anticipation.

Poor little thing. She escaped a wolf and she ran right into the lion's den.

The minutes go by, and as I look at my watch, I realize she's taking far too long in the bathroom. How hard could it be to remove some food bits from her teeth?

My eyes narrow.

She wouldn't think to escape, would she?

Could she perhaps have realized my intentions? No, impossible. For one, I have a pretty damn good poker face. And I've been nothing but kind to her.

I stand up abruptly and head straight for the bathroom. As I reach the women's restroom, however, the same annoying waitress from before catches up to me.

"You can't go in there, sir. It's the women's bathroom!" she calls out, placing herself in front of me.

"Move," I tell her in a low voice.

She blinks, and for a moment, fear enters her gaze. But she stands her ground, squaring her shoulders and staring me right in the eye.

Releasing a sigh, I grab her by the shoulders and deposit her a few feet over.

She regards me with a shocked expression as I lift her up in the air with the barest of effort, and I take advantage of that moment of inattention to barge inside the facilities.

"Minnie?" I call out.

The sink area is empty, but there are three stalls on the right.

All the doors are shut.

I tilt my head to the side and listen for noises.

"Minnie, where are you?" I ask again.

There it is. A small sound. I cannot make out what it is, but that confirms there's someone inside.

I lean into the first stall, placing my ear to the door.

Nothing.

I move to the second.

It's then that I see a shadow from under the third stall.

I take a step forward, and my senses tell me something is wrong.

The shadow is far too large to belong to Minnie.

At that moment, another low sound erupts in the air.

My nostrils flare.

Taking a step back, I put all my strength into my leg and kick the door.

The lock still holds, but the weak wood cracks down the middle.

Another kick, and the crack widens.

That's when rage overtakes me.

Inside, there's a dirty-ass man holding a hand over Minnie's mouth. Her shirt is in tatters, her gaze petrified. My eyes go to her jeans, and I note that the button has been ripped and the pants are hanging low on her hips.

The man's belt is unbuckled.

I see red.

With another kick, the lock breaks, and the door slams inward.

I barely give the man time to react as I step inside and grab him by the neck. He's a little shorter than me but on the heavier side.

Doesn't matter.

He dared to touch *my* little project, and that means all bets are off.

Pulling him forward, I wrench him with enough force to separate him from Minnie.

"Minnie, out," I grit out as I drag the man by the throat.

She's trembling, but she gives me a tight nod as she scurries out of my way. Yet she doesn't leave. She backs away against the wall, watching.

The door to the bathroom is wide open, and the staff are now crowding the entrance, together with the waitress from before, who keeps babbling about me going into the women's restroom.

But where the fuck was she when *this* creep got in?

The man flails his arms around, trying to land a punch on me. His silly attempts would have amused me if it wasn't for the fact that he dared put his dirty-ass hands on Minnie.

Clenching my other hand into a fist, I bring it down over his half unbuttoned pants, hitting him hard. Once is not enough, though. His moan of pain is not enough. I ram my fist into his dick again and again. Until the bastard is begging me for mercy.

A twisted smile pulls at my lips.

Mercy? *Mercy?* Don't fucking make me laugh.

I drag him by the neck to the sink, in front of the mirror. I give him one second to realize what's in store for him before I smash his face against the mirror.

Once.

Twice.

Blood pours.

Not enough.

I grab him by the hair, pull him back, and slam his face into the mirror again.

Shards of glass fall to the ground. Some are embedded in his ugly-ass face.

I slam him again.

One shard penetrates his eyeball.

More blood.

Good. Now we're getting somewhere.

There are horrified gasps flying around, together with cries for help. But they're all drowned out by a rage unlike any I've ever felt.

I let his body fall to the ground. Limp. Fucker has no tolerance for pain.

He's barely moving.

But oh, I'm far from done.

Assessing the different-sized shards of glass, I pick up a long and thin one from the ground.

Straddling the bastard, I cut through his jeans until I reach his underwear.

Fuck. This is gross as fuck.

I should be wearing gloves.

I shouldn't have blood on my hands.

I shouldn't have blood anywhere near me, nor should I have had to touch his slimy-ass hair with my fingers.

A ton of bleach won't be able to wash away the disgusting slime from this lowlife.

The disgust is there. But so is the rage.

And the rage wins.

I grab the motherfucker's genitals through his briefs and jab the sharp end of the glass into his groin. Bringing it down toward his bulge, I make a succession of rapid cuts until I feel the flesh peel off.

More blood soaks the material.

It soaks my hands.

Fuck. I hate this.

But I fucking hate this guy more.

I put more strength into my cuts until there's nothing left to cut.

There are no more sounds coming from the man. He's out.

Weak fucker.

Breathing harshly, I get up, the rage slowly clearing away.

My lip twitches.

Blood is everywhere.

On the walls, on the floor, on me.

But as I glance up and see Minnie's bedraggled state, another fresh wave of fury washes over me.

I bring my arm back and fling the shard of glass into the man's chest, right about where his heart is.

I have a good aim if I do say so myself.

But just to make sure the glass is deep enough, I press onto it with my foot until it's fully embedded inside his chest.

"Minnie, come," I call out, jumping over his corpse.

She nods and follows me out.

There's a crowd of people whispering in the hallway, but as I exit the bathroom, they all fall silent and make room for us to go.

Good.

One unplanned murder is enough for today.

Rounding up the counter, I spot the bags with our leftovers and grab them on the way out.

Minnie follows behind. As we exit, I feel her small hand slip into mine.

I startle.

But my other side of the brain knows there's no time to dally.

I open my car, dump the food in the back, and order Minnie to buckle up. The car roars to life and we're back on the highway, leaving that goddamn town behind.

I drive for half an hour, taking a few odd turns here and there before I find the edge of a forest and pull over.

All the while, Minnie hasn't said a word.

I get out of the car and open my trunk.

There are a few emergency license plates inside, and I get to work to replace them.

When I'm done, I take my shirt off and throw it in the trunk before closing it and sliding back into the driver's seat.

Fuck, it's cold.

I'm breathing hard.

The adrenaline is wearing off and I realize the extent of my mistakes.

So many, I can't even count.

I turn to Minnie and stare at her.

"What did he do?" I snap.

She jumps in her seat, her expression terrified.

"He... He didn't get to do anything... But he was about to..."

Her voice is so light and soft. So damn melodious.

I stare some more at her, as if by staring I can figure out what it is about this pocket-sized girl that made me break so many of my rules tonight—that will make me break even more of them.

"Tell me in detail what he did."

She swallows.

I should probably gentle my tone. Maybe soothe her or something.

But I don't know the first thing about soothing, so this will have to do.

She raises those big eyes of hers and looks at me.

Fuck. What the hell is it about her eyes?

"He cornered me outside the bathroom," she starts. Her hands are in her lap, and she's fidgeting with her fingers again. "When he saw it was empty, he pulled me inside and locked the stall. He groped me a little and tried to get my pants off. But then you came in..."

"Is that all?" I demand.

She nods.

"Are you sure you're telling me the truth?"

Another nod.

"It's not as if you can go back and kill him again," she adds with a nervous laugh. "You killed him, didn't you?"

I shrug. "Perhaps."

She blinks.

"Does that scare you?" I ask.

She wets her lips as she takes her time to answer. Yet for some reason, I don't want some politically correct answer that she thinks might be the *right* one.

I grab her by her nape and bring her closer. Our faces are inches apart—familiar, isn't it? A dry laugh bubbles in my throat.

Three hours ago, I would have never imagined I'd be willingly touching someone like this. But three hours ago, I was still on my self-imposed killing exile, and I was certainly not planning to beat a random man to a pulp and kill another in public.

Bloodily kill him.

Disgust rolls over me again. But it's only at having touched that dirty-ass man.

It's not directed at her. Now.

Interesting.

Perhaps I *can* develop a new killing technique after all, and she'll be the perfect muse.

Perhaps therapy was never the key.

I didn't need to stop killing. I just needed to find the perfect victim.

"The truth, Minnie. Do I scare you?"

She shakes her head.

"You saved me," she whispers. "Bad guys deserve bad things."

I maintain the eye contact for a few seconds as a smile curves my lips.

"Indeed." I chuckle. "You're a good sport, aren't you, Minnie?"

She presses her lips together. Her eyes are so dark in the dim lighting of the car, they're like two infinity pools striving to pull me inside.

"I can be," she says after a moment's thought. "If you want me to..."

"Good." I nod and release her.

I glance at my hand. There's an odd tingling sensation where my skin touched hers.

I frown.

Odd.

She is odd. My reaction to her is odd.

Every goddamn thing that happened today was odd.

Yet for once, instead of letting my obsessiveness for order rule me, I decide to embrace the chaos.

"You're coming home with me," I declare.

I don't give her time to voice a protest, though it doesn't seem she wants to.

This is it. The moment I've been waiting for all my life.

The perfect murder.

I will kill her.

And I'll relish every single moment of it.

FIVE

WE REACH my house around nine in the evening.

Only two hours left until my scheduled bedtime.

Two hours in which I'm unlikely to enjoy any *Supernatural* episodes.

My lips flatten in disappointment.

As the car comes to a stop, I glance at my little passenger.

Her eyes are wide and full of curiosity as she glances around. Surprisingly, she doesn't appear afraid.

Today, she was the victim of two assaults, yet she willingly agreed to come home with a stranger.

That's...confusing.

Does she have no self-preservation at all?

Does she not realize that the world is not a kind place for women?

By her own admission, she's been through some rough situations in the past—things that should have hardened her toward the world and made her distrustful of everything and everyone.

But as she looks at me, there's none of that. There's only an odd, unwavering trust, as if she were ready to jump off the top of a building if I said so—though I will not.

Maybe. I've yet to decide what I'm going to do with her.

She claims she's been to prison. But there's a softness in her features that belies that. There's an innocence to her that's almost intoxicating, and perhaps what makes her such a magnet for predators.

On any other day, I would have said I was immune to it.

Now? I'm not so sure.

"This is your house?" she asks in that soft voice of hers.

I grunt.

"Come," I say, opening the door. She follows behind me as we head toward the entrance to the house.

"Wow," she whispers as she stops in the middle of the foyer. "Is this a castle?"

"Mansion," I correct.

"Victorian?"

"How did you know?" My brows go up in surprise.

"I have a thing for old things." She gives me a shy smile.

My features harden—or, rather, I force them to do so.

Do not react, Marlowe. Do not even think of it.

"Really?" I drawl.

She nods, her features suddenly animated.

"How so?" I surprise myself by asking. I shouldn't want to know things about her, yet curiosity gets the best of me.

Her lips tremble.

"Old houses are generally abandoned." She gives me a tremulous smile.

I stare at her. "You've been sleeping in abandoned houses?"

"When I could find one." She shrugs.

I do my best not to reveal the shudder that goes down my spine as I think of the dust and dirt she must have slept in, not to mention the mold and other vermin. The more I think, the more horrified I become.

"Minnie." I clear my throat. "When was the last time you've had a bath?"

She raises those big eyes of hers to look at me as she mulls over the answer.

Immediately, I regret my question.

I don't want to know.

Knowing will just make me more anxious about the fact that I've had this creature in my car, wearing my coat. Fuck! She touched me with her hand.

"It's winter. I don't sweat that much," she answers shyly.

Right. The answer is a long fucking time ago.

I wrinkle my nose in disgust.

She's in my house—my sanctuary. An unwashed little heathen.

We must rectify this right away.

"Come," I command, bypassing her to head up the stairs.

I go up exactly five steps before I realize she's not following behind.

I half-turn and pin her with my gaze.

She's standing behind the railing, her teeth raking over her lips as she hugs herself with her arms.

"Did you change your mind?" she asks as she slowly looks at me.

I raise a brow in question.

"About having your way with me," she murmurs softly.

"No," I snap.

Her eyes widen at my tone.

"First off, I've already told you that I have no designs on you. And second..." I pause, pursing my lips. I'm usually direct without having to mince my words. But that's because I don't care about people's feelings. I don't care whether I offend them or not. But with her... The way she's holding herself as if seeking some defense from the world makes me hesitate.

I scowl at myself and continue, "Even if I were, I would not touch you within an inch of my life considering you don't even know when the last time you bathed is."

Her lips part. "Oh."

"Yes, oh," I repeat in a dry voice. "Come. I'll show you to your room."

"My... My room?" Her lashes flutter in confusion.

"Yes. You will not sleep with rats anymore. You can thank me," I say with a nod.

Her steps drum across the polished floor as she chases up the stairs after me. Her mouth is wide open in an exuberant smile.

But then she suddenly stops when she's a step behind me and frowns.

"But there are no rats at this time of the year," she mumbles, almost as if disappointed. "All the ones I've seen were frozen to death."

"Thank God for small miracles," I grumble under my breath.

"Hey, that's not fair!" She punches me lightly in the arm. "Rats have their uses, too."

I tilt my head and watch her with an amused smirk.

"Really? Do tell me what use they have aside from being disease-infested vermin."

New-York-sized rats in particular. They can reach the size of a fucking raccoon. Don't tell me those things aren't disgusting or unhygienic. They have a loose bladder, for God's sake! If a rat makes its home somewhere, there isn't a place it won't urinate on.

I rake my gaze over Minnie.

No, I cannot think of rats peeing on her. That will make me physically ill.

"Well," she starts. Her chin juts forward as she straightens her shoulders—a sign she's about to say something that's important to her. "They're food for other predators. Everything has its use in nature."

She has a point. But although I like animals, I will draw the line at those who live in their own filth.

"I may be able to appreciate their use, but that doesn't mean I want them anywhere near me or my house."

She sighs.

I narrow my eyes at her.

"Please tell me you didn't eat rats to survive," I add before I can help myself.

This is too much information that I do *not* need to know. So why the hell am I mentioning it?

Her lips flatten.

"You know what, don't. Don't tell me. I don't need to know," I quickly say, scrubbing a hand over my face.

Based on her expression, I'll wager a guess that she did, and having a vocal confirmation of the fact will give me nightmares for weeks on end.

"You're an odd man, Marlow," she mentions with a shake of her head.

"I think you're even odder, Minnie the dumpster diver," I quip back.

She stares at me.

I stare at her.

It's almost like a battle of the wills to ascertain who is the oddest among the two.

And I. Do. Not. Give. Up.

The staring contest lasts minutes on end, and just as I knew it would happen, she cracks first when a light giggle escapes her.

The tension seeps out of my body, and I reluctantly smile.

"Enough talk about rats. Let's go."

I continue up the stairs and she follows closely.

When we reach the second floor, I take her down the hallway to the right where the guest bedrooms are.

Yet another great thing about this house. The master bedroom is housed in the left wing with a room I converted into my office, while the other three bedrooms are in the right one. Even if by some odious chance my family found out my address and came to visit, I could dump them far away from me so they don't disturb my carefully crafted routine.

Which, glancing at my watch and seeing that another half an hour has passed, this little heathen is about to do.

Deep breath, Marlowe. You're just being a Good Samaritan— paying it forward and the like.

Two bedrooms are moderate in size, but the third one is almost the size of a master. It has its own private bathroom and terrace attached to it.

I stop in front of the door and unlock it. Stepping inside, I invite Minnie to do the same.

Her eyes widen in shock as she takes in the room.

I smile to myself.

These bedrooms might not be occupied, but that doesn't mean I didn't have them fully renovated when I moved in. I don't like things half-done.

There's a king-sized bed in the middle of the room, with a bedside table on each side. Against the external wall, there's a study and a chair, and next to it is the door that leads to the terrace. The bathroom, too, is fully functional, with a tub and a shower.

"I take it that you like it?"

She nods, her lips trembling.

She takes a step farther into the room as she peeks at the terrace. Then she goes to inspect the bathroom.

I lean against the door as I await her verdict.

"You will let me live here?" she asks as she slowly makes her way toward me.

"That depends."

Wariness enters her features. "On?"

"You must abide by my rules," I tell her.

"Oh, okay. What are those?"

"First, you'll shower daily. Second, you will *not* eat any more contaminated food. Third, you will not make any noise from eleven in the evening until seven in the morning. Fourth, you will not disturb me while I'm working. Fifth, you're allowed to wander around the house, but you're not allowed to come to my room. Sixth—"

"Why am I not allowed into your room?" She interrupts me.

"Because I don't like strangers in my personal space," I reply.

She considers my words.

"Do you have a wife?"

"No."

"A girlfriend?"

"No."

"A lover?"

"No." I scowl. "What's with these questions?"

She shrugs. "I was curious."

"Well, you're *too* curious," I grumble.

"I would not like to step on anyone's toes," she adds.

"You'll step on mine if you do any of the things above," I counter. "I'm a very private man and I value my routine. You already are a disruption in that routine." I pause as I look again at my watch. Ten more minutes have gone by. I should wrap this up soon so I can go take a hot bath and scrub the grime off me. The blood from that creep has dried on my skin, and just thinking about it makes me sick.

"If I'm such a disruption, then why are you helping me?" she asks in a small voice.

"Because clearly you cannot care for yourself. You need someone else to do it for you, and fortunately, you caught me in a charitable mood today, so I shall be that person for the time being," I explain. But as the words are out of my mouth, I mentally berate myself. How the fuck did I even *get* in a charitable mood? I'm *never* charitable, at least not with people.

She gawks at me. I wait for some feminist outcry that she's her own person and she can care for herself—even though the evidence at hand proves otherwise.

"You're odd," she mutters.

"So you have said."

"And a bit of a control freak," she adds, a hint of a smile pulling at her lips.

"Make that a whole lot of a control freak." I chuckle. It's not an insult. I am what I am, and I require full control over all areas of my life. Well, now hers too.

She gifts me with a full smile.

"You're also kind. Thank you. But I cannot in good conscience live here for free."

"May I remind you that you have no money?"

"Yes, but I could pay you in other ways—"

"No," I cut her off, putting my hand up. "I will not require *those* services from you," I add, my face screwing in disgust.

Has she not realized it by now that I'm not interested in her physically? She must be too used to men demanding that of her that she still suspects I have ulterior motives for taking her in.

"I wasn't offering!" she cries out, taking a step back and covering her chest with her hands. She has a scandalized look on her face that I would think to be genuine except I suspect this is exactly how she's been living so far.

My lips tighten in a scowl. Somehow, the thought of her with some dirty bastard is unpalatable. It makes me shudder in renewed disgust, but this time it's the type that crawls under my skin until I feel the need to scrub my skin with sharp nails to remove all traces of discomfort.

"I was thinking of something along the lines of cleaning. You like cleanliness, don't you? I can do it for you," she adds eagerly.

I take a moment to consider her proposition.

I don't have a maid or a cleaner. I never had. The thought of another being in my house is too horrifying for me to allow that. But that also means I've had to make sure my cleanliness obsession doesn't take over my life, which is why I spend far too much time scrubbing this place around. Perhaps a helping hand would not be so bad. She's already going to be here.

I nod to myself. Yes, that seems like a sensible idea. However, I must first determine *how* she cleans.

"You may clean the common areas and the kitchen. That's the whole of the first floor," I eventually reply.

Her eyes shine with optimism.

"However..." I put a finger up. "I'll need to assess your skills first. You may start tomorrow."

"Okay. I can do that." She nods, offering me a bright smile.

"Can you cook?"

She blinks and licks her lips. "Of course I can cook."

I nod. "Good. Then I shall make you in charge of cooking, too. I'm very specific about what I eat and when. I'll provide you with a schedule sheet tomorrow."

"Thank you! Thank you!" she exclaims effusively. Out of nowhere, she launches herself at me to give me a hug.

My eyes widen in horror as I hold myself still.

She's dirty. She hasn't bathed in days, mayhap more. She ate things from the *floor*.

Using only my thumbs and forefingers, I grab her shoulders and push her back.

"I don't like being touched," I grind out.

"Oh," she whispers, confused.

"There's also the matter of your...condition," I say as I nod at her body.

"My condition?" She frowns.

It would be uncouth of me to state the obvious, but it seems she soon understands my silence.

"But you're dirty too. You're covered in blood!" she points out.

My lips flatten.

"Perhaps. But that doesn't erase the fact that you've been living on the streets, and you..." I trail off, cursing under my breath.

"And me?"

"I have another stipulation," I suddenly add.

Her brows pinch together.

"You'll also need to get a medical exam done to make sure you don't carry any disease."

"W-what? Disease?" she stammers, dumbfounded.

I take a step back—just in case.

"You could have contracted anything from the streets."

"But—"

"And there's also the matter of your muddy past. Since we'll be sharing a space—to an extent—I want to make sure you're disease-free. That will put my mind more at ease, since even a small contact with your bodily fluids could prove fatal—though don't get me wrong, I don't plan to be anywhere near your body fluids. This is just a safety measure," I explain.

"What kind of diseases do you think I have?" she asks, her voice going down an octave. Her hands are curled into fists by her sides, and her entire body is full of tension.

I shrug.

"Venereal diseases and any other infections that can be passed on."

"Venereal? What do you mean?" She frowns, stumbling over the unfamiliar word.

"What do you think it means?" I ask drily as I let my gaze roam over her body.

"Y-you..." She blinks rapidly. "Did you just imply that..." She swallows audibly. "How dare you?" she cries out before she comes charging at me, all five feet of her. She jabs her finger into my chest, backing me into the hallway.

Damn, this tiny creature has some strength.

"Don't take it personally, pet," I say, brushing her finger aside, then wiping my hand on my pants. "I will not hold it against you if you do, but then we'll have to reassess this situation."

"I don't have any disease," she continues, her tone that of outrage. Of course it is. I must have offended her feminine sensibilities. But it's better to be blunt upfront than encounter issues later on.

"That will be for the doctor to determine." I give her a fake smile.

"But... But..."

I'm already down to one hour before my scheduled time to sleep. I should wrap this up quickly and be on my way.

"Venereal diseases means that..." she stammers.

"They're transmitted through sexual activities. Yes," I add with a roll of my eyes.

"Is that what you meant by my murky past?" Her eyes flare up in shock.

I merely smile.

"Do you think I'm some kind of trollop? I already told you I'm *not* a prostitute!"

"And that's what a prostitute might say," I remind her calmly. "But prostitution is not the only way you could have acquired a disease. After all, you don't have to always be paid for it," I continue.

Why the hell did I even bring this up? Why am I even continuing arguing about it when I should find a way to extricate myself from this situation faster? Yet I'm oddly interested in this subject —in *her* and her past. Why? I cannot say. But I find myself more and more curious with each word we exchange.

She must have a past. Everyone does—well, I suppose I may be one of the odd exceptions. But the mere thought that some dirty-ass man would have put his slimy hands on her rattles me—to an uncomfortable degree.

"You..." Her body shakes with anger. "Damn you! I've never engaged in s-s-sexual activities with anyone else! So take your prejudices about me and stick them somewhere," she yells before she does something unexpected. She stomps hard on my foot with her heel before she turns and leaves.

I stare at her in shock. I barely have time to process what she just said because this damn little heathen is leaving.

She's fucking leaving.

"Minnie!" I call out and chase after her when I see she's already on the first floor and heading for the exit.

She's fast, I'll give her that. For such a little thing, she's quite nimble.

"Where do you think you're going?" I demand as I reach her and grab her by the arm.

She turns those big eyes toward me and they're full of animosity. Her lips are pressed tightly together in annoyance and I wonder if she'll hit me.

Not that I don't deserve it. I probably do.

Hell, I almost *want* her to hit me.

"I'll find another old house to sleep in for the night," she says as she pushes her chin up.

"No. You will not. You'll stay here."

"Why? So you can insult me more? I've already told you I'm *not* a prostitute, but you're stuck on this idea that I must be some dirty and disease-infested person..."

She's not wrong there, but I will not confirm it to her face—again.

"Why would you even offer me a place to stay if you're going to be such an asshole?"

"Being an asshole is a specialty of mine," I say and flash her a smile.

It doesn't seem to move her.

A part of my brain tells me that perhaps this is for the better, that I should let her leave and wash my hands clean of her. After all, she's nothing but a troublesome little thing that I have neither the time nor the disposition for. I offered, so I did my duty. If she refuses, then it's on her.

Yet I can't bring myself to do that.

It would be the easy way out.

But the more I look at her, the more I don't want to *ever* imagine her sleeping in a cold, dirty-ass place or eating food from a dumpster.

It's for your own peace of mind, Marlowe.

That's right. If she's here, living comfortably and eating clean, healthy food, then I will not have to obsess over her situation for days, maybe weeks—perhaps months—to come.

This is the *smart* choice.

"I'm not the most pleasant individual to be around. I admit," I reluctantly say. "And I apologize if I offended you in any way."

There it is. It wasn't so hard. I can't remember the last time I apologized to someone. Yet here I am, saying those words to someone I've just met—someone to whom I'm not indebted in any way.

Odd. But it's another odd thing in a string of odd occurrences. As long as I can prevent spiraling down into another one of my episodes, I'll have to make this concession.

She narrows her eyes at me.

"Do you mean it?"

I smile. But before I can say anything else, she continues.

"I suppose I overreacted," she says in a low voice. "But I didn't like your insinuations."

"Noted. I will not make similar assumptions in the future."

She nods. "You're very concerned with cleanliness, are you not?"

"I am."

"I was acting like a brat, wasn't I?" She sighs. "You opened your home to me and offered me a place to sleep and here I am, being ungrateful. I'm sorry."

I blink.

That's it? *She* is the one apologizing now?

"I'm thankful for everything you've done for me." She smiles. "And I'll do my best to conform to all your stipulations."

"Good. Shall we head back up then?"

She wets her lips as she regards me for a moment. There's something in her gaze, something I cannot put my finger on.

"Okay."

We go up the stairs and I drop her at her door.

"There's unlimited hot water. Take advantage of it," I mention with a wink. There, I managed to find a more palatable way of telling her she needs to wash—for a *long* time, too.

I give myself a metaphorical pat on the back.

Minnie giggles and nods before she closes the door.

Once in my own wing of the house, I enter my room and discard my dirty clothes, then jump straight into the shower.

I spend thirty minutes scrubbing all the grime off my flesh before changing into a fresh set of clothes.

Glancing at my watch, I note I have ten more minutes before my scheduled bedtime, so I grab my phone and dial my secretary.

"Giles, there was a situation at Wendy's diner," I say and give him a quick description of the location. "See to it that nothing gets out."

"What kind of situation are we talking about?" he questions in that posh manner of his

"Code orange. Perhaps red. There were witnesses."

"I see." He pauses. "I'll take care of it."

"Thanks, Giles. Good night."

I hang up and put my phone to charge before I slide into the silky sheets and close my eyes.

What would I do without my precious routine?

SIX

THE FLOOR CREAKS.

I shoot up and my eyes collide with the electric clock on the desk across from my bed.

Four o'clock. In the middle of the fucking night.

More noise.

Steps thud on the floor, followed by a rapid descent onto the stairs.

My features harden.

Not even one night and she's already breaking my rules.

Getting out of bed, I put on a pair of sweatpants and a shirt and head downstairs to investigate.

I barely reach the top of the stairs when I hear a loud bang, followed by a muffled whimper.

I stifle a groan.

What the hell did this girl do this time?

Ready to give her a lengthy lecture about her rule breaking—and maybe throw her out into the snow, I march down the stairs with determination. The source of the noise is coming from the kitchen.

But just as I reach the entrance of the kitchen, I stop in my tracks, my eyes wide with shock.

"What the..." I trail off. I blink once, twice—just to make sure I'm seeing this right.

My little heathen is standing in the middle of the kitchen next to a broken plate. But it's not the shards of porcelain on the floor that grab my attention.

It's the fact that she's naked.

Fully naked.

Naked like the day she was born naked.

My body freezes, my eyes zeroing in on her breasts.

For such a slender woman, her breasts are on the heavier side. They're full and round, with light pink nipples. They'd probably fit in my palms. And I have large palms.

I swallow uncomfortably.

Heat travels up my neck.

I force myself to look away from her breasts, but instead of averting my gaze completely, my eyes follow the contour of her body. Her stomach is taut and her abdominal muscles are showing. Yet I don't think that's a consequence of exercise, but rather of starvation. Her ribs, too, are poking through.

Fucking hell!

She will not go hungry anymore—that's a vow I make to myself. I don't know where that's coming from or why I feel so protective over this slip of a girl who goes against every rule I've set for myself.

I should focus on ways to kill her to satisfy my bloodlust, not ways to protect her and see to her every comfort.

To my dismay, my eyes betray me once more as I glance lower. There's a dark triangle of hair at the junction between her thighs, hiding her most private part.

I've never believed myself to be the type swayed by such a sight, but there's a part of me that wants to know the secrets it hides.

I swallow again, and this time, it's like a knot forms in my throat.

I shouldn't notice her nakedness. I shouldn't react to it in *any* way—I've never been prone to such an affliction before. Yet the more I stare at her, the more I feel my body come to life in unfamiliar ways. My clothing becomes restrictive. Even my baggy sweatpants do little to keep my reaction in check.

Fuck! This is blasphemous!

And why the fuck is she not covering herself?

She just stands there, staring back at me with those big doe-like eyes of hers. Her arms are by her sides, and she makes no effort to shield *any* part of herself.

Is this on purpose?

I narrow my eyes at her.

Is she doing this on purpose in an attempt to seduce me?

Did someone put her up to this?

My family?

My thoughts go around in circles as I think of a myriad of reasons as to why she'd be in my kitchen, naked, and gazing at me with an inviting look in her eyes.

I think back to the many times she asked me if I find her irresistible and how she's repeatedly brought up the fact that I may expect something physical from her. Then there are also her claims to be untouched.

If my mother had a hand in this, then she would have instructed her to say that, thinking it would appeal to my obsessiveness about cleanliness. My mother has been trying to set me up with women for years now—all attempts a failure. But that doesn't mean she's given up. Maybe she's just changed her tactics.

But how would she have known that I'd stop to help her? That in itself is antithetical to my behavior. I don't help people. I don't step out of my way to be *kind*. I certainly wouldn't risk getting out of the comfort of my warm car to go out into the cold and get involved in something that's none of my business.

Yet that's exactly what you did.

I scowl.

This is odd. Something about Minnie is suspicious, but I don't know what.

Unfortunately, with that suspicion also comes curiosity. And I've never been one to leave any stone unturned when my curiosity is piqued.

"What are you doing?" I rasp out.

She blinks. She looks down at the broken plate, then back at me. Two pink dots stain her cheeks.

"I'm sorry," she whispers. "I was hungry, and you didn't bring the leftovers from the car, so I was trying to find something in the fridge. I'm sorry if I woke you up."

"You're naked, Minnie," I state the obvious since she's still not making any effort to cover herself.

Her brows furrow.

I gesture to her body.

"You have no clothes on."

"Oh," she says as she glances down at her naked body. "I didn't have any clothes to put on since they were dirty. I did wash them in the shower but..."

"Are you not in the least embarrassed?"

"Why?" She frowns.

"Because you're *naked.*"

"You keep saying that." She scrunches her nose—and it's too damn cute.

"*Because you're naked*!" I throw my arms up in exasperation.

"And? Why is that an issue?" She appears perplexed, which in turn makes me even more confused.

What the hell is happening?

"Do you always walk around naked in strangers' houses?"

"Well, no," she answers blankly. "You're not a stranger." She gives me a brilliant smile.

I sigh and scrub a hand over my face. This isn't working.

"Do you walk around naked in other people's presence?" I rephrase my question.

She shakes her head.

"Then I'd appreciate it if you didn't do this again. Put on some clothes."

"But they're wet," she answers with a pout. "And I don't understand why you're so hung up on my nakedness. It's a natural state. There's nothing to be ashamed of," she chides.

"Minnie!" I groan aloud.

"What? I don't understand why you're so upset with me."

Shaking my head, I shrug my shirt off and throw it to her.

"Put that on."

She mumbles something under her breath but does as told. With her height, my shirt is more like a dress on her and it finally covers everything that might have tempted me to gawk like a goddamn horny teenager. Of course there are still her legs, and they're very nice legs indeed.

Focus, Marlowe! It's not the time to admire her legs.

Perhaps her time in prison changed her views on nakedness since she wouldn't have had much privacy there.

When she's covered, I finally dare to get closer to her. I lean down to pick up the pieces of broken plate so she doesn't cut herself on them. She gets to her knees to help me clean up and through this proximity, her scent wafts toward me.

She's...clean.

I inhale deeply.

There's the scent of soap, but there's also something else. A sweet scent that tickles my senses.

"I'm sorry," she whispers again.

"It's just a plate." I sigh. "Did you find anything to eat?"

She shakes her head.

I throw the broken pieces into the trash bin and go to the fridge. I take out a couple of premade sandwiches and hand them to her.

She licks her lips as she stares at them.

Good God! You'd think she hasn't eaten in forever when just a few hours ago she had a full meal. But just as that thought crosses my mind, I berate myself. She probably hasn't eaten in so long that she's perpetually hungry.

Glancing back at my fridge, I realize I'll need to restock it soon.

"Thank you so much," she exclaims as she grabs them.

She quickly unwraps them and wolfs them down in a few bites. And when she's done, she licks her fingers for any remaining trace.

"We'll get more food tomorrow," I find myself telling her. "We'll go grocery shopping and you can pick up whatever you want."

Her eyes widen with wonder.

"Really? I'm not that picky. I can eat *mostly* anything."

"I can see that," I mutter drily.

She doesn't notice my jibe, still sucking her fingers dry.

"Come with me," I say as I turn to leave the kitchen.

For the thousandth time in one day, I ask myself what the hell I'm doing. I should already be planning her murder—something novel and exciting—but instead, my new fantasy seems to be to fatten her up.

I'm out of the kitchen when I realize she's not following. I turn, raising a brow at her.

Her hand is covering her mouth, her entire body shaking with amusement.

"And what's so funny?" I ask as I tilt my head to the side.

"You," she says and points a finger at me. A loud giggle erupts and she places an arm around her midriff as she bends over with laughter.

My lips press together in annoyance.

"Me?" I ask slowly.

She nods vigorously.

"Now *you* are naked!" Another giggle.

I blink and look down at myself. I'm shirtless, it's true. But I'd hardly call this naked.

"It's different," I mutter.

"How so?" she asks, an amused smile still painted on her face.

"I'm a man. I don't have...breasts." Heat climbs up my face. Why the hell am I getting flushed over saying the word *breasts* aloud? It's as if I were still a child being told off by my mother for saying a bad word. Alas, perhaps washing my mouth with soap did pay off after all.

Minnie sobers up. Striding toward me, she stops in front of me. Before I know what she's about to do, her finger is poking me in the chest, right over my nipple.

She's barely touching me, but her flesh is so hot, it's almost burning a hole through me.

A shudder goes down my back.

"Yes, you do," she states, quite pleased with herself. "Why aren't you embarrassed then?"

"I told you. It's different. I'm a man," I repeat as I—reluctantly—remove her finger from my person.

"No. It's not," she reiterates, placing her hands on her hips and staring at me defiantly. "You're just mi-mi-mi..." Her brows scrunch up together. Her mouth remains open as she tries to think of the word she's going to use to insult me.

"Misogynistic?" I offer.

"That word! You're mis-miso—"

"Misogynistic," I repeat, laughing.

"See, that right there." She points accusingly at me. "Why should you be allowed to be naked but not me?" she demands with a humph.

"Because this is my house and I make the rules. Now come along, little heathen. I'll clothe you for the night," I say, turning once more and heading for the stairs.

My lips are pulled up in an amused smile, especially as I hear her muttering something inaudible under her breath—likely cursing me some more.

"Just for the record. I'm *not* a misogynist. But I'm a stickler for rules. I gave up my own clothing so you could hold onto your modesty."

"I didn't ask you to," she mumbles in a low voice.

I shake my head. She's an amusing little thing.

We get to my wing of the house, and I ask her to wait for me outside my door. She's about to ask why, but I close the door in her face before she can muster up some more inane arguments—I really need to get back to sleep soon.

I rummage through my closet and find a pair of unworn boxer briefs and a couple of white shirts. I would give her a pair of pants, too, but unfortunately, they would likely reach her neck.

Damn it. I suppose that since I've made myself in charge of her, I might as well clothe her too.

I open the door and hand her the clothes.

"We'll go shopping tomorrow for clothes. But these should work until then. You still have your pants, no?"

She studies the clothing, giving me an absentminded nod.

"They're wet. But they should dry up until the morning," she mentions, her eyes still on the clothes—particularly on the boxer briefs, which she regards with skepticism.

"I've never worn them," I feel compelled to add.

She purses her lips, and I swear I almost hear her say *pity*. But who the hell would say that about worn underwear?

Gross.

A shudder goes down my back at the mere thought.

"Thank you. It's very kind of you." She smiles, then turns to leave.

"Wait!" I call out.

She raises her brows as she angles her body toward me.

"The laundry room has a washer and a dryer. Grab your jeans and follow me. I'll show you to it."

"But they'll dry eventually," she says with a frown.

"They might, but they also might not. I'm not sure how well you were able to wash them in the shower. It's better if you wash them again and then dry them properly—all within a couple hours too."

What I don't say is that *I* would feel better knowing her jeans are properly washed. Who knows how long she's been wearing them? A quick wash in the shower doesn't count. They probably need bleach or disinfectant at this point. If it wasn't her only pair of pants, I would have trashed them immediately.

Alas.

I take a deep breath.

Just a few more minutes. I'll show her to the laundry room and she can take care of herself. Even better, with it being on the right wing of the house, under her bedroom, that should keep the noise to a minimum and allow me to get back to my sleep.

She grabs her wet clothes, which frankly, still look dirty, and she follows me to the laundry room.

"Here," I say as I open the door.

There are two washers and two dryers. When I start cleaning, I wash everything I encounter in my path, so one would have never been enough. Alas, one is for my personal clothing while the other is for household things.

I open the cupboards in the back to reveal my prized stash of detergent.

"You can choose which scent you'd like."

I'm even allowing her to use my stash. That in itself is revolutionary.

"And here are drying sheets," I continue as I open another cupboard.

Minnie stares at me with wide eyes, slowly nodding.

"You'll use this one," I say, pointing toward the machine designated for household things. At least that way, I'll have *some* peace of mind. "You know how to use a washing machine, right?" I ask, just to make sure.

She wets her lips.

"O-of course. Piece of cookie!"

"Cake."

She frowns.

"Piece of cake," I correct.

Her mouth forms a small O before she nods.

"Piece of cake," she repeats, smiling brightly.

Before I go, I find myself mentioning, "You should go for the heavy soil and double rinsing setting. And don't be too stingy with the detergent."

Those clothes need all the help they can get. Even though they're going to be burned the moment she has a new wardrobe.

"Marlowe?" She calls my name just as I'm about to leave the room. I stop in the doorway and turn.

"Thank you. For everything. You have no idea what this means to me." She gives me a shy smile as she crosses her legs and tucks a strand of hair behind her ear.

I gulp down.

Now that she's clean, I can let my eyes roam over her face without the previous disgust—not that I could even call it disgust, which in itself was surprising. There's something striking about her. I wouldn't call her a beauty, not in the traditional sense. But there's something warm about her presence, something that goes beyond her physical appearance. Something...that puts me at ease and I'm never at ease with other people.

I grunt, unable to form a coherent sentence, and before I say something I might regret, I get out of the room and close the door behind me. Spotting a slight trail of wetness on the floor, I grab a mop and wipe it clean until everything is spotless again—until balance is restored.

You need to sleep, Marlowe. You need your eight hours of sleep. Otherwise, the next day will be ruined.

After I make sure the kitchen and living room are clean—since I will not be able to sleep otherwise—I force myself to put one step in front of the other until I reach my room. I lock the door—for my safety and hers—I take my sweatpants off and slide between the sheets. I close my eyes and start counting, knowing sleep will come.

One hundred eighty-nine, one hundred ninety, one hundred...

Just as I feel my lashes heavy with sleep, a loud screech penetrates the stillness of the house.

I shoot up, and my eyes collide once more with the clock.

It's almost dawn.

Fucking hell! I'll never get any sleep at this point.

I get out of bed, shrug on my sweatpants and a shirt and go investigate what went wrong *this* time.

Yet just as I get closer to the laundry room, I spot wetness seeping through the door, followed by small bubbles.

My eyes widen in horror.

Surely no...

I swallow hard as I push the door open.

"What the fuck, Minnie!" I thunder.

The entire floor of the laundry room is covered in bubbles. Minnie is sitting on the floor, drenched from head to toe. Her hair too is wet and the white shirt I'd handed her before is now clinging to her skin, once more leaving nothing to the imagination.

A pop resounds in the air before more bubbles exit the machine.

And to make matters worse, instead of trying to do something about this insanity, this damn little heathen takes her finger and sticks it in the bubble, then giggles.

She turns to me then, her entire face lit up with mirth.

"It's bubbles, Marlowe! So many bubbles!"

Good fucking Lord! I must have bubbles for a brain for thinking it would be okay to leave her alone for one moment.

"Right. So many bubbles," I mutter drily.

It's not too late to kill her, no?

SEVEN

MY FEATURES MUST BETRAY the rage I'm feeling because her smile dies on her lips.

I clench my fists.

The water from the washing machine continues to leak out, now brushing against my ankles.

I should fucking strangle this little heathen. Wrap my hands around her neck until the life seeps out of her features.

Or, even better, I should just grab her, wet as a rag as she is, and dump her in the freezing cold. Then I'd stand at my window and watch as the water droplets slowly turn into icicles and the color of her pallor changes to blue.

It would be nothing less than she deserves.

I take a step forward, ready to throw her over my shoulder and have my way with her—just not in the manner in which she undoubtedly desires.

Her lips tremble as she regards me and she does her best to give me a reassuring smile.

It won't work.

I'm angry, sleep-deprived, and on the brink of a mental breakdown. All because this slip of a girl decided to turn my house upside down. And the main issue is that *I* allowed her to.

Fuck. I should have never gotten involved with her in the first place. I should have minded my fucking business on that road and ignored her signs of distress.

But I didn't.

Instead, I'm now one step away from losing my calm—something I usually try to avoid at all costs.

I spot a towel by the washing machine and grab it, thinking I could use it to smother her. As I step toward her, however, instead of wrapping the material around her neck or suffocating her with it, I drop it in her lap.

"Your hair is wet."

Her mouth hangs open in shock as she stares at me. Her reaction is delayed, but she eventually takes the towel and wraps it around her hair, murmuring a low *thank you*.

"Are you going to sit in this puddle the entire night?" I comment when I note she's not making an effort to move.

"Uhm..." She looks left and right. What the hell is there to be indecisive about?

Shaking my head, I lean and offer her my hand.

Her eyes widen. She bites her lower lip as she reluctantly reaches out and places her hand in mine. I pull her up. But the invasion of bubbles has other plans.

I must have moved my foot while pulling her up because one moment she's halfway up, the next I feel my heel slip on the slick liquid. In my attempt to balance myself, I pull her down with me, and we both crash to the floor.

The water makes a loud, splashing noise.

My clothes become as drenched as hers, the water seeping into the material. The bubbly liquid reaches my skin, settling in an uncomfortable layer on top of it.

I'm on my back, blinking as I stare at the ceiling.

Minnie is by my side, half of her body on top of me. I can feel her weight and the way her chest moves up and down as she breathes.

She's still breathing. Because I didn't kill her when I should have.

And now here I am. Not only in the middle of a disaster of epic proportions but also wet to my bones.

Bathing in detergent-diluted water has never been on my bucket list before regardless of my obsession with cleanliness. And considering the way it sticks to my skin, it's never going to be either.

Her hand is draped across my midriff. She fists the wet material of my shirt as she brings herself closer to me. She brings her head to my chest, nuzzling her face against my exposed skin.

What the hell is this woman doing?

"Minnie," I say her name, my voice harsh.

"Yes?" she asks innocently.

She grabs onto my side and moves her entire body on top of me, resting her head on my chest and regarding me from beneath her lashes.

Which she flutters.

Repeatedly.

I narrow my eyes at her.

"What the hell are you doing?" I grit out.

She gives me a smile as she continues to flutter her lashes.

She's on top of me. Her body is flush against mine.

She's wet. So am I.

The white shirt she's wearing is almost transparent at this point, and I can make out the shape of her ass as she wiggles on top of me.

Fucking hell.

I must be going mad because for a moment, I can't tear my eyes from that sight.

Just for a moment.

I shake myself and grab her. In the span of a few seconds, our positions are reversed. She's on her back and I'm on top of her. This time, my hand is around her throat as it should have been from the beginning. My fingers massage her pulse before I start applying pressure.

But she doesn't react.

If anything, she keeps looking at me with a mix of curiosity and innocence. Good grief, does she not recognize the danger she's in? Does she not realize that in less than one second I could snap her slender neck with barely any effort?

She keeps staring at me.

Deeply. Penetrating.

Her eyes on mine.

She doesn't blink, nor move.

She just stares.

As if one look from her could communicate what words cannot.

They're dark, her eyes. So, so dark. Even with the light reflecting from above, they're like two bottomless pits of tar.

As if following her cue, my eyes, too, don't move.

I don't blink, nor move.

I stay like that, with my hand around her throat and with my eyes on hers.

Everything blurs in the background until there's only one perpendicular line of contact, from my irises to hers. As if there's a whole other world behind our retinas—one that seeks to speak and to be listened to.

Even my breathing slows down until I'm not sure if I'm breathing at all anymore.

There's something unnatural about my stillness—about the fact that I can't bring myself to tighten my hold over her lovely neck and kill her once and for all.

I force my muscles to react, but they fail me.

I'm trapped.

Trapped by two black eyes that are sucking the soul out of me.

It's only when she finally blinks that the spell is broken and I'm once more in control of myself. Yet it's in vain as I soon realize that this position, though a good idea when my intent was to kill her, now works against me. Her legs are spread, and my body is cradled between her thighs.

Her so very warm thighs.

The heat is so potent, it transfers through the wet material of my pants until it reaches my skin.

A groan escapes me.

This is dangerous.

She is dangerous.

I tighten my hold over her neck. Her lips part, and she blows hot air against my lips.

My eyes widen, and once more, I find myself caught in a maddening spell.

Before I can once more recover and bring my plan to fruition, she surprises me.

Again.

Out of nowhere, she grabs a fistful of bubble water and throws it at me. A giggle follows. Then more splashes of water.

"What…"

I release her, shielding my eyes instead. She continues her bubbly assault, and I can do nothing but withstand it for I'm too shocked to even move.

"You lose," she adds in between giggles.

Somehow, I end up standing in the rising puddle, my body frozen in place and my anger simmering on the inside.

Water keeps splashing against my body as she continues this *game*, but I don't even try to dodge the bubbles anymore.

Because a sudden realization dawns on me.

I'm losing.

I'm allowing this damn little heathen to turn my house and my routine upside down, and I can't even do what I do best—kill.

For fuck's sake. What the hell is wrong with me?

She prepares to throw another fistful of bubbly water, but just as she throws her arm back, I catch her wrist. I pull her forward, my gaze icy.

My lip twitches in annoyance.

"Are you done?"

She feigns innocence as she shrugs lazily while still batting her lashes at me.

"Are *you*?" she counters.

"What are you talking about?" I frown.

Without wrenching her wrist free from my hand, she leans in.

Our noses are almost touching.

"You need to relax, Marlowe," she whispers, her voice suddenly a different flavor from before—still sweet but somehow veiled in confidence. "You're too tense. When is the last time you've had fun?"

That sobers me up.

I narrow my eyes at her.

"I don't do *fun*," I grit out and push her off me.

She falls in the puddle of water with a splash.

Finally cured of this momentary insanity, I get up and wring my shirt dry.

"I'll put a mop and a bucket by the door. I want this mess cleaned up within an hour," I tell her sternly.

She regards me curiously, but I don't stick around to hear her reply. I turn my back and leave the laundry room, heading straight for my suite to take a shower and wash this pollution off my skin.

When an hour on the dot has passed and I'm freshly showered and dressed in clean clothes, I go downstairs to check on Minnie's progress.

To my surprise, the entire laundry room is spotless, and Minnie appears to be halfway dry. She's changed into another of the shirts I gave her, and the washing machine is once more running normally.

I grunt a reluctant approval.

Perhaps not all hope is lost.

What is lost, however, is my sleep.

The sun has already risen, and I hate sleeping while the sun is up. That means I'll have to face the day sleep-deprived.

I let out a loud sigh.

That's what I get for trying to be *kind*.

"Come," I tell her, motioning toward the kitchen.

She regards me for a moment, perhaps waiting for some praise, which will not be forthcoming. Eventually, she follows behind.

She hesitantly takes a seat at the table while I move around the kitchen and start the coffee machine.

"Coffee?" I ask, glancing back at her.

She's fidgeting with her fingers on the counter.

"Do you want coffee?" I ask again.

She bites her lip.

"I've never had it before," she answers slowly.

I nod, then go about making two cups of coffee. I take mine black but just in case, I rummage for some milk and sugar and place them on the table. When the coffee is done, I hand her one cup and take a seat across from her and drink my own.

She watches the steam rising from the cup with an odd amount of curiosity before she leans down to sniff the liquid. She scrunches her nose.

After a few moments of deliberating, though, she brings the cup to her lips and takes a sip.

"Ew," she cries out, making a face and pushing the cup away from her.

A smile pulls at my lips. I expected that. Perhaps I didn't warn her on purpose—payback for being a messy little heathen.

"How can you drink that?" She wipes her mouth with the back of her hand.

My lip twitches.

Has she no concept of etiquette?

"Here," I say and point to the milk and sugar. "You can sweeten it and add milk."

She's skeptical, but I'll give her bonus points for not giving up.

She takes the sugar and dumps almost half the container in the coffee. She then takes the milk and fills the cup to the brim.

My eyes widen.

What in the diabetic coma is this?

Satisfied, she takes the cup once more and takes a sip.

I wait for her to screw her face up in disgust again. Any normal person would after that amount of sugar.

"Oh, this is nice!" she exclaims. Placing both hands on the cup, she takes another long sip, smacking her lips together as if it's the most delicious thing in existence. Then she just downs the entire thing in one go.

I glance at my cup. I've barely taken a few sips and she's already finished.

Once more, she wipes her mouth with the back of her hand and lets out a satisfied moan.

"May I have more?"

"More?"

"It's so good. Sweet. I like sweet things."

I *don't*.

"I suppose you can have another," I grumble, getting up and fixing her another cup.

Like before, she pours the rest of the sugar container before adding milk to the brim. Then she drinks it in big, greedy gulps.

I'm halfway through my cup when she's done with her second.

"May I—"

"That's enough, Minnie," I cut her off, already anticipating her question. "If you've never had coffee before, then you likely don't know how you react to caffeine. You may have some more later."

She pouts before eventually nodding.

The washing machine finishes up its schedule, and I show her how to operate the dryer.

After that, I tell her the plan for the day.

"We'll go shopping for clothes for you first."

She opens her mouth to say something, but I shush her.

"You don't have to worry about money. I will not expect anything in return either except for you to abide by my rules—which you have ignored so far."

"Sorry," she murmurs, averting her gaze.

"You may buy a full outfit for each day of the week, warm coats, boots, and whatever else you need."

Girls need a lot of stuff, don't they? Not that I'm an expert, but my mother has a closet the size of a two-bedroom apartment.

"Do I need so many things?" Her voice holds a tinge of wonder.

"I will not allow you to wear dirty clothes again," I tell her sternly.

"But—"

"No buts. We leave as soon as your jeans are dried."

And with that, I end the conversation. Knowing the dryer cycle will take another half an hour, I head to my room to change my clothes for the day. I put on a pair of slacks, a white dress shirt, and a black sweater on top of it. I grab my watch from my nightstand and fasten it around my wrist, then add a touch of cologne.

I may not like to go out and interact with people. But if I have to, then I must at least make an effort to look presentable.

Before I head downstairs to meet Minnie, I grab a merino wool cardigan from my closet. My sweaters would be too big on her, but this should work.

To my surprise, Minnie is waiting for me at the bottom of the stairs. She's wearing her jeans and my white shirt tucked in the band of her pants. It still looks oversized, but somehow, she makes it appear chic.

"Here," I say and hand her the cardigan. "It's too cold to go out in just a shirt."

She murmurs a low thank you as she takes the cardigan from my hands. But instead of putting it on, she first brings it to her nose and inhales deeply. She nuzzles her face against it for a solid five seconds before she smiles and shrugs it on.

Odd.

She's *too* odd.

Perhaps she wanted to make sure it was clean?

Alas. I don't think I want to know what goes inside that messy brain of hers.

The cardigan reaches her knees, but she somehow makes it work.

There's only one more issue.

Her shoes—or lack thereof. She's still wearing the slides from before, but that's unacceptable in this weather.

My lips flatten as I contemplate what we could do.

"What's your shoe size?"

"Uhm..." she stammers. Grabbing one of her slides, she reads the number on the sole. "Five."

I nod, filing that information away for future use. Until then, however, she needs socks, which I'm generous enough to lend to her. At least this way her toes won't freeze off.

With that done, we go to the garage and get in my car.

Next stop, a department store.

Minnie is rather quiet the entire journey. She's staring out the window with a look of pure wonder. She marvels at every single thing on the highway.

On the fucking highway. What is there to even see?

I find myself scowling the more she reacts to her surroundings, and it takes me a moment to realize I'm not scowling because she's a rather ignorant little chit but because her attention is not on *me*.

"Minnie," I call her name.

Her head turns to me, her brows going up in question.

"What's your last name? You didn't mention it."

"Oh." Her eyes flare with concern. "My last name..." She trails off, her hands in her lap, her fingers working furiously buttoning and unbuttoning the cardigan.

She's...nervous.

Why?

I should have asked her this earlier so I could do a background check on her. Why did I not think of it last night? I let the little heathen sleep in my house, for fuck's sake. You'd think I'd take more precautions with something so important.

Yet that never once crossed my mind.

My hands tighten on the steering wheel.

"A-A..."

"A?" I raise an eyebrow.

She gulps down.

"An'yan."

"Minnie An'yan?"

She nods.

Interesting.

Looking forward to see what the internet has to say about you, Minnie An'yan.

We arrive in the city and soon park at Bloomingdale's.

My mother shops there. And if nothing else, at least I can trust her fashion choices.

A valet comes to take our car, but as we get out, he seems to forget his duties as his eyes become glued to Minnie.

He has a silly smile on his face as he makes a beeline toward her.

What the fuck?

Minnie's eyes widen, and she takes a step back, surprising me when she uses me as her shield.

"You're so beautiful, miss," he gushes in a sickeningly sweet voice. He barely notices me, or if he does, he pays me no mind. His focus is entirely on Minnie. "The most beautiful woman I've ever seen," he continues.

I frown and glance at her.

The most beautiful woman? I scoff. This man needs to get his eyes checked. Her features are pleasant and I might even call her pretty when she's freshly showered, but the most beautiful? That's stretching it.

Minnie wraps her fingers around my arm and gives me a worried look.

At the same time, the valet continues walking toward us. It's almost as if Minnie is his entire focus, and nothing can shake that. Not even the honking of cars or the fact that I'm raising my voice at him. "What the fuck do you think you're doing?"

He ignores me.

It's almost as if he's bespelled as he continues to spout nonsense about how beautiful Minnie is.

"I must touch you," he suddenly says. He reaches with his arm forward, but I don't give him time to do anything as I catch his arm and twist it behind his back, all the while keeping Minnie behind me and away from him.

"The only thing you'll touch is a wooden casket, if you're lucky," I tell him in a low voice. "Now get lost before I decide to bury you alive—no casket for you."

Minnie is completely shielded by my body at this point, and I note that the man finally gets to his senses. His eyes are wide with shock as he regards me.

"I-I'm sorry. I don't know what came over me," he stammers.

I pin him with my gaze, and that's enough to get him moving. He puts distance between us, all the while apologizing and making excuses for his behavior.

When he's a few steps away, he all but dashes inside. It takes a few moments for a different valet to come out to help us, this time a woman.

She, too, apologizes for her coworker.

I give her the car keys and ignore her babbling. Taking Minnie's hand in mine, I lead her to the entrance of the department store.

"Are you okay?" I ask when we get to the lobby. It's early in the morning on a weekday, so there are not too many people around.

She strains a smile.

"Yes. Just a little shaken," she whispers.

"Don't worry. As long as you're with me, nothing will happen to you. No one will touch you, all right?"

Thoughtless idiot! What the hell are you promising her?

But just the way her face lights up makes me glad I said those words and I promptly push my inner voice aside. Perhaps for once, I should let my instinct lead me rather than my intellect.

"That's kind of you," she murmurs shyly, tugging a strand of hair behind her ear. "But..." She takes a deep breath. "As long as you're with me, that will keep happening."

"What do you mean?" I ask, perplexed.

"Men," she answers with a defeated shrug. "They see me and they...want me."

What?

I blink.

Then I throw my head back and laugh.

This little heathen has quite the sense of humor.

EIGHT

"WHY ARE YOU LAUGHING? I'm serious," Minnie says with a frown.

"Sure, pet, sure." I pat her on the shoulders. "We should get you some shoes first. Just seeing you in those goddamn slides makes me physically uncomfortable."

"But—"

"Come," I tell her and grab her hand.

I'm not too familiar with women's brands, but I spot a shoe store close to the entrance, so we head there.

As we enter the store, all eyes are suddenly on us. There are mostly women inside, but the few men who wait around while their wives shop stare openly at Minnie.

I suppose they're equally offended by her battered slides.

"We'll get you some sneakers and boots for now. You can pick more items if something catches your fancy," I comment as I accompany her to the sneaker display.

Her hand is still in mine. She's incredibly close to me, sliding even closer when someone looks her way. Perhaps this is a sign of her trauma, too. She's already been through too much. And for some reason, she finds me safe.

My chest fills with pride, and I'm surprised to realize how delighted I am by the prospect that I'm her safe haven. Despite having an issue with strangers coming into my personal space, I don't mind it so much with her.

I pull her closer.

She gives me a shy smile.

There. Smart girl.

We browse around the sneaker selection for a while, but Minnie doesn't know what to choose.

"What do you like?" I ask her eventually.

"I like white. And red."

"What type of shoe do you like?" I amend with a laugh.

Her brows furrow.

"I just want something comfortable."

Right at that moment, a sales associate clears her throat as she comes to our side.

"Is there anything I can help you with?" she asks with a sickeningly sweet smile.

Despite the fact that we're looking at the female section of shoes, she's not even looking at Minnie or directing the question toward her. Instead, she's trying to work her wiles on me.

Ah, she probably thinks I'm the one paying, so she needs to be in my good graces.

Alas, I don't like the way she's ignoring my little heathen. She's the customer after all.

"What do you have in size five?" I ask brusquely.

"Size five?" she repeats, a frown pulling at her features. "The smallest most brands carry is a six. You should go to the kids' section."

Then she smiles. The same fake-ass smile.

Minnie gawks at her.

I narrow my eyes, my cheek twitching in annoyance.

"What about these?" I pick up the pair of sneakers that seems to be the smallest visually. Looking at the sole, I note they're a size thirty-five—the European equivalent of five.

"Uhm…" The sales assistant clears her throat.

"Bring us the other pair for this one."

The woman looks as if she wants to say something else, but she holds her tongue and mutters an *I'll be back*.

Minnie raises herself on her toes to peek at the shoe. I realize I'm holding it too high for her to see, so I hand it to her.

"Oh," she murmurs. "They're white *with* red."

There's something about the cadence of her voice that makes my breath stop. It's a combination of wonder and excitement that I don't think I've ever felt for something as mundane as a shoe. But just as that thought crosses my mind, I berate myself.

I was fortunate enough to be born into a wealthy family and even more fortunate to be able to start my business with the inheritance I got when I turned eighteen. I've never wanted for anything in my entire life. Not too many people can say that.

Minnie has probably worn hand-me-downs her entire life, especially since she grew up in the system. I doubt she's bought herself many new things.

Not wanting to mar her happiness, I keep a finger on the price tag so she doesn't feel bad about it.

"You like them?"

"Of course I do! They're so pretty! And look, they have a high heel," she says excitedly as she points to the platform, which by my estimates looks to be about two to three inches tall.

"That's a platform, pet. But I'm glad you like them. Sit down and try them on," I mention as the sales assistant comes back with the other shoe.

Minnie sits down on a round cushion and takes off her worn slides, placing them carefully aside. I don't know why that gesture in itself sends a sharp pain in my chest.

She takes the left shoe and undoes the laces before gingerly sliding her foot inside. She does the same with the other shoe and then proceeds to utterly fail at tying the laces back.

"Let me," I murmur and get to my knees in front of her. I tie one shoelace, then the other.

"They fit well?" I ask after I'm done.

She moves her feet around to test the shoe before getting up and walking a few steps.

"Oh, yes!" she exclaims. "And look, Marlowe. I'm taller," she says as she plants herself before me and shows me that now she's *slightly* taller.

"Yes, you are," I chuckle. "We'll get these," I note to the sales assistant.

She nods.

Minnie does a pirouette. She has an effusive smile on her lips as she skips around me, thanking me profusely for her new pair of shoes.

If she's this easy to please...

I go around looking for more shoes her size, and I find a pair of rain boots, a pair of normal leather boots, a leather loafer in white, and a pair of flats in red.

I take them and head back to Minnie so she can try them on. But as I turn toward her, I note that she's now surrounded by a group of men.

What the fuck?

I turned my back for a couple of minutes and this happened.

"Come on, miss. Tell us your name."

"Please leave," Minnie whispers, her eyes stuck to the ground.

"You heard the lady. Leave," I grit out as I reach her side.

They're the same men who'd been eyeing her when we came in. And to make matters even worse, their wives are a few steps away, ready to blow up at their inappropriate behavior.

"But I've never seen someone so beautiful before," one of the men says, his gaze roaming over Minnie's body.

"And you will not *see* again if you don't fucking move." I lower my voice, the threat clear.

"Marlowe," Minnie whimpers as she all but throws herself into my arms. "Make them go away, please."

The men follow her with their eyes, almost as if they're drunk on the sight of her. They take a step closer. Fucking hell, they look like zombies who've lost all capacity for reason.

"Security!" I call out.

At the same time, the wives try to pull their husbands away, their shrilly voices echoing in the store as they dare insult *my* Minnie instead of their lascivious husbands.

"Lady, shut the fuck up," I snap, pulling Minnie behind me to shield her once more. "One more word about her and I'll forget you're a woman and that sometimes I'm a gentleman."

That seems to shut her up. And as soon as Minnie is out of sight, the men suddenly regain control of their faculties. They appear aghast at their actions, and they let their wives lead them, who continue to nag and chide.

Security just now arrives in the form of a brawny man. But I don't know if he's supposed to help in any way considering the way his eyes widen when he spots Minnie. His entire body language changes. From a professional stance, he now looks like a lovestruck fool as he advances toward us.

"Stop!" I order him, hiding Minnie again.

The glaze covering his eyes vanishes and he blinks.

"Leave us."

He mutters something but does as told.

Turning to the sales assistant who is still by our side, albeit just as shocked as everyone else, I say, "Pack those shoes too." I point to the ones I'd picked out earlier. "She'll keep these platform sneakers on."

She stares at me.

"Hurry!" I bark out.

Nodding, she takes the shoes from my hand and runs to the back.

Minnie squeezes my hand.

"I wasn't joking earlier," she whispers, gazing up at me with those soulful eyes of hers. "Men see me and…"

"I got it," I answer tightly.

I'm still perplexed as to *why* this happens. She's pretty, yes, and her eyes have an otherworldly quality to them. But she's hardly the type to make men go mad with desire.

One person could have been a fluke. But three men at once trying to get close to her and telling her she's the most beautiful woman they've ever seen? Coupled with the two assaults I saved her from?

Something is odd.

And I don't like it. Not one fucking bit.

"Please don't be mad at me," she whispers, pulling on my hand.

"I'm not mad at you, pet. I'm mad at those fucking losers."

"It always happens," she says with a sigh. "I think we should go back home. I'll just get you into more trouble."

"No." I'm surprised at the firmness of my tone. "We came here to get what *you* like. And we're going to do exactly that. If someone tries to get close to you, they'll have to get through me first."

She bites her lip as she regards me wide-eyed.

"I don't think you realize it, pet. But I'm not an easy guy to get past."

"You're strong," she murmurs. "You can protect me."

"Damn right." I nod.

Smart girl. Perhaps my initial assessment of her was not entirely accurate. She might be ignorant about many things, but at least she can recognize that I'm the *only* one who can protect her.

Because I'm the only one who can claim her life, too.

"I knew you could protect me, Marlowe," she says before she

wraps her arms around my midriff in a tight hug. "You're the bestest ever."

"Best," I correct, though my tone is nowhere as harsh as before. "It's already superlative."

She shakes her head against my chest.

"Superlative will never be enough."

Odd little creature.

I sigh.

For all the trouble she creates in her wake, she's proving to be quite the entertaining little thing. Perhaps I could put off killing her for a while—only as long as I derive entertainment from her.

My therapist was right. I need to meet new people, for they're the only way I can grow and learn. And in a way, I took her advice.

I met *her*. Killing Minnie is *not* going to be anywhere near my usual *modus operandi*. It's going to be a glorious new start, and I'll relish every single moment of it.

I've never personally known my victims before.

With the exception of Mr. Rhodes, my old neighbor, though I'm not sure he counts. He was only someone within my proximity, not someone with whom I interacted. Then there was also... No, he doesn't count either.

Minnie is different. She'll change *everything*.

"Why is your heart beating so fast, Marlowe?" Minnie's voice puts a stop to my train of thought.

A slow, insidious smile spreads across my lips.

"I was thinking about something exciting, pet," I murmur.

She leans back to look at me, blinking curiously.

"What?"

"You," I answer.

"Me?"

"Yes. You, pet."

I smile then. A smile to lure the prey. A smile to get her comfortable.

And she smiles back.

Ah, my little heathen, I have grand plans for you. So grand, I cannot help the giddiness bubbling inside of me.

This is a foreign feeling for me.

Excitement.

Yet as I look at her, so small, so trusting, I can't help but picture the future.

Her, unmoving. Her, on display.

All for me.

"Sir, your order is ready," the sales assistant calls out.

I sigh when that exhilarating image dissipates.

If I killed women, I'd kill that annoying sales assistant in a heartbeat.

But I don't.

Except for Minnie.

She'll be the only one. *My* only one.

Because she's special. The *mostest* special.

I chuckle to myself as I lead Minnie to the counter and pay for the shoes.

As long as I disguise myself as her protector, she'll never know what truly awaits her.

With the shoes paid, we leave. I ask for our purchases to be taken to my car while we go browse other stores.

Minnie is almost bursting with happiness as she keeps staring at her new shoes. But that all changes when we go up the escalator and more men turn their sights on her. She huddles closer to my side, burying her small hand in mine.

I keep my focus razor-sharp in case anyone decides to approach. Her claims don't seem as ludicrous now as I note the way men eat her up with their eyes, almost as if they were bewitched by her.

Somehow, the prospect of others watching her like this enrages me.

They will not get to touch her—not on my watch. But even their eyes on her are more than I can stand, and the violence in me stirs.

I take a deep breath.

I must calm down.

The last thing I want, *or* need, is to create another scene like the one from the diner. Luckily, that had been in a remote location. The same shit won't fly in the middle of New York City.

Spotting a hat store, I take Minnie with me and buy her a cap, instructing her to keep it low on her face—perhaps this can help us avoid attention.

Alas. It might mitigate it, but it doesn't stop completely.

"I'm sorry," she whispers again.

"It's all right, pet. We'll buy you some clothes and leave."

She gives me a tight nod but doesn't seem too reassured.

We head into a ladies' clothing store to try to avoid more male attention. There are still a couple here and there trailing after their wives, but hopefully, they'll mind their own business.

I do my best to keep Minnie shielded by my side, and the moment another man tries to look her way, I give them my signature glare that makes them swiftly avert their eyes.

First, we shop for layers: leggings, tights, and undershirts.

"Do I really need that much?" she asks when she notes the pile of clothing mounting in our cart.

I raise a brow at her.

"I have money," I tell her pointedly.

"You do, but I don't. I don't want to take advantage of your kindness," she murmurs.

I stop her.

"Minnie, this is *not* kindness. I'm doing this for myself because I get cold the moment I see you without any clothes. So no. You're not taking advantage of anything."

Her lips flatten and she brings her gaze to the floor.

"You're a bit controlling," she mumbles under her breath.

"What was that?" I ask and tip her chin up.

"You are...controlling," she says the words louder. "You're

always saying Minnie come here, Minnie let's go there, Minnie do this, Minnie follow me—"

"Damn right," I cut her off. "My house, my rules."

She narrows her eyes at me before she releases a long sigh. "I suppose you're right."

"Don't look too down about it. You're quite good at following orders," I add with a wink.

Her cheeks flush a deep red before she averts her gaze. But I don't miss the little smile that plays at her lips.

"You need jeans, shirts, sweaters, and a few dresses. A coat as well. And underwear..."

"Oh, like those?" Before I can reply, she dashes to the other side of the aisle where the lingerie is and haphazardly picks up a few pieces. She seems quite proud of her selection. A mix of white-and-red frilly things, including some lace underwear and a rather provocative bra.

"That won't fit," I note to the bra she just threw into the cart.

"What?" She blinks.

"I think you need a bigger cup."

She glances down at the bra and then back at me.

"You think so? I've never worn a bra before," she adds pensively.

"Never?" I ask, horrified.

She shakes her head.

"But it looks nice, so I wanted one." She points to the ad pictures on the wall featuring models in lingerie.

I stare at her. I didn't think she could surprise me more, but here she is.

"Get a few sizes and you can try them on," I say.

She does as told, and then we fill the cart with more clothing items for her to try on. When there's no more space in the cart, we finally head to the changing rooms.

I've been shopping with my mother before. Many times, in fact. Before I left my family's house, that was her favorite pastime.

I always hated it.

It was dull and boring, and it consisted of my mother spending hours on end trying on clothes before leaving an exorbitant amount of money at check-out.

I should have hated this *too*. But for some reason, I find it rather interesting—sans the overwhelming male attention. Frankly, I could do without any of that.

But I like observing Minnie. It's an opportunity for me to learn what she likes and what she doesn't—to learn what makes her tick. It will come in handy at some point.

The more I know, the easier it will be to manipulate her and make her behave as I want her to.

I take a seat while Minnie goes inside the dressing room.

One after another, she tries on the outfits and comes out to get my opinion.

I tell her honestly which ones look good on her and which do not. She doesn't seem particularly impressed with my frankness, but alas. If I'm footing the bill, I will not have her walking around in cheap, ill-fitting clothes.

We're almost done sifting through the clothes when Minnie is down to the bras she's chosen.

"Uhm, Marlowe?" she calls out, a tinge of worry in her voice. "I don't think this works," she adds in a defeated tone.

"What do you mean?"

She doesn't come out, so I feel compelled to go after her. Pulling the curtain aside, I stop dead in my tracks.

This is my fault. I walked into this trap with my own two feet.

She's wearing a lacy red bra that's one or two sizes too small, her breasts spilling out of the cups. Luckily—for my sanity—she's still wearing her pants.

"This is the biggest size I got and it still doesn't fit." She sighs as she turns to me, motioning toward the generous cleavage that's now directly in my line of view.

I gulp down.

Just like before, Minnie is not at all shy about her nudity. She's almost intentionally tempting me to feast my eyes on her assets, which to my everlasting shame, I do.

Did it suddenly get too warm in here?

"I can go look for bigger sizes. Do you want this model and color?"

She nods.

"Yes, please. It's so pretty," she gushes.

I press my lips together. She might not be the most beautiful woman in the world, but damn if she's not the cutest. Even to my jaded eyes, she's too compelling to ignore. So off I go in search of other bra sizes.

The women around give me odd looks as they see me browsing, with one older woman whispering, "He must be one of those perverts."

I pick out three bigger sizes of the red bra and turn. Putting on my best smile, I look her dead in the eye.

"Not my fault I can wear this better than you, darling," I say in a high-pitched voice, waving around the red bra. I wink at her and head back to the dressing room. A smile pulls at my lips as I hear the outraged cries of the older ladies in my wake.

God, how I hate people.

"You're so wicked, Marlowe," Minnie says with a chuckle.

I shrug.

"If the situation requires it..."

She continues laughing as she proceeds to try on the other sizes.

"So? What's the verdict?"

"One of them fits!" she exclaims enthusiastically. "Oh my, Marlowe, look!"

She pulls back the curtain and steps out, letting *everyone* see how well that fucking bra looks on her.

My body is in motion before my brain can catch up.

She's barely taken one step into the open before I push her back into the cabin and pull the curtain to cover us.

Tension rolls off me in violent waves as I realize that anyone could have seen her. Men and women alike, and for some reason, I take issue with other women seeing her like this, too.

My hands are on her shoulders, my fingers digging into her warm flesh.

It's bad enough that men go crazy with just one look at her face. They'd probably launch a million ships if they got a glimpse of her body.

Her back hits the mirror as she gazes at me with concern.

"Marlo—"

"I get it that you're not bothered by your nudity. But I am."

"W-what do you mean?" Her lip trembles as she whispers. A look of hurt crosses her face. Another thing I don't seem to like.

"I'm adding another rule to our agreement," I add in a tight voice. "You may *never* show your naked body, or naked body parts to anyone."

Her tongue peeks out and she licks her bottom lip.

The sight is unnerving, and warmth spreads through my body like wildfire.

It's odd, isn't it? I'm always hot when I'm in her presence. Me, who's been cold my entire life.

"Anyone?" she murmurs softly.

"Anyone," I confirm. Her eyes flash at me. "Anyone but me."

NINE

SHE STARES AT ME, unmoving.

I cannot seem to move either, even though a few moments ago my body was more than capable of moving without intending to.

Her cheeks are flushed.

My eyes are drawn to the swell of her breasts as her chest rises and falls with every breath.

This is dangerous.

Far too dangerous.

I wrench my gaze away from that tantalizing sight, only to see her lick her lips.

Her pink tongue peeks out, and my pulse quickens.

However, the loud ringing of my phone destroys the moment.

I scowl and pull back, though I'm relieved for the intermission.

That is until I see the call ID.

I close my eyes and release a long sigh before I pick up.

"Mother," I grumble. "Why are you calling? I'm busy."

"Marlowe, dear, that's not how you speak to your mother," she chides. "Can't I call to see how my favorite son is doing?"

"I'm not your favorite son and you know it," I counter.

"Well, second favorite. But it should count, no?"

"Mother," I groan. "You know I have a job. You can't be calling me every day just because you're bored."

"I'm *not* bored. Perhaps lonely. But that's because neither you nor your siblings ever bother to spend time with me," she whines.

"You're a retired rich old lady. I'm sure you can find some rich old lady stuff to do."

"Marlowe!" She releases a scandalized cry. "I raised you for eighteen years. The least you could do is answer when I call and keep me some company. It's not as if that job of yours is too time-consuming. All you do is sit in front of a computer and delegate tasks," she continues.

I roll my eyes. Here it goes. While all my siblings have standard careers—lawyers and doctors—my mother has never forgiven me for abandoning my studies to start my own tech company. She thinks it's *beneath* our family name. Never mind the fact that I make more than all my brothers combined *just* from sitting in front of a computer and delegating tasks as she calls it.

"Fine. What did you want to talk about?"

I give Minnie another look before I exit the dressing room and take a seat on the couch. I suppose I can entertain my mother for a while until Minnie gets changed.

Despite my grumbles, I do have a soft spot for my mother.

"Well, Giles called," she starts.

"When does he not?" I fire back. "You forget that I know he visits you almost daily, Mother. Why you don't openly date him, I have no idea."

"W-what? Date Giles? Are you mad, Marlowe? What would people think?"

"I assure you that most people already know you've been sleeping with him for years."

"Marlowe!" She gasps. "What are you talking about?"

Of course she'd feign ignorance. It's been an open secret for the last twenty years, so I don't know why she's still bent on denying it.

"Of course, Mother. Forgive me for implying such a thing. You can continue to hide your affair in plain sight and think no one knows about it."

"M-M-Marlowe..." she sputters. "That's what I get for calling you," she mutters.

"Happy to be of service." I chuckle.

"Back to the topic at hand," she resumes in her stern voice. "Giles told me about your *incident*. He said he handled it, but he also let it drop that there was a lady with you?"

I curse under my breath. Of course Giles would tell Mother that.

"She's a friend."

"You don't have friends. Much less of the opposite gender," she replies, tongue in cheek.

"I have now."

"Fabulous! Oh my, dear, you have no idea how long I've waited for this day. I thought it was never going to happen. When I heard Giles, I could not believe it, of course, but then he showed me some of the footage from that diner."

"He was supposed to get rid of that," I mumble.

"He did, after he showed it to me, of course."

"And you say you're not involved in any way."

"That's neither here nor there, dear. I must say I was surprised to see the state of the girl. She was barely clothed, for God's sake. Where did you find her, Marlowe? Not that I'm complaining. God forbid. I'm very happy to see you in the company of someone else, regardless of whether she's a little street urchin or not. She isn't, is she?"

"And if she were?" I ask, just to bait her.

There's no point in lying to her now since Giles must have told her all the details already. If he weren't so damn good at his job, I would have stopped using him the moment I heard about his involvement with my mother.

Alas. Even if I prefer to keep my distance from my family, at the end of the day, what happens in our family, *stays* there.

"Well, I can't be picky now, of course. If that's what you like..." Her voice wobbles. She takes a deep breath and continues. "I'd like to meet her. I have already made a reservation at the Atera for the end of the month."

"Now wait a moment. What did you just say?" I stand up and pace around.

"You don't think I'm going to miss this chance for anything in the world, do you? I had already resigned myself to never seeing you with anyone before I die," she says in a dramatic tone. "So imagine my surprise when not only did I see you with a woman, but you held *hands*! You barely let *me* touch you and you held hands with that young lady? Well, I must meet her."

"Mother." I take a deep breath. "There will be no meeting of any sort. I'll see you at your birthday party next month. That's enough."

"How can you say that? Once a year is never enough, dear. No, I will not have it. The reservation is for the last Wednesday of this month at seven in the evening. I shall see you there, with your young lady."

"And if I don't?" I drawl.

"Then I'll get your home address out of Giles and I'll never leave you alone until the day I die. I'll put up a tent in front of your house and you will not be able to kick me out."

"Did you just threaten to annoy me for the rest of your life?"

"Precisely." She releases a loud humph.

"May I remind you that you would not last a day in a tent?" I laugh.

"Then it shall be a battle of wills," she confidently replies. "May the strongest win."

Fucking hell. I'm never going to get rid of her until she meets Minnie, that much is for sure.

"Fine," I eventually agree. "But remember. She's *just* a friend. You will not make her uncomfortable."

There's a pause on the line before my mother chuckles.

"Of course, dear. I'll be the picture of decorum. Just make sure she's wearing something more...appropriate."

Shaking my head, I end the call and place the phone in my pocket.

Minnie exits the dressing room and regards me curiously.

"My mother wants to meet you," I tell her.

She blinks. "She...does?"

"She somehow found out about you and now she wants to get to know you over dinner. But it's fine if you don't want to come," I quickly amend.

What I wouldn't give to get myself out of this mess, but the truth is that it's very unlikely I'll be able to.

When my mother puts her mind to something, it's impossible to dissuade her. I have no doubt she would make good on her threat to camp outside my home, in a tent no less.

My lips flatten in annoyance.

"No, no. I would love to," Minnie says, her lips slowly spreading into a smile.

I grunt.

"Let's go," I tell her, helping her with her clothes.

She pulls her cap lower to hide her features and follows behind me.

We get to the check-out, but there are at least ten people in front of us.

I curse under my breath.

I should have asked someone else to come shop with her—a personal stylist or whatever women use. Perhaps I should have ordered her something online and be done with it. But it would have taken days for it to arrive and she needs the clothes and shoes now.

I take a deep breath.

I hate waiting.

From the corner of my eye, I spot the Halloween clearance section, and something catches my attention.

A maid costume.

A flash of Minnie wearing that around the house while she cleans appears in my mind, and I hum in approval.

That would not be a bad sight at all.

It would be her work uniform, no?

"Wait here. I need to get something," I say before I leave the queue.

There are a number of variations of maid costumes. Some are downright skimpy, with skirts that are not longer than the width of my palm.

No, that would not do.

I don't need more temptation.

I browse the costumes until I find a more conservative one. The black dress is knee-high, with white lace detail around the hem, sleeves, and collar. There's a white apron included.

I check the back label and note that it's made out of one hundred percent cotton.

Good. This should be gentle on her skin.

I grab one of them and head back to the line.

I'm a few steps away when I note another woman talking to Minnie. I can't hear what she's saying yet, but Minnie's body language tells me this is not a welcome interaction. The woman grabs her hand and whispers something in her ear.

By the time I get to her side, I can only hear one sentence.

"They will come for you. You need to leave—"

My lip twitches.

"Any problem?" I ask as I slap the woman's hand aside. Immediately, I pull Minnie to my side, holding her tightly against my body.

The woman in question glares at us. Her hair is a deep shade of red, and her dark eyes flash red too.

I blink. What the fuck?

"He doesn't know who you are, does he?" The woman's lips curve into a smile.

One glance at Minnie, and I see the way her shoulders stiffen. Her lips tremble, and I swear I note some moisture clinging to her lashes.

"You need to leave. Now," I grit out.

The woman's laughter echoes in her wake as she steps away from us. But at no point does she take her eyes off Minnie, nor is her gaze any less threatening.

"What was that about?"

Minnie shrugs.

"I don't know. She scared me," she murmurs as she huddles closer to my side.

I wrap an arm around her shoulders.

"What did she mean by that? Who will come for you?"

Another shrug, though this one has less conviction.

"Some people are just weird, no?" She attempts a laugh.

I narrow my eyes at her.

She was scared. Of that I have no doubt. But there's more to this interaction than meets the eye, and for some reason, Minnie refuses to tell me the truth.

Hmm.

I don't press her on it. I should have plenty of information on her and her entire life once I do a deep dive into her.

We reach the counter and I unload our cart.

The cashier starts scanning the items, and the total ends up somewhere in the five figures. I give her my black card, and she completes the payment.

Minnie's eyes widen and her hold on my arm tightens.

"That's a lot, isn't it?"

"It is," I agree.

"Are you sure you don't want me to pay you back somehow?"

Ah, the little heathen fell right into my trap.

"You don't have to pay me. But," I say as I take out the maid costume from one of the bags. "This is your uniform. From now on, you'll clean my house wearing this."

She takes the package out of my hands and studies it with a frown.

"Oh. I can do that." She nods confidently. "It's pretty, too."

"Of course it is. I chose it personally." I grunt.

That went...better than expected. Suddenly, my head swims in visions of Minnie wearing that maid uniform—unnatural visions that I should put an immediate stop to.

Alas. I'll only admire the sight from afar.

Perhaps there's something rather...irresistible about her. Otherwise, I don't see why I'd change decades-long worth of convictions for her convenience.

As we leave the store, the same thing happens again. Men turn and stare. One by one, they look at Minnie with an inscrutable expression on their faces. Those who get a better look at her get that same glazed look in their eyes and they stop whatever they're doing to follow us.

"You were not kidding when you said men suddenly want you," I add in a dry voice.

It takes everything in me not to stop and make a scene, perhaps beat one or two of the men on our trail to a pulp. Agh, my blood is boiling just thinking about my fist making contact with their faces. And for once, I barely remember my revulsion about touching them barehanded and making contact with their blood. In fact, I'm almost craving it.

I look back and note five men currently on our trail. They appear to be in some kind of trance since they bump into people but barely acknowledge it. Their eyes are solely on Minnie, and their sole focus is getting closer to her.

"I'm sorry," she whispers, glancing back. A shiver goes down her back.

"Is it always like this?" My voice is a little rougher than intended, but I still can't wrap my mind around it.

Is she a goddamn siren? Because I can no longer deny that not only does she have a strange effect on those of the male variety, but she has a strange effect on me too. How else would anyone explain the fact that I let her live in my sanctuary, that I overlooked her egregious breaking of my rules, or that I took her shopping?

Or, the most outrageous thing yet is that I find her *cute*.

I scowl as my frustration mounts—at myself and at those fucking losers who think to follow her.

She gives me a guilty nod.

"I try to avoid populated areas," she answers. "But it's not always possible."

Of course it's not fucking possible if she's homeless. Good grief, what has this slip of a woman had to endure while living on the streets? I can hardly imagine, and to my surprise, a surge of protectiveness appears in my chest.

We pick up our speed. As soon as I get the keys to my car from the valet, we load the bags in the trunk and get inside.

The men are not far behind, so I start the car and steer it out of the parking lot.

"And you're telling me you've never been with a man?" I raise a brow.

That in itself is strange with the amount of attention she attracts. But even stranger is my reaction to the thought of her being with someone else.

She immediately shakes her head.

"Why not? You're twenty-five. That's unusual at your age, is it not?"

My focus is on the road, but I still glance at her from the corner of my eyes every now and then.

"Is it?" She shrugs. "That type of intimacy is only reserved for someone special."

"Someone special?" My brows go up in question.

A wistful smile appears on her face.

"My soulmate," she continues. "It's reserved only for my soulmate."

I narrow my eyes at her.

My blood pounds aggressively against my temples.

"You speak as if you already know who that is," I mention slowly.

Her smile grows brighter.

"I do. He's someone from my past. I hope to get together with him again at some point," she answers sweetly. The moment she mentions him, the cadence of her voice changes.

And I don't fucking like it.

Not one bit.

"Who?" The question comes out as aggressive. My mistake.

She startles at my tone and regards me with apprehension.

"If you know who he is, why not seek his help?"

She takes a deep breath.

"It's...complicated."

My nostrils flare.

"I don't see how it's complicated," I bite out. "If he's your *soulmate* or whatever, he should have helped you in some way, no?"

She purses her lips and starts fidgeting with her hands—a sign she's getting nervous.

"He would if he knew," she murmurs in a low voice.

"If that were me, I'd make it *my* business to know. Not knowing is not an excuse," I continue, though I have no clue where this is coming from. Yet as soon as the words are out of my mouth, I realize that this *is* the truth.

If I had such a person, I'd cross mountains and seas to get to her. Hell, she would not be lost to me in the first place because I'd never let her out of my sight.

"You don't know him." She glares at me.

I shrug.

"Have you ever been in love, Marlowe?" she suddenly asks.

I turn to look at her.

"No," I answer immediately.

"Why?"

"What type of question is that?"

"A simple one. You're old enough. Why haven't you been in love until now?"

I don't like where this line of questioning is going.

"I don't have the interest, nor the inclination for it."

She tilts her head to the side and studies me. She crosses her arms over her chest as if to tell me she means business.

"And what type of inclination would that be?"

"I'm not the sentimental type."

It is what it is and I don't plan to make any excuses for it. I prefer to live in solitude and secrecy, although that will prove to be harder now with her around me.

I scowl as I once more ask myself why I'm allowing this little stranger to invade my life thusly.

"Have you ever been in a relationship?" she counters with another question.

"Minnie. For fuck's sake, what's with all these questions?" I ask angrily.

"You're swearing again." She shakes her head at me. "You asked me private questions. I think it's only fair I ask you the same."

"What, next you're going to ask me how many women I've fucked?" I roll my eyes at her.

"How many?" she asks pointedly. She wiggles in her seat and comes closer to me, her eyes boring a hole in me.

"It's none of your fucking business," I grit out.

"How many, Marlowe?" she repeats, this time with more emphasis. Her eyes flash at me, and before I know it, she pulls my steering wheel to the left, almost causing us to have a direct collision with another car.

I curse aloud and maneuver the car to the side, parking it by the side of the road.

"What the fuck is wrong with you?" I call out, grabbing her by the shoulders and shaking her. "You almost killed us, Minnie. For fuck's sake."

Her lips are pressed in a tight line as she glares at me defiantly. There's a fire in her eyes that burns so hot, my body unwittingly reacts.

I should be mad.

I should be fucking fuming.

But instead, there's only an ardent desire for...more.

What the fuck is wrong with me?

"How many, Marlowe? Tell me," she demands.

I've gotten used to the meek version of Minnie—the soft temperament that fits her outer appearance. Yet seeing her now, like this, makes me wonder just how much of that was true. What truly hides behind her sweet face?

"What's your body score?" she asks as she leans forward. She's the epitome of seriousness, but how can I take her seriously when she's always using the wrong idioms?

"You mean body count?" I repeat jokingly.

She doesn't laugh. She just openly glares at me.

"Body score, body count. Whatever. What is it?"

"Are you sure you want to know?" I wiggle my brows at her suggestively.

"Tell me!" she demands impatiently.

"One hundred and fifty-seven," I answer with a straight face.

Her mouth drops open in shock. She blinks repeatedly, swallowing hard.

Slowly, she moves away from me, settling back into her seat and staring into open space. There's a slow tremor that goes down her spine, and she places her hands in her lap, fidgeting with them.

"Satisfied now?" I attempt to lighten the mood.

She doesn't even look at me. She continues to stare in the distance as she gives me a tight nod—one that's seemingly filled with pain.

I frown.

Her reaction is strange and I don't know what to make of it.

Yet I also can't tell her the truth. My body count *is* one hundred and fifty-seven. As in one hundred and fifty-seven people that I've killed.

But she doesn't need to know that.

TEN

SHE DOESN'T SPEAK to me for the rest of the day.

Even when I hand her the list of cleaning tasks, she just nods, glances at it, and then puts on her maid costume and proceeds to clean.

I can't even find fault with her cleaning. She follows my instructions to a T, scrubbing the floors until they shine and dusting the furniture until there's not one speck of dirt left.

Throughout the day, I try to ask her how she's doing, but she just glares at me before resuming her cleaning duties.

I decide to get some work done while she's busy, but I can't seem to focus on anything. Staring blankly at my computer, I find my thoughts straying to her as I wonder what she's up to. It takes me a few consecutive tries to get into a work mindset before I give up.

To make matters worse, I cannot even focus on a *Supernatural* episode—my usual pastime when I don't work.

Instead, all I can think about is her.

I scowl at myself.

I bought her shoes and clothes and now she's not speaking to me.

What the hell is wrong with her?

Don't girls like those things?

She should be thanking me profusely, perhaps on her knees. Now, that wouldn't be such a bad sight. Especially in that maid outfit of hers.

Before I can contemplate how my obsession with her is ruining my things, I click on the camera feed to see what she's up to.

Maybe it was a premonition, but she *is* on her knees in the bathroom on the first floor, scrubbing the floor. She's just started by the looks of it. There's only one small shining patch of tile among other dirty ones. Alas, she has her work cut out for her.

Although the dress covers most of her, from the angle of the camera, I can see her slender ankles. And as I rake my gaze over her body, my eyes land on her ass.

She thrusts it backward as she swipes the cleaning rag back and forth.

A groan slips past my lips.

This is madness.

Pure and simple.

She takes a deep breath as she leans back, wiping her forehead with the back of her hand. Usually, that would disturb me since her hands are undoubtedly drenched in a mix of filth and detergent. Yet for some reason, there's no revulsion.

My pulse quickens as I watch every small move she makes.

She gets to her feet and dumps the cleaning rag to the ground. Placing her hands on her hips, she looks around as she shakes her head.

She must be tired.

She's already cleaned most of the ground floor. I know firsthand how energy-consuming that is. But she hasn't complained once.

Hell, she didn't need to clean everything *today*. But it seems to be a way to rebel against whatever I did.

And I'm still left scratching my head as to what the hell I must have done or said wrong.

She was so happy this morning when we went shopping. But after the car ride home, she suddenly did a one-eighty.

Is she mad about what I said about that soulmate of hers?

Maybe that's it.

But the moment I think of that, my entire body tenses. Just who the hell is that wimp who would leave this poor little girl to fend for herself? She has no one in the world. Seeing how men flock to her and give her unwanted attention, she has most likely been living with danger looming over her head at all times. It's no wonder she went to prison for assault—a well-deserved assault if I do say so myself.

It's clear her entire life has been one struggle after another.

So where the hell is that knight in shining armor of hers? If she knows who he is, why has she not gone to him? And why the hell has he not tried to find her?

If that were me...

No. I shake my head at my own thoughts. I will not go there.

She's not my responsibility, nor is she my concern.

But deep down you want her to be...

That's partially correct. The only reason why I'm so interested in Minnie is because I've never met someone quite like her before. And she has all the makings to be the perfect hundred and fifty-eighth victim.

With one exception...

She's never done anything *truly* bad in her life. Yes, she might not have anyone who would miss her. But I don't kill innocents. And the more I learn about her, the more I see her for the pitiful creature she really is.

My lips flatten in annoyance.

This is a quandary I must solve, and soon.

I suppose I could keep her as my maid. She's certainly not bad on the eyes in that outfit of hers. She can clean and cook, and I'll take care of everything else.

I'll keep her fed and clothed, and I'll ensure she's never in danger from creepy-ass men.

I slowly nod to myself. That's not such a bad idea now, is it?

And to make sure she's still of use to me, I can use her to attract my future kills—all in a safe and contained environment, of course.

Perhaps a tad different than what I initially had in mind, but she'll still have her use.

Take that, wimpy soulmate of hers!

In the grand scheme of things, I win.

I chuckle to myself.

And if he perchance shows up, then I must, of course, get rid of him. After all, he is no innocent if he left this poor girl to suffer alone.

"Marvelous idea," I say to myself, a satisfied smile appearing on my face.

I won't kill her. I'll just kill her soulmate instead.

The camera feed suddenly buzzes out, and a static appears on the screen.

I frown and try to refresh it, but it doesn't work.

It lasts a total of ten seconds before the feed comes back on.

I blink in shock.

Minnie smiles to herself as she looks around the sparkling bathroom—the same one that was previously ninety-nine percent dirty.

What the...

I stare at my screen, unsure of what I'm seeing.

She couldn't have cleaned everything in ten seconds. There's absolutely no way.

Muttering a curse, I get up and go downstairs to investigate. But the moment I reach the landing of the stairs on the ground floor, a strong scent wafts toward me.

My nostrils flare.

I stomp to the kitchen, convinced she's up to no good again.

To my surprise, however, she's not doing anything wrong.

She's cooking.

There's a big pot on the stove, and she sways from side to side in that alluring maid costume of hers as she stirs the food.

When the hell did she have time to cook?

It must have been only a couple of minutes since I saw her finish with the bathroom.

"Minnie," I bark out.

Perhaps she had the pot on the stove *while* she was cleaning? But that doesn't explain her swift transformation of the bathroom. And unless I'm mad, and frankly, I don't think I am, something is wrong here.

She startles, turning to look at me. Her eyes widen and she swallows. Then she plasters a fake smile on her face.

"What are you doing?"

"Cooking." She shrugs. "It's in my responsibility sheet."

I narrow my eyes at her.

Her tone is flippant, as is her answer, and her body language tells me she wants me nowhere near her.

I scowl.

"How did you finish cleaning so quickly?" I ask.

"How do you know I finished?" she counters.

"I checked," I lie automatically.

Her tongue clicks against her teeth.

"It's to your liking, I assume?" She raises a brow as she leans back against the kitchen counter.

Who is this Minnie and what did she do with my sweet little heathen?

Well, not mine. She's not mine.

But she is, isn't she?

She's of my home. That's different.

No, it's not. You're losing it, Marlowe.

The sound of her mocking laughter brings me back to the present.

"You have done fine." I clear my throat and look around. "What are you cooking?"

"Beef stew," she answers curtly before she goes back to stirring in her pot and ignoring me.

The smell is stronger now, and I instinctively lick my lips.

I have yet to taste her cooking, but based on that scent, I have to say I'm looking forward to it.

Grabbing two plates and spoons, I place them at the table and take a seat.

She half-turns, giving me the side-eye.

"You've been ignoring me the entire day," I state. "Why?"

She doesn't reply. She turns off the stove, and putting on gloves, she brings the pot to the table. She pours some stew in her plate but pretends she doesn't see my own.

Ah, petty, I see.

"Minnie, I'm talking to you," I say again as I add some stew to my plate.

Despite our feud—that I still don't know the root of—the food smells mouthwatering.

"And I don't want to talk to you." She releases a loud huff.

"Why?"

"Because you're a hypocrite." She glares at me. "And a h-hoe."

"W-what? A hoe?" I repeat, unsure I heard her right.

"Yes. You're a hoe. You accused me of being a prostitute, but you're the true hoe."

I blink.

That's why she was so put off? Because of the answer I gave her to the body count question?

But she's not done with her rebuke. Placing her hands on the table, she looks me dead in the eye as she continues.

"How does someone even get to one hundred and fifty-seven

bodies? When did that happen? Where do you find them? Better yet, who were they? Tell me!"

My lips twitch.

"If you started at eighteen, that would be..." She pauses as she screws her face in concentration. She uses her fingers to do the math, and soon she reaches a conclusion. "Almost sixteen a year. How?"

"Seventeen," I correct. "I started at seventeen." Well, technically, a bit younger, but I don't count that.

Her mouth hangs open in shock.

"Seventeen?" she repeats, dumbfounded. "Who was it?"

I lean back and shrug.

"A neighbor."

A fucking asshole who deserved what was coming to him.

She blinks rapidly. Her breathing accelerates and as she picks up the spoon, I fear she may break it in two.

For some reason, this amuses me. Not her anger in particular. But the object of her anger. Don't tell me she's...jealous?

"Marlowe!" she cries in a scandalized tone.

"Jealous?" I wiggle my brows in question.

"Y-you..." Her lips are set in a mutinous line. She glares at me some more before she suddenly takes her bowl of stew and turns her back to me.

I shake my head at her behavior. As much as it annoys me that I don't understand where this is coming from, it's rather amusing. And if it *is* jealousy, then what about that soulmate of hers? Has she forgotten about him already?

"You're being absurd, Minnie. Why are you fixated on my body count? It's not as if it has any effect on you."

At this point, I've already started the game, so I can't back out and tell her it was all a lie—a misunderstanding, rather. Then, she'd want to know the truth, and while she might agree to keep staying with me while thinking I'm a *hoe*, I doubt she'd have the same opinion if she knew I'm a killer.

She might not have reacted that badly to me beating the creep from the diner to a pulp, but he'd tried to hurt her. It's different. I don't think she'd offer me the same grace if she saw my jar collection containing the ashes of my victims in the basement.

She glances at me. Barely.

"I don't agree with your morals." She shakes her head. This time, however, her expression morphs from one of anger to one of disappointment. And somehow that hits the mark because my chest tightens with discomfort.

"It's the twenty-first century, pet. Welcome to modernity." I wink at her in an attempt to make light of the situation.

She scrunches her nose in disgust.

"Convenient excuse." She bristles. "You said you've never been in love. So why?"

I raise a brow at her question.

"If you didn't care about them, then why would you..." She clamps her mouth shut, tipping her chin down and glaring at me aggressively.

"Right. I forgot you're waiting for that soulmate of yours."

She grinds her teeth at the mention. "Maybe I should forget about him, too, and get my body count up. Twenty-first century, right?" She sneers. "It wouldn't be much trouble to find volunteers anyway."

The words are barely out of her mouth and I'm out of my seat, planting myself in front of her and caging her with my arms.

"I'd like to see you try," I grit out.

She slowly raises her eyes to look at me, and the sheer sadness I note in them strikes me. There's moisture on her lashes as if she's one moment away from crying.

"Remember my conditions, pet. There will be no nudity in front of any man."

She tilts her head to the side.

"I'm sure it can be managed without nudity, no? I've seen

people in parking lots, you know. They didn't have to take their clothes off to get down to work."

Business. I'm pretty sure she means to get down to business. But the moment is too tense for me to correct her, especially since she looks as if she's on the verge of jumping on me—literally.

The little feral cat. Somehow, I'd like to see her try that.

"Well, then I'm adding another condition to our agreement. You will *not* see or entertain any men. You will not go out without me, and you'll keep your face covered at all times when we're in public so you don't attract any attention."

She scoffs.

"You and your conditions. What is it to you if I do any of that? Just like I shouldn't care about your past, you shouldn't care about what *I* do."

"Don't test me, Minnie," I say in a low voice.

"Or what?" She lifts a brow just as she rises from her chair. She brings her face close to mine, so close, I can feel that sweet scent of hers drift toward my nostrils again.

"Or you will not like the consequences. You live here now."

"Your house, your rules, no?" She laughs.

"Precisely. And I will not let you bring any disease in here," I find myself saying. The most ludicrous thing. But it's better than acknowledging the real reason *why* I don't want her anywhere near another man.

"You're one to talk? How can I be sure *you* don't have any disease from all those one hundred and fifty-seven bodies?"

I smirk.

"I always wear protective gear."

After all, I never interact with bodily fluids.

I like to stare at blood. I don't like to feel it staining my skin.

Too sticky. Too...personal.

"I can wear that too," she counters.

Over my dead body.

"You will not."

"You can't stop me."

"Oh, trust me. I can."

"I'd like to see you try. What are you going to do? Lock me in here? Chain me in your basement somewhere?"

She's not too far off from the truth. A dry laugh slips past my lips.

"Don't tempt me, pet."

"What if that's what I *want* to do, Marlowe?" she asks sweetly.

"What? Tempt me?"

"Uh-huh," she murmurs, getting closer. So close, her lips skim the surface of my cheek.

A shudder goes down my back. Her lips are soft. Hot. So fucking hot.

And once more, I find myself freezing and in need of warmth.

"What do you think you're doing, Minnie?" I rasp.

"What does it look like I'm doing, Marlowe? Tempting you," she whispers, blowing hot air on my cheek.

My body tenses. My brain malfunctions.

"It won't work," I reply. My voice is rough and I feel my control slipping.

Years of mental training going down the drain. Just like that.

She leans back, satisfaction gleaming in her eyes.

"Oh, I think it did." She chuckles as she nods to my body.

I frown.

But then it dawns on me what she means.

She's pointing to my tented pants.

Because I'm hard. For her.

Fucking hell!

I mutter a string of curses and wrench myself from her side.

She smiles triumphantly, but there's still a tinge of sadness in her features. One I cannot explain.

Clearing my throat, I take a seat once more at the table and decide to focus on the food. Perhaps that will alleviate the discomfort in my pants—something I've never had to worry about before.

The stew has gone cold by now, but the smell is not any less inviting.

I dip my spoon in the stew and bring the food to my lips.

I freeze.

What the fuck…

I barely swallow before I take another spoonful, then another, until I'm scraping the bottom of the bowl.

It's the best thing I've ever eaten in my life. Rich with flavor and spices, the sauce is absolute perfection. Couple it with the tender beef and I'm already salivating for seconds.

This is not normal.

I don't do seconds.

I'm very disciplined in my eating. Three meals a day, two snacks. Every meal is portioned to perfection to contain the right amount of nutrients.

I don't do *excess*.

But it appears this is another personal rule I'm breaking because of her since I don't even bother with the bowl anymore. I grab the entire pot and place it in front of me, ready to dig in.

"You approve of my cooking?" she asks at last.

I raise my eyes. For a moment, I forgot she was there. So absorbed I was in that stew that I lost track of everything around me.

I hum in approval.

"This wasn't one of my approved recipes," I note, though I'm not mad in the least.

"No. It's my own recipe," she mentions.

"It's good." No, it's *very* good. Bordering on orgasmic.

Fuck.

I've never thought of food in those terms before. In fact, I thought it was an idiotic phrase coined by horny people who wanted to make everything in their lives about sex.

But now I get it.

"What did you put in it? It's very…unique."

She smiles.

"It's a secret."

"No, seriously. How did you make it so good?" I ask in between mouthfuls. I can't seem to stop myself.

"What if I told you"—she places her elbows on the table and rests her chin in her palms as she looks at me—"that I added magic inside?"

I snort. "Magic? Really? That's what you're going with?"

"You don't believe me?"

"There's no such thing as magic," I tell her resolutely.

"Are you sure about that, Marlowe?"

"You don't want to tell me? Fine. Got it." I roll my eyes at her.

"Why are you so skeptical? Magic is everywhere," she murmurs.

"I'm not skeptical. I'm a realist. There's no such thing as magic except in fiction."

She chuckles.

"Or maybe you're too blind to see it."

I place down my spoon. The pot is now empty.

I take a deep breath and look her in the eye.

"If there were magic in this world, why would there be people suffering everywhere? Why would the people who inflict that suffering upon them walk freely with no punishment? If there were magic out there..."

Her eyes widen, her lips slowly parting in surprise.

"If there were any magic in this world, then why is it so fucked up?"

ELEVEN

I PACE AROUND THE HOUSE.

Aimlessly.

Like a lunatic.

Minnie is at her post, scrubbing the floors away and ignoring my presence.

She's been doing this for the past week.

One week.

One fucking week in which she has barely said a word to me.

And now I'll go mad if I listen to the jarring sound of my own goddamn breathing one more fucking time.

I stop at the top of the stairs.

It's almost ten o'clock.

My curfew is approaching, though this would not be the first time I'd miss it.

Ever since Minnie came into my life, my routine has greatly suffered, one way or another. My sleep, most of all.

I no longer go to sleep at my designated time, nor do I sleep as much as my body needs to.

My dreams are always plagued by her scornful expression every time I try to talk to her, to the point that I'm now wary to close my eyes for fear of another nightmare.

I scoff at myself.

Hear that. Me, having nightmares about a slip of a girl because she's ignoring me.

I suppose you could say I don't like being ignored, but that would presume that I interact with people enough to warrant that ignoring.

I don't.

At most, I delegate tasks and communicate my business needs online, or if need be, through Giles.

As such, I can't say I've ever experienced being ignored.

Perhaps this is why it's so striking. It's simply the novelty of it.

I nod to myself. Yes, that must be it.

Straightening my back, I start down the stairs.

Minnie is in the hallway, on her knees. She doesn't react to the sound of my footsteps. She simply pretends I'm not there.

Goddamn it.

It appears I do *not* like this business of being ignored. It must be remedied immediately.

"It's late," I comment, hoping it would draw her into conversation.

She doesn't reply.

"How late will you work?" I rephrase my question, since now she'll *have* to answer it.

A small sound erupts through the empty hall, something between a scoff and a grunt. She raises her eyes to look at me, her gaze murderous.

If looks could kill, I'd be dead and buried. Perhaps even tortured before said death.

I clear my throat.

"You don't have to work so late."

She glares at me then huffs aloud and turns her back to me. Correction, since she's on her knees, she turns with her ass to me.

I gulp down.

Her dark stockings hug her shapely legs. Her uniform has bunched up her body, the hem barely covering her ass.

Goddamn.

I find myself rooted to the spot as I cannot wrench my gaze away from her. It's almost as if I've been bewitched. There's no other explanation.

There's no other time in my life that I can remember where I've reacted to a female like this.

She continues scrubbing the floor, seemingly oblivious to my struggles.

I take a deep breath.

I should look away. Perhaps leave.

I continue staring.

She moves forward, and the dress bunches farther up her ass, so much so that I get a hint of the color of her panties.

For fuck's sake! I've seen her naked. It's not like I don't know what she looks like. But as I keep watching her, I find myself wishing for another small peek.

Mumbling a string of curses to myself, I pivot and stride out of the house. The only way I can deal with my growing obsession with this little heathen is to put some distance between us. Otherwise, I'll keep pacing around the house and turn into a pathetic bastard who begs for a modicum of attention. Well, unfortunately, I think I've already crossed that bridge.

I scowl.

Pathetic? Me?

How the hell did I get here?

It's all her fault.

In my mental battle with myself, I don't even realize as I slide behind the wheel of my car, or the fact that I steer it out of the garage.

I only gain some awareness of the situation when I'm on the highway, aimlessly heading *somewhere*.

It seems my body knows me better, since it leads me away from her, knowing how weak and *pathetic* I'm about to become, even more than I already am.

More curses slip past my lips, together with a few punches into the car's dashboard.

The days when I used to be calm and collected are long gone. Chaos has slithered its way into my life, turning it upside down and making me feel like a damn stranger in my own skin.

I drive without a destination for what seems like forever. The need to turn the car around and go back to demand an explanation from Minnie is overwhelming. But I fight against it. It wouldn't yield any results.

As I drive by a small town, I find myself stopping in the parking lot of a pub. Not my scene, but for the first time, a glass of something to numb my thoughts sounds mighty fine.

I get out of my car and walk into the pub, where I take a seat at the bar.

"Give me your strongest stuff," I say in a gruff voice to the bartender.

I'm not much of a drink connoisseur. My father was the expert in the family.

Compared to most teenagers, I never had a phase of experimentation.

I stayed at home, kept to myself, and studied.

Boring, I know.

I must have only tried a sip or two of wine when Mother left her glasses unattended, but that was it. I never developed the taste for it.

So for me to be sitting here, asking for alcohol of my own volition is...unheard of. But I suppose this is what my father must have felt like when he couldn't withstand his own thoughts anymore and he needed to numb them. Or, perhaps, the drink amplified the thoughts? Can't really say since I tried to keep my distance from the old man—it was the only way to keep your bones intact.

The bartender slides a glass of amber liquid in front of me.

I stare at it.

Even as I realize what a bad idea this is, I cannot escape this unnatural urge to escape my own feelings.

It's too much, and all at once.

I'm sleep-deprived, annoyed, but too invested to stop. That would describe my current condition. And it's all *her* fault.

Minnie.

That little heathen who thinks to control me with her attention—or lack thereof. That slip of a girl can hold a fucking mean grudge. In turn, that only calls to my obsessive side more, making me want to get to her, find out what goes on inside her head— what makes her tick.

And I *will* do that.

Once she decides to start talking to me again.

Fucking hell. I'm the most pathetic bastard in existence.

I groan aloud as I pull the glass toward me.

I'm a sad excuse for a man, much less for one who considers himself to be at least of above-average intelligence.

Nowadays, though? A dog might beat me on an IQ test. It's that dire.

"Damn you," I mutter as I bring the glass to my lips to take a sip. "Damn you, Minnie!"

The liquid barely touches my tongue when a man in his forties slides into the seat next to me. His hair is gelled and combed back in a slick style meant to make him appear younger—it fails. He's wearing a dark navy two-piece suit that has seen better days, which is surprising considering the fact he's wearing a genuine Rolex on his wrist.

"Women trouble?" he inquires in a lazy voice.

I put my glass down and narrow my eyes at him.

Did I allow him to talk to me?

Do I seem like I need his advice? He'd more likely benefit from someone pointing out that hair gel doesn't replace old-school shampoo and clean hair.

I wrinkle my nose in distaste. I don't suppose he's that well acquainted with shampoo and soap, and the obnoxious perfume he's wearing does little to mask that.

"I can relate, man." The man releases a long sigh as he continues. With a hand gesture, he asks for a glass of the same I'm having. "Women are more trouble than they're worth."

Again, why is he talking to me?

Do I look fucking approachable? I doubt it. I spent years training my facial muscles to exemplify the male equivalent of a resting bitch face, which I have come to call resting brooding face —see, even the acronym is the same.

The concept is simple. One glare and people scramble from my vicinity.

Not this man, apparently.

"That's why I always say, get them while you can."

I raise a brow. I still have not made one sound of acknowledgment and this man goes on as if we're long-lost friends.

Does he have a death wish?

"They think they're too good for us. They send us signals and then they complain when we respond to them..."

I flatten my lips as I turn to stare at him.

"What are you talking about?"

"What's the name of your girl?" he asks.

I glare at him.

Instead of scrambling away, he reaches inside his coat and takes out a business card, which he slides in front of me.

Alpha Academy.

Lead Instructor, Paul Barnes.

"I can recognize heartbreak from a mile away. I can help." He winks.

He fucking winks.

"Is that so?" I drawl.

Great. Just what I needed. A fucking pick-up artist trying to teach me how to woo women. Granted, I might need some lessons on that front. But the last person I'd consider learning from is fucking mister gelled hair over here.

I bet that hairstyle alone acts as a repellent to all women.

"Tell me what the problem is," he continues, giving me that slimy salesman smile.

"You're rather confident it's about a woman," I note.

"There are only two things that bring a man here at this hour. Women and money. And I don't think it's money you're trying to forget." He winks, again.

I suppose that's not a hard assumption to make. That it happens to be correct is pure luck.

When I don't speak again, he continues.

"You don't have much experience with women, do you?"

I don't reply, merely look at him.

Fuck. Do I have the word *inexperienced* tattooed on my forehead?

I hate people.

"You'd be surprised just how many good-looking and successful men have trouble getting the woman they want. Especially them, I would say, since they have no way of knowing if a woman is with them for their money or themselves." He keeps going as he takes a swig of his drink.

"Yeah, well, I don't have that problem," I mumble under my breath.

I look at my glass. It's barely touched. Alas, I don't think drinking is for me. I'm about to get up and leave this lunatic when he speaks again.

"Ah, I see." He chuckles. "Is she not willing then?"

I freeze. Something about his tone rubs me the wrong way.

"What if she's not?" I ask, slowly turning to him.

His lips curl up. Leaning in, he whispers, "I can fix that, too."

"And how would you do that?"

He carefully assesses his surroundings before he speaks.

"A few drops in her drink when she's not looking and she'll be putty in your hands," he whispers. "I have a new product that's even more effective than the old stuff on the market."

My blood grows cold.

He's talking about date rape drugs, out in the open. We've barely exchanged a few words and he's already trying to sell me this shit. If that's the case, he must have done this countless times before. His delivery is smooth, his speech rehearsed.

Fuck.

"Color me intrigued," I answer slowly.

"Two hundred a mil," he mentions. "That's enough to use on ten girls, or, if you'd like, ten times on one girl." He laughs.

I force a smile on my lips, though inside I'm seething.

This fucking asshole.

"How do I know it works as you say? Have you tried it yourself?" I ask, probing further to see just how much of an asshole he is.

"Of course." He scoffs. "See that girl over there—" He points to a young girl at a table, who's doing her best to keep her eyes open. She sways sideways, grinning when her head hits the table. "She's my ride for tonight."

That wink again.

"I see it works," I reply, measuring my words.

"Of course it does!" he sputters, offended.

I smile.

That seems to put him more at ease.

"I don't have that much cash with me here. Come to my car and I'll give it to you."

He beams.

"Say no more." He chuckles. "We'll head out too."

I pay the bartender for my drink and wait for Paul of the Alpha Academy to do the same. On our way out of the pub, he grabs the girl he drugged and more or less carries her out of the building.

To my surprise, no one bats an eye.

They turn and look, but they don't question whether she's willing or not. They simply shrug and move on—it's a regular occurrence after all.

Anger simmers inside of me.

Today, of all days, when my temper is threatening to get the best of me, I happen to stumble over this bastard.

An insidious smile spreads on my face.

Alas, maybe this was fate—and now I'm starting to sound like Minnie and her magic talk. But it could prove a nice distraction and an opportunity for me to blow some steam.

Paul leads the girl to his car and dumps her on the back seat before following me to my car.

"You won't regret it, I promise. All of my customers come back for more," he mentions when he sees me open the front drawer of my car. "You have my card. You can always call..."

He says something more that I tune out. It's unnecessary details of his deeds that I don't want to listen to.

Instead, as I open the glove compartment, I take the time to scout the area.

There aren't people outside. Good.

There's one camera at the front of the pub and one by the side. I do a quick calculation.

I always park my car in the outside radius of the camera, but he's standing *by* the car, so any sudden movement could get him back into the camera's coverage.

I click my tongue against my teeth in annoyance. The only way to do this is to ensure he doesn't struggle.

"Here," I say in a bright voice, lulling him into a sense of security. Just as I turn to give him what he thinks is cash, I strike.

Using the back of my palm, I hit him against the chin with enough force to rattle him. He barely makes a sound.

As he sways on his feet, I grab him, pulling him toward me and wrapping my arms around his neck. I apply just enough force to knock him out before I quietly deposit him in my car.

That was rather easy.

There's one issue, though. The girl in his car.

I debate what to do for a few moments before I cave in and call Giles.

"There's a drugged girl at..." I pause to look at the name of the pub and the address on the GPS. "The car is a black SUV with the plate numbers ending in seven-three-nine. Make sure she gets home safe."

A pause.

"Do I want to know how she ended up there?" he asks in his usual bored voice.

"No. But I'm taking care of the owner of that car."

He chuckles.

"Fair enough. I'm on my way."

Hanging up, I stick around until Giles is a few minutes away and leave. I can't have my new prisoner wake up before he ends up in his prison, now, can I?

As I drive back home, I access the camera feed from the house to see where Minnie is. Luckily, she took my advice and stopped working. She's now lounging around in her room.

Did I install another camera in her room? Yes, I did. And I'm not sorry about it.

After the incident with the faulty footage, I've been more wary of her. And what's the best way to get a read on her if not by seeing what she does in the intimacy of her room?

Creepy? Maybe. But at least I'm not as creepy as mister gelled hair in the back, who's no doubt stinking my upholstery with his cheap perfume.

I shake my head in disgust. I suppose tomorrow I'll need to take the car out for a wash.

Minnie struts up and down her room as she tries on the clothes we bought for her last week.

It takes me a few moments to realize she's pretending to be on a catwalk, walking like a model.

I chuckle.

She's cute. *Too* cute. *Disturbingly* cute.

Fuck. Maybe mister gelled hair was right. I do have a problem. And it's one I have yet to find a solution for.

Instead of paying attention to the road like a responsible driver, my eyes are on Minnie and her antics.

It's even worse when she takes some clothes off to put on the others because though she's not fully naked, she's naked enough for me to feel my clothes becoming too constricting.

Goddamn. I've become a pervert.

If she only knew what I've been doing lately instead of sleeping...

Gelly Paul moans in the back. I sigh. Ten more minutes until I get home.

Pulling over, I lean back and give him another blow to the head to ensure he stays put—and quiet—until we reach my basement.

After he goes back to sleep, I continue driving until I get home.

I park the car as usual, and holding my phone with the camera feed in one hand and dragging Paul with the other, I use my hidden entrance to go to the basement.

The first room is the decoy—of sorts. There's a functional fireplace—cough, furnace, cough—and a wine cellar.

Behind the cellar, however, is my playroom.

I drag Paul into the playroom and dump him on the floor while I go about setting up everything for his *comfort*.

He'll find my playroom *very* welcoming. As welcoming as the girls he's raped in the past were.

Although I made sure to cover my tracks, my actions were still reckless because I can be put in the same location as Gelly Paul over here.

If I hadn't been so high-strung recently, I would have let him go—sans the girl, of course—and stalked him for a week, all the while planning the perfect kidnapping *and* punishment.

As it stands, I might not be as creative as he deserves since I don't have enough time to think of a fitting punishment for him.

"I promise you, Paul, that I'll give you a night you won't forget," I murmur as I put on my suit and gloves.

Setting up the screen on the wall to show me Minnie's room, I start undressing Paul until he's stark naked, and then I drag his body to my favorite chair—that can convert into a bed, too!

It feels almost profane to have Minnie's exuberant beauty in the background while I have to stare at nasty Paul's genitals, but I suppose this is a good reminder of what lies beyond the walls of my house.

Minnie could have very well encountered a slimy Paul, too, and she would have been hurt.

My anger spikes.

She's not safe, anywhere but here, with me.

The outside world *will* hurt her. Men *will* hurt her.

Men like fucking Paul.

The thought drives me insane.

Instead of seeing the unknown girl he'd drugged, I see Minnie.

She's such a gentle soul that every fucking depraved bastard is drawn to her like a fucking moth to a flame.

But that will not happen.

I found her first.

She belongs to me now, which means no one else can harm her —me included.

To think that only a week ago I entertained the idea of killing her.

Unacceptable.

How could I have ever thought of something so disgraceful is beyond me.

I purse my lips, mentally berating myself for it.

But then another thought arises.

Mister gelled hair did get one thing right. I have no idea how to behave with women.

Murder is all I know.

Maybe my first thought was to kill her because I had no idea how else to translate my interest in her. After all, for more than a decade, my only interest—besides trashy TV—has been killing.

From the start, she didn't fit the profile. She was an innocent—someone who needed saving, not damning.

Clarity explodes in my mind.

My eyes widen and I stop.

My lips slowly curve up into a smile.

Minnie, Minnie. Minnie mine...

Has a nice ring to it, doesn't it?

I grab a sharp knife and get to work as I hum my new favorite melody, which might or might not be *Carried Away* from a certain cartoon character that shares her name.

TWELVE

THE FIRST INCISION wakes him up, ready to scream. He's unable to, of course, since I've already gagged his disgusting mouth.

I've doubled up on gloves for this particular task. Holding on to his limp dick, I cut transversally from proximal region to distal.

"Good on you to wake up, Pauly boy. What do you think of my work so far?" I ask with a smile as I point to his butchered dick.

It's now spread open like the loaf of an Italian sandwich, waiting to be filled with delicious salami, roasted peppers, and mozzarella. Alas, I don't know why I'm likening his disease-infested dick with an Italian sandwich... Perhaps because I aim to fill that gap with a corrosive agent to give him pain to rival that which he's inflicted on others.

My stomach growls in hunger.

Ah. That also explains it. Hopefully, Minnie left something for me to eat since I predict I'll be rather famished after I finish with this exertion.

Paul wiggles in his seat. I've left his chair on an incline so he can admire my handiwork while he still has time left on this earth.

As I busy myself around, gathering the necessary materials for the *filling*, Paul continues to struggle, perhaps thinking he actually has a chance at escaping.

I take my materials and lay them out on a table in front of him.

There are only three materials: a bottle of water, a bottle of chlorine, and a pack of concrete mix.

When Paul sees the items, his eyes bulge like crazy, and he renews his efforts, this time with more vigor.

It's useless.

Those straps can hold someone double his size with no issue. Scrawny Paul won't be able to make them budge.

But because his reaction to the items was so amusing, I decide to give him a chance for last words—or, perhaps, a delayed apology.

"You fucking psycho," he cries out when I remove the gag. "W-what the hell do you think you're doing? I'll have you fucking arrested. Fucking creep."

"Now, Pauly, I think you have the places reversed. *You* are the creep, not me." I smile.

"You're s-sick," he mumbles, sweat gathering atop his forehead from the pain.

His dick is still bleeding, and I note he can barely stand to look at the mess in his groin.

Slow shudders take over his body.

The moment I'll pour the bleach, he'll likely pass out again.

I sigh.

That's not fun.

"How many women have you drugged and raped?" I raise my brow in question.

He just stares at me.

"If you answer, I might take pity on you..." I lie. Of course I'd never take pity on someone like him. But perhaps his answer will enrage me enough to get even *more* creative with his punishment.

"I-I don't know..." he stammers. "I never counted."

"You never counted? I find that hard to believe. A man such as yourself needs the validation to feel like a man, no?"

His lips flatten.

"Ten, twenty?" I ask, though I imagine those to be low estimates. Then again, figuring in the numbers of the people he supplied with the drug would make the numbers much higher.

He scoffs.

I smirk. There he goes.

"Fifty?"

"As if," he mumbles under his breath.

Ah, it seems he still has the strength to do so. Perhaps I should remedy that.

Grabbing the bottle of chlorine, I pour it generously over his split dick. The moment it makes contact with his open wounds, I push the gag back into his mouth to muffle his scream.

Then, just in case, I look at the screen that shows Minnie in her room.

She's finished her fashion parade and she's now in her pajamas. Her hair, too, looks to be freshly washed, which I appreciate.

Despite not speaking to me much in the last week, she's held her part of the deal. She washed every single day.

I checked, of course. And by that I mean I went close enough to her to sniff her.

On second thought, perhaps I am a bit of a creep, but it's not in any malicious way. It's just to check if she washes daily. There's also that natural scent of hers that always goes to my head. See, I have honorable intentions, unlike slimy Pauly over here.

Her pajama is a cute set comprised of silky white shorts and a button-up shirt. The pants are short enough to emphasize her legs, and for a moment, I forget that I'm supposed to be torturing a rapist.

Minnie, Minnie... Why are you so distracting, little heathen?

I watch her for one more minute while Paul's thrashing subsides. As I predicted, he passes out from the pain. Alas, that was my aim with it.

Although bleach can help prevent an infection, it's also a highly caustic substance that burns through tissue—especially an open wound.

I'll allow Pauly here a few seconds to rest while I prepare the cement mixture.

Very magnanimous of me, I know.

I resume my humming as I use a small bowl to mix water and the cement powder until it's a homogenous substance. From the corner of my eye, though, I continue to watch Minnie, focusing in particular on her features.

She's in bed now, reading a book. Her expression is one of pure rapture, and I'm immediately curious to know what book she's reading.

I told her she could avail herself of my library as long as she didn't damage the books—no doggy ears, markings, or torn pages. So far, she's been well-behaved, which I do appreciate.

Once the mixture is done, time is of the essence before it hardens.

Grabbing my electric wand, I plug it in and power it on. Pressing it to the dampest portion of slimy Pauly's body, I send a couple of powerful shocks that startle him back into a state of consciousness.

Once more, he tries to scream. And once more, he cannot.

"I can't have you missing the most important part of this session, Pauly. You see, there's nothing I abhor more than a cowardly son of bitches like you. And you know what I hate the most? Creeps who hurt women," I tell him with a smile on my face.

I've always detested rapists, but since Minnie has arrived into my life, my distaste for them has reached new heights. Perhaps it's because she was almost a victim twice. Or perhaps it's because I know she's a magnet for men and their unscrupulous desires.

Every single woman this slime bag hurt was a potential Minnie, and that makes me even more enraged.

"Since you used this particular organ to commit your crime," I start, pointing at his split dick, now red and swollen from the chlorine that's seeped into the tissue. "I shall have to punish it first."

Grabbing the bowl, I place it over his dick and slowly tilt it. The substance pours down between the two halves of his dick, filling it up like the sandwich it reminded me of.

This is a fast-drying concrete, so it will take around half an hour for it to harden.

Paul's eyes are once more wide with horror as he attempts to push against his bounds.

He's barely conscious, and liquid pours out of the split dick—not blood, something else. It seems that his urethra burst, and that's urine.

I shake my head.

"Disgusting." I tsk at him. "That deserves a punishment, Pauly boy."

Leaving behind the terrified rapist, I head over to one of my cabinets and open it. I browse the selection of tools as I think what would be the most fitting one for what I have in mind.

I suppose a saw?

Hmm.

But as I contemplate how to hack Pauly apart, I happen to glance upon a funnel. My gaze remains fixated on it.

"Aha!" I exclaim, giddiness erupting inside of me.

This is all new territory. And despite my rather absentminded state as of late, Pauly's kill is the best I've had in forever.

Since two years ago, as a matter of fact.

Perhaps I *have* finally gotten my mojo back.

My mood is soaring as I pick up the funnel and go back to the table. I pour more cement powder into the bowl and make the mixture more watery.

Pauly is beside himself with fear as I remove his gag and place the funnel in his mouth. He tries to move, but it's useless. He even tries to bite down on the narrow end of the funnel—how he still has the strength to do so, I don't know.

Alas, with a bit more force, I manage to shove it down his throat so he cannot get it out. Taking advantage of this position, I pour the mixture from the bowl down his throat.

He makes some choking sounds, as one would expect. He gags and thrashes some more. I suppose that's what his victims experienced, too, on that drug.

"How does it feel to be helpless, Pauly boy? Not so great, no?"

I don't know how long it will take for the cement to fortify inside his body. There's a lot of wetness there, after all. But hopefully, it will not be too long. I still want to sleep a few hours. And it will take me quite a while to slice up his body and dump the parts in the furnace.

I release a deep sigh.

It seems this night will be a long one.

Another glance at the screen has me smiling. Minnie is on her belly on top of the duvet, holding the book with both hands as she reads.

Cute. So damn cute.

I spend a few moments admiring her, which strengthens my resolve to get rid of this little pest. This way, the world will be safer for her and women like her.

Since I'll have to wait for the cement to grow hard inside of him—and that's quite the pun—I decide to watch an episode of *Supernatural*. This one has been long overdue, and as I play the show, I realize how much I was looking forward to it. That was before Minnie, of course. Since she's barged into my life, I've barely given it any mind, except when I recall how messed up my previously perfect routine is.

By the time the end credits roll on the screen, I'm yawning.

Have I gotten too old for this torture business?

While I admit it was fun while it lasted, now that I have to clean up and cut him into pieces, I'm almost...reluctant.

It's late. Minnie seems to have gone to bed too.

Maybe I can wrap this up quickly and get some hours of sleep as well.

Going to my tool cabinet, I grab a medium-sized saw and head back to Paul.

Let's see if he's still alive after that cement soup.

As I reach his side, I note that his dick has fallen off. The cement was too heavy for the skin holding it together, so gravity did its thing.

Pauly, too, shows no signs of life.

I check his pulse.

Nothing.

His abdomen is distended. His neck, too, is solid to the touch.

I just hope the cement won't make it harder for me to cut his body.

Plugging the saw in, I start with the bottom. First are his feet, which I cut at the ankle. Easy enough.

Then I slowly work my way up.

Even with how tired I am, the sound of the saw is music to my ears as it cuts through Paul's bones. Blood splatters all over my gown and goggles, and I smile at the result of my work.

I dump the cut body parts in a bucket at my feet, which fills just as I dump the thighs inside. All that's left is the torso and his head, but it seems I'll need a new bucket.

Taking a small break to find another bucket, I glance again at the monitor to see what Minnie's up to—or mostly to watch her sleeping.

I stop dead in my tracks.

She's not in bed. In fact, she's not in her room.

I grab my phone and go through the different cameras in the

house in an attempt to locate her. And when I see where she is, true horror grips me.

She's in the basement—in the furnace room. She's looking around, her expression tense. Slowly, she raises her eyes and looks straight at the camera.

Panic unlike I've ever known swells inside of me, and I quickly scramble to hide all the evidence.

It doesn't matter that there's a huge block of steel separating us. The mere thought that she might find out the truth about me and decide to leave me makes me act irrationally.

I cover the bucket with Paul's lower body with a towel, and I dump his torso into another bucket without bothering to cut it up some more—she might hear the sounds of the saw.

But that's more difficult than I imagined. Instead of going in smoothly, I have to cram it inside, using my weight to push against it. Just when I think I've made some progress, a loud crack erupts in the air and his neck snaps.

Paul's head rolls on the floor.

Fuck!

I run after it, grab it, and stuff it back in the bucket before covering it with another towel.

Then there's the mess on the floor.

That's a lot of blood.

I won't be able to clean that up in time.

Fuck.

Why is she in the basement? And why is she now poking around the hidden entrance to the *other* side of the basement?

"Marlowe? Are you there?" she calls out.

More panic.

How the hell does she know I'm here?

I look right and left for a way out.

What if she somehow finds the way in? What if she sees me standing in the middle of a sterilized room that's currently stained with blood, with butchered body parts lying in buckets?

No. I cannot have that.

She'd get scared then. She'd run off. And she has nowhere to go —nowhere safe.

That cannot happen.

She cannot leave.

Not now, not ever.

In a burst of desperation, I grab a white sheet and lay it on the floor. I head over to Paul's lower body and grab his thigh, which should still have plenty of blood inside it.

Puncturing a few strategic spots alongside the inner thigh, I spray the blood all over the sheet, mimicking a Pollock design.

I've never been the artistic type, but I do think this might be a Pollock.

If nothing else, I'll go with some modern nonsense. No one knows what those mean either.

"Marlowe? Where are you?"

Minnie's voice intensifies as she walks around the ante-basement room. As she studies the area, she stops right in front of the door to *my* room.

Her eyes narrow in suspicion and she places her hands around the surface of the door, feeling it out.

The door won't open to anyone but me, since it requires biometric information. But if she finds out that *is* a door, she'll want to know what for, what I'm hiding.

She'll grow suspicious, and that will feed into her negative feelings about me. It won't be long before she grows to fear me and decides she's much safer far away from me.

No. No. No.

She cannot leave.

She'll stay here. With me. She'll clean my house, cook my meals, and give me something pretty to look at. A little misogynistic, I know, but do I get a pass if she's the only one who's ever made me feel that way?

Probably not.

Goddamn it.

In my panic, I'm once more getting lost in my thoughts and the many what-ifs.

Perhaps if I wait, she'll leave.

So I wait.

Minutes trickle by. My ADHD runs rampant, making me pace around like a madman—not that I am not one.

Minnie remains in front of the door, studying it. I can tell the wheels in her brain are turning.

She's a smart girl. If she brushes her hand against the right part of the door, a screen will light up, asking for log-in credentials.

Fuck.

Then I'll be truly fucked.

Odd how my last concern is the fact that she might go to the cops. No, my *only* concern is how she'll react if she knows this side of me.

So what if she also hurt someone in the past? That was legitimate self-defense. What I'm doing here might technically be considered self-defense by proxy since I'm defending her and women like her, but I doubt she'd understand my reasoning.

Lately, I barely understand it myself.

She touches the door again, dangerously close to the screen.

This is it. I need to make a decision.

Taking off my goggles, gloves, surgical gown, and all the stained equipment, I dump them on top of one of the buckets and cover them neatly with the towel.

The plan is to convince her to go back without inquiring about this room. The Pollockesque charade is a last resort.

Making sure I look presentable and that there's not one drop of blood on my body or clothes, I go out.

I open the door and close it behind me, not giving Minnie any time to see what's inside.

"Marlowe!" Minnie squeaks, jumping back when she sees me. "What are you doing?"

"Why are you here, Minnie? You should be sleeping."

"I didn't hear you come home," she mentions. "Where were you?"

"Who says I went anywhere?" I counter.

"Your car was gone."

I smirk.

The little heathen's been tracking my movements? Beneath that facade of nonchalance lies some interest.

"I was out." I shrug.

She glares at me.

"Out where?" she asks in a low voice.

"You ask a lot of questions for someone who's barely spoken to me this week, Minnie," I note.

"Where were you?" she repeats more emphatically, taking a step toward me. Her eyes blaze at me, so much so I feel like she's going to jump me any moment now.

"Do I have to give you a rundown of all my whereabouts?" I raise a brow.

"*Where*?" she asks again, aggression oozing from her tone.

I roll my eyes and sigh.

"If you must know, I was at a pub."

"You don't drink," she mentions, her eyes narrowed.

"And how do you know that? Maybe I do."

"You don't. I know you don't."

Before I get to mull over how she knows that, she continues.

"Who were you with? You don't drink, so you must have been there for another reason."

"Minnie..." I groan.

What the hell is with her? This morning she could barely spare me a glance and now she's interrogating me about my whereabouts.

"Was it a woman?" she asks as she taps her foot against the tiled floor. She's only wearing her slippers, and as I look down, I make the mistake of also glancing at that little silky pajama she's dressed in.

Big. Mistake.

I gulp down.

My thoughts immediately scramble as my gaze becomes fixated on her legs. Very fine legs, indeed.

"Did you bring a woman here? Where is she?" Her vicious tone brings me back to the present.

"What?"

"You're hiding a woman in there, aren't you? Move aside," she demands.

"There's no one there, Minnie." I sigh.

"I don't believe you. Y-you're so secretive, you must be hiding something. Who is it?"

"No one," I say. "Let's go upstairs. I'm hungry and I want to know what you prepared for dinner."

A little late for dinner considering it's the middle of the night, but maybe this can distract her long enough to forget about the basement.

What the hell got into her, anyway? Why is she so convinced I have a woman in here? She's been with me long enough to see I don't entertain guests.

But maybe...

Does she think I'm trying to replace her?

Sure, her cleaning has been ninety percent accurate, but her cooking more than makes up for that ten percent. I doubt I'd ever find a better cook than her. Not even restaurant food tastes as good.

Perhaps she's merely insecure about her work. She doesn't have anywhere to go after all, and though she hasn't been exactly cordial with me, she must want to protect her position.

"No," she states staunchly, placing herself in front of me as I try to move. "Show me," she repeats, pointing at the door. "I want to see with my own eyes. You and your one hundred and fifty-seven bodies. What's one more to that collection?" she mumbles under her breath.

My lips curl around the corners and I barely stop myself from chuckling. Technically, she's right. I did add another body to that collection. But if I were to say that, she'd once more misunderstand me—not that I did anything to *clear* that misunderstanding in the first place.

I step around her to leave, but it seems her stubbornness knows no bounds.

She plops herself on the floor, her back to the door.

"I'm not leaving. I'll stay here until you open the door and show me," she mentions, crossing her arms over her chest.

"Minnie, you're being outrageous."

"Not more than you. You can just show me and I'll leave you alone."

"Why do you care so much if I am or *not* with another woman?" I ask, my blood pounding in my ears as I await the explanation.

Her eyes widen. Her mouth drops open and she doesn't answer for a moment.

"Well?" I repeat.

"I d-don't care," she mumbles, flustered. "It's all your fault and your rules. I'm not allowed to see other males, but you can go out to pubs and find other females? You think I don't know that's where you humans find your one-night stays?"

"I think you mean one-night stand," I say, a smile pulling at my lips. "And what's with the *you humans*? What are you? An alien?"

She blinks in shock.

"Uhm...erm... Anyway, I am *not* leaving until you show me what's behind that door. And if it *is* a woman..."

"If it is a woman...?"

"You won't like what happens then," she states, her cold gaze finding mine. To say I'm surprised by her demeanor would be an understatement. But it's not the first time, is it? Minnie can be both soft and cute but also sharp and alluring. A deadly combination, if I do say so myself—for me in particular.

I stare at her.

She stares right back at me.

We engage in a silent battle of wills and as the minutes pass, I realize she won't give up.

To be more precise, after ninety-eight minutes pass, I realize I'm fighting a losing battle. And I'm hungry. And tired.

Murder does that to people.

With a weary sigh, I walk to the door and unlock it.

Minnie is sporting a triumphant smile as she strides inside, her eyes taking in every inch of the expansive room.

"There's no woman," she mumbles to herself.

"Told you." I chuckle.

"But what's that?" she asks as her eyes zero in on the middle of the room where my fake Pollockesque painting lies. "You paint?" she asks, her lashes fluttering at me.

That's rather...distracting.

I clear my throat.

"Occasionally," I lie.

"And what is it supposed to be?" She walks toward the painting, eyeing it with great interest.

But as she gets closer, she trips on something and loses her balance, falling to the ground.

"What..." she whispers.

I look with horror at what she tripped over and force my brain to come up with *some* sort of an excuse.

"What is this?"

"Don't touch it!" I shout, rushing forward and grabbing it before she can do so. The mere thought that she'd touch Paul's dick makes my blood boil, and I can't even kill him again. "It's silicone and cement," I hurry to say. "And the cement is still wet. I don't want you to get any on your hands."

She nods slowly.

"Another art project?"

"Yes... Something like that," I mumble awkwardly.

"Oh." She purses her lips. "I'm sorry I accused you, then. I didn't realize you had a secret art room."

"That's right. No one knows I paint," I say. The lies flow from my mouth with increasing ease. "It's not something I share with people."

"I see." She scrambles to her feet and directs her attention to the stained sheet in the middle of the room. Glad she moved on from the cemented dick, I quickly discard it in a nearby bin and follow behind her.

"Is it because you're not very good?"

"Excuse me?" I cough, not sure I heard her right.

"I suppose if I painted like this I wouldn't want others to know either," she mentions thoughtfully as if she's not just roasting me to my face. She walks around the *canvas*, looking at it from different angles and scrunching her nose in distaste.

I blink repeatedly.

"It's modern art. You wouldn't understand," I mumble under my breath. Though that was my first encounter with anything remotely artistic, I find myself rather protective of my blood splatters. They had intention behind them, purpose.

She half turns, raising a brow at me as if asking *really*. She knows it's bad and she's not afraid to say it to my face. Hell, I know it's bad. But it's for a good cause, no? I mean, I did rid the world of a rapist to build this art piece. For that alone, it should have value.

"And what is it supposed to mean then? Enlighten me."

"Loss of life. Blood spilled. It's a metaphor," I answer with whatever comes to mind first. Though, I must admit, it's not completely false.

She frowns.

"With real blood?" she asks in a provocative tone.

"O-of course not."

"Hmm…"

Crouching down, she swipes her finger over the sheet, picking up some blood. She brings it to her nose.

"It smells like blood to me," she comments.

"And you know what blood smells like?" I counter.

"Doesn't everyone?"

"No."

She smiles at me. It's a knowing smile. One that's as mysterious as it is beguiling. Not for the first time, I wonder just how much I know about Minnie. One moment she's one person, the next she's a completely different one.

"Is it because of what happened to your foster father? Did you smell the blood when you stabbed him? What was it, twenty-eight times?" I inquire, purposefully getting the number wrong.

She shrugs, but she doesn't correct me.

Interesting…

"You forget that I'm a fertile female, Marlowe. I happen to be well acquainted with the smell of blood."

Her lips curve up in an enticing smile.

So enticing, it's making my body react in odd ways.

Why did she have to put it that way? And why is the word *fertile* echoing in my brain on repeat?

Just as I am rooted to the spot, staring at her and seeing her in a very *fertile* way, she waves her blood-stained finger around before bringing it to her lips.

"No," I snap. Rushing to her side, I grab her finger and stop her.

Her lips twitch.

"So it is blood. Whose?"

"Animal blood," I lie.

"I see." She meets my gaze head-on, as if to communicate she knows this is all a lie. "So you like to paint with blood," she muses. "Was this your big, bad secret?"

"So what if it was?"

"Don't get so defensive, Marlowe." She tsks. "I like it. It's hot."

Hot?

Is this the same Minnie as before?

She slowly gets up, her eyes never leaving mine. She reaches out with her hand and cups my cheek.

"You shouldn't hide, Marlowe. I see you. The *real* you."

I freeze.

Just how much does she know?

THIRTEEN

MINNIE AN'YAN.

I stare at the computer screen pensively.

Zero hits.

There's no one with her name on the face of the earth. No birth records, no foster home records as she claimed, and certainly no prison records.

For all intents and purposes, Minnie An'yan doesn't exist.

Either that or she gave me a fake name. And that begs the question: what is she hiding?

Unable to find anything on the name she's given me, I decide to try the police database. I log in some of her characteristics and narrow the search down to the surrounding area. If she's given me a fake name, then she must have something to hide. And the best place to start is with police records.

The program registers my criteria and starts the search. I tap my finger on my desk as I await the results.

Normally, finding out about such a deception would have me raging. I've been living with this little heathen for almost two weeks now. Weeks of cohabitating with someone who *lied* about who they are. That in itself should get me riled up enough to add her on my murder list—again. Especially since she's barged into my life, I've barely done *any* real work.

All I've done is sit in front of my computer and watch the house feed or do impromptu walks through the house to get a glimpse of her, then get flustered when I get caught staring.

Why am I getting fucking flustered? It's my house. I'm allowed to walk around my house, no?

The mere fact that she's made a mockery of my well-crafted routine and has reduced my productivity to zero should have me ready to murder her on the spot. Instead, I only find myself more intrigued by her and the secrets she hides.

She's an enigma. And I've never been able to back off from an unsolved puzzle, no matter how difficult it might seem.

Odd, isn't it?

I've gotten so used to getting rid of everything that inconveniences me that it's absolutely mind-blowing that Minnie not only still lives with me, but that she enjoys a lot of privileges even when she breaks my rigid rules.

Yes, she can clean. And oh, can the girl cook. But other than that, she's a disaster waiting to occur with her clumsiness.

Just the other day, I was walking through the kitchen—for no other reason than to check up on her cooking, of course, and perhaps find out what her secret to those delicious dishes really is. The little klutz got startled by my presence and cut her finger.

I stood there in shock, not knowing whether to tell her off for contaminating the meat, or lick the blood off her finger and tell her I'll make it better.

Ludicrous. I know.

In the end, I went with a mix of the two. I chastised her for not paying attention and contaminating my food *and* my kitchen, while gently holding her finger and dabbing it with disinfectant. Then, of course, I bandaged it up so she wouldn't contaminate anything else.

It may have taken me the better part of an hour to get it right. I know how to separate body parts, not how to put them together. But eventually, after finishing up an entire box of bandages, I managed to do a decent job.

On the bright side, I got a little taste of her blood, though I doubt she realized it.

Oh, fuck. I sound like a goddamn creep.

But it was there, leaking out of her cut, free for the taking.

What's a man to do when the opportunity arises right in front of him?

Besides, wasn't she the one who said blood was hot? I'm sure she wouldn't mind. If she does bring it up at any point, I'll tell her it's rent.

I smile to myself at that particular memory. Though I always avoid contact with bodily fluids, the redness of her blood had been quite a hypnotizing sight. A dark red bordering on burgundy, it had been unlike anything I've ever seen. And God, had it been sweet.

I'm almost ashamed to admit how sweet and potent it had been.

For someone who's never had a vice before—bar murder and compulsive cleaning—this looked very much like the beginning of a dangerous addiction.

I don't know how I wrenched myself away from her long enough to fumble with the bandage, or how she didn't notice the way my attention was clearly somewhere else. But in the end, I managed to disguise my growing desire with another rude comment—my M.O. at this point—which of course, she didn't appreciate.

I expected at least some thank you. Perhaps another kiss on the cheek, not that I enjoyed the first one *that* much. But it should be common sense, no? I patched her up. I deserve at least *something* in return.

She only glared at me, muttered something under her breath, then proceeded to ignore me while she continued cooking.

Because she's still mad at me.

That little heathen can certainly hold a grudge.

Things seemed to get better when she spoke to me in the basement, but after that, she went back to ignoring me.

I wonder if she's worried I might replace her with someone else. She's been making fewer mistakes in her tasks and it's obvious she's been putting more effort into her cleaning. Hell, lately I've been nothing short of impressed with her work ethic and the number of hours she dedicates to cleaning everything according to my instructions sheet. And for someone like me, it's *hard* to be impressed about anything, let alone cleaning.

Perhaps she *was* worried I'd sack her. Though I wish it would have been jealousy that prompted her to be so mad about the basement, the more I think about it, the more I'm sure it's her being worried about her position.

She wants security, I can tell. But surely she'd realize that the best way to get in my good graces is to actually *talk* to me. Every day, I can count on two hands the amount of words she directs toward me.

Is it any wonder that I've resorted to surreptitiously following her around the house? Or that I've become glued to my computer screen to see what she's doing when I'm not around?

I think not.

But by not speaking to me, she's only making me more intrigued.

Fuck. I'm dying of curiosity.

The computer releases a loud beep, and a list of matches appears on the screen. There are over a dozen results that match her physical description, but I can easily filter through them based on the mug shots.

And then I finally find *her*.

Her identity is unknown. She's listed as Jane Doe and a person of interest in a number of criminal proceedings from the past couple of weeks.

The criminal cases range from petty theft to assault and they're all in different jurisdictions. But she's only on the list of potential witnesses.

Interesting.

I click on the first case, which is that of theft from a convenience store a few towns over from where I live. The case description notes that someone entered the convenience store at 10:00 p.m. and stole a week's worth of food and some Christmas decorations. But the report highlighted that a certain brand of chocolate cookies was stolen in unusual quantities amounting to over five hundred dollars in losses. The cashier could not remember who it was that came inside to steal, and the CCTV cameras malfunctioned for a short period of time—exactly when the theft occurred.

The only footage is that of before and after the incident, and a girl fitting Minnie's description is seen entering the store shortly before the cameras malfunctioned, and she exited sometime before they started working again. For that reason, the police are looking into her as a potential witness to whoever had robbed the place.

Hmm.

I click on the footage from the outside of the convenience store.

It's night. It's snowing heavily, and the ground in front of the convenience store is covered in ice. The time stamp shows the date as two and a half weeks ago. It's 9:55 p.m. when Minnie appears in the frame. There are a few other people in the parking lot, but they seem to be departing the store.

I stop the video, my eyes growing wide with horror.

If when I found her I thought her mad for being so scantily dressed in that freezing weather, what she's wearing in the video is much worse. Or, rather, I should say what she is *not* wearing. She has on a thin layer of what looks to be like a shift. She's barefoot. Her hair is long, almost reaching her ankles. She must have cut half of it between then and when I found her.

I frown. This girl... She really knows how to get on someone's nerves.

How the fuck does she go around in freezing temperatures wearing only a thin layer of material and *no* shoes?

She doesn't seem cold, either. There's nothing indicative of it in her body language. There's no huddling or holding her arms close to her body. She appears perfectly fine.

She enters the store.

I quickly click on the second video—the one from inside. It captures her entering the store, but as she looks up, almost directly at the camera, the footage becomes unintelligible. Static appears on the screen, and it doesn't stop until ten minutes later, when the video refreshes. The cashier is at his post, looking bewildered. There's no trace of Minnie.

I narrow my eyes. This is...intriguing.

The next case happened a few days after, in another town. This was outside a small clothing shop. Three items were stolen from it. A pair of jeans, a shirt, and a pair of slides.

My cheek twitches.

The person fitting Minnie's description was seen around the store at night, but once more, the cameras malfunctioned. This time, they didn't catch her entering or exiting the store, so they only want to question her if she saw anything.

Since these are all small-town cases of petty theft, there isn't much urgency. In fact, I'd be willing to bet they're not even trying that hard to find her.

The third case is the most interesting, though.

Three men were assaulted in front of a movie theater. Once more, the same pattern emerges. The cameras outside the movie theater had malfunctioned exactly when the incident took place. More interestingly, though, none of the men could remember exactly what happened to them. They just recalled spotting a pretty young woman with dark hair and dark eyes and that was the last thing they remembered.

One of the men had both of his arms broken.

The second had multiple lesions, broken bones, and had to be put in neck braces.

The third had his head repeatedly banged against a hard surface, which resulted in intracranial pressure and required immediate surgery.

All were said to make a full recovery.

This time, the police seem more involved. It isn't just stolen goods. Three burly men were put in the hospital.

I click on the video, and there are very few snippets of Minnie, always walking a distance away from the movie theater. But as I read more through the report, I find out that the CCTV inside the location had been malfunctioning for a week straight and always at night.

I tap my finger against my chin.

Cold facts are my specialty. They don't lie. And in this case, I'm sure the person in the videos *is* Minnie. But more than that, I'm also sure that she's the one who somehow got the cameras to malfunction. She did it here too, didn't she? And multiple times too.

Opening my own camera feed, I write a quick code to scan for any static in the last week.

Just as I expected, there are numerous instances throughout the day when the camera stops recording. It's not just one isolated incident. It's tens, if not hundreds.

I'll be damned.

She likes sweet things. When she broke into the first store, she stole a bunch of packs of chocolate cookies. When she broke into the second place, she stole the clothes she was wearing when I first met her. And in the third case...

She couldn't have beat those men up, that's for sure.

But her frequent sightings around the movie theater, especially at night when the cameras wouldn't record tell me one thing—she was sleeping in the movie theater.

But these are just a few cases in which she happened to be named a person of interest because she happened to be nearby. Who knows how many more times she did this before and was never caught on camera? She's been living on the streets for a long time by her own admission.

A smile spreads up my lips.

My little heathen is smart. Very, very smart. And potentially a criminal.

And while she lied about her identity and her past, I'm not even mad. If she can hack into CCTV feeds like that, then she must be a hell of a hacker.

Enthusiasm bubbles inside of me.

I've never felt like this before. Like I might finally have an equal—someone I could go up against but also share my thoughts with. Someone who would understand.

Ah, but the things we could do together... The chaos we could create...

Minnie, Minnie. My lovely little liar.

You're lucky I've developed a fondness for your brand of deceit—and your unmatched cooking skills.

Now I just need to lure her in until she reveals everything by herself. After all, what's the fun in confronting her when the chase will prove to be so much more exciting?

Yet until then, I'll have to throw my mother off her trail. That wretched dinner is in just two days, and I have no doubt she'll ask Minnie all sorts of questions which she'll then go on to try to corroborate.

My mother might be the more sentimental of the two of us, but she's just as careful and shrewd as I am.

After closing my computer, I head downstairs.

Minnie is in the kitchen preparing lunch.

As soon as I step inside, the mouthwatering scent hits my nostrils and I gulp down.

I don't know what the hell she puts in those dishes of hers, but after eating her food for almost a week, I might even believe her when she says it's magic.

I can't explain it otherwise. Every single thing she's made has been perfect. It's gotten to the point that I got rid of the recipe sheet I gave her on the first day and instead instructed her to cook whatever she wants.

In fact, maybe it *is* magic because the only explanation for my obsession with her entire persona is that she bewitched me. How else can I justify my unnatural interest in all things *her*? How else can I justify this change in my behavior that's absolutely unprecedented?

"What are you making?"

She doesn't turn to look at me. Her attention is on the stove as she watches the sauce simmer.

"Lentil curry," she answers in a dull voice.

I suppose the first thing I need to do before she reveals her true self to me is to get back into her good graces. And I think I know just the thing that might...sweeten her a little—literally.

"Is it done?"

"In five minutes. But it will have to cool down," she mentions, still not looking at me.

I wait the requisite five minutes. When she turns off the stove, I tell her.

"Come."

That's when she finally *turns*.

It's been a few hours since I made contact with those big eyes of hers, but every time is like the first time. They're so striking, it's impossible not to be shaken by the sight of them.

If in the beginning I would have said she was cute, perhaps pretty, now that I know more about her—and I've tasted her food—I can confidently say she is...stunning.

I stare at her, salivating worse than I did five minutes ago when I got a whiff of the curry.

But this new information showed me a new side of her. One that I'm looking forward to exploring more.

Minnie takes off her apron, folds it, and drapes it over a chair. She follows behind me and asks, "Where are we going?"

"You're going to put on some nice clothes," I instruct.

"Why?" She stops in the middle of the hallway, her hands on her hips as she glares at me.

For some reason, this mutinous glare of hers has grown on me. It's quite...cute. And although I don't like the way she always ignores me, I have to admit she's damn cute when she's angry—not that I want to anger her more. On the contrary. From now on, operation make Minnie happy is in motion.

"We're going to grab some dessert."

Her eyes light up despite the fact that she tries to curb her excitement.

Aha, I was right. Sweet things are the way to her heart.

"Dessert?" she repeats, licking her lips.

"Yes. There's a really good cookie shop in the next town over. We'll grab some and come back to eat." Not that *I* would know. But a quick search put me on the right path. And for once, I'll even indulge in the sin of chocolate—as long as she indulges with me, too.

She smacks her lips together and I can already see the cookie signs reflected in her eyes.

"I suppose that's a good idea. We do need dessert," she murmurs. She's trying not to seem *too* eager, but I know she's probably already tasting that sweetness.

She dashes to her room and in less than ten minutes, she's back downstairs, dressed and ready to go.

I smile to myself.

So far, she hasn't really had the chance to wear the new clothes she got. We haven't left the house since.

She's wearing a pair of dark jeans and a cream cashmere sweater, together with her platform sneakers. As we head to the garage, she puts her coat on and places a long scarf haphazardly around her neck.

I stop her.

"Let me," I murmur as I take hold of the scarf, wrapping it around her neck and tying it neatly in front of her.

She blinks fast, but as my eyes meet hers, she averts her gaze. A blush creeps up her cheeks.

"Let's go," she mumbles under her breath as she all but runs to the car.

We get in the car and I start driving.

It's been a while since I've been in such close quarters with her, and I find the air growing hotter and threatening to suffocate me. Especially with this deafening silence.

Minnie is looking out the window, ignoring me.

We're a few miles away from the house when I clear my throat.

"I got you something," I add, feeling rather uncertain.

She turns, raising her brows at me.

Damn, she's pretty.

I stare at her for a moment, forgetting my train of thought.

"What?" she asks.

I take a deep breath.

Don't screw this up, Marlowe.

"Open that compartment," I tell her and motion to the compartment in front of her.

She does as told and fishes a small red bag from inside.

She frowns.

"Look inside," I add.

She slowly pulls on the white ribbon at the top and takes out the perfume box.

I'd ordered that for her days ago but never found the perfect moment to give it to her since she's barely been acknowledging my existence.

I had been planning to give it to her before the dinner with my mother, but I suppose now it's a good time too.

"It's a perfume," I feel compelled to mention when she's just staring at the box.

She blinks, wets her lips, and then finally speaks.

I prepare myself for that thank you I've been waiting to hear from her lips.

"I've been washing daily, as per your rules," she says.

"I know but—"

"If this is your way of telling me I still smell, then no, thank you," she grumbles. Before I can say anything else, she places the box back in the bag and stuffs it in the compartment.

I look at her, dumbfounded.

"That wasn't my intention..." I mumble, aware I screwed up again.

She must notice my expression because she immediately changes her mind.

"I suppose I could try the perfume," she murmurs. She plasters a tight smile on her face as she grabs the gift bag again and takes out the box.

She's doing this to appease me.

My heart is pounding in my chest.

Minnie struggles to get the perfume bottle out of its box. Keeping one hand on the wheel, I use the other to help her.

"It's caramel-scented," I mention awkwardly as I try to regain my composure.

She likes sweet things. She should like this too.

"Oh."

She takes the cap off and sprays the perfume around her.

I hold my breath while she's deliberating, hoping she'll like it.

Her brows furrow as her nostrils flare. She scrunches her nose. Then sneezes.

Repeatedly.

One after another, she won't stop sneezing.

My eyes widen.

I pull over and open the windows to the car.

Her entire face is flushed, and the tip of her nose is bright red.

"You don't like it." I release a deep sigh.

"It's n-not"—*sneeze*—"that." *Sneeze.* "It's j-just t-too"—*sneeze*—"strong."

"That's fine. You don't have to wear it," I tell her.

She attempts a smile, or I think she does because her sneezing fit resumes.

I get out of the car and go to open her door, then pull her out so she can inhale the fresh, crisp winter air. She takes mouthfuls of air, all the while scrubbing her nose, making it even redder.

I forget about the cold or the fact that the snow must be six inches around us. Waving my hands in front of her face, I do my best to help get the toxic fumes out of her vicinity.

Goddamn it. Women are supposed to like perfumes. I spent hours scouring the internet for the best sweet fragrance, but I never once considered that she'd be allergic to it.

"I think I'm good," she murmurs after about ten minutes of sneezing. Her eyes are damp, and a few tears run down her cheeks from too much sneezing.

I press my thumbs to her face to wipe the moisture away. She gazes at me from beneath her lashes, giving me a tentative smile. She sniffles, and more moisture drips out of her nose. My arm is next to her face and my sweater the closest thing to a handkerchief.

I don't even get to react before she's using my clothes to blow her nose.

I can only stare at her in shock as shudders rack my body.

"Thank you," she mentions when she's done, wiping her nose a couple more times on the material of my sweater. "That was thoughtful of you."

Then, as if nothing happened, she turns and gets back into the car.

That little heathen...

FOURTEEN

WE EVENTUALLY REACH THE STORE.

How I didn't turn the car around to go back home, shower and change, I don't know.

I thought about it.

I was one step away from doing it.

But then she looked at me.

And smiled.

I couldn't screw up again after giving her an allergy fit with that wretched perfume. I'm still mentally cursing myself for my oversight. Perhaps I should have asked her first instead of just buying it because the internet told me so.

I park the car and look around.

The streets are busy.

Even though it's a small town, it's the middle of December and people are strutting up and down the street, browsing shops for gifts.

The *worst* time to go out.

I glance at Minnie.

She has stars in her eyes as she looks at the beautiful Christmas lights adorning the shops and trees. She's eager to get out there and explore—I can tell.

But she cannot.

"Stay here. I'll be just a moment," I tell her.

She flutters her lashes in confusion. "But—"

"There are people around, Minnie. Men," I state emphatically. "You cannot go out."

"But, Marlowe, I—"

"I'll get the dessert for you. Just tell me what you want."

"How can I tell you when I have no idea what options they have?" She pouts.

For a second, I waver. But then I see a group of men walking down the sidewalk and glancing at my car. I pull her toward me so all they can see is her back.

I seriously don't need to kill someone tonight. And with the not so ideal developments from the last week, I don't think I'll be quite as gracious as I was during our visit to the department store. One lustful glance from a man will likely set me off and that will set off a chain reaction that will either end up with me on the news or at the police station—or both. Somehow, her proximity makes me take leave of my senses and when engaging in murder—in the *perfect* murder—the presence of one's senses is of utmost importance.

The unfortunate truth is that since she's appeared in my life, I've most definitely lost brain cells. I am dumber, I feel dumber, I do dumber things.

She's converted me into a blundering idiot. And though I'm annoyed at that particular development, every time I think of ways to combat that, I spot her and I'm back to being a dumb, primitive male.

That's the main issue. As long as I'm alone, I can plan a myriad of ways in which I'll get rid of her and of the ridiculous ways in which she continues to bewitch me with her soulful eyes, her orgasmic food, and that little ass of hers that she keeps shaking while she's cleaning. But as soon as I come face to face with her, I forget all my plans until only one goal remains.

Gaining her approval.

Fuck. I shouldn't have taken her with me. But I was too excited at the prospect of giving her a surprise that I didn't think too long about the implications—yet another thing that I've stopped doing since she's come along in my life.

My lips flatten into a thin line as I look into her beguiling face.

She's giving me puppy eyes.

Double fuck.

How can I resist that? How can *anyone* resist that?

"You like chocolate. What else do you like?"

She scowls but soon realizes arguing with me is pointless since I will not budge on my decision.

"I like vanilla, too. Oh, and red velvet. That one is divine."

I nod.

"I'll be right back," I say as I get out of my car and lock it.

Her expression has now changed to that of a wounded puppy and I want to fucking kick myself for upsetting her. I doubt that will win me *any* sweet points with her.

I sigh.

I better get as many cookies as I can fit into my arms and hopefully a sugar high will make her see me in a different light.

Inside the store, I browse the selection and tell the clerk to pack two dozen chocolate and vanilla. Luckily for me, they have red velvet, too, so I get a dozen of that, as well. As I wait for them to pack my order, I also spot a red velvet cheesecake, and I smile to myself. That will be a good surprise. She'll have no option but to allow me back into her good graces once she sees the sweet fare I have prepared for her.

After I pay the bill, the clerk stacks four boxes in my arms and I return to the car.

I barely open the trunk to deposit the boxes when I notice something is amiss.

Minnie is not in the car.

Panic flares in my chest. I slam the trunk shut and look around me.

"Minnie?" I call out, my voice loud enough that it makes everyone pause. "Minnie, where are you?"

She's nowhere to be seen.

Did she... Has she left me?

Was my clumsy attempt at a gift such a turnoff that she decided to leave, once and for all?

But no, that can't be.

Where could she go? Where would she sleep? She has no money, and her only possessions are the clothes on her back.

"Minnie!" I continue yelling as I run up and down the street.

My heart is racing, and my sight begins to cloud. Fear unlike I've ever known floods my insides, causing me nerve-wracking anxiety.

I bump into people right and left as I keep calling out her name.

Where is she? Where the hell is she?

She can't have run away. No. I refuse to believe that.

People passing by become a blur in the background as I suddenly stop. I'm out of breath. My head is pounding, and my heart threatens to burst in my chest.

I bang my fist against my ribcage to alleviate the discomfort. But the mere thought that she might be lost to me has me hyperventilating.

What if she didn't leave of her own volition? What if someone took her?

What if a *man* took her?

Her allure to the male species is a curse. Someone could have easily seen her through the window and become obsessed with her. A concept I might have laughed at a week ago, but one that could be very much a reality now—a frightening reality.

Fucking hell!

What if she's cold? She left her coat in the car. She's only wearing a sweater.

What if she gets lost and doesn't know how to reach me or how to get back home? She doesn't have a phone—which I now realize to be an oversight on my part and something I mean to rectify as soon as possible.

The more she'll wander around, the colder she'll get. Then she'll be hungry.

She can't go hungry.

I gulp down hard and try to push those intrusive thoughts away. I'll solve nothing if I let the fear overtake me.

What if something happens with Minnie? What if I never see her again?

My veins are about to pop at my temples, but I force myself to focus.

She can't have walked far. I was only inside the shop for a few minutes.

I look around me again, trying to see my surroundings with a clearer mind. It takes me a couple of deep breaths to dispel the fog trying to lay claim over my mind.

Walking a few feet over, I hear a sharp cry.

Minnie!

I push my way through the crowd, letting her voice guide me. I don't even care that I'm brushing against other people at this point and letting them brush against me. The pain is ephemeral compared to the regret of a lifetime I'd have if I don't find her.

The crowd becomes more sparse, and Minnie releases another cry.

I run at full speed, rounding the corner to an alleyway nestled between two tall buildings. It's dark and hidden from sight.

My eyes widen at the sight before me.

There she is.

Her knees are digging into the icy snow. She's hugging a furry little thing to her chest as she glares at the man in front of her. He's in his mid to late forties, dressed respectably in a medium-priced parka and wearing a woolen hat tipped over his face.

"Minnie," I rasp, my voice harsh and out of breath.

She turns to look at me, her lips tipping up in a tremulous smile. Her eyes brighten.

"Marlowe. You have to help!"

I stride to her side, grab her by the arm, and pull her up. I deposit her and her little furry friend behind me and turn to stare down the man who dared to threaten her.

"What happened?" I ask as I give her a cursory glance to ensure she's all right. Aside from the new addition in her arms, she seems unharmed.

"Look, Marlowe," she murmurs in a low, tight voice. She motions toward the little dog in her arms. Gently pulling him from her chest, she shows me the gashes running all over his back. I press my lips in a tight line. The length and width of the gashes are consistent with the impact of a belt against his skin. The dog releases a whine as if afraid she's going to release him from her arms. He nestles closer, burrowing his snout against her neck.

He's trembling. And it's not because he's cold.

This can only mean one thing.

"Now listen here, miss. You can't just kidnap my dog," the man interjects.

"Shut it." I give him a deadly glare as I hold one finger in front of him.

"Continue," I tell Minnie, needing to hear the rest of her story so I can adjust the punishment accordingly.

"He"—she wets her lips—"he kicked the dog because he wouldn't move. That's when I ran after him. And when he saw me..." She takes a deep breath. "Well, first he threatened to call the police, but then he got a better look at me and he said I could have the dog if I paid for it..." She trails off and I get the gist of it as well as what the man was implying she pay him with.

The man has the decency to flush.

"It's not my fault," he cries out. "I don't know what came over me, I swear. I don't go around propositioning young girls."

I let out a dry laugh.

"But you go around abusing animals?" I raise a brow.

He averts his gaze.

"I wasn't abusing him. I was disciplining him. He needs to learn—"

"No, you need to learn. The dog seems perfectly behaved to me."

He's snuggling tightly against Minnie's chest, and for a moment, I envy the little bugger. Now that's one body I wouldn't mind brushing against. But it's unlikely that will happen anytime soon since she's still pissed at me.

"No, you don't understand," the man cries out. "He won't pee outside. He only pees inside."

"He's a small dog!" Minnie exclaims. "He has a small bladder. You do, don't you, little baby," she coos at the dog, who rejoices at the attention he receives from her. Another stab of jealousy spears against my chest.

For fuck's sake, Marlowe! Being jealous of a dog is low, even for you.

"Maybe he would learn to pee outside if you walked him more often and made an effort to teach him instead of punishing him," I mention.

"You have no right! It's my dog! I'll call the police!"

"Please do. Here, I'll even help you," I say as I pull out my phone and dial 911.

"W-wait..." the man mumbles then jumps at me to try to get the phone from my hand.

I'm at least a head taller than he is, so I simply raise my arm. My lips twitch as I watch him try to jump up and down to grab the phone.

"What do you say, Minnie? Should I give him the benefit of the doubt?"

"No," she answers immediately.

Good girl.

"He doesn't deserve to own a pet," she continues.

"You heard the lady." I smirk and press call.

I might not be able to murder him on the spot for his offenses, but I can certainly do...something. And getting the authorities involved will at least give him a taste of that punishment he's so fond of inflicting on a little creature. But it will also help me save face with Minnie, since I doubt she'd warm up to me if she sees me murder someone in cold blood.

I want her forgiveness for whatever I did wrong. The last thing I need is for her to recoil in fear if she knows just how far I'd be willing to take this—well, only as far as having his body chopped up in small pieces before feeding them to wild beasts. It might be an affront to said wild beasts to eat something so unpalatable as this coward, but it would be a kind of poetic justice.

"Nine-one-one, what's your emergency?" the operator speaks.

The man pales and right as I start reciting what had happened, he gets ready to run.

He makes a couple of steps before I'm on him, grabbing him by his coat and pulling him back, half lifting him off the floor.

Scrawny-ass coward.

He squirms and wiggles in an attempt to free himself, but he's only battling the air at this point.

"We'll send a car over," the operator says after I tell her our location.

The man begs me to let him go, his words more fervent with each passing moment.

I chuckle and shake my head.

One glance at Minnie, though, and I thank all the known and unknown deities that I resorted to a non-violent method to make sure this lousy coward gets his comeuppance.

Her expression is soft, and a sweet smile appears on her lips as she regards me—as if I were her hero.

It finally dawns on me that's exactly what I want to be—and maybe what I've been subconsciously trying to be all along.

Her hero.

In his desperation to escape, the man tries to kick me but misses. I shake my head at him and his feeble attempts. What I wouldn't give to be able to teach him a lesson—one that he would never forget. But just as that thought becomes more and more tantalizing, the blaring sirens dispel all my fantasies.

Damn it.

The police arrives, and upon confirming the validity of our allegations, they arrest the man and take the little frightened dog to a veterinarian for urgent care.

Minnie pouts when she has to hand over the dog to the police-woman, but she eventually relents when she learns it's for the best of the dog.

As the police car drives away, I quickly text Giles and ask him to monitor the case for me. In my experience, the police won't do too much, so I'll have to intervene at some point. It doesn't matter if it's two or ten years later. If it means doling out the proper justice, I'll do it.

"You like animals?" I ask Minnie as I lead her back to the car.

I keep her to my side to avoid getting noticed by other people.

"Of course. Who doesn't?" she asks as if this were the most natural thing in the world.

"I'd think the incident that just occurred would have answered your question."

"Those are not people," she mentions, scrunching her nose in disgust. "They're far below animals as far as I'm concerned."

I raise a brow in surprise at her staunch statement.

"They are," I agree. "Unfortunately, the law is not enough to keep them in check."

She nods.

"Human law is so peculiar to me," she muses to herself.

"Human law?" I repeat, amused. "You speak as if there was some other type of law out there."

Her eyes widen briefly and she clears her throat.

"I was just thinking of what ideal law would be like. There was this book I read," she mentions, not looking at me. "In it, when a trial would be held, a deity of truth would be called to ascertain whether the accused was guilty or not. Then, that person would be executed."

"A deity of truth? That's interesting. I suppose it's in a book with magic, since you seem to be quite fond of that."

She smiles.

"The deities of truth are the ones in charge of divining the truth. They use an ancient relic called the mirror of truth that shows the unadulterated facts," she continues.

"So they're interpreting what the mirror shows them?" I ask.

"Yes, they're trained to do so."

"But doesn't that skew that meaning of *objective* truth? Since the mages use their training and personal experience to translate what the mirror is saying. Isn't that another way of manipulating facts?"

She stops in her tracks.

Slowly, she glances up at me.

"Unfortunately, objective truth cannot account for emotions, can it?"

"I don't believe there's such a thing as objective truth, pet. Once it passes through the human lens, truth loses any objectivity it might have had."

"But they're deities. Not human..."

"Doesn't matter." I shrug. "They're still beings that process information and emotion. Even a computer only does as much as it is trained to do, and the bias from the coding becomes visible in the final product."

"You're so smart, Marlowe. You're right. There isn't really an objective truth, but they do disguise it as such." She shakes her head. "I've always wondered if there's true justice out there, or if it's only the justice of those who get to define it."

My mouth curls up in a lopsided smile.

"No." I shrug. "As far as I'm concerned, there's no true justice, just as there's no truth. But I'm a selfish bastard and I don't care about *other* people's truths. I have my personal justice system based on a number of factors, the most important being firsthand evidence. Like what we just witnessed. That's enough for me to reach a verdict, whereas for the justice system that might not even be enough to make it to trial."

"But if everyone operated based on a personal code of justice, chaos would ensue. There would be an unending cycle of retribution. Would that solve anything?"

"That would never happen," I say confidently. "People are much too comfortable, much too complacent. Very few people are brave enough to take matters into their own hands to achieve what they see as justice."

We reach the car and get inside. She's silent and biting on her lip as if she's mulling over the issue.

"I don't know, Marlowe." She sighs. "This law you have going leaves too much room for interpretation. That divine law? I fear it leaves too little. I wish I could have strong convictions like you, but sometimes..." She takes a deep breath. "Sometimes it's only a matter of survival."

I slowly turn toward her. She gives me a tremulous smile.

I stare at her, returning the smile with a devious one of my own.

Yes. It *is* a matter of survival. *Her* survival. The more time I spend in her presence, the more indispensable she becomes to me —after all, who would willingly give up her spectacular cooking?

Minnie is small, gentle, soft. She needs me to protect her; to keep her safe and happy. I'll willingly become both the judge and the executioner if it means keeping men who mean her harm away from her. With her penchant for attracting all sorts of attention, she needs me to serve as a buffer between her and the world. And I will do it.

For her, I'll continue killing—not that it's a hardship.

But for her, I'll even break my rules.

As we get inside the car, I hand her a box of cookies from the trunk.

She opens it, and the moment she spots the contents, her entire face lights up.

My chest, too, lights up.

In an odd way.

An inconceivable way.

I never thought I'd want someone of my own.

But Minnie? She's the perfect pet. The perfect companion. Sweet, loyal, and entertaining.

My lips pull up in a satisfied smile as I watch the way she's reacting at those cookies—as if it's the best thing that's ever happened to her.

And in my mind, a new definition of justice forms—*her*.

From now on, she'll be my standard for justice.

FIFTEEN

UNFORTUNATELY, the cookies don't help my case *that* much. We get home, she opens the boxes, eats half the cookies, then bids me goodbye so she can go nap with a full stomach. She even had the gall to lick her lips and pat her full belly as she blithely announced her departure.

I'm left staring at the half-empty boxes. Muttering a string of curses, I grab a cookie and shove it into my mouth.

Soft, crunchy, and chocolatey. Everything I hate.

I eat another one.

It's all her fault. Making me eat chocolate and sweets when I've avoided a sugar addiction my entire life.

I finish the first box and turn to the second, all the while blaming her for this.

If I didn't need to impress her, I wouldn't have all these cookies in front of me, beckoning me to eat them. And if I didn't watch her mere minutes ago eating them with so much gusto, I would not be so tempted right now.

But I am.

And what's worse is that with every taste, all I can picture is her lips as she bit into the cookie. Her luscious mouth as she chewed on them.

Fuck.

I need to stop.

Getting to my feet, I close the cookie boxes and put them away. Then I stalk up the stairs and go to her room. Planting myself in front of the door, I knock.

The seconds trickle by and my pulse starts drumming in my ears.

At last, Minnie opens the door.

Big mistake.

She's wearing a black oversized shirt that I gave her when she first came here, and nothing else.

Her legs are bare, and as she notices my gaze drifting lower and lower, she wiggles her toes. They're small and dainty. Just like her.

I gulp down.

"Do you need anything?" she asks in a monotone voice.

Do I? I can't remember *why* I came here.

As I rack my brain for something to say—something that won't make me look like the dumbass I already feel—she continues. "If you need me to clean the kitchen, I'll do that later. I don't think you have anything against me taking a short nap, do you?"

She narrows her eyes at me. Just how tyrannical does she think I am?

I straighten my back and attempt to infuse some confidence in my stance, though I don't even know why I'm here other than to ogle her. Although, if I'm honest, she's rather nice to ogle and that in itself makes the visit worth it.

Fuck. I must be losing my fucking mind because there's no way I'd entertain that train of thought unless there was something clearly wrong with me. Something like...magic.

This girl... What if she has bewitched me? Because under no circumstances would I have eaten more sugar in the span of a few minutes than I have in my entire life.

My stomach rumbles in approval, and I can feel the sugar high poking its head to the surface, which for someone with already bad ADHD, that can only mean one thing.

Chaos.

Unless I have been possessed by a sugar ghost, there's absolutely no way I would have willingly engaged in that. Nor would I have been standing here, watching Minnie as if I've never seen a woman before in my life. Which, granted, I've never seen someone like her before, but maybe that's the issue.

She must have done something to me, something that logic cannot explain.

She wormed her way into my house, and that wasn't enough, so she concocted to invade my mind too.

What if it's her food? What if she's been feeding me something that altered my brain chemistry in such a way that I've become addicted to her presence?

"Marlowe? Are you going to stand there all day and brood?"

"I wasn't brooding," I lie.

She places her hands on her hips and tilts her head to the side.

"What do you want?" she asks with a sigh. "I really want to nap."

It's on the tip of my tongue to ask, *can I join you*? But that would be low, even for me. So instead, I end up muttering something worse.

"Did you put a spell on me?"

The words are out of my mouth before I can think them through.

Her eyes widen slightly. "What?"

"You heard me. Did you put a spell on me?" I ask, watching her with narrowed eyes.

A faint blush appears on her cheeks. Suspicious.

"Where would you have gotten that idea from?" she mumbles, but she averts her eyes.

Even more suspicious.

"I'm rich, objectively good-looking, and at the right age to settle down. I'm the perfect target for that *magic* of yours."

"You..." Her lips tremble with mirth. "You think I used magic to what?"

"To get me to become obsessed with you, of course. You want a ring on your finger. Admit it," I tell her squarely. "Well, I feel compelled to tell you that you've made a bad gamble when you chose to work your wiles on me."

She blinks a few times before she bursts out laughing.

"So let me get this straight. You think I must have put a spell on you to get you to become obsessed with me because I want you to marry me?"

"Indeed. And I'm here to tell you it won't work."

"So you're obsessed with me?" she asks as she wets her lips and takes a step forward.

I take a step back. "Have you not heard what I said? It will not work on me."

"If it doesn't work on you, then how do you know there's anything at all happening to you?"

"Because you're a witch," I say accusingly.

"Marlowe, with all due respect," she starts in a serious tone. "I know your favorite show to watch is *Supernatural*, but that doesn't mean everything around you has a supernatural explanation."

How the hell does she know that? I don't recall mentioning it to her.

"You're the one who mentioned magic first."

"As a joke." She chuckles. "Are you sure you're not trying to find an explanation for something that's already happening to you? Something you may *not* want to happen to you?"

Once more, she takes a step forward. This time, I don't move, letting her chest brush against mine. I barely hold back a groan.

"Something like the fact that you might...like me?" She bats her lashes at me.

I place my hands on her shoulders.

Hope blossoms in her features.

Lifting her up, I deposit her in her room and put some space between us.

"I don't *like* you, Minnie. I merely tolerate you," I grumble as I pull the door closed to her room, trying to ignore the stricken expression on her face.

MINNIE'S BEHAVIOR the next day tells me that I mucked things up once more. This time, even worse. If before she would at least mumble something back to me or acknowledge my presence —at times—now she straight up pretends I'm invisible.

As for me? Frankly, I have no idea why I went to her room in the first place, let alone why I felt the need to accuse her of being a witch. After my sugar haze cleared, I could see that I was not in full control of my faculties when I made those accusations, a fact that I communicated to her as well.

She didn't answer.

Well, to be more precise, she did answer, but not directly.

She just left behind a piece of paper with a blood-red pentagon on it and my name written in the middle.

Now she's not *just* ignoring me. She's mocking me as well.

I would too, since everything I told her was pretty much nonsense.

On top of that, when I went to look at her search history, it was all about spells on *how to make him love you*, but also one search hit for *how to turn him into a toad*.

Safe to say, she's not a witch. If she were, I would have become a toad a long time ago considering the times I've made her mad or straight up insulted her.

Alas, the damage has already been done. Now I need to find a way to fix it. Especially since the dinner with my mother is... tomorrow.

Fucking hell!

I spend the entire day morosely stalking up and down the stairs of my house, half to catch a glimpse of Minnie as she does her *magic* with food, and half to find a solution to my dilemma: earning her forgiveness.

Ultimately, I end up in my car and driving away from the house in an attempt to clear my head—and also get Minnie a present so she'd stop ignoring me.

The perfume was a bad idea, so I'm crossing that off the list.

She has clothes and shoes, but girls love that stuff, so I'm sure she won't mind more—especially since she doesn't have a specific outfit for *this* occasion. And now that I think about it, I haven't gotten her a bag, have I?

I need to remedy that, too. Girls love designer bags.

The stores are nearing their closing times, so I hurry to find something to her liking.

Her favorite colors are white and red. I'll just get something in those colors.

Easier said than done since most of the dresses in white are bridal, while the ones in red are far too sexy and sultry for me to be comfortable going out with her like that. Even if my mother rented out an entire space, there will still be people seeing her when she walks into and out of the restaurant, as well as the serving staff.

I curse in annoyance.

This is not going well.

Eventually, I settle on an off-white dress with a modest length and neckline, but which should flatter her figure nonetheless. Although I'm reluctant to have anyone see her like that, it's the only thing I deem acceptable, which she might also like.

A nice pair of white heels is easy enough to find, and since her entire outfit is white, I think she can add a red bag to it—that way, she'll have *both* of her favorite colors.

Luckily for me, I spot the perfect red Chanel bag in a window and go inside to buy it. The sales associates are not very accommodating at first, saying the items in the window are not for sale. But a few phone calls later and I'm walking out with the red bag.

I don't want to be gone for too long, so I jump into my car and drive back home. Excitement simmers inside of me as I think of her reaction when she'll see these gifts. She'll smile, that's for sure.

Or at least, I hope she will.

I love her smile.

I'll love her smile even more if I'm the one to put it on her face.

I hum along to the song on the radio as I drive just under the speed limit—another first.

It's fully dark out by the time I get back.

I don't waste any time after I park the car in my garage and I head straight for her room, gift bags in tow.

"Minnie?" I ask as I knock at her door.

No answer.

I wait a few more seconds before I knock and call her name again, this time louder.

No answer.

Frowning, I pull the doorknob to the side. The door slides open.

I walk inside, only to find the room empty. I put the bags on her bed and walk around the room.

"Minnie?" I call out again, stopping in front of the bathroom and listening for any sound.

Nothing.

She's not here.

At this point, I'm not overly concerned. She could have very well returned to cleaning.

Leaving the bags on her bed, I head to my office and pull up the camera feed from around the house.

I scan every single frame, looking for her, but she's nowhere to be found.

I gulp down.

Something slides beneath my skin, worming its way right

under the surface of my epidermis. Discomfort settles deep in my gut.

She wouldn't leave.

Where would she go?

We're basically in the middle of nowhere here. She'd have to walk miles to reach the highway.

Once more, panic pokes at my usually calm demeanor, causing me to become frantic in my attempt to find her—any trace of her.

I rewind the video footage until I see her exiting the house. I access the feed from the outside cameras, but they only show her going into the back field before the same static as before appears on the screen.

Fuck.

I need to get the system checked out. It's not normal for static to appear so often, even after countless upgrades.

Cursing at the fact that technology is failing me, I head outside, looking for Minnie in the last place I'd seen her go—the field.

It's cold out.

Much colder than I expected. So cold, in fact, that I wonder how the fuck Minnie would have gone out wearing only my old shirt. As she exited the house, her legs and arms were bare. The flimsy material of the shirt would have hardly provided any boundary against the chilly wind.

Fucking hell. The moment I get my hands on that little heathen, I might just wring her neck.

I stride across the field determinedly, looking right and left for her. The entire expanse of the field is covered in white, so a small, black dot would certainly be rather conspicuous.

Except, what I see is not only one small black dot but two.

I can spot her in the distance, some five hundred feet away.

She's close to the fence surrounding my property. But she's not alone.

There's someone else with her. Someone not so small. Someone who looks like...a man.

A man who is *hugging* her.

I can't make out more than his stature and build and the fact that he's wearing all black.

Despite the cold, my blood boils in my veins. I increase my pace.

I'm around three hundred feet away when Minnie half-turns, almost as if she can hear me—though it's impossible from that distance. She makes some gestures with her hands and just as I blink, the other person disappears.

I don't even get to process my disbelief as pure rage overtakes me.

She was talking with another man. On my land. While living with me.

Who was it?

How did he know to come here?

Did she call him here?

Is it that soulmate of hers or is it someone else? Maybe a lover. Maybe she's been lying to me all along and I was far too blind to see it. Maybe this was all just one giant set-up. Cozy up to me, learn everything about my house, then bring her lover so they can both rob me blind.

It's not a far-fetched scenario.

I may be a very private person, but unfortunately, there's plenty of public information about me thanks to my high-profile family. My family name alone would attract all kinds of attention, most often the negative kind. I suppose I should have thought about that before I picked up a stranger from the side of the road.

For fuck's sake, there are no records about her online. None whatsoever.

Even knowing that, I've decided to ignore the rational side of my brain that was yelling at me that this is a disaster waiting to happen. She was a liability from day one and I could have kicked her out at any point after I found out about the inconsistencies in her story.

The more I think of it, the more mad I am at myself. But not as mad as I am at her and *this* betrayal.

Yet it's not the thought that Minnie lied to me about her identity that guts me, it's the fact that she may have colluded with another *man* to achieve this plan of hers—whatever it is.

The more I think of her and that shadowy figure together the more I find myself slipping.

I don't do anger.

I don't do disappointment because I never expect anything in the first place.

I don't do emotions at all—they're far too troublesome.

Yet since she came into my life, every fucking rule I've had for myself has gone down the drain.

I crack my knuckles as I march toward her. I *hate* the way tension knots in my gut, in my veins, in every goddamn organ. The urge to smash my fist against a hard surface is *almost* irresistible. I need to feel the physical pain as a way to make sense of this ineffable emotion that's bubbling inside of me. Because physical pain is the only pain I should be acquainted with, the only one to fit the definition of pain.

Not...this.

My insides are getting twisted up in pain the closer I get to her.

"Marlowe, what are you doing here?" Minnie asks me in a soft, quivering voice when I reach her.

"I should be asking *you* the same thing," I retort.

"I thought you'd left..."

"Who was he?" I ask, barely containing the rage in my voice.

Her lashes flutter in confusion.

"Who was...who?"

She's a great actress, I'll give her that.

She appears genuinely surprised by my question.

"The man you were meeting. Who is he?"

"What man?" She frowns.

"Cut it out, Minnie. I saw you. Who was he? That soulmate of yours? An old lover? A *current* lover? Who the fuck is he?"

She regards me with those innocent doe-like eyes of hers and my heart stills in my chest. Yet the image of her in that man's arms is fresh in my mind—so fresh, it's making my blood boil with anger again.

I grab her shoulders. Her skin is warm. Hot. She's only wearing a shirt in this freezing weather, but she's hot to the touch.

The rational part of my brain that would have questioned this is long gone. If I weren't so mad, I may have paused to ask myself how this is possible—especially since it's not the first time. But how can I think coherently about anything but this infuriating situation? How can I still have any thought in my brain when *she* is my sole focus? When I need to know whether she was meeting a lover or not more than I care to take my next breath?

It's fascinating on a deep level—perhaps I should ask my therapist about this. First, I need to find another therapist, I suppose. And quite urgently.

The way Minnie can play with my emotions is dangerous—far too dangerous. And this isn't just about my mental peace—though I have not had any since she came into my life—it's also about keeping my urges in check. That used to be something I was good at.

Before.

Now?

I fear no one in my vicinity is safe as long as I'm constantly in a murderous mood. But more than anything, *I* am not safe as long as I allow her to have such control over me.

"Who. Is. He?" I demand again, my voice dropping to a low octave. She shivers, but it's not from the cold.

"I don't know what you're talking about, Marlowe," she whispers. "You're scaring me."

"Good. I should scare you," I grind out. "I should fucking

scare you, Minnie. Because it seems I've been far too lax with you if you thought you could meet with your fucking lover in my home."

"What lover? Are you insane?" She shakes her head as she tries to deny it.

I tighten my hold on her arms, feeling the way her plush skin molds to my bruising grip.

My mouth curls up in a sick smile.

"Oh, I *am* insane. Perhaps you should have realized that earlier. Before you started fucking with my mind. Before you turned me into *this*."

"Marlowe..."

"Who. Was. He?" I repeat.

"I told you. I don't know what you're talking about," she murmurs, gazing up at me with concern.

"Stop lying, Minnie," I grit out. "Stop fucking lying to my face. I know what I saw."

I let my gaze scan the surrounding area behind her, and sure enough, there's a pair of foreign footprints.

"What's this then?" I ask as I pull her toward the trail of footprints that lead into the neighboring land.

She loses her equilibrium and falls to her knees in the snow. Her chest rises and falls as she looks up at me.

"Marlowe, you're worrying me. There's nothing there," she says in a small voice. Raising one hand, she points to the pristine snow.

I blink.

No fucking way.

"What the fuck..." I mutter under my breath.

"I don't know what's going on with you, Marlowe, but there was no one here. No man. No woman. No one. Absolutely no one," she continues in a calm voice.

I let go of her arm and take a step back.

What the fuck?

What's happening?

There were clearly prints in the snow, just as there was a man with her minutes ago. I saw it. I'm sure I saw it.

But...

Minnie slowly gets up and dusts the snow from her body. Her movements are slow, calculated. She's not trembling. She's not grimacing from the cold.

Her expression is as serene as ever as if the coldness could never reach her.

My heart pounds in my chest. Faster and faster. A vein throbs in my temple.

Confusion swarms inside my mind.

She takes a step toward me.

"There's no one here, Marlowe. There never was."

"But I saw—"

"Maybe you didn't see properly," she offers as she stops in front of me, placing a hand on my chest. She gives me a worried smile. "Are you all right? Do you need to lie down? I can make you some hot soup and you can take a nap."

I gulp down. Uncertainty flickers across my features. Yet another emotion I haven't experienced before, but that now seems to have possessed me.

"I think you're right," I say as I take a deep breath.

Maybe I *did* see wrong. Maybe I've been too stressed about her being mad at me that I just imagined things. It's not as if I don't think daily about the effect Minnie has on other men and the fact that I'll very well end up killing someone soon for looking at her the wrong way.

Perhaps it's just my subconscious telling me that I need to be more careful with her—keep her close to me and away from the world.

"Let's head back inside." She takes my hand and leads me back to the house.

As soon as we reach the warmth of the house, I release a deep sigh. I regard her warily, an apology brewing in my mind.

Yet when the moment comes to verbalize it, I find it hard to do so.

I open my mouth to speak, but no sound comes out.

"Come, I'll make you something hot to eat," she says.

I don't move. I simply stare at her. The anger from before hasn't abated. If anything, it's intensified.

"Marlowe?" she calls out when she notices I'm rooted to the spot.

She tilts her head to the side in question.

"I saw you," I repeat. "You were not alone."

"And I showed you there were no footprints in the snow. Come on, Marlowe. I don't understand why you're making such a big deal out of this."

In two long strides, I'm in front of her with my hand around her throat. I don't squeeze. I merely push her chin up with my thumb so she's looking me in the eye.

"I don't care whether there *was* someone there or not. But trust me when I say that if I *ever* see you with another man, I'll kill you both."

"W-what?" She blinks.

I smirk at her and slowly tighten my grip on her neck.

"You will not talk to other men. You will not smile at other men. And you will certainly not *hug* other men."

"What are you talking about?" she asks, confused.

"Tell me you understand me, Minnie," I drawl, slowly getting back to my comfort place. If everything else fails, then there's only one answer—murder.

"But... You don't even like me," she stammers.

"I don't need to like you." I shrug. "You belong to me."

She stares at me with those big eyes of hers before her expression slowly morphs in front of my eyes. Her lips curl up in a secretive smile.

"So you will kill me, too?"

Is she...taunting me?

I narrow my eyes at her.

"I'm a selfish bastard," I whisper, moving my hand up her cheek and caressing her skin. "I'd rather kill you with my own hands than know some other bastard laid *his* hands on you."

"So you're a killer, huh?" She raises a brow.

"That's an understatement, little heathen." I let out a dry laugh.

"I know, I know." She giggles. "You're a big, bad killer, aren't you?"

I freeze. My eyes slowly widen.

"What did you just say?"

"I know who you are, Marlowe," she whispers as she leans forward. Grabbing my hand, she keeps it against her cheek, grazing my thumb with her teeth. "I know what you've done."

"What do you know?"

She chuckles.

"For starters, your silly story about art. But I know why you did it. And I approve," she purrs softly. "Then there's that story about my foster father? It was a lie. I was never in the system, nor was I in prison."

"I know you've been lying about your identity," I say, my eyes narrowing at her. How the hell does she know about slimy Pauly? "As for the prison, it's only a matter of time," I lie. "The police are actively looking for you for shoplifting." Another lie, since she's technically only a person of interest.

She shrugs, her expression nonchalant.

"They can't prove it," she adds with a smile. The little heathen... She must know about the faulty footage then. Her presence around those sites is the only thing tying her to the crimes, but that would not stand in court since it's just conjecture.

"So you never stabbed your foster father, did you?" I ask, leaning back and watching her intently. Though I'd already guessed she lied about that, I'm curious why she'd been so specific. Had there been someone else she'd stabbed? Another man who hurt her? Because then I'll need to know. She mentioned he was still alive.

Not for long...

"Nope," she answers, popping the P in such a cute way that I momentarily forget I need to be mad at her. "I never stabbed anyone. I'm not a fan of knives, truthfully." She feigns a shudder. "I prefer swords."

"Then why the specific lie?"

"Well, it wasn't technically a lie..." she starts.

I raise a brow.

"*You* stabbed him," she states confidently.

My brows knit together in confusion. What the hell is she on about?

"What are you talking about?"

"Was it two years ago? It was snowing that night too," she mentions.

My eyes flash at her.

Two years ago. A snowy night.

The memory assails me as if it were yesterday.

How could I forget the incident that rattled me so much I lost my usual calm? That day marked my official decline. Since then, I have not been able to kill anyone cleanly, methodically...

"That man was beating his wife. She was full of blood and begging for her life, but no one dared to intervene. People watched, but they ignored it. But you didn't," Minnie continues.

My body tenses. That's too specific. Almost as if...

"How do you know that?" I demand sharply.

She smiles.

"I was there. I saw everything. The way you charged at him, the way you stabbed him over and over, staining the snow with red..." She closes her eyes as she releases a sigh of satisfaction. "Truly a work of art."

It's as if I'm staring in the face of a stranger. But I find that I don't care about the fact that Minnie knows the truth about me, or that she's lied about her past. The most deranged thing is that regardless of who she is, my heart has never beat faster in my chest.

My dick has never been harder either.

"Who are you?" I rasp out.

She smiles.

"A fan."

I narrow my eyes at her.

Ambiguous answer, but a spear of excitement goes through me.

I need to know more.

"Is your name really Minnie An'yan?" I ask skeptically.

"Well…" She wets her lips. "Minnie is short for Minerva. And my last name is, indeed, An'yan. I didn't lie about that."

Minerva. I regard her intently. Minnie suits her better.

Minerva is much too prim and proper. Minnie is…cute, playful, unexpected. Just like her.

Yet when her expression becomes serious and she challenges me…

Maybe I can see some traces of Minerva in her.

And that duality is fucking hot.

"Then why is there no record of you anywhere on the internet?" I ask.

"Hmm, I wonder," she murmurs as she shrugs. "You know all this, yet you still allowed me to live in your house?"

"Minnie…"

"But you have nothing to be afraid of, do you?" She continues, "Because you can kill me anytime you want. And because there's no record of me, then no one will ever look for me, either. Easy kill, isn't it?"

"You're not wrong," I say with a chuckle. "But that doesn't mean I'm not curious about who you are."

"You will know who I am. In due time," she says cryptically.

"And until then, I should just allow you to stay here with me, no?"

She gives me a proud nod.

"Why?"

"Because I belong to you," she states seamlessly as she flutters her lashes at me.

The tension from before melts away as I throw back my head and laugh.

"You're amusing, Minnie. For that alone, I'll keep you around."

"And here I thought it was because I'm so irresistible that you simply couldn't bear to *not* look at me ever again," she adds jokingly.

I clear my throat. She's not too far off the mark, but she doesn't need to know that.

"You're not bad to look at," I mumble.

She smiles and shakes her head.

"There's a present waiting for you in your room," I add after an awkward pause. "You'll wear that tomorrow for dinner with my mother."

Her lips form a small O and her cheeks flush a pretty pink.

I turn to go back to my room, ready to renew my search into Minnie's identity. Perhaps the name Minerva might yield more information.

I only take a couple of steps before she calls my name.

"Marlowe?"

"Yes?"

"Did you mean it? That you'd kill me if you saw me with another man?"

"What do you think?"

"I don't know," she admits honestly. "A part of me hopes you wouldn't." She takes a deep breath. "But the other part of me loves that you would."

SIXTEEN

STRANGE CREATURE.

I cannot get her words out of my head for the rest of the day.

And the following night.

I twist and turn, unable to sleep despite following my nightly routine to a T.

In the morning, instead of feeling refreshed and ready to battle the dinner with my mother, I'm about to snap someone's neck. Preferably Minnie's since the image of her hugging that man hasn't left my mind. It progressed into a nightmare last night as I saw her doing more than hugging and with a great deal fewer clothes than before.

Blasphemy.

It was pure blasphemy.

I have to do something about this, and fast.

Yes, she belongs to me—technically. But I need to find a way to tie her to me permanently. Perhaps I can find some magic spell to serve that purpose since everything in the mortal realm is too ephemeral for my liking.

I chuckle at my own thoughts.

Magic and hallucinations.

What's next?

Ghosts?

Was the man she was seeing a ghost?

But that wouldn't explain the missing footprints since I'm sure of what I saw.

I sigh as I complete my morning ablutions and head out to work. God knows I'll probably end up doing nothing, but at least I can devote more time to stalking Minnie online. Now more than ever I need to know everything there is to know about her. Not because it would change the fact that she now belongs to me, but because I need to know every single man who's ever been in her life. Family, friends... lovers?

I scowl at that thought.

She better be telling the truth about never having had a lover because by God, I'll scour this Earth for the man who dared touch her and I'll kill him slowly and painfully.

Fuck my rules. I'm officially throwing every single rule I've ever had out the window. So what if he's innocent? The mere fact that he's put his hands on her means he's guilty in my eyes, and thus worthy of a fitting punishment.

Heading to my office, I turn on my computer and start a new search into Minnie.

Minerva An'yan.

I type in her name and check the police database first.

No hits.

I turn my attention to Google, genealogy sites and other databases, but that's equally fruitless.

She doesn't exist. Plain and simple.

But she can't not exist, especially in this day and age. Everything is on the internet. The fact that she's not is rather concerning. And it can only mean one thing. Someone made a deliberate effort to erase all traces of her from the internet.

I could, of course, torture the answers out of her. But where's the fun in that? There's also the unfortunate issue that I don't want to harm her—a first, I know.

She said I'd find out her identity in due time, but the curiosity is killing me.

Thinking about this issue for a few more moments, I grab my phone and dial an acquaintance who owns a security company. He's developing a state-of-the-art software to aid background checks, which is supposed to revolutionize the industry. As far as I know, it's still in beta testing. Still, it's worth a try.

Clearly, a simple Google search will not yield anything. The police reports gave me some new information but not nearly enough to find out who she is.

"What?" he answers with a long drawl.

"Does your background check software include facial recognition?"

"Straight to the topic, I see." He chuckles.

I grumble something under my breath.

I don't do people and I don't do friends. But in my industry, Leonidas is the only one I'm on friendly terms with, perhaps because both of us hate going out. To this day, we've never met face to face, but we've talked plenty via email and phone calls.

"As a matter of fact, it does. We've patented a new AI technology that can scour the entire internet archive in a matter of minutes and find all available matches. However, the program is nowhere near finished. We still have a lot of glitches to fix and—"

"Can it find me info on a person based only on their picture? I'll take anything," I cut him off.

He pauses and clicks his tongue.

"I suppose it could, though I would not trust it to be one hundred percent accurate just yet."

"That's fine. I need to use it for something. Personal, not business."

"It wouldn't kill you to say please, you know." He laughs.

"You owe me one," I remind him. I did him a favor last year

when his company was being blackmailed with sensitive information. And I'm not one to not cash in on the debts I'm owed.

He groans. "Fine. I'll have my team send you an invite into the beta. If you have more than one picture, that will help. A video would be even better so the AI can do a 3D scan."

"Thanks," I say and hang up.

Sure enough, a few moments later, I get a notification that I've been invited to join the beta version of the software.

I upload a video from my surveillance feed in which Minnie's features are visible from all angles. Just like Leonidas said, the software isn't without its glitches, and before I can run the search, I have to refresh it a few times so the video can upload.

Once the results loading window appears, I lean back in my chair and wait.

I can't say I'm very hopeful at this point. If someone went to such lengths to erase every record of Minnie from the internet, I doubt I'll be able to find anything. But I won't know until I try, and truthfully, I'm too damn curious to let this go.

If I wait for her to tell me her identity, then I'm putting all the power in her hands. She could make up anything, and I'd have no other choice but to believe her.

The software finishes running the search, and to my surprise, it pulls up a number of hits. The first few ones are the same ones I'd found when I hacked into the police database. The last two hits, however, are new.

I frown as I click on the first one.

It's a scanned photo from the Library for World War II Studies dating back to 1943. This must be wrong. Why the hell would it show me a picture from the mid-twentieth century?

There's a short description next to the picture.

Red Cross nurses outside an infirmary.

Confused, I pull up the picture.

It depicts some ten women dressed in Red Cross uniforms posing for the cameras in front of a makeshift hospital.

Why the hell would the software give me this result?

I scowl. Maybe the software is more faulty than I gave it credit for.

I'm about to exit the window when one of the women catches my eye. She must be in her late teens, early twenties by the look of it. She's smiling brightly at the camera, excitement shining in her features. Her hair is tied in a tight bun at the base of her head and she's holding her nurse's cap in her lap. All the others are wearing their caps on their heads.

I zoom in a couple of times so I can get a better look at the girl.

"What the fuck..." I mutter to myself in disbelief.

Now I realize why the software pulled up this picture. She looks eerily similar to Minnie. She's smaller than the other women next to her, and the uniform hangs loose around her body. Almost as if she'd borrowed someone else's clothes. Around her neck rests a silver necklace with a small cross pendant.

It's striking just how much the girl looks like Minnie. It's not just her diminutive stature, although I suppose historically women were much smaller back then.

It's her eyes.

They're the same.

Big and expressive, almost filled with wonder.

I've spotted the same expression on Minnie's face before, the latest being when she opened the box of cookies.

Maybe it's someone related to Minnie?

I continue to peruse the photo.

Her lips, too, are the same shape and size. There's even a small black dot atop her upper lip just like the mole Minnie has.

I freeze.

That's one too many coincidences, isn't it?

Even if by any chance it's her grandmother, how could she look exactly the same, down to the placement of the mole?

Yet the alternative is simply ludicrous.

The photo is from 1943, for fuck's sake.

And no matter how much I've been toying with the idea of magic recently, the logical side of my brain refuses to believe there's such a thing as immortality. Or time travel.

It's scientifically impossible.

There must be an explanation for it. Like the fact that the photo could have been edited. Although, why someone would have gone to that extreme, I can't say.

I mutter a string of curses under my breath. Although the entry has a short description, aside from the mention of the Red Cross, it doesn't say who the individual nurses are.

"Come on, Marlowe," I mumble to myself. "Maybe it's just a case of a historical doppelgänger. It's happened before, no?"

There are all sorts of articles circulating on the internet on celebrities and their historical doppelgängers. And those resemblances are quite uncanny too.

Convincing myself that it's only a case of a look-alike, I click out of this entry and pull up the last result. The source is some obscure archive in French. There's a short description attached to the photo, but it's not in English.

I click on the photo. It's black and white and it depicts the same woman from before. But she's not alone. She's accompanied by a man dressed in a military uniform. They're posing for the camera. Behind them, there's a monochrome background, which suggests this was a professional photo shoot.

The girl is no longer wearing her nurse uniform. Instead, she's dressed in a long, dark cotton gown. Her hair flows down her back, long and luxurious. Although her outfit is rather simple, it does nothing to detract from her natural beauty, which is further emphasized by her wide, effusive smile. Around her neck is the same necklace with the cross pendant as before, confirming this is, indeed, the same person.

The man by her side looks to be around her age. He has a long scar running down the right side of his face, and what's visible of his left hand appears to be riddled with scar tissue.

They're standing close together. The man has his arm over her shoulder, holding her possessively by his side.

Are they lovers? Perhaps husband and wife?

Maybe these are Minnie's relatives.

I nod to myself. That must be it.

Wanting to see if the description of the picture might give me more clues, I copy and paste it in a translator.

Lucien de Vitry with his fiancée, Mina Anyan, in Paris.

There it is. The same last name, or at least a variation of it. It must be her family, after all.

I end up going down a rabbit hole investigating both Lucien and Mina.

There isn't any information on Mina Anyan, though I already anticipated that. There is, however, a small entry on Wikipedia on Lucien de Vitry. A first generation French American, he was a decorated B-17 commander of the Eighth Air Force of the U.S. Army Air Forces in World War II. He completed over forty-one missions before being shot down on German territory and becoming a POW.

But as I read on, I see that despite surviving the war camps, he died of tuberculosis right before the end of the war.

He was only twenty-four.

Damn.

If that's the case, I wonder if he managed to marry Mina.

A little curious, I go back to the photo and zoom in to look at Mina's face.

The woman is identical to Minnie, and just as beautiful.

Now that I have confirmation that they're related, I feel more at ease.

I chuckle to myself. Of course that's the only explanation. It's not as if Mina is Minnie and she ended up time-traveling to the twenty-first century. It's even more ludicrous to think of her being over a hundred years old. If anything, the girl barely looks eighteen.

But even as I convince myself about the impossibility of the matter, I can't stop looking at Mina and seeing my Minnie.

Mina holds herself straight in front of the camera, but her gaze is directed at the man. She's watching him intently. The corners of her mouth are slightly curled up in a smile, lighting up her entire face.

The same mole is above her upper lip.

Her eyes are wide and bright, her expression that of a woman in love.

She's stunning. The simplicity of her outfit highlights her natural beauty.

My cursor hovers over the X button, but I suddenly stop when I notice something else.

There's another black dot on her cheek and one on her forehead, right below her hairline.

I frown.

Turning to my other monitor, I pull up a video of Minnie and wait until I find a frame that shows her right cheek.

"The fuck..."

There it is. The same mole on her cheek. And to make it even more absurd, Minnie also has a mole on her forehead, right below her hairline.

I stare in disbelief at the two women. I cannot wrap my mind around how they're so identical. Even if they're related, I doubt they'd have the same moles in the same positions.

That dilemma prompts a search into the genetics of moles, and while some are genetically inherited from parent to offspring, there's still not enough information to say for sure whether mole placement is inherited too.

But I'm still not convinced.

How is it that the only records of Minnie on the internet are those police records that list her as a Jane Doe and the two pictures featuring someone who looks exactly like her but who lived almost one hundred years ago?

There's also her name. Minerva, Minnie, Mina...

It's all too close for my peace of mind.

Add to that the odd things happening all around Minnie. Men seem to fall into a trance the moment they see her, almost as if they were bewitched. Technology glitches around her, and it always happens at very opportune moments. I still haven't forgotten the time she supposedly cleaned the entire bathroom in a matter of minutes. I may have relegated it to the back of my mind, but it's been bothering me ever since.

Then there's also perhaps the most glaring detail. Her ability to withstand the cold. Whereas a normal person would get frostbite from being exposed to the cold in nothing but a shirt, she was perfectly fine—warm to the touch even.

That is...not normal.

A knock interrupts my thoughts.

I barely look up as the door opens and Minnie steps inside.

She's wearing the outfit I bought for her. As expected, the dress fits her like a glove. Her lips tremble as she smiles at me.

"Thank you for the dress. I love it," she murmurs.

I grunt. "It looks good on you."

She stands awkwardly at the entrance of my office, balancing from one foot to the other. The shoes, too, fit her, the heels making her legs look longer.

I berate myself for noticing every single thing about her when I should be concentrating on her deception.

"Shouldn't we...go?" she asks after a lengthy pause in which we just stare at each other.

"There's still time," I reply, glancing at my watch. "I'm working," I mention.

"Oh. Do you want me to go? I can come back later."

"Not at all," I add, forcing a smile. "Please, take a seat." I motion to the sofa by the wall.

She nods and reluctantly advances into the room, taking a seat on the sofa. She places her red bag in her lap, holding it with both hands as if it were something precious.

My chest rumbles with satisfaction. It appears she did like my surprise.

She holds herself perfectly still, her back straight, her shoulders square. She's the picture of decorum, yet I have to wonder how much of that is true.

Yesterday, I saw her mask slip for the first time.

I have to take into account the fact that she *knows* about me, too. She was there two years ago. She saw me kill. Keeping her ignorant is no longer an option.

Pretending to work for another half an hour, I surreptitiously watch her from the corner of my eye. Her hair is freshly washed and full of volume. As I study her, however, I note she has some hint of eyeshadow on her lids, as well as some reddish color on her cheeks and lips.

I frown. I don't remember buying her any cosmetics.

"Where did you get the makeup from?" I suddenly ask.

Her lashes flutter as she turns to look at me.

"This?" She motions to her face.

"Yes, that. We didn't buy any makeup, did we?"

Did she buy it when I wasn't looking? Did she get it so she can wear it to meet that mysterious man? My hands curl into fists, and I already feel rage burning inside of me.

I force myself to breathe. There was no one there last night—there couldn't have been. But even as I tell myself that, there's a part of me that still believes there was someone there last night—or something.

"No, we didn't," she murmurs and bashfully tucks a strand of hair behind her ear. "I made it."

"You made it?"

"Yes." She nods. Pride shines in her voice.

"How?" I ask, genuinely curious.

"Well," she starts as she wets her lips. "For the red, I used some of the vaseline you keep in the bathroom cupboard and I mixed it with some blood from the beef I cooked you for lunch."

"You…" I swallow. "You're wearing cow blood on your lips and cheeks?"

She nods exuberantly.

"Ingenious, no?"

I stare at her. I'm not sure ingenious is the word I'd use.

"And the eyeshadow?" I'm almost afraid to know the answer to this, but hopefully, it's something innocuous.

"It's ash," she declares, her face brightening with joy.

Horror grips me.

"And where would you have gotten ash from?"

Please tell me you burned some paper and used *that* ash.

"I was cleaning the basement and there's a fireplace there. There was still a lot of ash left behind and it was the perfect pigment for my eyes. Do you like it?" She gets up and comes toward me, batting her lashes and inviting me to check her makeup.

"Ash from the fireplace in the basement," I repeat like a broken radio.

Shudders go down my body.

"Yes! Back in the day, ash was used for cosmetic purposes."

"Minnie…" I take a deep breath. "That wasn't a fireplace in the basement," I tell her with great reluctance.

She frowns.

"But…"

"It's an incineration furnace."

"What's the difference?" she asks.

"That furnace is not used for heating the house. It's used for…"

I scrub my hands on my face. How the hell do I tell her she's wearing dead people's ashes as eyeshadow? I should probably just lie and let her believe it was normal ash.

She looks at me expectantly.

"You said you know what I do." I clear my throat.

"You work in tech," she answers.

"Not that. The thing you were a fan of," I mutter.

She blinks. Slowly, her lips part and make a small O.

"Punishing bad people?" she asks, a hint of excitement in her voice.

Interesting word choice. I wonder what she thinks that punishment entails.

"Yes, you could say that. I punish bad people."

"Okay? I don't mind it, you know. Just in case I didn't make it clear last night," she mentions, her lips pulling up in an exuberant smile.

Fuck, she's beautiful. I stare at her and my mind goes blank.

"Bad people *should* be punished. Your human law is too corrupt and so many bad people go free." She shudders. "It's good there's someone like you out there to save the world. Like you saved me." Another smile. "I knew you would. You're my hero, Marlowe. And though they may not know it, you're other people's hero, too. Like..." She trails off. Her nose scrunches in concentration. "Super..."

"Superman?" I offer.

"Yes! That one!"

"You don't think it should be handled by the police?" I ask by way of testing her.

"If there was such a thing as a fair system, maybe," she answers without missing a beat. "But there's not. That's why the world needs heroes like you." There she goes with that smile again.

It's too blinding. Too...distracting.

I swallow.

"I'm not a hero," I grumble.

"Oh yes, you are! Trust me. I'm a good judge of character, and you're the bestest person I've ever met."

My eyes widen at her proclamation. What? She thinks I'm the best person she's ever met?

Did I end up in an alternate dimension where I'm *not* a killer? Where I'm not a selfish bastard who'd kill someone without any reason other than the fact that they'd look at her the wrong way?

I avert my gaze. Heat climbs up my cheeks.

"Back to the furnace." I clear my throat again. "I don't just punish bad people. I get rid of them. Do you realize what that means?"

She nods effusively.

"As you should," she replies.

Okay, she's not reacting badly to this. Perhaps she's desensitized to violence? She didn't seem to mind me beating the crap out of that creep at the diner or the dude abusing his dog.

But I don't think she's made the connection between the two quite yet.

"I get rid of them in that furnace," I add slowly.

Her brows furrow and she bites on her lower lip as she digests my words. Realization slowly dawns on her and her entire demeanor changes.

"You mean that..."

I nod grimly.

"Oh," she whispers.

"Here." I open a drawer and take out a pack of wet wipes. She glances at it warily and debates what to do for a moment. Then she shakes her head.

"It's fine," she says with a sigh. "I want your mother to like me, and I look nice like this. It's not as if it's an issue, no? They're already dead."

My lips flatten as I stare at her. Right. She's already wearing cow blood on her face. The ashes of a few dead people on her lids should be child's play compared to that.

I make a mental note to keep my distance from her face, regardless of how pretty it might be.

"Right," I mutter under my breath. "Let's go."

She gives me a full smile as she clutches onto her red purse and follows me to the car.

We get inside and I set the coordinates on my GPS to take us to the restaurant.

The first half of the ride, we're both silent.

Minnie smiles to herself every now and then, distracting my attention from the road.

What is she thinking about?

For someone who just found out she's wearing dead people on her face, she sure seems rather cheery.

"What are you thinking about?" I suddenly ask.

She fidgets in her seat and her smile grows wider.

"You," she whispers softly. "Being your fan was the best decision I ever made." She giggles.

She seems so pleased with herself that I don't even know what I should reply to that.

It's an odd thing—having a fan.

I still cannot fathom how she found me or how she became my fan. That, coupled with all the other abnormalities surrounding her, makes me wary.

But also goddamn excited.

I mean, who the hell would have thought to use cow blood and dead people's ashes as makeup? Disgusting, yes. But as she said. Ingenious. And a little disturbing.

But would she be so intriguing to me if she weren't a little disturbing?

Somehow, I doubt that.

I've never felt more alive in my life. And it's all because of the entertainment value Minnie has brought to my life. At this point, I'm willing to overlook her shady past as long as she's not hiding a lover or, God forbid, a husband.

I scowl.

Just thinking about a potential lover sours my mood.

She can lie to me about her identity, about her background,

about everything. But if she's lied to me about her history with men, then all hell will break loose.

My fists curl under my desk as I think of the bloodshed I'd unleash on anyone who's ever touched her. Especially that soulmate of hers. He'll be the first because he means something to her. He claimed a part of her heart when the entire thing should be mine and mine alone.

A sudden thought flashes in my mind and I tense.

She said she's never fucked anyone, but that doesn't mean she hasn't done something else with that soulmate of hers, or with others.

My lip twitches and my vision goes red.

"Minnie," I bark aloud.

She startles. Turning her head, she raises her brows in question.

"Yes?"

"How many people have you kissed?"

"W-what?" She blinks.

"Answer the question," I demand harshly.

She gawks at me. I suppose I'd gawk too since I must look like a madman suddenly bringing this up. But I must know—so I can plan accordingly, of course.

"What do you mean?" she asks slowly.

"A simple question. How many men have you kissed?"

"Only one," she answers in a soft voice.

My hearing dims until the only sound I hear is the pounding of my own blood.

"Who?" I rasp out.

<h1 style="text-align:center">SEVENTEEN</h1>

"WHO WAS IT, MINNIE?" I ask again, more pointedly. "Who did you kiss?"

She appears taken aback by my vehemence. She licks her lips as she prepares to speak.

Bad idea.

Now I'm staring at her lips.

Imagining another man's lips on hers.

Thinking about her sighing another man's name while he plunders her sweet mouth.

My pulse is through the roof, and I press harder on the gas pedal.

"Marlowe," she yelps, holding on to her seat.

"Who was it, Minnie?"

"It was you, you idiot!" she screams. "I kissed you on the cheek, didn't I?"

I blink. A deep sense of relief envelops me and I'm able to breathe properly again.

"Just me?" I ask, just to make sure.

Did it suddenly get too hot in here? I pull on my collar to loosen the tie.

"Just you," she confirms.

"Good. Make sure it stays that way," I grumble, though inside I'm gloating.

Pleasure spreads through me as I let myself enjoy this small win.

"What about you?" she asks in a vicious tone. "How many women have *you* kissed, Marlowe?"

She crosses her arms over her chest, her eyes narrowed as she looks at me. If those beautiful eyes could shoot daggers, I'd be riddled with holes right now.

Veering to the right, I stop the car by the side of the road and turn toward her.

She's still glaring at me.

"How many, Marlowe?" she repeats in an icy tone.

Fuck. I've always hated the cold, but if it's coming from Minnie, I suppose I can learn to like it.

Minnie is probably thinking the number is in the hundreds, and she's waiting for me to voice that number aloud so she can give me the cold shoulder treatment for another week.

Alas, I have a surprise in store for her.

I smirk at her and cup her cheeks. Her eyes widen and her brows pull up in confusion.

She blinks repeatedly, fluttering those long and pretty lashes at me. I ignore the fact that she's wearing dead people's ashes on her lids. Even human remains look good on her.

Leaning in, I press my lips against the corner of her mouth, just as she'd done to me before.

Her skin is soft and warm. And as I make contact with the corner of her lips, a jolt of electricity shoots through me. It stings, but it's a sweet pain that I'd gladly seek more of.

This close, her scent invades my nostrils. She's not wearing perfume. I've already ascertained she's allergic to it. But there's something absolutely delectable about the way she smells—as if she just bathed in a mix of cherry blossoms and musk. My nostrils flare, and I get the urge to move my lips to the left until my mouth covers hers—until her breath becomes my breath.

My clothes are suddenly too tight, too stifling.

Just a small contact, and I find myself on the verge of losing control.

Would her mouth taste heavenly too?

I linger for exactly five seconds. I count it. Much longer and we'd never make it to dinner with my mother, that's for sure. Not when I'm certain her taste would be a hundred times more addictive than her cooking.

I pull back.

"There," I whisper. "We're even now."

She's frozen on the spot, her eyes on me.

She presses her lips together, her tongue peeking out to lick the place I just kissed.

"What do you mean we're e-even?" she stammers.

I smile.

"It means exactly what you think it means." I wink at her.

I start the car anew and steer it back onto the highway.

Minnie opens her mouth to speak but then closes it. A myriad of emotions plays across her face, but the most conspicuous one is confusion.

She doesn't know what to make of my confession.

The rest of the journey, she mulls over my words as she stares out the window. She fiddles with her fingers continuously, biting on her nails.

I pretend I don't watch her, but I do.

To my surprise, the fact that she's eating her nails doesn't faze me. Why, I put my mouth on top of her blood-stained one. Cow blood. And I still haven't retched.

Why, I haven't even reached for my mouthwash.

That in itself is a miracle.

Maybe I don't need therapy. Maybe all along, I just needed a Minnie.

Correction. Not *a* Minnie. This Minnie. Because there's only one of her.

Only one in the entire world.

And she happened to fall into my lap.

I've never considered myself much of a lucky person. I mean, sure, I recognize the privilege I have in being born into a rich family, but aside from that, I don't think I've ever been happy in my life.

If I were to think back on my childhood, I can't remember a time when I didn't live in fear—for myself or for my family. Perhaps that's the reason why I don't remember laughing or smiling like this before.

But since Minnie came into my life...

It's almost as if I'm no longer the old Marlowe.

I'm just...*her* Marlowe.

WE REACH the restaurant and as we get out of the car, the manager greets us.

"Keep your head down," I advise Minnie.

She does as told, a surprise in itself.

"Welcome, Mr. Spencer-Astor. Please follow me."

"Thank you," I say and incline my head.

To ensure our privacy, my mother has booked a private room. On the way there, we pass by a few people, but Minnie remains glued to my side, shielding her face from everyone.

The manager tells us we've arrived at the destination before taking his leave.

"Wait," Minnie suddenly says. "What if your mother doesn't like me? I want her to like me."

"I don't think you have to worry about that," I mutter drily just as the door to the private room opens to reveal my mother.

"Marlowe!" she cries out and all but jumps on me, hugging me to her chest.

I tense, but I allow her this moment.

Physical touch is important for her. It's always been her love language. And though I may not be the biggest fan of skinship, I don't have the heart to tear her from me. Usually, I allow her this once a year, on her birthday. It's the one thing she desires that money cannot buy. This year, though, it seems she'll be getting *two* hugs.

She should consider herself lucky—which, of course, I aim to tell her.

I stand there, still as stone while she holds me tight and rubs my back.

I grit my teeth.

She coos some words into my ear as if I were a baby—another thing that my mother does every time she sees me. Again, I allow her this since she's a rather sensitive soul. Any other and I might put a bullet through their heads.

After what feels like an eternity, she finally draws back.

Her green eyes are glistening with tears, and she dabs her fingers on her cheeks to remove the moisture.

"You look so good, dear. What has changed?" she asks sheepishly as her gaze finally moves from me to Minnie.

"And this is your little friend? Oh, Lord, aren't you a darling. What's your name, pretty girl?"

Minnie blushes profusely and brings her chin down.

"Hello, Mrs. Spencer-Astor," she murmurs shyly. "My name is Minnie."

"Nonsense, call me Simone," my mother says. "I'm so happy to meet you, Minnie. You have no idea just how much. I almost gave up on the hope that this rascal will ever get himself a girl."

She takes a step forward and gives Minnie the same treatment. She wraps her arms around her slight frame and gives her a bear hug.

If possible, Minnie turns even redder. She bites her lip and glances at me from the corner of her eyes, not knowing how to respond to it.

I smile, pleased.

Before, I would have quickly chimed in to say she's *not* my girl. But I have since reformed. And to my surprise, the term *my girl* sounds entirely too good. Perhaps I should use it more often in the future.

I'm in danger of losing myself to my musings when I realize that my mother is still hugging Minnie, who's now starting to look a little uncomfortable.

"Mother, I think this is enough," I intervene, slowly pulling her off Minnie.

My mother scoffs at me and rolls her eyes, but as she looks again at Minnie, she smiles brightly,

"Come, child. I can't wait to know more about you."

Minnie reluctantly returns the smile.

We step inside the room and take a seat at the table in the middle.

Minnie sits by my side while my mother is across from us.

Just as we make ourselves comfortable, though, a knock resounds at the door and a man dressed in a server uniform comes in with our menus.

I grab Minnie's hand and squeeze it.

"Could we have a female server this evening?" I ask aloud.

The server blinks in surprise but acquiesces.

"Of course. I'll have one of our female staff come to attend to you."

I grunt a thank you.

All the while, my mother is watching me with a wicked glint in her eyes.

"Do you have any food allergies, darling?" Mother addresses Minnie.

She shakes her head.

"Any preferences then?"

"I can eat mostly anything. I can't eat a lot of meat since it can make me sick, but otherwise, I'm not picky."

"Really?" My mother's eyes widen and she looks at me questioningly. "This rascal of mine is the pickiest eater I've ever met in my life. How do you put up with it, dear?"

Minnie blinks.

"He's not picky, though," she adds in confusion. "He eats everything I cook. He hasn't refused any of the things I've made so far."

"You cook his meals?" My mother gasps.

"Of course." Minnie nods in all seriousness. "It's part of my duties."

I squeeze her hand tighter. I don't think this is the time to tell my mother about our arrangement.

"Oh my, aren't you a little gem!" my mother gushes. "You're exactly what I envisioned for my son." She dabs again at her eyes. "You're so pretty and sweet, and you *cook*! I don't think there's anything else I could have asked for."

"I also clean and do laundry," Minnie chimes in, proud of herself.

I give her a pointed look.

"You do! Good Lord! He let you in his house?"

I shake my head at Minnie. Damn it. I should have instructed her not to say *anything* about our relationship.

"Of course. We live together," Minnie answers matter-of-factly.

My mother almost faints at the news. She gasps for air, holding on to her chest as if she's about to have a heart attack. Tears are streaming down her face and she releases an audible sigh.

"You *live* together? Oh, dear God, this is absolutely astonishing but so wonderful to hear. Minnie, darling, I'm so happy you're here today." More tears. "I cannot express in words the joy I feel at knowing my child has someone by his side. He's always been so alone…" More sighs.

I flatten my lips as I wait for her theatrics to end. I love my mother, I do. But she can be a bit…much. And while she's genuine, her way of showing emotion is just too direct for my taste.

"So tell me, how did you two meet? Marlowe never told me anything about a girl until I had to pry it out of Giles. I can't even imagine him going out on his own to meet someone. He rarely even goes out these days," my mother continues.

Perhaps Minnie and I should have agreed on a narrative for this dinner. The oversight on my part is unforgivable, but lately, my focus has been otherwise occupied.

"He saved me," Minnie answers buoyantly.

"He did? My Marlowe?" My mother's eyes widen.

I sigh.

"Oh, yes. He was so cool. You should have seen him. He was like one of those superheroes from the movies. I've stuck by his side ever since."

"And he allowed it?" Mother raises a brow.

"He offered," Minnie quips, satisfied with herself.

"This is fascinating," my mother comments. "I've never known Marlowe to be this…altruistic."

"I'm not," I mumble.

"Of course you're not, dear. I know that," my mother says as she reaches out to pat my hand. "But I'm glad there's an exception to your surliness."

I glare at her and remove my hand from the table.

"See, this is what I mean. He's so…asocial. He always keeps to himself and hates human interaction. Even with his own mother, for God's sake! All he does is work, work, work. Out of all my children, he's the one I've always worried about."

"Really? I haven't seen him work that much. He's always

walking around the house and mumbling things to himself. I assumed he was on vacation," Minnie adds innocently.

I grimace.

My mother beams.

It seems my loitering didn't go unnoticed. And here I thought I was being careful about it...

"It's an uneventful time at work." I clear my throat as I try to explain.

But it's in vain. The glint in my mother's eye tells me she knows exactly what has been causing this.

"He's really not that bad!" Minnie interjects. "Please don't think badly of him. He's the bestest, kindest person I've ever met. I don't even care that he swears too much, or that he's a clean freak, or that he can be a bit controlling. Did he tell you he saved a puppy?" she adds eagerly. "He did. He's a hero, Mrs. Spencer-Astor." Turning to me, she gives me a bright smile. "*My* hero," she emphasizes.

I blink, taken aback by her defense of me.

No one's done that before.

Ever.

I've always been the weird one in the family, and while they accepted me, they never made excuses for me and criticized my eccentricities every time they could. Even my mother, who I know loves me, has never shied away from pointing out my flaws.

This is the first time someone's focused on the positives instead of the negatives.

And I don't know how to react.

Heat travels up my neck, and I look away.

Minnie, however, is not deterred.

She continues to smile brightly at me as she seeks out my hand under the table and covers it with hers.

A current of electricity travels from her skin to mine, causing a sweltering heat to take over my entire body. Yet it's the type of heat

I've always yearned for. The type of scorching heat that reaches deep within me until not just my body is warm, but also my soul.

My mother watches us closely.

There's a smile on her face, but it doesn't reach her eyes. She has a calculating look, and I know she's trying to ascertain whether Minnie's proclamation is genuine. In her mind, just as in mine, something like this is simply...impossible.

"Minnie darling, I have to ask. Are you with my Marlowe for his money? I do admit he is a good-looking boy, but he is..." She pauses as she purses her lips. "Well, odd is putting it mildly. He's my son and I love him, but he's not the dreamy hero you speak of. I should know. I've raised that rascal for almost eighteen years. He's cold and detached, and quite frankly, I don't see him saving a dog, let alone a human. So please excuse me for being curious about the nature of your relationship and your interest in him."

There it goes. Straight to the point.

I expected this.

No matter how much my mother might want me to settle down, she also knows *why* it's not likely to happen. It's a hypothetical scenario in her mind—a wish. It's not something she ever thought would really happen.

Minnie blinks, taken aback by the question.

"No, no," she quickly answers, waving her hands back and forth. "I don't care about his money, and I don't need a lot to live comfortably. Of course I do like that he's rich." She nods. "Because that means he can buy me cookies. Lots of cookies. Those things are so delicious, but I never realized how expensive they can get in this world." She shakes her head to emphasize her disapproval.

My mother stares at her, her mouth agape.

Minnie continues.

"I can cook, but I can't bake. And the one time I tried, the cookies weren't as delicious as the ones from the store. But Marlowe's been very good. He gives me chocolate cookies daily.

Rather than being with him for his money, I think you could say I'm with him for the cookies he can provide." Then she smiles.

My mother stares at her for another moment before she throws her head back and laughs.

"I love her, Marlowe! Cookies, hear that." She continues laughing.

"But it's true!" Minnie protests. "Cookies are really the bestest."

"I can't fault you there, darling. Cookies are the best." My mother chuckles.

Meanwhile, the female server comes to our room to get our order and brings over a bottle of red wine. I decline, but Minnie regards the bottle longingly, so I encourage her to have some.

"I've never had any before," she whispers as she takes her glass with both hands and takes her first sip. My mother, too, sips her wine slowly as she studies Minnie and me.

"How is it?" I ask her.

She smacks her lips together a couple of times before she gives me a thumbs-down.

"You don't like it?"

"I love it!" she exclaims, then proceeds to take another big gulp.

Smiling, I grab her hands and change the position of her thumbs so they're pointing upward. It takes her a moment to realize she got it wrong, after which she chuckles and moves her thumbs up around in my direction, then my mother's.

I shake my head at her antics, but she's too cute, so I don't mind it. Not one bit.

My mother doesn't seem to, either. In fact, she seems to like Minnie, which makes my chest tight with emotion. I didn't realize how much her approval meant until now, but to know that she also likes her carries a lot of weight.

"So tell me then, Minnie. What do you like about my Marlowe? Aside from the fact that he buys you cookies."

Minnie is still gulping down her wine, finishing her glass and leaning over the table to grab the bottle and fill it up again.

I hope she's not a lightweight.

"Easy," I murmur softly.

She gives me a brilliant smile and I don't have it in me to stop her as she starts sipping on her wine again.

"I like everything about him," she declares. My eyes widen. "Aside from the fact that he cheated on me," she mutters in a sour voice as she slams the once-more-empty glass on the table.

"W-what?" I sputter.

I cheated on her?

When? How? With whom?

"Marlowe cheated on you?" my mother exclaims, horrified. "Are we talking about the same Marlowe? How could he have cheated on you when he's never so much as looked at a woman before?" She turns to me. "Marlowe, explain yourself!"

Before I can recover from my shock, Minnie speaks.

"He"—she points at me—"was a hoe. His body score is *over* a hundred!"

She gives me a disgruntled glare and it's like we're back to square one.

I stare at her in disbelief. She's still hung up on that? I thought we moved on from it, for fuck's sake. Haven't I already endured days of torturous silence and scathing indifference because of it?

Now looking back, I regret making that joke since it continues to follow me around like a hungry ghost.

"I'm appalled that he'd do something like that," Minnie continues. "I've been pining for him for so long, only for him to do something like this to me?" She stifles a sob.

What the fuck?

Pining?

Since when?

She admitted she's known *of* me for years, but she *pined* for me? Does that mean she's been following me? Longing for me all this time?

And does that mean that our first meeting was not fortuitous, but rather a calculated one on her part? The idea of it doesn't enrage me as it should. In fact, it makes me rather warm on the inside.

While I was stalking my victims, I was being stalked in return.

And I never even knew it.

That in itself should bother me. But it only makes me hold Minnie in a higher regard.

For all her bubbly personality and ignorance about the world, she's quite the scheming little thing.

Fuck. That's hot.

She can stalk me anytime she wants. But I can't say that aloud as it would scandalize my mother more than she already is.

Pity. But I'll make sure to tell her later.

"Marlowe! How could you?" my mother demands sharply, rising out of her chair and placing her hands on her hips.

Minnie crosses her arms across her chest and she tips her chin up at me in a *explain yourself now* gesture.

Is it wrong that her anger makes me hard?

I look between the two of them and realize I'm caught between two *very* scary females. And while Minnie's anger is rather hot and I wouldn't mind having some more of that, preferably when we're alone, with a few less clothes, my mother is another issue altogether. She'll grasp onto this idea and she will not let it go until she goes into her grave. Alas, I fear she might even go as far as to write on her gravestone—*poor mother of a shameless cheater*. Of course she wouldn't want to let me live it down even after she's no longer here.

The worst thing? I'm innocent.

But how the hell do I even begin to tell them that without explaining what I truly meant by my body count?

EIGHTEEN

"FIRST OFF," I say as I look at Minnie. "We're not in a relationship for me to cheat. And second, even if we were, which we are not"—I make sure to emphasize—"I never did anything wrong. Where the hell did you get that idea?"

"Marlowe!" my mother exclaims in outrage. "I thought I raised you better than this!"

I roll my eyes.

"I didn't cheat, Mother," I repeat, exasperated.

"That I believe," she says. "It's the fact that you live with this darling girl but you haven't made it official yet. How ungentlemanly!"

I gawk at her.

Minnie does too.

"But he slept with all those women," Minnie mumbles again. Confusion swathes her features as she looks thoroughly lost. "Women who were not me," she whispers desolately.

My conscience roars to life unexpectedly.

I don't like that look on her face. I don't like that I put it there.

And it was only a harmless joke...

Yet the more I think about it, the more I realize it wasn't a joke to Minnie. For some reason, she was truly hurt by it.

I scowl.

How was I to know she'd take it to heart? And now to claim that I cheated on her? That would imply there was an understanding between us.

You're a fucking idiot, Marlowe!

My lips flatten as I mentally replay everything from day one.

It's my fault, isn't it? Because I fucking suck at social interactions and everything of a more emotional nature, I didn't see what was right in front of me.

Minnie's behavior toward me and the way she reacted whenever she thought there was another woman flashes in my mind.

She was fucking jealous! She wasn't worried I'd fire her. She was worried I'd be with another woman.

I mutter a string of curses to myself.

I must be the biggest idiot who ever lived for not seeing this earlier.

Yet despite my anger at myself for letting things degenerate this badly, excitement builds inside of me.

I don't dislike this. I don't dislike this at all. Didn't I already decide Minnie belonged to me? I suppose it's only fair to belong to her in return.

My lips spread into a smile.

But while I'm lost in my thoughts planning to redress the wrongs I have committed in the past and woo Minnie once more, the matter of the bodies still hasn't been resolved.

Fuck.

"And where did you hear about those women, dear?" my mother asks sharply.

"He told me himself," Minnie replies and points at me.

My mother's shrewd gaze turns to me.

"To make matters worse, he's been telling me details about it, too. Like how he started at seventeen with a neighbor!" Minnie continues, her expression one of true horror.

My mother raises a brow at me and shakes her head.

"Dear, don't believe that." She snorts. "We only had two neighbors back when we lived in that house. One was an elderly lady, who I doubt could spend five minutes without dozing off. She also had a slew of health issues and my Marlowe wouldn't have ever gone near her. He's too much of a germaphobe for that. The other one was a vile, vile man who ended up dying in a horrific accident." My mother pauses. "That happened around the time you were seventeen, though, no?" She raises a brow at me.

I purse my lips.

She knows too damn well it did. Hell, Giles took care of it.

"Oh," Minnie murmurs. "It was a man then? Not a woman? You also betrayed me with a man? A bad one at that?" she suddenly asks, the fire in her eyes blazing anew.

"Is that all you got from this?" I mutter.

I don't like explaining myself. Truthfully, I don't have any experience explaining myself. But in this case, I'm afraid I'll just make matters worse if I open my mouth to say something.

"I think you're misunderstanding him, dear," my mother interjects.

"What am I misunderstanding?" Minnie cries out, and her eyes glisten with unshed tears.

I immediately sober.

What the hell? She's not going to cry, is she?

Panic takes hold of me.

"There are other types of...bodies," I hurry to say.

I'll take anything but her tears.

Never her tears.

Minnie stares at me.

"I don't understand," she adds in a defeated tone. Her lips tremble and a lone tear slides down her cheek.

Something pricks at my heart.

Fuck. My chest tightens.

All I've wanted to do was keep her safe from the outside world, but I was the one to hurt her.

I was the one to make her fucking cry.

That's unacceptable.

"My body count is strictly reserved for the bodies that end up in my fireplace," I explain. Then I hold my breath while I wait for my meaning to sink in.

She blinks. Then frowns. Then her mouth parts in realization.

"You mean..."

I nod.

"So you lied to me?" Suddenly, her tone is once more aggressive.

"I didn't technically lie. You misunderstood me." I shrug.

"Me?" Her eyes widen. "*You* let me misunderstand it on purpose! Why would you do that?" She stands up, her cheeks flushed, her entire body vibrating with anger. "I've been torturing myself these past weeks with thoughts of you and those one hundred-plus bodies. Damn you, Marlowe! You're a wretch and I don't like you anymore."

"You just said you like everything about me," I protest.

"I *liked*. Past tense. I changed my mind," she mutters belligerently. "I don't want to talk to you anymore."

She huffs at me, takes her chair, and moves it to the far end of the table. My mother watches the entire exchange with an amused smile.

"Minnie!" I call after her.

She scowls at me.

"Wretch!" she insults me before she decides to ignore me.

My mother takes her hand and consoles her.

"There, dear. Don't fret too much. I told you my Marlowe would never do that. He's a handsome devil, I'll give you that. Just like his father," she says, her eyes slowly rising to meet mine.

My body tenses.

"But I knew since he was a boy that he would *never* be like his father. He might be odd and reclusive, and he certainly harbors one too many compulsive tendencies that I've told him to seek help for, but he's not a bad one." She smiles. "He's my little knight in shining armor. Always there to help me, even when he thinks I don't know it."

Minnie sniffles a sob. She grabs a napkin off the table and blows her nose. I suppose this is neither the time nor the place to tell her that napkin is supposed to go on her lap while she's eating.

"He's been so bad to me," she whimpers between sobs. "Tricking me into believing he had a harem of women out there. How was I to stand a chance against that?"

My mother gives me a sharp look.

Why do I suddenly feel cornered?

Also when the hell did I imply I had a harem of women?

"He's more likely to have a harem of dead bodies than a harem of women, dear. Why, the rascal can barely bring himself to hug his own mother and you think he'd do that with another woman? Multiple women?" My mother scoffs aloud.

"Thank you for the vote of confidence, Mother," I mumble.

At the same time, Minnie looks at my mother with wide eyes.

"You know about the harem of dead bodies?" she asks, her voice tinged with awe.

Fuck.

My mother blinks.

"I was speaking figuratively, of course," she says in a low voice before she glares at me.

"Oh," Minnie gasps. "I—"

"Marlowe! Didn't I tell you not to collect dead bodies anymore? Damn it, dear. That habit of yours will bring nothing but trouble."

"You *know*?" Minnie asks.

"I'm his mother. Of course I know everything that goes on with him."

"As in, you have Giles to spy on me for you," I mumble.

"Spy is a very harsh word, dear. I cannot help it if Giles decides to share." She smiles brightly. "But now I'll need to have a word with him about this. I don't like you living with dead bodies. It's all right if you have a distaste of the living, but really, Marlowe? I don't even know how you can stand it with that obsession of yours with cleanliness..." She pauses. "Then again, last time, you kept them frozen in an industrial fridge," she adds pensively.

Minnie's mouth drops open in shock.

"He had a fridge full of dead people?" She marvels.

"Oh, yes! He even placed them around to make them look as though they were engaged in a theatrical scene. It was a very odd period of his life."

"Oh, tell me more!" Minnie says eagerly.

"I've never been there, of course. He doesn't want me at his house." Another glare. "Perhaps it's because of the dead bodies. He knows I don't fancy the smell of rotting flesh."

"They were frozen. They didn't smell," I interject.

"Anyhow. Giles told me all about it since we had to find a way to convince Marlowe to get rid of them. He was collecting them almost like figurines."

"Like figurines?" Minnie intones.

"Yes! They were arranged hierarchically according to the crimes they committed. I did quite like the idea of it, but the execution?" She shakes her head.

That's it. This is getting out of hand.

"Mom!" I groan. "I'll have you know—both of you—that I do *not* have a harem of dead bodies in my house, okay?"

"Well, technically they're not bodies anymore, no? They're charred bones," Minnie adds, her expression serious.

"I have heard." My mother nods. "That's a very good idea, indeed. But you still cannot keep those charred bones around, Marlowe. Technology is quite advanced these days and they can even get DNA from badly damaged bones."

"I know that, Mother. I get rid of them, don't worry."

"No, he doesn't. He left the ashes in the fireplace," Minnie quips. "See"—she points to her eyes— "I'm wearing them on my lids."

My mother's lashes flutter in shock. She looks stricken.

She's a strong woman who's not easily put off by death—she's experienced plenty of it in her lifetime. But this might be her breaking point.

"You...do?" A trembling smile pulls at her lips.

"Yes! I didn't know about it at first, of course. I thought it was just regular ash. But I'm not mad. I mean, at least they're useful for something, no? And this way, I'll help Marlowe get rid of the remains." Minnie beams.

"By wearing them?" my mother asks, half-horrified.

"Well..." Minnie bites her lip. "I don't have any makeup. He didn't buy me any," she says and points her finger at me, her expression once more belligerent. "So I had to make do. But it's quite pretty, no?" She bats her lashes to emphasize her eyeshadow.

"Very," my mother murmurs.

"And it's all natural too! Aren't you humans concerned with that? Although I'm not sure if this would be considered vee-gan," she continues, her tone pensive. Her pronunciation, though, is a little off as she elongates the E in vegan too much. "It's clearly not cruelty-free, but is it vee-gan if it's just ash? I suppose it could be up to interpretation, but it is an animal by-product, no?"

Both my mother and I stare at Minnie.

"I don't think the issue is if human-derived eyeshadow ash is vegan, dear. It's murder."

"Well, yes." Minnie frowns. "But what *isn't* murder? Aren't you guys killing nature all the same? Plants, people, what's the difference?"

Once more, Minnie has rendered both Mother and me speechless.

Slowly, my mother turns to look at me. She just stares for a few moments before she finally speaks.

"I don't know where you found this young lady, Marlowe, but this is perfect. So perfect! You two are made for each other," she exclaims, clasping her hands in front of her.

Minnie smiles. But then she remembers she's mad at me and scowls.

"I'm not talking to him," she mutters under her breath.

"Hear that, Marlowe." My mother chuckles. "You should apologize for making your girlfriend sad."

"She's not my girlfriend," I mutter.

"That's right. You two live together already. She's more like your wife than your girlfriend. Ah, this is just marvelous. I didn't expect this, especially since it's...well, you. But now I can die happy."

Though she does her best to hide it, Minnie is quite pleased by my mother's words.

"There will be no dying, Mother. You're young. Stop the dramatics."

"I'm not as young as I used to be." She sighs.

"You look wonderful, Mrs. Spencer-Astor," Minnie interjects, nodding effusively. "Your taste in clothes is very nice, too. I must get Marlowe to buy me some of this too. The color is quite nice and vivid," she continues as she inspects my mother's tweed two-piece set. She touches the red tweed with reverence and I make a mental note to buy her some.

"You have a good eye, dear." Mother winks.

They start talking about fashion and completely ignore me.

The waitress brings us our appetizers, then the main course.

My mother and I went for steak, but for some reason, Minnie declined to get meat. She opted instead for *vee-gan* pasta.

"I didn't realize you've suddenly become vee-gan," I note as I watch her eat her pasta with gusto.

"I didn't." She shrugs. "It's just the meat here doesn't seem to sit well with me. If I eat too much, I get sick."

I frown. That's one odd way of putting it. But then I recall that aside from the first few days when she ate nearly everything, she's been eating meat very sparsely. I berate myself—I should have noticed that.

"What do you mean? What type of meat?"

"I used to be fine with it years ago," she continues. "But I think it's all this weird stuff they put in it. The GTFO one. It's not natural."

"What?"

"I'm quite sensitive to meat in general, but that's because of my age and training level. Back home, I can only eat one type without feeling the side effects. In the past, I could eat the beef here, but with these GTFO stuff you humans put inside, I get quite ill if I have it too often."

I still stare at her. My mother, too.

"Do you mean GMO?"

She stills. Then frowns.

"Genetically modified?" I offer.

"Oh, yes. That!" She nods. "I think that's why I cannot eat the meat here." She continues eating.

What the hell? I'm racking my brain as I try to make sense of her words when she puts down her fork. Her meal is only half finished.

She tips her chin up and tilts her head to the side, as if listening for something.

"I have to go," she says as she suddenly stands up.

"Are you all right, dear?" my mother asks, concerned.

"Y-yes. I must go to the bathroom." She smiles sweetly as she retreats and exits the room.

The door barely closes when my mother starts talking.

"Lovely girl, Marlowe. A bit odd, but I suppose it's only fair when you're so odd yourself. But she's quite the beauty, isn't she?"

"She is," I grunt. My mind is still on her abrupt departure. It looked as if she had somewhere to go. But where?

"But her accent..." She frowns. "Where is she from? Her accent sounds rather..."

That gets my attention. I've wondered about her accent from the beginning, but I could not quite place it. At first, I thought it might be a Boston accent or thereabouts. Later, when the mystery of her background grew, I simply suspected she was faking a British accent to throw me off her trail—but she hadn't done the best job mimicking it.

"Rather?"

"Mid-Atlantic," my mother says. "But no one speaks like that these days."

"Isn't that the Old Hollywood accent?"

My mother nods.

"Maybe she liked it and taught herself how to speak it," I mention with a shrug.

My mother looks at me with a glint in her eyes.

"You don't know," she states. "You don't know where she's from."

My lips flatten. This is the last thing I want to discuss with her considering my own frustrations with Minnie's identity.

"I know enough," I grunt.

Of course, my mother doesn't buy that. If anything, she's probably thinking of ways to find out who Minnie is and why she's close to me.

"Marlowe, darling. I like the girl, I really do. But don't you think it's rather premature to tell her all your secrets if you don't know hers?"

It's the mothering tone.

I take a deep breath.

"Mother. I know what I'm doing. Please don't interfere. And by that I mean don't ask Giles to spy on us, and most importantly. Do *not* try to hurt her."

"How could you think that of me, dear?" Her eyes widen in affected shock.

I roll my eyes.

"Don't try anything. I'm serious. I'm not in the mood to argue with you. Just know that I will not allow anything to happen to her."

"My, my! Is that a threat, dear?"

I shrug.

"Marvelous! You do like her." She chuckles. "Fine, fine. I will not meddle as long as you bring her to my birthday party."

"Done," I reply.

"And," she continues, a mischievous smile appearing on her face. "I want a spring wedding."

"W-what?" Did I hear her right?

"I'm not getting any younger and I do want to see you settled down. Minnie is a wonderful girl and perfect for you. I approve. Now we can move to the wedding. If Minnie doesn't mind, I can help organize it..."

"Now, wait a minute. Who said anything about a wedding?"

"That's right. You haven't even asked her to be your girlfriend, yet you live with her. Shame on you, Marlowe! You need to rectify that immediately so you can move to the next step. Preferably within the next month so we can set a date."

And just like that, once my mother gets something in her head, it's very hard to dissuade her. She continues talking about this fantasy wedding, describing everything she envisions for the occasion.

I look at my watch and note that Minnie's been gone for a good ten minutes now.

"I'll be right back," I tell my mother as I suddenly stand up.

Getting out of the room, I find a server and ask where the women's bathroom is. There are still people around here—men in particular—and that means my Minnie is *not* safe.

A server points me in the direction of the bathroom, but just as I reach the hallway, I spot Minnie at the corner. She's standing with her back against the wall. Only half her body is visible.

What the hell is she doing there if she's going to the bathroom?

I stride toward her. But I only get midway before I see she's not alone.

There's a man dressed entirely in black with her. A man resembling the one in the snow from a few days ago.

From this distance, I can see him better.

He's around my height, putting him at a foot taller than Minnie. But the man is packed. His forearms alone are stacked, his muscles bulging through his fitted shirt. His hair is a dark brown, cropped around the sides and longer at the top. There are two swirling tattoos on each side of his scalp.

"You don't understand," he tells her in a rough voice. "You need to leave. It's not long before they find you."

She shakes her head.

"I can't. Not yet. I let you convince me to leave two years ago and I've regretted it ever since," she murmurs. "There has to be a way, Kai. I've been good about keeping my shields up."

"Minerva," he rasps and takes a step closer to her. "For now, it's only sentinels. But next, it will be Commander Azerius. And no shield will keep you hidden from him—"

"But I just started to live again, Kai. How can I leave now? How can I abandon everything..."

"You don't understand what's at stake. I've done my best to cover for you, but even my influence can only do so much." He grabs her arm, his fingers tightening over her flesh.

I see red.

Regardless of how interesting their conversation is and that it might give me more insight into Minnie, I cannot stand still when another man touches my woman.

"Minnie!" I thunder, stalking toward her.

My body is tense, my fists clenched by my sides.

I'm ready for *war*.

She jumps back, hitting the wall. The man she's with, that Kai, assumes a fighting position.

"Get away from her. Now!" I call out as I near them.

He places an arm around her protectively, but that barely registers as I swing my fist at him.

His eyes flash at me as he moves his head to the side and avoids the blow.

"Kai, don't," Minnie pleads in a low voice, pulling on his shirt. "Don't hurt him, please!" Turning to me, she bites her lip. "Marlowe…"

"Who is he, Minnie? Who the fuck is he?" I grit out, preparing to hit him again. I don't care if we're in public, or if anyone sees it. I don't care about anything but the fact that he laid his hand on her.

"Minerva, control your human," the man drawls in a bored voice.

My nostrils flare at his condescending tone.

I swing another fist at him, which he evades again. But I already intuited he'd dodge, so as he leans back, I bring my other fist to the back of his skull.

He manages to move last minute, but my knuckles still make contact with his flesh.

His lip twitches in annoyance.

I smirk. Come on, tough guy. This is just a warm-up for me.

He takes a step back, but I don't give him the opportunity to retreat. I punch him again, but this time he catches my fist in his hand and twists it.

I grind my teeth at the sudden pain, but I ignore it.

"Kai. Stop this!" Minnie cries out, launching herself at the other man. "You too, Marlowe. He's my brother!"

NINETEEN

"HE'S MY BROTHER, YOU IDIOT!"

Her voice echoes in my brain and it takes me a few moments to digest the new information.

Brother.

He's her brother.

That means they're related. Which further means he's not interested in her, nor does he want to hurt her.

I stare at him. He stares at me.

Minnie pries my fist from his hand, but I barely register that as I'm busy staring down this man that she claims is her brother. It's not that I don't believe her. But I don't think I like him touching her regardless of whether they share blood or not.

I narrow my eyes at him. Now that I see him up close, I suppose I can see the similarities. They have the same dark eyes.

But she never mentioned a brother, did she?

Then again, up until a few days ago, she was still claiming to be an orphan and an ex-con.

"Brother, eh," I mutter, narrowing my eyes at them. "Introduce us," I demand.

Minnie appears conflicted as she looks from her brother to me.

She's standing between us now to prevent another conflict. Too bad for her, I'm still contemplating how I can use my surroundings to teach this man a lesson.

Brother? And he left her like that, on the streets? Homeless, with no clothes and no money? Something is not adding up.

Minnie clears her throat.

"Marlowe, this is Molokai, my older brother. Kai, this is Marlowe, my..." She bites her lip as she pauses to think of a proper term. "My friend." She smiles.

What?

Friend?

I'm her friend?

Once more, a red haze covers my sight.

"Boyfriend," I correct.

Minnie gives me a look.

Molokai, on the other hand, frowns.

"I'm not familiar with that term. Is he your human guard, Minerva?"

"Uhm, you could say so?"

He takes a deep breath.

"I would have thought you'd stopped messing with humans after the last disaster."

"It happened. Marlowe is a great guard, though. He's been protecting me against the males in this world," Minnie adds.

"He has?" Molokai narrows his eyes at me, his tone suspicious.

"He's immune to my charms. It's why I asked him to be my guard in the first place," Minnie continues.

Their discussion is...odd. I have no fucking clue what they're talking about. Why am I suddenly her guard?

"And what does he get in return for guarding you?" Molokai asks. "You have nothing to offer in Anthropa. Unless..."

Anthropa? What the hell is that?

"Kai! You're being offensive." Minnie scowls. "I make food for him. It's a fair exchange."

Her brother freezes.

"You...cook?" he asks in a disgusted voice. "For a puny human?" The mood changes as his voice thunders through the hall. "You forget your position, Minerva."

"You know my position very well, Kai. And it's not as bad as it seems. I happen to enjoy it." She shrugs. "I really am fine. You don't have to worry about me anymore. At least not for a while."

He glares at her, then at me.

"I don't approve."

"And I don't care if you approve or not," she quips. "Now go. It's not safe for you to be here either."

"But—"

"Kai..." She gives him a pointed look. "Next time, only make contact if you find something. Otherwise, it's too dangerous."

He purses his lips as he crosses his arms over his chest.

"Minerva, this is unacceptable."

"I think we're long past what is acceptable, Kai. I'm no longer the naive little sister you knew, nor are my circumstances what they were before. Now please... Don't make this harder than it already is."

He doesn't move, still staring at her.

"Please?" she repeats.

He releases a deep sigh.

"All right. I shall return if there are new developments."

Minnie nods and gives him a shy smile. But as she goes to give him a hug, I stop her and pull her back.

"Goodbye, Molokai," I grit out.

He gives me a mutinous look, but as Minnie nudges him, he eventually retreats and leaves.

Then we're finally alone.

"Brother, huh?" I add skeptically.

"Yes! You didn't have to be so violent." She shakes her head at me.

"Maybe I would not have been if you had told me you had a

brother," I argue. Though of course I would have been just as violent. I don't care if they're related. He put his hand on her. That's all I need to know to act.

"We rarely talk." She shrugs. "He lives abroad."

"He has a different accent than you," I note. After Mother's comments, I paid more attention to her speech, and as a consequence, to her brother's. Where hers is what my mother would call a Mid-Atlantic accent, her brother's is a very standard American one.

Odd.

Then again, what isn't odd about Minnie?

Her cheeks redden.

"That's... Well..." she stammers. "As I said. We live in different countries."

I narrow my eyes at her.

"I'm getting tired of all this secrecy. Who is after you?" I demand sharply.

She takes a deep breath.

"It doesn't matter. Not now," she says with a smile as she turns to go back to the dining room.

I follow after her and grab her arm.

"It matters to me. I need to know who you are, Minnie."

She raises her eyes to meet mine.

"Your girlfriend."

My eyes flash at her statement.

"You were the first to say it." She smiles, fluttering her lashes at me.

"You—"

"I'm glad you're coming around. I was wondering how long it would take you to realize how perfect we are for each other," she whispers. Raising herself on the tips of her toes, she brushes her mouth against my cheek, rendering me speechless.

A flush climbs up my neck and I suddenly feel too hot.

"We are?" I repeat awkwardly as my heartbeat intensifies.

"Oh, yes," she murmurs seductively. She blows hot air on my cheek and a shudder goes down my back. "You're my murderous Marlowe and I'm your mischievous Minnie. See how well we fit?" She trails her lips all over my cheek.

Her lips are soft. Hot.

I gulp down.

"I suppose so," I mumble, my mind going blank.

The only thing I know is that her body is flush against mine, her mouth on my skin. Her scent is assailing my nostrils until her presence overtakes my entire universe.

Girlfriend.

I repeat the word in my head, unused to the ring of it.

She's my...girlfriend?

Flashes of being near her, of exploring her lush mouth and naked body assail me. Because that's what couples do, no? They share everything.

Hmm. The idea is more appealing than I would have thought.

I've never dwelled much on what couples do since I've never really felt drawn to the institution. But I suppose there are perks to it.

And as my mother noted, we're already living together and doing the mundane things couples do. All that's missing is physical intimacy.

Fuck.

The moment I open that door, a barrage of images assaults me.

Minnie, naked, in my bed.

Sweat pebbles on my forehead the more I think about the countless things we can do.

Damn it, but I can't wait to trace my lips all over her body and find out how she tastes everywhere. I have a feeling she's going to be even more addictive than her food.

And then I'll be truly in trouble.

I've been thinking of this for far too long, and now that my fantasies are close to being fulfilled, I'm worried I might not...be good at it.

Fuck. Double fuck.

I need to watch some porn. Maybe read some romance novels.

While I'm lost in my head, I barely realize that Minnie has stepped away from me and is now looking at me with an amused smile on her lips.

"I think you need to take care of that before we go back to your mother," she murmurs seductively.

I look down at where she's pointing and I'm not surprised to see that she's referring to my erection.

"Now?" I ask.

"Of course now!" She chuckles. "Come, the bathroom is over there," she says as she grabs my arm and steers me toward the men's bathroom.

I didn't think my fantasies would come to life so quickly, but damn...

My excitement increases with every second as I picture Minnie's small hands wrapped around my dick as she tries to take care of it. But then, the picture morphs into her on her knees, those pouty lips of hers parted over the tip of my cock...

Fucking hell.

At this rate, I won't make it to the bathroom. The mere idea of my cock in her mouth has me close to coming already.

In fact, I'm so lost to lust that I forget about wanting to question her further about her brother or her identity. All I can think about is my impending release. And the fact that she looks so fucking hot in that dress.

I picture what she looked like naked.

I was a fool for telling her she should keep her clothes on. She wouldn't have objected to working naked around the house.

Back then, unacceptable.

Now? It would be heaven.

I mentally berate myself for my previous uptightness—not that I've shed much of it, and only when it concerns Minnie.

We reach the bathroom, and I'm happy to see it's single use. I'll make sure to put paper towels on the ground so Minnie won't sully her knees or her dress.

Normally, I'd question the cleanliness of a random bathroom and I'd never see myself setting foot inside it.

But this will be an exception.

I might have nightmares about it and I might over-scrub my skin tonight in the shower, but a little pain is nothing compared to the bliss that awaits me.

I open the door to the bathroom and motion for Minnie to go in first. I do my best to not seem overly eager, but it is what it is.

We're boyfriend and girlfriend at this point, no?

"Why won't you go in?" She frowns.

"You go first," I mention. Can't she see I'm being a gentleman? Does she have any idea how hard it is to remember to be gentlemanly when your dick is about to go off?

Her frown deepens.

She stares at me, then at the bathroom, then back at me.

"You..." She swallows, her cheeks turning a deep shade of red. "You want me inside? To help you..."

I nod. Why is she suddenly playing coy? It was her idea.

She balances herself from one foot to another.

She doesn't seem so sure anymore.

Before I can ask her to clarify, she shoves me inside the bathroom and closes the door.

"Pervert," she squeaks, then giggles as she runs away.

I can hear her heels clicking against the floor at a very high speed.

I stare at the bathroom mirror, confused.

Goddamn it.

There goes my fantasy. I knew it was too good to be true.

I stand there for what feels like an eternity as I think of the most boring things imaginable—though even that proves difficult when my mind keeps flashing me tantalizing images of Minnie.

Even my organized thoughts about cleaning are now marred by her presence. Instead of going over the different steps to disinfect my basement, all I can think about is Minnie in her maid outfit, on her knees, thrusting her ass backward...

Fuck.

This won't work.

I turn on the faucet and spray water all over my face.

This would be the perfect time for a cold shower.

I could, of course, take care of the issue as Minnie suggested. But my hand would be a paltry imitation for her touch. And it's her I want.

It takes me about ten minutes of breathing exercises to get my erection to go from a full mast to a half mast. Still uncomfortable, but not nearly as noticeable.

As I head back to the private room, I note that Minnie hasn't gone inside. She's standing by the door, waiting for me.

"Done?" she asks as she rakes her eyes over my body. Her cheeks are stained with a deep red.

"Not thanks to you," I mumble.

She flushes again and averts her gaze.

"I..." She wets her lips. Her hands are behind her back and she balances herself from one foot to the other. She appears... uncertain?

"Was it...good?" She has the gall to ask. She's biting on her lip, looking like a goddamn siren. The sight of it alone sends another jolt to my cock.

Damn it. It's the proximity. It's messing with my head.

Of course that's not to say that my loitering around the house and watching her twenty-four seven didn't send me into a sexual frenzy, which I have yet to quench. But it's nothing compared to the feel and smell of her in front of me.

Have I been bewitched? Or have I simply fallen into...lust?

I fear it might be a combination of both.

"No. It was so bad I may have caused permanent damage to my cock," I reply wryly.

Her eyes flash at me in alarm. She blinks repeatedly before she launches herself at me.

"W-what? Are you all right?" she quickly asks, her voice tinged with worry. "Please tell me you didn't break it..." She's close to panicking as she pats her hands all over the front region of my pants.

She accidentally touches my dick, and it immediately twitches under her palm.

She freezes but keeps her hand in place.

Blood rushes down to my cock at her touch, so it moves. Again.

She draws back, her eyes wide.

"Oh my! It's bad, isn't it?" She continues, almost frantic. "Now it's moving on its own!"

While she's getting increasingly agitated, I can only stare at her. Does she not know that's how dicks work? I suppose she doesn't.

And that pleases me. Immensely.

"It's all your fault," I continue, somehow unwilling to end her torment. "If you had helped me..." I sigh, feigning a forlorn expression.

"But... I don't understand..."

"You made it hurt. You should have taken care of it, Minnie. It's only right."

She swallows hard.

"But we aren't bonded yet. I can't do that..." she mumbles to herself.

"Bonded?" I frown. "What does *that* mean?"

"Joined by a vow," she explains, her tone even more serious.

"You mean married?" I croak, once more surprised. When will this girl not shock me with her behavior?

She nods.

"We must be bonded to touch each other, of course. But now that you've damaged it... Oh, Marlowe. What are we going to do? I was quite looking forward to it. After we bond, of course."

Her expression is one of pure horror and she appears to be close to tears.

What the fuck...

"It was a joke," I quickly say before she sheds any tears. "Nothing's broken."

She raises those big and beautiful eyes and stares at me.

And stares.

Moments on end, she stares.

"You...made a joke?" she inquires in a small, disgruntled voice. "You?" she repeats as if it's absolutely out of the ordinary for me to make a joke.

It's not, is it?

I frown as I think on it. When was the last time I joked with her? With anyone, for that matter?

The answer comes to me easily.

Never.

I don't joke around. Just like I don't go to public restrooms with a fucking hard-on caused by a little heathen who won't even take responsibility for it.

I don't get to reply to her as she takes me by surprise and stomps her heel on my foot.

Fuckk! That hurt like a bitch.

"You wretch!" she cries out. "How can you joke about that? I really thought I caused you permanent damage!" She starts pacing around. "But it was just a kiss on the cheek! It wasn't anything lewd," she continues as if trying to make sense of it.

"Have you thought that a kiss on the cheek might be just as potent?" I ask in between pained breaths.

"But it wouldn't break your...thing..." She trails off.

"My thing?" I raise a brow, amused at seeing her so disconcerted. "You seem overly concerned with my cock, pet."

She reddens even more.

"I d-don't. That is to say I… It's n-not like that." She takes a deep breath to compose herself. "I merely wanted to make sure you aren't hurt," she mumbles.

"You wanted to make sure my cock works before you married me. Do I have that right?"

"Well…" She bites her lip.

"Good God, Minnie. You'll only marry me if my cock works?" I ask in feigned outrage.

Our waitress just rounds the corner when she hears me. Mortified, she immediately turns to leave.

"Keep it down, Marlowe. You can't keep saying c-c-c…"

"Cock?"

"That. Stop saying it."

"Or what, you won't marry me?"

Her eyes flash at me, shooting me daggers.

"Perhaps I won't," she quips.

"I didn't ask." I shrug.

"You will ask."

"I have no plans of getting married."

"Yes, you do," she states more emphatically. "I'm your girlfriend now. The next step, the obvious step for you humans, is marriage. You will bond with me."

"You're getting ahead of yourself, pet," I say with a chuckle. But the truth is that her words leave me a bit flustered too—just a bit, though.

So she wants to marry me, huh?

This time, the prospect isn't as daunting. In fact, it might prove to be quite exciting.

She'll be mine then. On paper. In front of the law.

No one would be able to take her away from me.

"You'll bond with me, Marlowe," she continues, straightening her back. "If you want to get in my dress, you'll have to bond with me."

"I think you mean in your pants," I add dryly.

"I'm not wearing pants." She narrows her eyes at me.

I open my mouth to point out it's an idiom but then remember idioms aren't her strong suit anyway.

"So that's it? If I want to fuck you, I must marry you?"

"Precisely." She pushes her chin up in defiance.

"Why?"

Not that I'm averse to marrying her. Perhaps I should look into that today. But there's still the matter of her muddy past. And now that aloof brother of hers. Just who the hell is her family?

And more importantly, do I care?

Surprisingly, not really.

"Because a true bonding is sacred," she adds with a small smile. "And if we do it right... The fates might look favorably upon us."

I stare at her for a moment. Then I sigh and shake my head at her. I knew she was a strange girl, but I never realized *how* strange. Next, she'll talk about astrology and zodiac signs.

As I think on a reply that will not offend her or her belief system—she might be a Wiccan or pagan or that type of shit for all I know—the door to the room suddenly opens.

My mother comes out, already wearing her coat.

"There you are, dear. I fear I must leave you two now. There's a matter that requires my immediate attention," she says apologetically.

She hugs me, then does the same to Minnie, who happily returns the hug.

"What happened?" I ask.

"Julius is ill. His fiancée is worried about him."

I click my tongue against my teeth.

Julius has always been an attention whore. I bet he heard about Mother's dinner with me and didn't like being overlooked.

"He's a fucking doctor. He can take care of himself," I mutter under my breath.

"Marlowe! You're swearing again." She tsks at me.

I shrug.

"He can't stop himself," Minnie quips, giving me a look.

"I knew I liked you, Minnie." My mother chuckles. "I'm sad to cut this meeting short, but I'll see you soon at my birthday party."

"Of course." Minnie nods and smiles.

A few more platitudes and my mother leaves.

Fucking Julius. He's thirty-five not *five*.

Then again, he's never liked when the attention was on me instead of him.

With Mother gone, I settle the bill and ask for some dessert to-go for Minnie. That done, we leave.

We get in my car and I start driving home.

Ten minutes into the ride, though, I note that she's pouting at me.

"What now?" I ask with a roll of my eyes.

"You might have noticed I'm a little dense when it comes to some things," she starts. "Not dumb. I'll have you know I came first in my theoretical classes," she makes sure to add.

"I know you're not dumb, Minnie." Sure, there seems to be a bit of a language barrier between us. But aside from that, she's a bright girl.

"Good." She nods, pleased.

"That's it? You wanted to make sure I don't think you're dumb?"

"Well, partially," she answers sheepishly. Wiggling in her seat, she turns toward me, her expression excited. The movement, however, hikes up her skirt and gives me a good eyeful of her shapely legs.

I gulp down. Is she doing this on purpose? Does she want to drive me insane?

She just told me she's not going to sleep with me unless I put a ring on her finger, so at this point, I can only conclude she's trying to torture me.

Alas, it's my fault for being such a weak soul.

Once upon a time, I thought myself above such temptation. But now I realize I'm just as weak as any other man.

I see her, I get hard. It's that simple.

I suppose I'd better start shopping for a ring.

"Why partially?" I clear my throat, doing my best to focus on the road and not on her legs.

Goddamn it, I want her. So much so I'm willing to risk my holy bachelorhood for her.

"I need you to clarify something for me. It's life and death, Marlowe, so don't think to lie to me again," she adds in a serious voice.

"What is it?"

"Your body score."

"Body count," I correct.

"Whatever. It's only dead people, right?" she asks, nibbling uncertainly on her lip.

"Yes, only dead people," I confirm.

"And by that I mean that you *killed* those dead people, you didn't do other...things with them, right?" She continues.

I blink, fearing I haven't heard her right.

"Did you just imply I'm into necrophilia, Minnie?" I ask, barely holding my laughter in.

"N-no. I mean... Just tell me the truth, will you?" she cries out in frustration. "Have you slept with any person, dead or alive?" She stares at me intently as she waits for my answer.

"No, I have not slept with anyone," I reply.

A smile tugs at her lips, but before she can breathe in relief, she frowns.

"No, no. I will not let you mislead me again," she mutters. "Marlowe! Have you f-fucked anyone, dead or alive?" she asks again.

I'm close to bursting out laughing, but I know that will only offend her further. I'm already in her bad books for my previous behavior, so I might as well give this round to her.

"No, Minnie. I have not fucked any person, dead or alive."

Finally, a big smile explodes on her face. She brings her hands together in front of her chest and she claps her palms repeatedly in excitement.

"Good. That's good," she whispers to herself.

Fuck. If I had known that would bring her so much joy, I would have told her the truth from the beginning. Then I wouldn't have had to withstand her cold behavior for weeks.

But then I wouldn't have known she was jealous either...

Ah, such a dilemma.

"And kissing. You said we were even. Clarify that for me, too," she adds, even more excitement echoing in her voice.

"It means exactly what you think it means, Minnie. I have not kissed anyone else, dead or alive. Unless you count kissing my mother on the cheek."

She waves her hand.

"Doesn't count."

She's so chirpy and happy, she starts humming to herself and dancing in her seat.

Cute. She's so damn cute.

"Now it's my turn," I find myself saying.

She raises her brows in question.

"That soulmate of yours. Are you still waiting for him?"

I brace myself for her answer.

"Nope," she replies, surprising me. "I've decided you will do."

My lips curve into a satisfied smile.

But I don't get to enjoy this victory as a dark shadow appears in front of my car, obstructing my view of the road. I pull on the steering wheel in an attempt to find some visibility, but it only makes it worse.

Minnie grabs my arm, her expression one of pure terror.

A loud bang erupts in the air and the car starts spinning uncontrollably.

I reach for her, pulling her in my arms to protect her. At the rate we're spinning, we're likely going to roll over. She's so fucking small and frail, the impact will undoubtedly injure her badly.

And I'm powerless to stop it.

I can only watch it happen in slow motion as I hold her tightly to my chest.

Her breathing intensifies.

"It's okay. It will be okay," I whisper in her hair, praying to all fucking known and unknown deities that my words will not become lies.

Her arms are tightly wrapped around my midriff, her head on my chest as she holds me just as tightly. We're jolted around a couple of times, but nothing too bad.

The trunk of the car collides with what I can only hope is a tree. The impact releases the airbags into our faces and stops the car from moving farther.

"Minnie? Are you all right?" I ask as I gently caress her face.

She nods slowly.

A howl resounds from outside, and we both turn to look in front of the car.

The dark shadows start to recede, but from their depths, a gray, ghost-like figure appears. Behind it, more of its kind follow until there's nothing else in the horizon *but* these ghost-like figures.

What the fuck...

"They have arrived," Minnie whispers in a low, ominous voice.

TWENTY

THE BEEPING SOUND of the machine is the first sound I hear when I wake up.

There's a flurry of movement around me, and as I move my hand, I feel resistance. There's something holding it in place.

"Mr. Spencer-Astor, you'll hurt yourself." A stern voice reprimands me, taking my hand and placing it by my side. "I'll get the doctor to come look at you."

I blink once. Twice.

White and blue swirl before my eyes, slowly taking the shape of people in scrubs.

Hospital.

This is a hospital.

And my arm is hooked to an IV.

"Minnie. Where's Minnie?" I croak.

My throat is dry, and my voice comes out broken. It's almost as if I've swallowed pieces of glass that embedded themselves into the walls of my throat.

I'm not sure when or how I ended up here, and frankly, I don't care at this moment.

The only thing I'm concerned with is the fact that Minnie is not here. She's not by my side, nor is she in my field of view.

And that's a problem.

Gritting my teeth, I force myself to stand up. Once more, the IV holds me back and I pull with enough force to rip it.

Blood flows down my arm.

Fuck.

"Mr. Spencer-Astor!" a nurse exclaims, scandalized. She places herself in front of me, trying to get me to go back to bed.

Her lips are moving, but the words don't register.

There's a deafening pounding in my head that makes my vision shaky. Still, my focus is unperturbed.

Minnie.

I need to find Minnie.

Pushing the nurse aside, I pull the curtain to reveal a crowded ER.

"Minnie. Where's my Minnie?" I call out, ignoring the jab of pain in my ribs as my lungs fill with air.

"Sir, please calm down," another nurse yells at me.

"Where is she? I need to see her. Now," I grit out.

The hospital is packed. That means there are tens if not hundreds of people around.

Men.

One look at Minnie and I know they'll fall under her spell. Fuck, I have firsthand experience with it.

But there's also the worry that she might be hurt, too. The last thing I remember was that we crashed the car, no? What if something happened to her?

"Minnie?" I shout, wildly looking around for any trace of her.

"Sir, please!"

People gather around me, and in the distance, I note security wading through the crowd and heading my way.

"I need to find her," I say as I turn to one of the nurses. I mellow my tone so I don't seem threatening—I won't achieve anything if security takes me away.

"Who?"

"The girl who was with me. Please…"

"Is there a problem?" a man dressed in a security uniform inquires as he steps closer to me.

I weigh my options.

The nurses appear terrified—for good reason. One of them nods to the security guy and he comes toward me, ready to restrain me.

Fuck.

I could fight him. At my normal capacity, I wouldn't have a problem winning.

But the pain in my ribs tells me I'm *not* at my normal capacity.

My entire body hurts, and there's still blood flowing down my arm from the ripped IV.

The man stops in front of me. Two other security guards are behind me.

Since I'm not about to allow them to take me away or restrain me, I suppose all that's left to do is fight.

Just as I'm about to throw the first punch, a melodic voice calls my name.

"Marlowe?"

I pivot, my breathing labored.

I blink a couple of times to make sure I'm not seeing things.

She's there.

Minnie. My Minnie.

She's wearing a face mask that obscures her features, and it appears to work because none of the men are yet in thrall with her.

She's dressed in a hospital gown, and there's a wide bandage wrapped around her forehead.

"Minnie," I mutter breathlessly as I rush toward her. "Are you all right? What's this? What happened?"

"Oh, this?" she says as she touches her bandage. "It's just a bruise from when the airbags got deployed. You have one too," she mentions. Reaching for me, she touches my forehead, tracing the contours of my own bandage.

"The airbags?" I frown. Images of the crash slowly come to me. But *why* did we crash?

I'm a good driver. I didn't drink. The roads were in fairly good condition.

Flashes of a fog appear in my mind, but I shake my head as pain stabs at my temples.

"Are you all right?" she asks worriedly when she sees me wince.

"Yes, yes. But what happened? Why did we crash?"

"You...don't remember?" she asks carefully.

I shake my head.

"Some animal ran in front of the car. You tried to avoid hitting it and the car slid off the road," she exclaims. "Come. You need to take care of that." She points to my bleeding arm.

Still out of it, I allow her to take me back to my hospital bed.

A female nurse comes to tend to my wound, but I instinctively shrink away, baring my teeth at her.

I hate people touching me, but this is more than that. I physically feel ill the closer she comes to me. And as she hovers over me, my stomach recoils.

I'm about to ask her not to touch me, but Minnie seemingly anticipates it as she intervenes.

Her arm shoots out and she stops the nurse.

"May we please have a male nurse treat my husband?" she asks in a sweet voice.

Husband.

She called me her husband. In a possessive way, too.

That's my girl.

She not only claimed me publicly, but she also put on a mask to make sure no other male can witness her beauty. Of course the least I can do is ensure that no other female touches me, too. I'd say it's a fair exchange.

My chest fills with pride—though that also sends a stab of pain to my ribs.

Alas, this is the type of pain I don't mind.

The nurse is taken aback by the request. She frowns as she looks around for help—most likely trying to signal security again that we're a couple of weirdos.

But if my Minnie is a weirdo, I don't mind being one either.

I sigh as I glance at her. Another sharp pain erupts in my chest.

Beautiful, poised, and jealous. What more can a man ask for?

"We're at full capacity, Mrs.," the nurse replies uncertainly. "He needs to get his arm treated—"

"I know, and I'm sorry to ask this of you. But my husband has a psychological condition that only gets worse if a female touches him. It's for his own good, you understand." The same sweet tone, but there's a tacit threat in the way she's staring at the nurse.

Fuck, that's hot.

I'd tell her that, too, if it didn't hurt to speak or move.

"She's right," I croak, followed by a groan of pain.

Minnie grabs my non-injured arm and places my hand in hers.

"Please?" She bats her lashes at the nurse.

The nurse sighs.

"I'll see what I can do," she mentions. "Until then, please apply pressure on the bleeding site."

Minnie takes her duty seriously as she presses a bandage against the bleeding wound.

"You're sure you're fine?" I ask, studying her intently.

"Yes." She rolls her eyes. "You should take care of yourself, first. How could you pull your IV out of your arm?" She tsks at me.

"You weren't here," I grumble.

She blinks, then looks away, blushing furiously. Even the mask cannot hide the redness that spreads up her face.

The male nurse comes over and takes care of my arm. I'm asked to undergo a few more tests to make sure my chest injuries are not life-threatening.

Oddly enough, only I'm forced to withstand a CAT scan. They barely pay attention to Minnie.

I argue with them, of course, demanding that they take care of her first. But I'm told she's perfectly fine aside from that one scratch. That's relieving. I vaguely remember taking her in my arms at the time of impact. That must have protected her quite well, a fact that makes me preen.

That should help her see that I'm the best match for her.

Rich—check.

Good-looking—check, if I do say so myself.

Smart—check, of course.

Strong—check as I've already proven it.

I can take care and provide for her, which considering how small and frail she is, that's something she really needs.

Even that brother of hers is useless, leaving her alone in this wretched world that wants to take advantage of her. How could he do that? She's his little sister, for fuck's sake.

I don't even want to imagine what would have happened if I hadn't met her when I did.

She'd still be all alone and defenseless.

That thought awakens my rage all over again, making me tense —a mistake considering my entire body is bruised. Alas, my pain and suffering should show her how serious I am about her.

That's not to say I'm in a hurry because I want to get in her *dress*. I mean, of course I do. It's been all I could think of for the last couple of weeks. But I've lived close to thirty years as a monk. What's a few more weeks?

Torture. That's what it is.

I'll need to make it days not weeks.

I might have been above temptation, but that was before she appeared into my life, showing me everything I've been missing.

A smile pulls at my lips, and once more, I'm told to stop moving or the CAT scan will not get a clear image.

I scowl.

It's not my fault Minnie occupies all my waking thoughts.

It's hers.

If anything, they should tell *her* off for making me take leave of my senses.

Hell, I should tell her off—again. And I would if I didn't happen to like having her occupy my thoughts. I know, strange.

Even stranger is the fact that I don't care anymore if she bewitched me or not, or if she fed me some type of magical potion to make me so obsessed with her. I've reached the point where I'm happy going with the flow. Frankly, I never even knew I had such a rich imagination before. But lately, the things my brain has managed to conjure up.

I whistle as I once more picture her in her maid outfit. But then the thought morphs, and I see her in a nurse outfit taking care of me, slowly, seductively...

"Sir! Stop moving!" the technician calls out.

I glance down at my tented pants.

Fuck.

Does he think I'm in control?

Not even thoughts of blood, or guts, or other bodily fluids staining my spotless floor can help me cool off at this point. On the contrary, I become even more excited at the thought of disemboweling every man who dares to look at my little heathen.

"Sir!" Another exasperated cry from the technician.

I sigh. It's going to be a long night.

Eventually, though, I manage to stay still long enough for the machine to do its thing. The results are good—bruised ribs but nothing broken. I'm given a bag of painkillers and the doctors discharge both Minnie and me.

Since my car is totaled, we take a cab home.

The pain is manageable at this point thanks to the pills, but my body is still sore. Minnie, on the other hand, is as spry as ever.

"Are you all right?" she asks worriedly as we make it inside the house. "Do you need anything?"

She's taken her mask off and is now regaling me with her full-on blinding beauty.

I smile like a fool.

"Marlowe? Did you hear me?"

"Agh, it hurts so much," I whine when I note this might be my chance to fulfill that one fantasy I got inside the CAT machine.

"It does? Where? We should get you to bed," Minnie hurries to say.

I slouch and limp up the stairs, gaining more sympathy points from her.

I'm not *that* bad. But she doesn't need to know that.

She takes me to my room and settles me on the bed before rushing to get me a glass of water.

I pretend to be unable to swallow—my throat hurts, but not as bad as before.

Her features tense and she panics.

"What can I do to help?" she asks in a small voice.

My lips flatten, and I pull my features into a pained grimace.

"Maybe... No, it's nothing..." I trail off.

"What is it? Tell me and I'll do it!"

"You're injured too. It wouldn't feel right." I sigh and turn my head to the other side.

"You heard the doctor. I'm perfectly fine. Tell me what you need, Marlowe," she hurries to say. "I feel great. My head doesn't even hurt. I can do anything."

She speaks with such conviction, I feel slightly guilty for my pretense—only just slightly.

I clear my throat, letting out a rough groan of pain.

She's once more by my side, assessing me with a frantic expression.

"I'm cold," I say and let out a visible shiver. The goal is to get her to warm me up with her body—though I don't know how amenable she would be to that considering her no touching rule before marriage, whatever that may mean. I'm still a little confused about her reasoning about that.

She kissed my cheek! That counts as touching, no?

Minnie is an enigma.

One moment she seems into me, the next she takes a step back and puts up boundaries.

I can never tell what really goes through her mind, or if she's been staying with me just because she has nowhere else to go—and the chocolate cookies, of course. Even if that were the case, I'm happy to give her chocolate cookies for the rest of her life as long as she remains by my side.

It's an odd realization for someone who's always preferred solitude. But since she's come into my life, I've seen myself change. And the biggest change is the fact that I'm experiencing happiness for the first time ever.

She quickly gets a couple of blankets and places them atop me.

"Better?"

I shake my head.

"Still cold."

Her brows bunch together. She bites her lips as she looks at me.

Going back to the drawer, she takes out another blanket and packs it on top of the others.

Fuck, that's hot. Almost *too* warm, and I love being hot.

"Now?"

I shake my head again.

She glances at the empty drawer. Good, maybe now that there are no more blankets, she'll get a hint.

I expect her to suggest to lend me some of her body heat. I'm waiting for it with my heart in my throat. Of course I'd prefer her to be naked when she does that, but for now, I'll take any crumb she gives me.

She debates with herself for a few moments and I see the

wheels spinning in her mind. Soon, she'll reach the unavoidable conclusion.

I'm bracing myself for it while doing my best to temper my excitement.

She finally nods to herself, but instead of climbing in bed next to me, she dashes out of the room.

I frown. But within seconds, she's back with another blanket—her own.

She places it on top of the others and smiles to herself, satisfied.

"Warm now?"

It's almost insufferably hot, but I shake my head.

"Oh no! You must be really sick, Marlowe. What are we going to do?" she whispers, her features torn. "There are no more blankets..."

I clear my throat.

"In the past, people used to warm each other with their bodies," I add slowly.

She stares at me, her lips parting in surprise.

"You mean... But..."

"It's fine, it's fine." I sigh and turn my head to the side.

Her breathing picks up as she contemplates what to do.

It might be manipulative of me to do this, but one thing I've learned about Minnie is that she likes to help. If she's willing to put herself in harm's way for a puppy, surely she should be willing to help an ailing man.

I release another heavy, pointed sigh.

"Is it that bad?" she asks in a small voice.

"I'll be fine," I mumble. Then feign a cough. That does hurt since my throat is still somewhat sore.

The minutes trickle by. Her indecision hangs in the air.

Then, without a word, she picks up the heavy blankets and slides under them.

At first, she's tentative about it. She doesn't come near me, maintaining a small distance between us.

I shiver intentionally and she slides closer. But still not as close as I'd like.

"You don't have to do this if you don't want to," I add weakly.

"It's not that I don't want to…" She trails off.

I turn on my side so I can look at her.

She's on her back, staring at the ceiling. The blankets are up to her neck, leaving only her beautiful face for me to feast on.

Now I understand why so many men become enchanted with her at first sight. It might not have been as instantaneous for me, but that's likely because I'm a blind idiot.

She's stunning.

All sunshine and warmth, and I so desperately need that warmth.

"But?"

She bites her lip as she slowly turns on her side too, her gaze meeting mine.

There are still a few inches of separation between us, but at this point, they feel like a wide ocean. I've never been fond of swimming—too cold. But for her, I might be willing to do it.

"I want to and at the same time I'm scared of getting too close," she confesses on a whisper.

"Why?"

"Because only tragedy awaits then." She gives me a sad smile.

I stare at her.

"Minnie, I hope you're not scared I'm going to hurt you," I suddenly say. I never realized this might be something I need to address, but given my proclivities, I suppose she has reason to be afraid. "I may kill people, but I will not kill you," I tell her. "Granted, I did at one point want to kill you, but not anymore. You should feel honored." I nod at her.

She blinks.

"You…wanted to kill me?" she repeats in disbelief.

"Well, only at the beginning. And for about a week or so after I met you. But I've come to my senses." I smile, waiting for her to realize how lucky she is.

She doesn't say a word. She just stares at me, so I feel compelled to clarify.

"I don't normally kill women. In fact, you were going to be my first female victim. That in itself is an honor, too."

"You don't kill women but you wanted to kill me?" she asks slowly, her expression slowly morphing into one of outrage.

"You're taking it all wrong. I was about to make an exception for you," I explain.

"I don't see how that should flatter me," she mutters in a dry voice.

"Well, you have to admit that when you first moved in, you were dirty and smelly. Let's not forget you ate from dumpsters, which by the way, I have never heard something so obscene before." That makes me pause. "I hope you brushed your teeth before you kissed my cheek that time," I add, narrowing my eyes at her.

"Marlowe! Even sick you manage to be an asshole," she cries out.

"But it's the truth! Would you prefer I lied to you?"

Okay, maybe I'm still not the best with words seeing as all I say offends her.

"Not everything needs to be said aloud," she chides.

"But I'm telling you this so you know how special you are. I've accepted you even though you have a not so clean past, although I do appreciate you've started to wash daily. And your cleaning technique has vastly improved."

Her mouth drops open in shock. I still have not received my answer regarding whether she brushed her teeth before she kissed me on the cheek, but I fear it might not be in my advantage to ask again.

"You just told me you wanted to kill me!"

"And that in itself is special since I don't kill women! I would have given you a very special death!"

"Special death? And pray, what would a special death look like?" She narrows her eyes at me.

"Well, you're not bad to look at, so I would have embalmed you. I wouldn't have frozen you, though, since I hate the cold, and my previous experiments with freezers failed. But I would have found a way to keep you alive-looking and—"

She presses her finger against my lips to shush me.

"I think it's in your best interest to stop talking," she mutters.

"But you need to understand. Both the fact that you would have been my first female victim and the fact that I decided *not* to kill you despite your state of uncleanliness makes you very special to me. I wouldn't make these allowances for just anybody..."

She presses her fingers insistently against my lips, stopping me mid-sentence.

"You're a very odd man, Marlowe."

I grab her finger, holding it in place. Parting my lips over the tip, I suck it in my mouth. I don't even pause to wonder what she might have touched with said finger. In fact, I rather hope it was a certain part of her body, thereby allowing me to taste what is otherwise forbidden.

Her eyes widen and she freezes. Her chest rises and falls with every labored breath and I find myself getting lost in those black eyes of hers. They're so dark, they resemble an obsidian mirror; one with mystical abilities that has the power to suck my soul right out of my body and consume it.

The moment is broken when she yanks her hand back and scoots over, putting even more distance between us. She swallows hard, and I note she's as rattled as I am.

"You're a very odd woman, too, Minnie. In fact, considering all the secrecy surrounding you, the fact that you're here, in my bed, and not in my basement, is a wonder in itself."

"You should sleep," she mumbles, turning with her back to me. "You're sick and cold and you need rest."

That's the last thing she says to me before silence envelops us.

I stare at the back of her head for moments on end, wanting to say more but being afraid of saying all the wrong things.

She confounds me to no end.

With a long, tired sigh, I get comfortable under the blankets—a little hard to do considering it's sweltering hot with four blankets on, and the added weight puts too much pressure on my battered ribs. Eventually, though, I fall asleep.

As soon as I close my eyes, though, strange images assail me. Flashes of strange creatures and dark shadows seeking to hurt Minnie. This all morphs into a clearer picture as I find myself back at the scene of the accident.

"They have arrived," Minnie says, right before both doors of the car are yanked by an invisible force.

TWENTY-ONE

A LOUD, shrilling sound erupts in my ear, almost as if a banshee had received notice of the coming death.

I don't know what could have ripped apart the car doors—what could have such strength to do it. But where my mind becomes muddled and confused in the face of failing logic, my instincts flare up.

I grab onto Minnie and hold her tight, whispering continuous nonsensical assurances.

Yet it's only a matter of seconds before we're ripped from the car, too.

I don't see who or *what* does it. I only feel a whoosh of air that grips me tightly and pulls me out of the body of the car, slamming me against the pavement.

Keeping my arms around Minnie, I take the brunt of the fall. Pain radiates from my back, and as we roll onto the ground, my side gets bruised too. The air is knocked out of me, and I gasp for breath.

But I don't let go.

I keep my grip steadfast, tight, and unyielding.

Even as the pain becomes blinding, I don't let go.

"Minnie," I say her name on a groan. "Are you all right? Talk to me."

She stirs in my arms. Her eyes open and she regards me with shock.

"Are you okay—"

I don't get to finish the question as she flexes her arms and pushes me away with astounding strength. My eyes widen in shock, but it's nothing compared to the disbelief that forms inside of me as I watch her get to her feet and face the monstrous shadows.

The fog from before slowly takes the shape of an army of anthropomorphic creatures. They're lined up in a triangle formation, with one creature at the front that's larger than the rest, but just as ugly and disgusting.

Their bodies are gray and gnarly, resembling mummified flesh. Ribs poke through the dried flesh, angling inward and pointing toward the hollow of their stomach.

There's nothing there. Only a black hole as if their internal organs had shriveled up and shrunk inside of the chest cavity.

Their pelvis is a mass of mottled flesh. They have no genitalia, only raised scar tissue that descends down their legs, wrapping around their feet like vines wrap around trees—close together, but not close enough to hide the bony skeletal foundation. Their arms, too, are a mix between bulging bone and dried, mottled flesh where muscle should have been.

But it's their faces that are the most terrifying—or, I should say, straight out of a nightmare.

Scar tissue abounds around the top and back of the skull, making for misshapen crania. The muscles of the face are prominent, but in the same desiccated way. They wrap around the cheekbones before thinning out in the lower part of the mandible. In fact, it's such a thin layer of dry flesh, that when they release a battle cry, opening their mouths wide—inhumanly wide—the skin breaks apart.

The sound echoes through the stillness of the night. It's the same sound we heard before. Right before we crashed.

Minnie's chest is rising and falling with each labored breath as she glares at the army of skeleton-like beings bellowing their cries of war. Her lips twitch in annoyance. Her expression is a far cry from the innocent Minnie who makes gooey eyes at me.

Her gaze is focused on them—observing, calculating.

She's not surprised. She doesn't seem afraid, either.

Just mildly irritated.

"What the fuck?" I mutter, convinced I must be making this shit up. "What are these?"

I slowly get up and stand next to Minnie, placing a protective arm around her.

The skeleton-like beings continue to howl, their mouths hanging low, unmoving. I don't know where the sound is coming from since their mouths are empty, black holes. Do they even have the anatomical apparatus to make sounds?

"Sentinels," Minnie answers. I turn toward her. Her body is tightly wound, her entire demeanor changed.

"Sentinels? What the fuck does that mean?"

"Soulless beings whose only purpose is to track a target. They're relentless, but they aren't very strong. At least not individually. This many, though..."

"This many?" I raise a brow.

I'm convinced that this is all a dream. None of it is real. It cannot be real.

Maybe I've been watching *too* many *Supernatural* episodes and this is the result.

"It might prove a challenge," Minnie says.

"A challenge for whom?"

She doesn't answer. She's watching the sentinels closely. Sliding one foot to the side, she assumes a fighting stance, balling her hands into fists.

Minnie. Fighting. I scoff aloud at the thought and shake my

head. We're talking about an actual bite-sized human who weighs a hundred pounds wet. Imagining her fighting anything puts an amused smile on my face.

But then I have to wonder *why* I'm dreaming about this savage side of Minnie. Perhaps my subconscious is trying to tell me something.

But what? That I quite like it when she becomes an aggressive lioness, baring her teeth at me and telling me that we're *meant* to be? When she becomes a possessive little heathen that *almost* rivals my own possessiveness?

Hmm. Yes. That must be it. I like the assertive part of her as much as I like the coy persona she has going on most times. Perhaps I even *want* her to be more assertive—to tell me in no uncertain terms that she wants me as much as I want her.

But fighting? Minnie fighting? It's *my* job to keep her safe, not the other way around.

"Right. Let's say these are some soulless creatures or whatever. Why are they here?"

She doesn't miss a beat this time as she answers.

"They're here for me."

"For you?" I chuckle. "These dried up mummies are here for you?"

Ludicrous.

Even more so than the image of her fighting.

I wonder if *Supernatural* had a creature that resembles these soulless beings. Perhaps I'm using that hidden knowledge to project them into my mind as the big bad that needs defeating. Although, to be perfectly honest, I don't remember seeing anything like this in my life. Not on TV or anywhere else.

That doesn't mean I'll let some imaginary ugly-ass beings get to my Minnie.

Extending my arm, I push her back behind me.

"Let me handle this," I tell her confidently.

It's my dream. That means I can defeat these creatures and save the day. Perhaps I'll even get a kiss for my valiant deeds—a kiss on the lips this time. I'm getting tired of those sample kisses on the cheek—even though I've only had two.

I'm getting greedy. I sigh.

It is what it is. I've come to accept my weaknesses where it concerns her.

So what if it's just a dream? I'll take what I can get. And if my mind cooperates, mayhap dream Minnie will be willing to shed some of her clothes, maybe even let me touch her...

Ah, the possibilities are endless.

And since I already have her naked form imprinted on my retina, it will not be hard to imagine her like that.

Once more, I berate my past self for being so uptight. I could have had her walking around naked all the time without too much effort if I hadn't told her off that day.

Focus, Marlowe. This is your moment to shine.

And besides, perhaps it's better that I told her to keep her clothes on at all times. It will make the victory that much sweeter when I finally get to remove them myself.

After I buy that damned ring, of course.

Fuck.

I glance at her and force my mind to manifest a ring on her finger in the dream.

I squint hard, but nothing happens. Her hand is as bare as before, no matter how much I try to picture a big diamond gleaming atop her ring finger—only the best for my girl.

Double fuck. Dream rules must be more stringent than I thought.

Alas, the big bad will not be defeated anytime soon if I dally too much.

Taking a deep breath, I run toward the formation.

"Marlowe!" Minnie screams after me, her voice tinged with surprise.

Watch this, dream Minnie! I'll save you from these disgusting creatures and then I'll claim my kiss.

Reaching the leader of the formation, I note that he's close to my height, with the other minions in the back a full foot shorter.

Piece of cake.

Flexing my arm, I throw the first punch, aiming for the head. They might look strange, but every creature, soulless or not, has a vulnerable spot, no? The head would be my first guess, but I suppose I'll find out if I'm right.

Just as my knuckles make contact with the dried-up flesh of the mummy, its skin becomes malleable, as do its bones. They curve and bend following the shape of my knuckles, thereby deflecting the blow.

My eyes widen.

But before I can think of an alternative, the creature opens its mouth to release another loud bellow. The air pressure from the scream hits me in the chest, throwing me back.

I hit the ground, but I'm not deterred.

So it's not the head...

"You idiot! You'll get yourself killed," Minnie shouts from the back.

I ignore her. Breathing hard, I get back up and move for a different attack.

My fist makes contact with the creature's sternum, and the same thing happens.

The surface of its body becomes gooey, almost absorbing my fist inside of it.

I quickly yank it back.

"Fuck!" I mutter.

The creature watches me, still unmoving. Its mouth opens for another bellow, but I'm ready, this time dodging the air blast.

Minnie reaches my side and places a hand on my shoulder.

"Stop," she whispers. "If you don't get involved, they won't hurt you. They're not allowed to harm humans."

"What?" I blink in surprise. There's so much to unpack from that statement, but we don't have time for it.

Just as Minnie moves, the sentinels move, too, stomping their skeleton-like feet on the ground and moving the formation so that the tip of the triangle is directly in front of her.

Before I can ask Minnie what she means, or what the hell is going on, the creatures open their mouths in tandem, sucking in air before releasing another shrilling sound.

This time, the air blast isn't released immediately. It builds up, gathering the strength of the entire formation.

Yet the aim is clear.

Minnie glances at me, her expression sad before she pushes me to the side just as the creatures release their blast.

It converges into a single line aimed at Minnie, and before I can do anything, it hits her.

Her mouth drops open in pain, her entire body seized by an invisible force.

She's not thrown back as I was. Instead, she's immobilized by that air pressure, held in place. She cannot move or do anything.

"Minnie?"

"Run," she mouths, a barely audible sound.

She tries to speak again, but she seems frozen on the spot. The air gathered around her is turning opaque, almost as if it's solidifying to keep her inside.

I don't even think as I use my entire body weight to slam myself against the forming wall.

It doesn't budge.

Her eyes are wide with shock as she does her best to signal for me to leave.

To hell with that! If she thinks I'm going to run away and leave her in danger then she doesn't know me at all.

I slam myself against the forming cocoon again, but it's in vain.

With every second, the shell around her becomes stronger, more impenetrable.

Panic swells inside of me as I wildly look around and force myself to think.

Despite it being a dream, it seems I'm not in control.

The creatures maintain their formation, not moving one inch. But there's something odd about their position. Their mouths are wide open, and their entire focus is on Minnie.

I move around them, baiting them.

But they ignore me, as if I weren't there.

My lips flatten in concentration as I go to the second line of the formation and try to kick one of the sentinels. Like before, it doesn't do anything to the creature, its skin molding to my kick to absorb the shock. But what's odd is the fact that it's not even turning to acknowledge me. It stands there, absorbing blow after blow. Mouth open, eyes straight forward, it stands still as a statue.

I narrow my eyes as an idea comes to mind.

To test it, I go to another sentinel and do the same thing, but this time, I hit the front of its body.

My blow doesn't do any damage, but it confirms my theory as I see its sunken eyes move slightly to look at me. Yet it doesn't do anything.

It keeps its mouth open, eyes facing forward.

Could it be...

The only way for them to keep Minnie captive is to not disturb the formation? By keeping their mouths open, they continue to reinforce the prison so Minnie cannot escape?

The initial blow had been accompanied by sound.

I stop, forcing myself to be still. Slowing down my erratic breathing, I tune in with the sounds around me.

It's dim, but there's a light vibration emanating from the sentinels. It's almost like a continuous hum that holds the exact same note ad infinitum.

Minnie said the duty of these things is to track something or someone, which means they're not here to hurt her, or us. They're only immobilizing her until someone else comes along to do that job.

Fuck.

That thought is sobering. The clock is ticking, and if these desiccated mummies are any indication of what's after Minnie, I don't want to wait around for the ultimate big bad to come along.

I glance back at her. She's now completely enclosed in the cocoon, the shell almost entirely opaque.

That means I don't have much time to act. And the only thing I can think of—the only thing that makes logical sense—is to disturb the formation. If that's holding the prison in place, then any disturbance within the formation should weaken it.

Easier said than done when these fucking mummies seem impervious.

I go back to my initial reasoning, though.

Every being has a weakness. I just need to find theirs. And fast.

The seconds trickle by as I force myself to think. When nothing comes to me, I decide that I might as well throw everything I have to them—starting with the last row.

If the biggest one is at the front, perhaps he's also the strongest. That means I may have a chance with the last row of creatures.

Dashing to the end of the formation, it is with horror that I realize just how big it is. It must have nine or ten rows, each one containing more and more creatures.

As I reach the end of the formation, I start with one of the creatures near the edge.

I throw in punch after punch to the front of his chest, but they do little damage. The skin bends once more, absorbing the energy of each blow.

The creature, too, remains focused on Minnie, its mouth wide open and emitting the same low frequency hum as the others.

Gritting my teeth, I put more strength into my punches, hoping at least one of them will hit.

Moments pass. My heart races like hell. Sweat pebbles on my

forehead, droplets falling down my face. My hair is damp from the effort, as are my clothes.

I take my coat off and dump it to the ground.

The cold of the night assails me, made even more potent by the sweat clinging to my clothes.

I shiver, but I don't give up. In fact, as I throw the next punch, I find I'm able to channel more strength without the weight of additional clothes. The cold too, although initially biting, only serves to spur me further.

I fucking hate the cold. But in this moment, it might be my biggest ally.

I take off my sweater, too, remaining only in a thin shirt.

My breathing grows labored, but I force myself to focus on the task. Just one. If I get one of them to stop interacting with the formation, perhaps Minnie's prison might weaken enough so I can pull her out.

I throw my punches haphazardly. But one of them lands in the hollow part of the mummy's stomach, right under the protruding ribs.

This time, the flesh doesn't bend around the contour of my knuckles. Although the cavity is deep, when I'm elbow deep inside the creature, I touch something.

Something that makes it stir.

I raise a tired brow.

Not wanting to lose momentum, I pummel into his stomach, one blow after another.

Dry, cold, snake-like flesh meets me at the bottom of the cavity. But with every blow, I get more reactions from this fucking walking mummy.

It takes me a couple minutes of repeated blows for the creature to move. At first, it's eye movements and a few facial cues. But eventually, it winces in paint with its whole body.

Seeing this as a breakthrough, I don't stop until he releases a sharp sound that goes against the collective hum of the formation.

One last punch that seems to penetrate the back of its stomach and he reels back in pain, breaking from his place in the formation.

His mouth slowly closes, his eyes losing all life. In a matter of seconds, he turns into dust, carried away by the wintry wind as if he'd never even been there.

Breathing hard, I turn to look at Minnie. The previously opaque cage has now become a little more transparent, giving me hope.

She still cannot move, but I note the hope in her eyes, too.

Not wanting to waste any moment, I hurry to the next sentinel, repeating the process and pummeling that hollow crevice until I make a hole through it. This sentinel, too, breaks from the formation and turns into dust.

I repeat the process until the entire last row is turned to ashes.

I'm close to fainting from exhaustion, but I don't stop. I simply go to the next row and do it all over again. Only when I'm halfway through this row does Minnie regain some of her mobility.

Removing my hand from one mummy's stomach, I watch as he steps back, screaming in despair before becoming dust.

"Marlowe..." A low sound reaches my ears.

I turn, wobbling on my feet. A smile pulls at my lips as I slowly walk to her.

But then something strange happens.

There's still a cage around her, but it's not as prominent as before. Inside of it, though, a blue light starts to shimmer.

At first, it's a light blue, barely visible through the milky-white walls of the prison. But as the light deepens into a darker blue, cracks appear all over the walls. Until one moment later, the entire prison shatters.

I have to shield my eyes from the blinding light.

Squinting to get a good look, I freeze as I see Minnie—like I've never seen her before.

That blue light? It comes from her. It surrounds her, emanating from every pore in her body.

The sentinel formation startles, and the sound stops. But it seems they're not giving up as they quickly prepare to send another air blast her way and trap her once more.

She only gives me a small smile before she moves. So fast, the sentinels cannot keep up with her. So fast, even my eyes cannot keep up with her.

I rub my eyes to make sure I'm seeing this right.

Why is my dream Minnie surrounded by a blue light? And why is she faster than the flash?

I only see glimpses of her as she goes from sentinel to sentinel, stabbing them with what appears to be a sword made out of the same blue light that emanates from her. She does it so fast, sentinel after sentinel shrieks before turning into dust.

What the fuck is going on?

When the wind swipes the last batch of dust, she finally stops.

She approaches me slowly, uncertainly.

"What the fuck, Minnie?" I rasp.

She bites her lip.

"I don't think I can stay here anymore, Marlowe," she whispers as she stops in front of me. She raises her big, beautiful eyes and I note the unshed tears lining her eyes. "Thank you for everything."

"What are you talking about? You're not going anywhere," I say as I grab her arm, needing to ensure she won't leave my side. But even that amount of force is too much for my worn-out body.

Fucking hell!

She flinches at my tone.

"They found me," she murmurs in a soft voice. "And now *you* know..."

"Know what?" I frown.

"That I'm not human."

I blink, fearing I haven't heard her right. I mean, it's not a stretch of imagination to equate what I've seen she can do and what I know of her with her being not human. At the same time, hearing it directly from her lips has me frowning.

I'm...confused.

"So?" I ask, raising a brow. "I'm a serial killer. You're not human. It's not the worst thing that could happen." I shrug. For some reason, my words are a little slurred. "I kill humans, and you're not human, so I don't kill you. See? Even better..." I mumble.

Does it make sense? It sort of does to my ears. But seeing Minnie's confused features, I don't think it does to her.

Holding on to her shoulders, I pull her into my arms and continue mumbling.

"Not human... If you're not human, what are you?"

She swallows.

"I'm a..."

She says something, but I'm not certain I can make out the words. My legs give out and my eyes roll out in my head. She holds on to me as we both fall to the ground.

"Marlowe... Marlowe..." she keeps saying my name.

I wish I could respond, but I find I cannot make my lips move to do so.

"Molokai, you need to help..." Is that her voice? "He can't know... His memory..." She continues, but I don't know what that has to do with everything.

"We need to leave, Minerva. Now. If they haven't communicated your location yet, the next troop of sentinels will when they find you."

A male voice. Molokai... Her brother, no?

"Molokai... Please..."

Why is she begging him?

That's my last thought before I lose consciousness.

TWENTY-TWO

I GET UP, drenched in sweat. My body aches, and I groan as I flex my arms.

What a strange dream.

Even stranger is the fact that the pain is located in similar places to where I was injured or exerted myself in that dream.

My back and torso hurt from being wrenched from the car. My arms from punching too many disgusting mummies. And my throat...

I frown.

My throat would be hurting from the cold as I kept breathing harshly while pushing myself past my limits.

Of course that would be the case if my dream was not a dream. But it was a dream, no?

I immediately glance over to my right.

The spot where Minnie slept is empty.

Fuck.

If there's any chance the dream was real and she thinks to disappear and leave me alone, then she's sorely mistaken. I jump out of bed and run out of the room.

I don't even bother to shower or change my sweaty clothes.

All that matters is to make sure that Minnie hasn't left me.

Because how *dare* she?

I saved her and this is how she repays me? Not even a kiss?

As soon as I reach the bottom of the stairs, a delicious smell assails my nostrils.

I follow the trail that leads to the kitchen. Minnie is in her maid uniform, her expression tense and focused as she tends to the pot on the stove.

"There you are," she says brightly as she gives me a wide smile. "How did you sleep? Any pain? You need to eat so you can take your meds."

I stare at her. "What are you?"

She blinks. "W-what am I? What do you mean by that, Marlowe?" she asks in a sweet voice.

"You're not human. So what are you?"

"Marlowe, are you all right? Do you have a fever?" She takes a step forward to touch my forehead, but I push her hand aside.

I narrow my eyes at her.

"You're a witch, aren't you?"

"That again?" She frowns.

"I remember," I tell her, watching her reaction closely.

She doesn't even blink. "What do you mean?"

"The car accident. We didn't hit an animal. It was some kind of dried-up mummies that were coming after you."

She blinks in confusion.

Her expression seems genuine, and for a moment, I fear I might be going off the rails.

But then I recall the list of injuries I sustained that match what happened in my dream. It couldn't have been my imagination, no matter how fucked up that might be. For one, I have no frame of reference for those creatures, not even with my addiction to *Supernatural*. Then there's everything else odd about her that cannot be logically explained—and oh, I've tried.

I'm not so obtuse as to believe that science is the only answer.

And though I'd classify myself as more of a skeptic, I can no longer deny what's in front of me.

Something is seriously wrong with Minnie.

And I've spent too much time denying it. It's time to face it head-on and get to the root of this mystery.

"Marlowe, I think you're confused. I don't know what you're talking about."

"You know perfectly well," I accuse. "You said it yourself. You're not human. So you're a witch, aren't you?"

"I never said anything like that." She continues to deny it, and to my dismay, I find myself wavering. Her expression is convincing.

But I'm not going crazy. I know I'm not.

She releases a deep sigh.

"That never happened. You must have hurt your head worse than I thought. We should go back to the hospital to get you checked again," she mentions, taking her apron off.

"I'm fine, Minnie. Nothing is wrong with me except some soreness in my arms and ribs. My head is fine."

"But you're spouting nonsense, Marlowe!"

I raise a brow at her. "Am I?"

She shakes her head at me.

"I can't put up with you like this. There's hot food on the stove. Help yourself to it," she mumbles as she moves to leave.

"I haven't finished talking," I grit out, my voice harsher than before.

She stops in her tracks, her back to me.

"But I did."

Before she can leave, I grab her arm and push her against the wall, trapping her with my body.

"You're not going anywhere until you tell me what you are."

Her eyes flash at me.

"If you're so sure I'm a witch, aren't you afraid I'll put a hex on you?" She smirks.

"I think you've already done that."

She raises her eyebrow at me. "I have?"

"I *know* you put a spell on me," I tell her confidently. "Now I just have to prove it."

"And what spell would that be?"

"You know fully well what you've done. You've bewitched me just as you've done to all the men who ever laid eyes on you."

"I seem to remember you weren't very bewitched when you laid eyes on me," she mutters drily. "Didn't you want to kill me?"

"That in itself suggests you bewitched me. How else would I otherwise deviate from my normal M.O.?"

"You're mad." She laughs.

"That's the issue, Minnie. I'm mad for *you*. And it's unnatural."

She blinks, taken aback. "You're mad...for me?"

"I'm disgustingly, disturbingly mad for you, to the point that I've started questioning my own fucking sanity," I grit out.

Biting her lip, she regards me with a curious expression on her face.

"This was your plan all along, wasn't it? Get me so fucking obsessed with you I cannot function anymore."

"Marlowe—"

"I was right from the beginning. You wanted my ring on your finger, and you cast a spell to get it."

"M—"

"Now that you got me panting after you like a dog in heat, you're withholding everything from me until I marry you. How Boleynian of you, Minnie. Classic strategy," I add wryly. "What do you want? My money? My family name? My—"

"You. I want you."

That stops my tirade. I swallow, suddenly overcome by a wave of emotions I cannot recognize. Heat climbs up my neck and I avert my gaze.

"Well, congratulations. Your spell worked. You'll have your ring and your marriage," I say uncomfortably.

She snorts.

"Thank you, Marlowe. That sounds like the most romantic proposal a girl can get."

I turn sharply to her.

"You wanted a ring, you'll have a ring," I tell her. "We're going shopping at the end of the week."

That surprises her. She stares at me for a few long seconds before she clears her throat.

"You still want to bond with me even though I might have put a spell on you?" she asks uncertainly.

I glare at her. That's as much of an admission as I'm going to get, isn't it?

"I want to fuck you, Minnie. If a marriage certificate is what you need to put out, I'll give it to you."

"You're crass." Her nostrils flare.

"I'm honest. I want to fuck you," I murmur as I let my fingers trace the contour of her waist until I reach the curve of her hip. Spreading my palm over her ass, I pull her closer to me so she can feel what she does to me. She's turned me into a fool ruled by his baser needs, and she needs to take responsibility for it—spell or no spell.

"I want to have you on my bed. Naked. Although..." I pause, letting my gaze roam over her glorious body. "A bed isn't that necessary."

She gulps down.

"I want to fuck you long and hard to make up for all the restless nights I spent going mad over you but with no relief in sight."

"T-that sounds like a y-you problem," she whispers, her tongue peeking out to wet her lips.

"And when you're my wife, it will be *your* problem, Minnie." I chuckle.

She blushes furiously and tries to push me away, turning her head so she looks anywhere but at me.

"I think you're still confused from your injuries," she mumbles. "I need to go..."

"You're not going anywhere until you tell me the truth, Minnie."

"What you're saying is absurd, Marlowe. And your language is so sordid and—"

"You think fucking is sordid?" I raise a brow.

"I mean... The word f-f-fuck is sordid," she murmurs in a barely audible voice.

"Ah, Minnie. I'll enjoy fucking that coyness out of you."

"Please stop saying f-f-uck..." she whispers, her eyes squeezed shut.

"Why? It's what married people do. And you want to marry me, don't you?" I ask in a smooth voice. "That's why you bewitched me. Because you want *me*, don't you, Minnie?"

"Yes, but..."

Aha, there it is. I smile to myself.

"But?"

"I should go. You're unwell and this is quite inappropriate and..."

"Why is this inappropriate, Minnie, when fucking is all we'll be doing? Morning, noon, afternoon, evening, night... Maybe a few times in between," I muse aloud.

"T-that many times?" she stammers, her eyes growing wide with shock. "Is that even possible?"

"I don't know. I haven't tried it." I shrug. "But I'm looking forward to." I wink at her.

She reddens even more, so much so, she resembles a cute little tomato that I wouldn't mind taking a bite out of.

"You're trying to scandalize me."

"If you think *this* is scandalous, my little heathen, wait until you're mine," I murmur seductively. "I have so many plans for you." Leaning in, I whisper, "And they all involve a variation of the word fuck."

She sputters.

"Marlowe!" she cries out. "I... I need to go. Please let me go," she says and renews her efforts to evade me.

I smile at her.

"Why should I?" I raise a brow. "I still have not extracted a confession out of you."

She blinks repeatedly, her eyes roaming around to find an exit. When she realizes she cannot escape, she comes up with the most outrageous excuse.

"I... I haven't washed today!" she suddenly says. "I'm *veryyy* smelly, Marlowe. I wouldn't want to offend your sensitive nose with my stench."

The little heathen... My lips curl up at her measly attempt to escape.

Leaning in, I touch the tip of my nose to the curve of her neck, inhaling her scent.

"I like your smell. A hint of spice. A hint of flowers," I drawl. "Soon, there will be a hint of me, too. Right here," I whisper as I place my finger atop her pulse point. "And here..." I continue, trailing up her neck until I skim the surface of her lips. "You'll be smelling of me everywhere, Minnie."

"I..." She trails off as she panics. "I ate garlic," she bursts out. Her hands cup my cheeks as she brings me to the same level as her face. Opening her mouth, she blows rancid air toward me.

I immediately wince and take a step back.

"Good grief, what's that odious stench?" I curse as I squeeze my eyes shut and rub my nose.

That's not even garlic. It's something so putrid I get full-body shivers from it.

Fuck.

"I'm sorry," she squeaks as she dashes up the stairs.

I'm left gasping for air as I watch her retreating form, yet something solidifies in my mind.

Her breath didn't smell before. I'm certain of it. Otherwise, I wouldn't have been fantasizing about devouring her lips the entire time we've been carrying this conversation. I was literally salivating for a small taste.

But that only proves my point. She must have done it on purpose to end this conversation.

There's something unnatural about Minnie. And I aim to find out exactly what.

A FEW HOURS LATER, and instead of working, I find myself going down a rabbit hole investigating witchcraft. The historical documentation goes back centuries, but I don't have time for that.

I need something more recent. Something I can use to prove with certainty that Minnie is a witch.

There are countless pages for *covens.* Apparently, they still have those. They're public, too.

Of course the main issue is that these are only wannabe witches who *think* they have powers.

I want the real deal, not some delusional people chanting *hocus-pocus.*

These websites even have membership sign-ups for a monthly fee.

I scoff aloud.

Witches my ass.

I resume my search, and by some stroke of luck, I end up on a forum for witches based in the state of New York.

Although the entries are mostly about medicinal plants and incantations, there seems to be a common thread. One poster, a certain *SarahJ,* is the one answering all questions posed on the forum. From the replies, it appears she's got quite the loyal following, with some referring to her as a *Grand Master*—whatever that may be.

Hmm.

I click on her profile and look at all the posts she's interacted with. It takes me a few minutes to comb through the useless herbal threads to get to some more interesting bits.

There's one post asking about divination, to which Sarah replies by giving her email address and encouraging the poster to get in contact.

I jot down the address.

I scroll more and find a different post talking about a love potion.

Aha.

I knew there must be something about Minnie's food that makes me lose my mind. She must have put the potion inside of it, making it so damn delicious that I can't help but consume enormous quantities of it until I'm absolutely mad for her.

The thread is talking about the different ingredients needed for a love spell, and it appears that once more, Sarah is the expert on the matter.

That settles it.

Opening my email, I type out a small inquiry, asking her if she'd be willing to meet me because I think I'm the victim of magic and I'd appreciate any help in combating it. I mention that money is not an issue.

I click send.

Then I continue to study these modern-day witches and what they claim they can do, looking for any patterns similar to Minnie.

It's not even five minutes later that I get a reply from Sarah.

Her email is short and to the point.

She writes that magic should always be performed for good and when someone consents to it. If I have not consented to anything and I feel that I'm under attack, she's willing to help me.

I shoot her back an email, telling her I have not consented to anything and embellish it a little by claiming I fear for my life after an eerie accident that may have had supernatural influences. I also tell her that I suspect my girlfriend is the witch who caused all of this and that I'm having an existential crisis about our relationship —dramatic, I know, but it does the job.

She replies within a few minutes, saying she'd be happy to meet with me. But for her investigation to be fruitful, she requires a personal effect of my girlfriend's so she can try to see if there are any traces of magic. After a little back and forth, she tells me that anything Minnie has worn for a significant period of time works, or even better, if I can acquire it, a strand of her hair.

I tell her I'll do my best to get it.

We exchange a few more emails and soon I have a location, date, and time. To my great surprise, she offers to meet me tomorrow, in the city, at noon.

I thank her and confirm the meeting before closing my computer as I contemplate how to get a strand of Minnie's hair.

Good Lord, look at me now. A few months ago, I would have gone to my grave swearing up and down that witchcraft is not real; that we live in an age of scientific advancements not one of superstitions. Even with my slight addiction to *Supernatural*—which I've barely been able to watch because my thoughts have been too wrapped up in Minnie—I would have never imagined I'd be in my current position.

My mind is clouded with doubt and confusion, to the point where I don't know what reality is anymore.

Of course I'm not about to blindly believe this Sarah lady, since she might very well be a crook, too. But I'll reserve my judgments until I meet her tomorrow.

Now onto getting that strand of hair.

Getting up, I go and take a shower. I put on a pair of sweatpants and a shirt and head downstairs.

It's almost five in the afternoon, which means Minnie should have prepared dinner already.

As I head down the stairs, I'm surprised to see that my pain has greatly subsided. In fact, compared to the soreness in my throat when I first woke up in the hospital, now I barely feel anything.

I probe at my ribs. They're tender but not nearly as painful. My muscles too are no longer as sore and I can move my arms with ease.

Odd.

I reach the kitchen, and Minnie is not there.

Nor is my dinner.

"Minnie!" I bellow. It doesn't matter that I'm about to consume again something that's likely contaminated with witchcraft. At this point, I'm so addicted to her food, it's pure blasphemy to miss a meal. Even stranger is the fact that she's not in the kitchen when she's *always* there at this time.

Sure, she might still be peeved with me. But that's almost at the back of my mind.

My intrusive thoughts tell me she might be sick. She might be experiencing side effects from the accident—well, accident is a misnomer seeing that we both got injured fighting off those sentinels.

I pivot, ready to go to her room when a sudden thought stops me.

She had a bandage around her head yesterday.

It was nowhere to be seen today, nor did she display any visible injuries.

I frown. Why didn't I think about this earlier?

Because you were too damn focused on resisting her siren's song to think of anything else.

Alas, not for the first time, I do seem to be rather scatterbrained and weak-willed whenever I'm in her presence. And she knows it, too, because she's always taking advantage of it.

Determined to get to the bottom of this, I stride toward her room.

"Minnie!" I call out again.

Before I reach her room, she opens the door and comes out, her arms crossed over her chest, her lips flattened in disapproval. She's changed out of her maid uniform and she's now wearing a pair of jeans that fit snugly over her hips—maddeningly so, might I add—and a white sweater.

"Why are you yelling?" she asks me with a pointed look.

"You weren't in the kitchen."

"Am I supposed to *always* be in the kitchen?"

I frown at her displeased tone.

"Well, yes. It's your job."

Her nostrils flare as she takes a step toward me.

"Is that all I'm good for? Cooking? Cleaning?"

I blink, the vehemence in her voice taking me aback.

"Well, you *are* my maid," I reply, scratching the back of my head.

She stomps her foot loudly as she releases an aggravated humph.

"Marlowe! Why do you even want to bond with me if all I'm good for is being your maid?"

"That's not what I said." I put a hand up.

"You just said I'm your maid so it's my job to clean and cook."

"Exactly. When we marry, you'll be my wife. Of course it will still be your job to cook. I'll take over the cleaning since I'm much better at that. But you'll have other duties too."

"Like what?" She raises a brow.

"Like warming my bed." I give her one of my charming smiles.

It doesn't do the job.

She glares at me.

"So cooking and warming your bed. That's all?"

I take a moment to reply as I think about what the best course of action is. Clearly, she's not satisfied with my answers so far, and the last thing I want to do is piss her off.

I need a strand of hair from her.

I'm also quite hungry. And if she's mad at me, she won't make me anything to eat.

"Well..." I start, clearing my throat.

"Well?" She taps her foot against the floor.

She's wearing the platform sneakers I bought her, which make her slightly taller. But she's still a little tidbit who's awfully cute when angry.

"You're highly entertaining," I finally say. I nod to myself—yes, that's good. "You provide me with daily amusement."

She gawks at me.

"Am I a circus animal to provide you with *daily amusement*?" she asks in outrage.

"Minnie." I sigh. "You're misconstruing everything I'm saying."

"Then say better things," she cries out.

"What do you want me to say? Tell me and I'll say it," I add, hoping to pacify her somehow.

My stomach rumbles. I was too lost in my research that I forgot to eat. It's been hours. And I don't want any other food than hers. I've gotten too used to it, and switching to anything else will be a huge downgrade. Nah, scratch that. Eating anything other than food cooked by Minnie would be both a tragedy and a betrayal—both to my stomach and to her.

"That's not the point, Marlowe. You have to say it because you *feel* it, not because I tell you to say it. Otherwise, it's not genuine."

My lips flatten in contemplation.

"I'm not good with words," I mutter under my breath.

"What's that?" she asks, taking a step forward.

"I don't know what to say because I've never had to say something like this before," I say with a sigh. "I don't know what you women like or what you want to hear."

"The truth," she simply states. "I want to know that you value me for more than the services I provide to you. Because anyone can do that."

"Now wait a moment," I interrupt her. "That's not true. No one can cook the way you do. No one can make me smile the way you do. And certainly no one can make me overlook my duties the way you do."

She flutters her lashes in disbelief.

"Thank you. The first two are positive. But the third... I'm not sure how it can be a good thing that I make you overlook your duties."

"But don't you see?" I grit out, exasperated. "I'm someone very set in my ways. I never stray from my routine. No one could make me do that—except you."

She's still staring at me, so I continue, trying my best to see things from my perspective.

"You're lively and cheerful and you find joy in the smallest things, which in turn makes *me* find joy them, too. I've never had that before," I admit. "You're like a ray of sunshine that's snuck through the grids of my window and I'm doing my damn hardest to trap it inside and never let it go."

She's quiet for moments on end as she regards me. I'm almost sweating thinking I might have said something wrong—again.

But then she speaks.

"That might be the nicest thing you've ever said to me," she murmurs.

My lips slowly spread into a smile.

Coming toward me, she raises herself on the tips of her toes and presses her lips against my cheek.

My heart stops in my chest.

I gulp down nervously.

Her lips linger on my cheek, and I have to fight against myself to not pull her into my arms and ravish her right then and there.

"Let's make dinner," she whispers as she leans back. Fuck. I've never in my life heard more erotic words than that.

I'm frozen on the spot, unable to find my words. But as she turns to go downstairs, I reach out and pluck a fallen strand of hair from her sweater.

She doesn't notice it, to my great relief.

But once the smell of food infiltrates my nose, I forget about everything else.

I should have asked her about her injuries—well, nonexistent injuries. But how can I ruin this dynamic when she smiles at me and hands me my bowl of food?

And I, like the poor peasant that I am, take it with both arms, worship dripping from my gaze.

A while later, my stomach thanks me. My brain, however, keeps berating me for becoming a mindless fool around her.

Alas, I don't think there's any cure for that.

TWENTY-THREE

AS I GET ready to leave for the meeting with the elusive SarahJ, Minnie almost knowingly awaits me in the hallway. Arms crossed across her chest, she looks at me suspiciously.

Her strand of hair, nestled inside a small vial in my pocket, bores a hole through my clothes as she studies me from head to toe.

"Where are you going?" she demands to know.

"Out. I have business to take care of," I answer glibly as I pass by her.

I barely take a step before she jumps in front of me, her brows drawn together in a frown.

"You never go out, Marlowe," she notes. "So where are you going?"

Damn it. Of course she knows my patterns by now and the fact that I rarely go out.

"I have some business to attend to. You may not believe it, but I still work daily."

"I don't believe you."

"I didn't ask you to believe me. I just stated the facts."

She narrows her eyes at me.

"I'm coming with you," she says after a moment.

"No. You'll do no such thing. This meeting is with men. A lot of men. I will not have them become obsessed with you. I happen to be recovering from grave injuries, as you recall. I cannot be out there fighting legions of men," I tell her matter-of-factly.

"I'll wait in the car."

"The answer is no, Minnie. I will not be long. You can clean the downstairs bathroom while I'm away."

I move to leave again, but once more, she stops me.

"That's it? You're leaving just like that?" she asks in disbelief. "No more questions about my witchery? Or those creatures you think you saw? Don't tell me you came to your senses?" She raises a brow.

"Of course I came to my senses. Yesterday was a mere lapse in judgment, and I trust you will forgive me given my incapacitated state?" I smile.

I can tell she wants to pick a fight by the way her upper lip twitches in annoyance. She didn't think I'd give up so easily on my claims, and although she'll never admit what happened at the accident site to my face, she's not above using the topic to stop me from leaving.

Ah, my little heathen. She has no idea how much it pleases me to see her so rattled by my departure. Unfortunately, I do have to go. Otherwise, I would have baited her further with this jealousy she has going on.

It's a big turn-on, what can I say.

Although... Thinking about it, maybe it's a good thing I'm leaving. Getting into a heated argument with her will only lead to one outcome—blue balls. And I've had enough time to realize she's dead serious about the no touching before marriage rule.

I sigh.

Alas, a man can dream, since dreams are all I'll be entertaining until I put that blasted ring on her finger.

"You're serious?" Her voice is tinged with skepticism as she takes a step forward, getting too close to me.

Damn, Minnie. Can't you see I'm suffering over here? A mere whiff of her sweet scent and I'm already sweating.

"Can we just forget that? It's embarrassing. Hear that, creatures and mummies..." I let out a dry laugh.

She stares at me unblinkingly.

Despite her diminutive stature, she can be quite scary.

Scary hot.

Stop it, Marlowe!

It's not the time to think about how hot she is, or how close, or how good she smells, or how good her lips must taste...

Fucking hell!

I take a step back and clear my throat.

"I'll be back shortly," I repeat and move to leave.

To my surprise, she doesn't stop me again. She's rooted to the spot, her eyes on me.

When I get to my driveway, a rental car is waiting for me. I let out a sigh of relief when Minnie doesn't follow me and I plug in the coordinates for the meeting.

It takes me some twenty minutes to get to the meeting location.

To my surprise, it's a legit office in an old brownstone with a huge logo on top of the building: Sarah Jade Potions.

Interesting.

Perhaps witchcraft is not as rare as I might have previously believed, nor as controversial seeing that this woman is flaunting it publicly.

Alas, we're not in the seventeenth century for them to warrant persecution.

Parking my car, I go to the main door and ring the bell.

"Who is it?"

"It's Marlowe Spencer-Astor. We've spoken via email."

A few moments pass before I hear movement on the other side.

Bolts and locks turn, at least five that I can count—odd. Then the door finally opens.

Sarah Jade is a woman in her sixties with white hair and a pair of thick-rimmed glasses perched on her nose. Initially, she's all smiles as she greets me. But as she gets a good look at me, a sour expression appears on her face.

"I'm sorry, I cannot help you," she mutters, ready to close the door in my face.

I slide my foot forward to stop the door from closing.

"Why? You said you'd help me when we talked," I say slowly, my attention on her to see what's brought on this sudden change in behavior.

"T-that was before," she mumbles. "I cannot have you in my home. I'm sorry."

"What are you talking about? If this is about money, I'm willing to pay for the consultation. In fact, I'll pay double."

She shakes her head.

"I cannot welcome your kind in my home," she repeats.

"My kind?" I frown.

"You're too...tainted," she whispers.

My eyes widen. Can she sense that I have blood on my hands? If that's so, then she's remarkably intuitive. That only strengthens my resolve to get her opinion on my dilemma.

"I will not hurt you," I tell her in the most non-threatening voice I can muster. "I mean no harm. I'm just seeking information. I brought the strand of hair," I say and remove the vial from my pocket.

She purses her lips.

"I'll pay triple," I continue.

She doesn't budge.

"Four times. This is really important, Mrs. Jade. I wish to know if I'm under any spell."

"Four times?" She bites her lip.

I nod.

"Wait here," she mentions.

The wooden floors in her house creak under her heavy steps. I stay where she instructed me, not wanting to cause her any distress that might make her unwilling to help—more than she already is.

A few minutes pass, and she comes back.

She pulls the door wide open, and I note she's carrying a small bowl in her hands.

Dipping her fingers inside, she wets them in a clear solution. She splashes me with the liquid from head to toe, going around me three times and chanting something in what appears to be Latin.

"You may come in. But you may not stay longer than ten minutes," she eventually says.

I suppose ten minutes will do.

I follow her inside and she leads me to the back of the house. The entire atmosphere is eerie, if I do say so myself. The scent of incense is strong, almost clogging my nostrils. The hallway is full of antiques, a tall rusty clock, a table that has seen better days, and a bunch of Victorian photographs.

Eerie, as I said.

The deeper I head into the house, though, the more I feel a tightness in my chest—as if something seeks to drive me out.

I take a deep gulp of air and try to focus on my surroundings.

There are shelves of books everywhere. Cracked, leather spines with foreign titles. In the middle of the room there's a case with a large vellum book inside. It's half open, and curiosity gets the best of me as I step forward to take a look.

There are colorful illustrations around the edges depicting thorny roses and some odd symbols. The letters have the distinct flourish of the early medieval days. There are two drawings, one on each page, and they both depict an apocalyptic scene. The first one shows seven shadowy figures watching the world burn while skeleton-like beings dance on top of people's graves. The second one depicts one man. His face is shadowy, but his eyes are a deep purple. He's standing tall over everyone, his sword ready to cut them down.

"Over here, Mr. Spencer-Astor." Mrs. Jade clears her throat.

I look over my shoulder to see her watching me intently.

"What's this?"

"My family's codex. You don't need to concern yourself with that," she adds snappily. "Follow me."

She continues walking past the library and into a small study. I don't know what I expected, but there are no magic bowls and the like. Instead, there's only a desk with a computer and a sofa. Quite normal for a witch—may even be the most normal part of the house.

She takes a seat at the desk and invites me to do the same opposite her.

I do as she says, and to my surprise, instead of asking me to give her the vial, she opens a drawer and removes a deck of tarot cards from it.

"Touch this for me," she says and hands me the deck.

I lay my hand flat on the top of the deck before she pulls back and starts shuffling. She barely spares me a glance as she places five random cards on the table face down.

She turns the first one.

"Seven of swords. There's a secret in your past. Something that haunts both you and your family. I see dishonesty." She frowns. "But it's not all of your making. There's an external force."

I swallow hard.

I didn't expect her to start with the hard truths.

"Go on," I say.

"Something isn't right." She looks at me pointedly. "It's something that goes against the natural order."

Yeah, I suppose I have done plenty of things that go against the natural order.

"Death. Change. Everything you've known so far has changed. And it will continue to change."

When are we going to talk about the spell? I'm getting bored of this vague shit.

The next three cards are The Tower reversed, The Chariot, and The Magician. She doesn't read them individually. Instead, she just stares at them. Then at me.

"The strand of hair. Hand it to me."

I hand her the vial, but as she takes out the strand of hair, she drops both on the desk. She pulls back, as if burned.

She gets up, her eyes wild as she looks right and left.

"You need to get out of my house. Now."

"I need to know if she's a witch and if I'm under a spell," I grit out. It's what I came here for and I'm not going to leave without that knowledge.

"She's cursed, as are you. The fires of hell would never be enough to cleanse either of you," she spews at me, the hatred in her voice evident.

"What are you talking about?"

"Leave!" she yells, her voice so high-pitched the entire structure of the house starts to shake.

What the...

She walks toward me, backing me out of the study. Her expression is crazed, and there's a strange aura surrounding her.

"I'll give you ten times your fee if you tell me what I came here to find out."

"Get. Out," she bellows. This time, a whoosh of air hits me in the chest. It's not enough to hurt, but it's enough that I feel it.

Sarah's eyes have turned a shade of white as she glares at me with burning hatred.

I back away, continuing to make her offers, but she doesn't even consider them.

"I won't take your dirty money. You're an abomination, that's what you are," she growls in a thick, almost unnatural voice.

Funny, with that timbre, I'd say she's the abomination, not me.

Yet I've seen how well I fare in the face of magic, so I decide to cut my losses. She's not going to answer any of my questions. But before I can leave, I quickly dash back to the study and grab the strand of hair. Even I know better than to trust a witch with something like this.

Sarah doesn't seem to take my short detour very well, and before I know it, books fly off the shelves as a strong gust of wind accumulates inside the house. It gathers up in the shape of a vortex, and it's aimed right at me.

Oh, fuck.

I duck just as a heavy book is about to hit me in the head.

"Get. Out!" Sarah continues to shout.

With tens of books flying off the shelves and aimed at me, I do my best to dodge them as I run for the exit.

Just my luck, though, as I reach the door, I note that there are a bunch of locks in place.

I start to unlock each of them, but the books keep flying toward my head, the intent to do me harm clear.

They knock against the wooden door with a thud, and I move right and left to avoid being the target.

Sarah comes into view, her hair standing up as if electrified. She glares at me as she does some movements with her hands. A ball of energy emerges from her palms, and I barely manage to pull the last latch and open the door before she decides to throw the blow my way.

But if that's not plenty of surprises for the day, as soon as I open the door, I come face to face with Minnie.

Her expression is dry as she stares at Sarah.

"Business?" She raises a brow as she looks at me.

"Not anymore," I mutter as I take her hand. I try to pull her away, but she won't budge.

Sarah chases after me, but as she sees Minnie, she stops in her tracks.

Minnie glares at her.

"She's crazy," I whisper. "We need to leave. Now."

"This is *my* man," Minnie states pointedly.

Sarah takes a step back.

Her hair is back to normal, and her eyes slowly return to their original shade.

She squares her shoulders and cowers back, her expression now one of fear.

"I apologize," she murmurs subserviently.

What the fuck?

"Please forgive me," Sarah continues, her knees bending until they hit the ground. She bows in front of Minnie, hitting her forehead against the wooden floor in a kowtow.

Double what the fuck!

At the same time, I have to admit that Minnie claiming me as her man is hot as fuck. Although now's not the time to be horny. A witch just tried to kill me and my almost lover seems to be a psycho stalker.

Hot. My stalker, that is. Not almost being killed by a witch. That kind of sucks.

Minnie nods at her before finally allowing me to draw her away from the house.

Sarah immediately rushes to lock the door after us, the sound of the bolts echoing in the air.

We don't speak until we reach the car, after which I'm compelled to get an explanation out of her.

"How the hell did you follow me here?" I ask when we're alone.

She gives me a bored look as she points at the back of the car. "I hid in the trunk."

I stare at her. Then I stare some more.

My ingenious little heathen. I should be outraged. But I would have done the same if I were her so I can't exactly blame her.

"You hid in my trunk?" I feign outrage.

Good girl, Minnie. Taking care of your man, as you should.

Perhaps I should be slightly disturbed that she would do that, but at this moment all I feel is a strong pang of lust.

Damn, she's hot.

"Of course," she quips in a sweet voice. "I wouldn't be a good girlfriend if I didn't support you in your business endeavors, right?" She has the gall to bat her lashes at me innocently.

Blood rushes to my cock.

"And you're the most supportive girlfriend, aren't you?" I ask wryly.

"Well," she murmurs as she bites her lip. "Any moment now I'll be your fiancée, no?"

Another bat of her lashes.

Oh, fuck! She must have thought I went shopping for rings behind her back.

"Right...of course."

"But really, Marlowe, what were you doing here? That old woman is cray-cray and a fanatic," she says.

I shrug.

"And how do you know she's a fanatic?" I raise a brow.

"Because I saw the books inside her house. They were all manuals on demon hunting."

"Demon hunting?" I raise a brow.

"People like her assume anyone with abilities *is* a demon when that's the furthest from the truth. But it is what the human church has indoctrinated its followers to believe. It's all the fault of that Vatican," she mutters under her breath.

That's surprising. And perhaps the first real piece of information Minnie has willingly given me.

"And what is the truth?" I inquire.

She smiles.

"There are a lot of beings in this universe that have powers, Marlowe. But it is wrong to assume they're all bad. Certainly, some are. But not all."

"What about you then? Are you good or bad, Minnie?"

I already know she has powers. She's aware I know, too. We're just pretending that's not the case because she's not ready to tell me yet.

If I were a better man, perhaps I'd wait until she's comfortable telling me.

But I'm not.

I'm a greedy bastard who needs to know everything there is about her. And if she's not yet forthcoming... Then my quest is not over yet.

"Oh, Marlowe." She chuckles. "Depending on who you ask, I'm perhaps the baddest."

"Worst," I correct.

"Baddest," she repeats, shaking her head. "I'm so bad, I need to add four more letters to the word to emphasize how bad I am."

I raise a brow at her. But then I laugh when I realize she's joking.

We both laugh until she suddenly stops. She shakes her head and sighs.

"I didn't put a spell on you, all right? I was actually surprised when you didn't find me irresistible from the first time you saw me. It was...refreshing." She smiles. But then she leans forward, her eyes on mine. "If you find me irresistible now, it's all on you. There's nothing supernatural about it. You want me."

"Is that so?" I croak.

"You want me," she repeats. "You said so yourself. Even if you claim you only want to sleep with me, I suppose that's all right too. Because I know that deep down, you care for me."

"You're that sure, eh?"

"Yes. I'm very sure. It's why I've chosen you to be my bonded male."

"And here I thought it was my good looks and my money."

"I suppose those come secondary, as long as you buy me cookies, which you haven't done in one day. You're slacking, Marlowe!

Soon, people will realize that I'm not a gold plower and my reputation will be destroyed." She feigns a scandalized expression.

I smile and shake my head.

"I think you mean gold digger," I add, amused.

"Same thing. Don't change the subject. I require my daily tribute, preferably in boxes of a dozen of each flavor."

"Forgive me, your highness. It is awfully bad of me to have forgotten to pay my tribute. I'll rectify that right away. How many flavors do you require?"

"I suppose I can be satisfied with three," she answers pensively.

"Thirty-six cookies? My, for a tiny thing, you surely can eat a lot."

"Of course," she quips, patting her belly. "There's always room in here for your daily tribute."

I stare at her stomach. Then swallow hard. I don't think she realizes where my thoughts are straying in this moment, or the fact that I'm thinking of an entirely different tribute that would fit inside of her.

Fucking hell.

I move uncomfortably in my seat in an attempt to keep the lust at bay.

Minnie, though, is oblivious as she continues to chat away about her favorite cookie flavors.

"Right. Let's go buy cookies," I declare. Anything to help me take my mind off the many ways in which I could fill her up with other things.

She beams at me.

As we drive, she appears deep in thought for moments on end. Eventually, she speaks.

"You're a very nice man, Marlowe." She pauses. "For a killer."

"I'll have you know I have a moral compass too," I interject. "I don't—"

She turns to me and places her finger against my lips. Then she shakes her head.

I should probably pay attention to the road. But that's very hard to do when my dick is still crying for her attention, my heart is hammering in my chest, and my eyes don't even want to blink because that might mean a second of not seeing her.

"Don't tell me again how you wanted to kill me. You'll ruin the mood," she murmurs softly.

"But it would have been a special death," I protest.

"You and your special death." She sighs and leans back in her seat. "See, now you've ruined the mood."

Unfortunately, my mood is anything but ruined...

"Minnie! I would have cherished your dead body!" I say, though retrospectively, that didn't come out right.

She gives me a stern look.

"I'd rather you cherish me alive," she adds drily.

"I think that can be arranged."

Her brows go up as she looks at me in surprise.

Then she smiles.

"I'll buy you *four* dozen cookies," I say, needing to keep that smile on her face.

She clasps her hands together in a sign of happiness. Her smile widens, too, and the entire car becomes bathed in the pure light she emanates. And the only thing I can do is bask in it.

Of course, by the end of the day, I'm once more too enthralled by her to interrogate her on her origins or ask her about Sarah's behavior when she saw her.

And that's how I realize it.

I'm bewitched all right. But it's of my own making.

That doesn't mean I'm not still curious to know what she is. But that can wait until I get some distance from her so I can think straight again.

TWENTY-FOUR

IF YOU'RE THINKING I've become an idiot ever since I met Minnie, you would be correct.

The more I should be suspicious of her and question her about her background, the more I end up foolishly acceding to all her wishes. Which is also how I currently find myself watching an episode of *Supernatural* with her while she's munching away on chocolate cookies.

She's already eaten two dozen of them!

But this is the least I can do after our failed shopping trip at the most illustrious jewelry shops.

When I'd said I'd get her a ring, I didn't realize she would be so hard to please. So far, she's been very accommodating and she's never once complained about the things I bought her.

But as soon as marriage rings came into question, she became impossible to please.

I first took her to Cartier. She found nothing to her liking. Then, we went to Tiffany's. Once more, nothing impressed her. We went to a string of other luxury shops with no success.

"I want something unique," she said as we came back home empty-handed. "Something of *your* making, not of anyone else's."

Great. Now she wants me to become a master jeweler as well. For fuck's sake, it's like she enjoys torturing me with blue balls. By the time I learn to make a goddamn ring, I'll likely die a goddamn virgin.

But do you think I told her no?

Of course not.

I assured her I'd find a way to personally make her ring. Because I'm an idiot. That's why.

I've already ordered all the necessary equipment, so now it's only a matter of learning how to craft it.

"You know, this show didn't get demons completely wrong," she mentions as she slurps on her Coke.

"That so?" I raise a brow.

We're currently huddled on the floor in my spare bedroom that acts as a movie theater. There's a huge TV with high quality speakers that ensures the perfect immersive experience—after all, how could I ever leave my house for a movie? Absurd.

We're sharing a blanket, though that wasn't the best idea seeing how tempting she is, even when she licks her fingers clean of the cookie crumbs—yes, I've officially lost it.

To my surprise, watching *Supernatural* was *her* idea. She wanted to see why it was my favorite TV show, and we've now binged almost an entire season in the span of three days. That's quite a feat.

On the downside, however, that means I've spent the last three days in very close quarters with her for hours on end, leading me to make repeated trips to the bathroom for a cold shower.

Alas, at this point, it is what it is—as much as it pains me to say that.

"Well, there are two ways to become a demon. You're either born one, though those are demons by designation only since they technically have divine origins too. We usually just call them the Sons of Tenebreis. But since they're the ones who control the other type of demons, they mostly get lumped in together," she explains matter-of-factly, popping another cookie in her mouth.

I stare at her.

"Right," I mumble as if that's common knowledge. "And what's the other type of demon?"

"The second type of demons are the made demons. That usually happens when a corrupted soul refuses to move on after life. The Sons of Tenebreis swoop in and form a thrall bond with them after which the demons go on a rampage."

"I see. And how is it similar to *Supernatural*?"

"Well, like in *Supernatural*, at first, the corrupted souls are amorphous, sort of like that smoke. But that's only a low-level demon. The only way for them to gain strength is to possess other mortals and corrupt them before they ultimately consume their souls. The more souls a demon consumes, the higher level it becomes, until it finally manages to take shape. Of course the intermediary shapes are rather monstrous. But the highest-level demons can take a humanoid shape. It's quite scary, really."

"Of course." I nod. "And where did you learn this?"

"In school. Like everyone else," she quips blithely before she realizes her error. She slaps a hand over her mouth and turns to look at me in horror. "Oops," she whispers.

I chuckle.

"I never learned that in school. It must have been a cool school that you went to."

"Not...really..." She smiles awkwardly.

"So you learned about demons in school. What else?"

"I..." She gives me a sheepish look. "I shouldn't have said that."

"Why?" I raise a brow. "Because it might give me insight into what you are?"

"Well..." She bites her lip. "It's not that I don't want to tell you, Marlowe. I really do. But I know that when you find out the truth about me, everything will change."

"Why?" I probe again, turning to look at her intently. "I

already know the sentinels incident was real." She opens her mouth to speak, but I press my fingers against her lips. "Don't try to deny it again. After what happened at Sarah's house, I'm more certain than ever that I didn't imagine that."

She sighs.

"You're right. You didn't imagine it," she finally admits.

"And the man in the snow?" I raise a brow, though I have an inkling of who it might have been.

"My brother," she confirms with a sheepish smile. "He visits me every now and then to give me information."

"What information?"

She presses her lips together.

"He tells me if the sentinels are close or not. And if they are... He helps me fight them."

"He was there, too, wasn't he? At the scene of the accident."

She nods.

"I should have called him earlier to take care of it, but I panicked because you were there too. And I was reluctant to use my powers because they act as a beacon to the authorities that are after me." She pauses. "I put you in danger. I'm sorry," she says with a sigh.

I wave a hand.

"Nothing happened to me. But I distinctly remember a blue glow around you when you were fighting the sentinels. What's that?"

"My energy signature. I can only use a small percentage of my powers without detection. I'm still not sure if the amount I used that time sent them a location signal, but seeing that we haven't had any visitors since, I'm going to assume I'm fine. For now."

"You have powers..." I trail off.

I'd already intuited as much, but to have her confirm it? It's quite unsettling. Not because she has powers, but because people with powers exist. That and witches, demons, and mummy-like sentinels.

I'm still wrapping my head around that.

Minnie is not the damsel in distress I originally thought her to be, but that doesn't diminish my attraction to her one bit. In fact, I find myself even more enthralled with her the more she shares about herself.

She's not human. She has powers.

Fuck. My girlfriend is a fucking supergirl.

I don't think I've ever been more aroused in my life.

"What can you do?" I find myself asking.

She gives me a hidden smile.

"Well, normally... There isn't much I cannot do. My family belongs to the ice clan, so my powers are predominantly based around ice."

"Is that why you're never cold?"

She nods. "My body temperature is higher than most. I can withstand the most extreme temperatures with little to no discomfort. I can also create and manipulate ice."

I stare at her in awe. I may hate the cold but damn if this isn't the one instance in which I'm willing to make an exception.

She's a literal ice queen. And she's fucking mine.

Heat climbs up my cheeks and I clear my throat.

"And this?" I say as I trace her forehead. "Did you even have an injury?"

"Yes. But I heal fast." She brings her fingers to her forehead. "I forgot to wear my bandage. Did that give me away?" She giggles.

"A little."

"Here, let me show you," she says and reaches for my set of keys. Using the sharp part of one of the keys, she places it against her arm, denting the skin.

"Wait. You're not supposed to use your powers," I say and stop her.

She shakes her head.

"This is not technically me using my powers. It's as natural to me as breathing is to you," she replies and digs the key again in her arm.

The metal cuts into her skin. At first, it's just a scratch, but as she keeps pushing it into her flesh, blood pools to the surface.

She points her arm at me, letting me see the small gash. In a matter of minutes, it's closed. The skin is once more smooth, with no hint of injury.

"Damn." I whistle.

"You're taking this way better than I expected you to," she adds nervously.

There it is. I can see the worry reflected in her gaze and her body language. She draws back, huddling into herself as if to protect herself from rejection.

Perhaps someone else wouldn't have taken this well. Perhaps I wouldn't have taken it as well if she had told me from the first—I might not even have believed her.

"Minnie, you're just confirming what I've been suspecting for weeks. I suppose I've had time to get used to the idea, though what you're telling me now is nothing short of extraordinary. Are there more people like you?"

"My brother."

"That's a given. Besides your brother."

"There are many of us," she says, but she doesn't elaborate.

I suppose I can let her off the hook for now. I'm pleased enough she's starting to trust me with information. Pressuring her won't solve anything.

Good Lord! I cannot believe how magnanimous I am. Old me would have had her strapped to the chair in my basement to torture the information out of her.

"You're really not put off by what I told you so far?" she asks again, wariness entering her features. "Others were not so kind in the past."

"You're lucky you came across me," I tell her proudly. "See, not only am I handsome, rich, and smart. But I'm also open minded and accepting. You got yourself a great deal."

"You forgot arrogant," she mumbles under her breath, but I detect a hint of a smile.

"That's a given," I scoff. "Though I prefer to call it confidence. Arrogance oftentimes lacks the substance, whereas I'm quite sure of my attributes."

"Of course." She chuckles. "You're just the epitome of perfection."

"Do you doubt me?" I feign outrage.

"No, no, of course not. You are, indeed, the perfect human," she adds in a mocking, deferential tone.

"You should be glad for it since it reflects on you, too. A perfect human such as myself could only choose another perfect being to be his partner. It's no wonder I never bothered with other women, since none of them were you."

She blinks at me, her cheeks slowly reddening.

"That is..." She swallows. "I'm grateful," she murmurs. "I've been worrying endlessly about how you'd take this, or whether you would shun me or not," she admits in a low voice.

I narrow my eyes at her.

"Who shunned you in the past, Minnie?" I demand rather harshly.

She shakes her head.

"It doesn't matter now. It's long in the past. But not all people are as tolerant as you are. It's something not exclusive to the human race, though your history is rife with it. Intolerance is something rather...innate. After all, the gods themselves are intolerant of most other beings," she adds carefully.

"Was it a man who shunned you?" I probe, not wanting to let this go.

"It doesn't—"

"Was it Lucien?"

Her eyes widen.

"W-where have you heard that name?" she whispers, her expression shocked.

I grab my phone and pull up the picture of *Mina* and Lucien and show it to her. My body is tense as I wait for her reply. Though I've kept this at the back of my mind, it's been something that's been bothering me from the beginning.

But now that I know for sure that she's not human, that means she could very well have a longer lifespan, especially with those healing abilities of hers. That in turn suggests it *could* be her in the picture and not a distant relative as I previously thought.

And that only makes my blood boil further.

Biting her lip, she takes the phone from me with trembling hands. She studies the picture for moments on end, but her expression betrays everything.

There's disbelief. But also something else...

Sadness.

Tears rim her lashes and I fear she might cry any moment now.

Taking a long and deep breath, she gives me back my phone and closes her eyes.

"This is you, isn't it?"

She gives me a small nod.

"Yes," she whispers.

"But you look the same." I frown.

"I'm far older than I look, Marlowe."

"How old?"

"Four thousand five hundred and fifty-eight years."

She watches closely for my reaction. But I don't betray anything—I'll have time to examine this conversation later. For now, I need to know the most important thing.

"Did you love this man?" I ask, and the words cause physical pain to reverberate through my body.

She smiles sadly.

"I did. But he's dead. Long gone. Ashes to the wind..."

The urge to smash something to pieces is unbearable. But I

bottle it all up since I need more information. I need to know exactly *who* he was to her.

"It says here you were his betrothed. How are you still untouched, then?" My voice comes out harsh, but even a saint would crumble in front of this insane jealousy I'm feeling.

"I said I never slept with another male before," she answers softly. "I didn't say I never loved one."

I stare at her, my cheek twitching. Somehow, the thought of her loving someone else in the past is more painful than the thought of her sleeping with another.

Because she should only love *me*. Not some random dude from the last century. She should only think of *me*.

"What happened?" I grind out.

"He died of consumption," she mentions tersely.

Then it dawns on me.

"He's that soulmate you kept talking about."

The realization cuts me deeper than I would have imagined.

"He is, isn't he?" I demand when there's no forthcoming answer.

"Marlowe, I think we should talk about something else. This clearly upsets you and—"

"No. We'll talk about this. Now. I don't care a damn whit if you're not human. But I do care that you apparently have another man in your past. Someone you *loved*," I spit the word love as if it were the most disgusting thing in the world.

And it is.

Because it belongs to someone else.

Someone who is not me.

She looks away.

"You said you were waiting for him. Why? How?"

"That was... It was to make you jealous," she stammers.

"Is that so?" I raise a brow. "I don't believe it."

"But it was... Marlowe, he's long gone. You don't need to overreact..."

"Overreact?" I echo as I get to my feet. "You just told me you loved another man. *My* fiancée told me she was in love with someone else in the past. How would you want me to react?"

Her lips tremble as she stares at me.

"Let me guess. He proposed to you because you wouldn't put out for him either."

"Marlowe!" she cries out, her mouth dropping open in shock. "That's uncalled for."

"Is it?" I snicker.

"He was a sick man. I cared for him and we fell in love. He died. That's the end of the story. I don't know why you're making this into something bigger than it has to be."

"Don't you know? Weren't you the one who gave me the cold shoulder treatment for weeks because you thought I'd slept with hundreds of women?"

"But this is different," she protests.

"No. It's not. You were jealous at the thought of other women having laid claim to my body. I'm jealous because I now *know* another man laid claim to your heart," I grit out.

A tear slips down her cheek, and immediately, I regret my tone.

"This is why I didn't want to tell you," she whispers. Her voice is muffled, as if she's trying to keep the sobs at bay.

Pain strikes in my chest.

"I knew you'd react like this." An audible sob. "I knew you wouldn't...like me anymore."

"Minnie," I whisper and get down on the floor next to her. "Please don't cry. I don't like it when you cry."

"Then why are you making me cry?" she asks in a small voice.

"Because I'm a fucking bastard who deserves a good whipping. And I'm also filled with an insane jealousy that's making me act like a prick."

She sniffles and wipes her nose with her sleeve.

Odd, but even that bit doesn't seem as repulsive as before.

Instead, I only want to punch myself repeatedly for making her feel like this.

"He's gone. You are not. You're here with me, and I *choose* to be here, too," she says in between sobs. "I'm in constant danger of being caught, yet I still *choose* to be here. Doesn't that count for anything?"

I stare at her, anger roaring inside of me and threatening to spill over.

I want to rage at her and ask her why she didn't wait for me like I waited for her—even without knowing she would come.

But there's also that part of me that wants nothing more than to console her.

A battle ensues inside of me and I wonder which side will win. My egotistical side that cannot accept that she'd give her heart to another man, or my other, dormant side, that wants her regardless of it?

I've never given much thought to women before or imagined how the one for me would be like—I never even thought there would be someone to match my idiosyncrasies as well as Minnie does. But if there's one thing I cannot fathom is being secondary in someone's affections.

I want it all or nothing.

I'm ready to tell her that, but as the tears keep spilling down her face, I find that the words will not come out.

A chasm opens in my heart at seeing her hurt, and I realize I'd do anything to comfort her. Even lie.

I tentatively touch her and bring her closer to me. Wrapping my arms around her, I hold her to my chest in a tight hug.

"I'm sorry," I whisper again. "I shouldn't have spoken to you like that."

It seems like forever before her tears finally subside. But now her eyes are red and swollen, and I feel even more like a prick for doing that to her.

"We won't talk about it anymore," I declare, though it's

another lie. Of course we'll be talking about it again, but when she's not as distraught and when I've had some time to gather my own thoughts.

We spend moments in silence, and I just hold her.

Guilt rams into my gut at the way I behaved, yet the jealousy is still there, lurking, ready to poke its ugly head and destroy this moment again.

I fight against myself, struggling to push those feelings away.

Minnie's right. She's here now. In my arms. That Lucien dude is dead and buried. I should focus on the present, not on the past...

I tighten my arms around her.

If Lucien had still been alive, he'd officially be dead again.

Flashes appear in my mind as I think of all the ways I'd kill him —torture him for daring to look at my Minnie, never mind make her fall in love with him.

What does he have that I don't?

My eyes widen as another realization dawns on me.

She stated in no uncertain terms that she loved Lucien. But she's never said the words to me. She's never indicated that she had any deeper feelings for me other than affection.

I scowl.

"Please tell me you're not mad at me, Marlowe," Minnie whispers. "I don't like it when you're upset with me."

"I'm not," I lie. "I'm not mad at you, Minnie."

She leans back and gives me a sad smile.

I school my features so she doesn't see how troubled I am by her confession. Instead, I choose to change the topic.

"Why are the sentinels after you?"

Her brows go up at my question.

"Because I did something bad," she replies. "I'm a wanted criminal." She lets out a dry laugh.

I narrow my eyes at her. Yeah, right, Minnie a criminal. That's the most laughable thing I've ever heard.

"Minnie, I'm a criminal, too. Why would you be afraid to admit that to me of all people?"

She tilts her head as she studies me.

"Because I wanted to live in this illusion for a while longer. I wanted to be normal, to experience normal things... I wanted to be with you," she admits in a soft, vulnerable voice.

My heart squeezes in my chest.

Well, that's certainly a little appeasing—just a little.

"And you *will* be with me. Don't think for a moment that I'm going to let anyone take you from my side."

She *chose* me. That's enough for me to know I'm never letting go of her. I don't care if that fucking Lucien comes back from the grave. I'll just kill him again.

Slowly. Painfully.

She's stuck with me now, for as long as I live—and seeing how she can live forever, I suppose I'll have to find a way to do so, too. I'm not about to die like fucking Lucien and leave her to find another man.

Nope.

No way.

Absolutely never.

And if I do have to die... Well, I suppose I should find out how to kill her too.

I can't believe that killing her is once more on the table, but I'm not going to allow her to *ever* move on. Besides, she's already wanted anyway. It would be a rather poetic death. We'd be like contemporary Romeo and Juliet but with a dash of supernatural sprinkled in the mix.

I smile to myself. Yes, that sounds agreeable.

If I die, I'm taking her to the grave with me.

Minnie shakes her head.

"It's not that easy. You saw what they're capable of, and sentinels are among the weakest beings that will be sent after me. Soon, it will be soldiers. And if that fails..." She trails off, her expression troubled. She gulps down. "If that fails, they'll send Commander Azerius after me, and there's absolutely no one in the entire universe who can defeat him."

"Commander Azerius? Didn't your brother mention him?"

She nods.

"He's the master executioner. One way or another, I *will* meet my end under his sword."

"Now wait a moment. I'm not about to let anything happen to you," I tell her roughly.

Only I am allowed to kill her, and only before I'm about to die myself.

"You're sweet, Marlowe. But there isn't anything you or I can do. We can only enjoy this little time we have together and—"

What the fuck?

"No. I refuse to accept that."

"And yet it will happen all the same. Do you think I haven't tried? I've been on the run for so long, always doing my best to stay under the radar. But they always track me down. Always. And then I have to run again."

"Then I'll run away with you," I state confidently.

That sound like a good plan. We'll run away and get married. I'll finally get to fuck her and once our time runs out, we can pull a Bonnie and Clyde.

Minnie's lips pull up in a sad smile.

"I'd never endanger you like that."

"Minnie," I start, doing my best to keep my emotions in check. "If I have to chain myself to you to prevent you from leaving me, then I'll fucking do that. So don't you even try to tell me you'll leave me because I will not let you."

In this life, or the next—if there is a next.

"But—"

"No buts. You belong to me. You are *mine*. Is that clear? I'm not going to let anyone take you from me."

"But, Marlowe, surely you can see that this is beyond you—"

"I don't care." I shrug. "I don't care who's after you. I don't care what you've done. I don't care about anything other than the fact that you are mine. I've chosen you as my person and no one is going to take you away from me."

"These are powerful beings, Marlowe—"

"I don't care," I repeat. "If they're so powerful, then I'll just have to be more powerful," I state as an idea forms in my mind. "I'll become one of those demons if need be. I kill. They feed on souls. It's not that much of a difference already. Then I'll be able to protect you."

Hmm, that's not a bad idea. My, my, but I'm teeming with good ideas today.

"Don't even joke around with that!" she exclaims in outrage. "Demons are awful, wretched beings, Marlowe. Your soul would be damned for an eternity—"

"I'm already damned, Minnie. What's a little more damning going to do to me?" I mutter drily.

"You're not taking this seriously," she chides.

"Oh, I'm taking this very seriously. I just found out my *fiancée*," I say pointedly, "is being chased around by supernatural beings. Seeing as I'm just a puny human, I'll need to acquire some supernatural powers of my own to protect you. That seems like the logical course of action to me."

"Marlowe!" she cries out. "Please be serious. Demons are not a joking matter. And even if you became one—which you will *not*—you'd just put yourself in danger. Demons are hunted. Just like in that show. They're a pest to be controlled."

"So? I'll just become the king of demons. Like Crowley," I say and flash her my most charming smile.

She smacks my chest and gets up, the blanket falling from her body.

"No. You will not."

"Yes, I will. You've got to admit, it's the best plan so far."

"No," she repeats staunchly.

"Didn't you talk about acceptance until now? Why are you so against demons?"

"Because they're evil. They're malevolent beings and there's not one ounce of goodness in them."

"So?" I shrug. "I'm not that good myself either."

"You are. There's good in you, Marlowe. And becoming a demon would only taint that."

"Minnie," I say and get up.

"No, Marlowe. You will *not* become a demon for me. Promise me."

"No," I reply. "I cannot promise you that."

"You must, Marlowe," she continues, an anxious edge to her voice.

"Why is that so important to you?" I frown.

Her lips flatten as she looks at me, her features tight with worry.

She takes a deep breath and meets my gaze. There's conviction there, one that's shadowed by sadness.

"If you were to become a demon, I'd be forced to kill you," she states in a low, sorrowful voice.

TWENTY-FIVE

SHE'S NOT A WITCH.

She's a fucking demon slayer.

Somehow that's hotter, but it still doesn't help my current dilemma.

I stroke my chin pensively as I stare at the equipment I've set up in my basement. Given how precarious her situation is, I don't want to waste any time in getting her ring and thereby marrying her once and for all.

It's not *just* that I want to fuck her—though that's a good enough reason seeing how I've been struggling to keep my arousal in check lately. No, this is symbolic.

That fucking Lucien didn't get to marry her, which will make *me* her first husband. She'll officially be mine in a way that she was never his.

Yes. A couple of days later and I'm still bitter about that—will likely be for a long time.

In fact, I've photoshopped Minnie out of the picture with Lucien and printed it for my target practice. It's been quite liberating to see him slowly get shredded to pieces.

Petty, I know, since the man's already dead. But if I could, I'd resurrect him just to have the satisfaction of killing him with my own hands. I'm not too sure Minnie would be pleased about that, but she'd have to make a choice—me or him. As it stands, I'm the only one available, which doesn't help with my peace of mind.

No, he deserves to die a second death, preferably with Minnie watching and cheering me on. Now *that* would be perfection. Unfortunately, I'm only left with desecrating his picture since I can't do it to him directly.

Or...

My eyes widen as an idea strikes me.

I get my phone and plug in Giles's number.

"Yes," he answers immediately.

"I need you to find something for me. By the end of the day."

"It's already noon," he answers dryly.

"I don't care. You must find it."

He sighs.

"What is it?"

"The burial place of a certain Lucien de Vitry. He was a soldier in World War II. I believe he died in France in 1945. I reckon he'd be buried somewhere around there."

Silence greets me.

"And why would you want me to find the burial place of a man who died almost a hundred years ago?"

"Just do it, all right?"

Another sigh.

"How did he die?"

"Tuberculosis."

"He might have been buried in an unmarked grave."

My lip twitches. I should have thought about that. But I doubt Minnie would have allowed his body to be thrown into a pit or in an unmarked grave.

"I'm quite certain he was not. You will find it."

"By the end of the day you said?" Giles asks in a bored voice.

"Yes."

"Fine," he reluctantly acquiesces.

"Oh and, Giles? I'll have my jet ready for use. Find a local grave digger to get the remains and have them flown to me here."

"You do realize that's a crime. Both of them. All of them."

"When has a crime stopped me? Or you, for that matter?"

"You've asked me for many strange things in the past, but I think this has to be the most deranged. Why would you need a century-old skeleton, Marlowe?"

"I just do, all right?"

He takes a few seconds to answer.

"Fine. I'll call you when I have something."

"By the end of the day."

"By the end of the day," he confirms.

Satisfied, I turn my attention back to the ring-making machinery. I put on a YouTube tutorial and I get to work. The band is easy enough to make since I already have her ring size from when we went browsing for rings. It's a tiny four and a half.

I spend a few hours polishing the band until the silver gleams. But this is just the base. The hard part is making it *unique* as she wants. To that end, I add an engraving on the inside of the band. I won't win calligraphy contests anytime, but I hope she'll be pleased with my effort.

Marlowe's. She'll get my meaning.

I nod to myself, satisfied. I wonder if this will yield me another kiss? I certainly hope so since I have the battle wounds to prove how much effort I put into this.

It's late afternoon by the time I'm done. It might have sounded easy, but I scraped at least five bands that I messed up. The sixth one seems to be my lucky one.

Yet even then, there's still something missing.

I could always add the most expensive diamond I could find. Perhaps a ruby. But she said *unique* and anyone can buy one of those—well, not anyone, but those who can afford it.

Since she's not impressed with my money aside from my

ability to provide cookies, I suppose she will not be impressed with an expensive jewel either.

I stare at the band for moments on end before I get an idea. Ah, but today is *my* day seeing as how I'm getting one good idea after another.

Doing a quick internet search, I find that it's possible to infuse a jewel with bodily fluids. There are even online kits for it! I quickly order a bunch of them—my ring adventure has shown me I need backups—and check out choosing next day shipping. I'm an impatient bastard after all.

I lean back, a silly smile on my face.

She wanted unique? I'll show her unique! And considering her favorite colors are white and red, I think we have a winner. One half of the jewel will be white, the other red—both bodily fluids courtesy of yours truly.

Giddiness surges inside of me, and I'm already counting down the minutes until the ring will be in her hands.

Ah, but I can almost imagine her expression. She might be confused at first—who wouldn't? But when she realizes I'm gifting her parts of myself—literally—she might swoon. And when she does, I'll be there to catch her like the gallant gentleman I am.

A sudden whooshing sound interrupts me from my—rather marvelous—thoughts.

Turning, I'm surprised to see Minnie's brother.

Well, now that's interesting.

He's wearing the same clothes as before, down to the same shirt and shoes. There's grime and dirt on the sleeves of his shirt, and I could swear I spot some caked blood on his pants.

I wrinkle my nose. I suppose this is where Minnie got her manners from. Alas, under my guidance, she has vastly improved. Perhaps I could recommend her brother a similar coach. Minnie is the only one I'd personally help, but I suppose finding a hygiene coach shouldn't be too hard.

He turns to glare at me.

Maybe I'll do that at our wedding since he doesn't seem to be in such a good mood today.

"Have you heard of knocking?" I raise a brow.

He grunts and comes closer to me.

"Does Minnie know you're here?"

He doesn't answer. He simply stares at me.

"I suppose not," I mutter.

His eyes flash.

And here I thought *I* would win the resting brooding face award. This guy here might just be a contender for first place.

"Well, Mr. Grunting, why are you here?"

This time, he gives me a warning looks. It seems he only knows how to communicate with his eyes. So like the accommodating gentleman that I am, I aim to do the same. After all, I cannot be a bad host to the brother of my future wife, can I?

I take a few steps until I'm in front of him. I widen my eyes and blink rapidly.

He frowns. Then scowls.

I tilt my head and continue to blink some more.

"Are you having a seizure?" he asks, then he tsks. "You humans are so fragile," he swears beneath his breath.

"I suppose your magical powers don't extend to eye reading."

He frowns again.

I roll my eyes to the back of my head.

"Are you mentally challenged?" His tone is serious as he poses the question.

I blink, then widen my eyes.

He narrows his eyes.

I squint in return.

He nods to himself. Placing his hands behind his back, he paces around the basement.

"I know my sister is not too bright, but to get herself a mentally challenged human?" He shakes his head. "And he called you her bodyguard. Absurd."

All semblance of amusement disappears.

"Don't insult her."

He stops and turns. He raises a brow at me.

"Don't insult Minnie," I grit out.

"Ah." He chuckles. "You're not just her human shield, are you?" He shakes his head. "I told her to stop getting involved with humans, but she never listens."

"Why are you here?"

The mere suggestion that she was involved with Lucien makes my blood boil.

He shrugs. "I wanted to know what stops her from leaving. You probably already know she's being hunted, don't you?"

"Yes."

"Then you should also know that staying here is dangerous for her."

"And?"

"She needs to leave," he states, his face expressionless.

"No," I reply firmly. "Minnie isn't going anywhere. She's mine, and I'm marrying her."

He stares at me for a second before he laughs. It's an odd laugh, since there's sound coming from his mouth, but his face is still.

"Marrying her?" He scoffs. "See, not bright. I was right."

"Stop fucking insulting her!"

"Or what? You'll kill me?" he asks in a mocking voice. "Like all those other weakling humans you killed?"

I don't get to ponder on how he knows about that because I'm still pissed about his implication that she's not bright. How the fuck dares he say that? She's his sister, for fuck's sake!

"What if I do?" I mutter under my breath, doing my best to keep my composure when I'd like nothing more than to snap his neck.

"I'd tell you to try." He chuckles. "But you will not succeed," he states in a low, ominous voice, as the same type of blue smoke starts emanating from him.

The temperature of the room drops. Damp areas around the basement immediately freeze. Icicles form around the pipes on the ceiling.

I start shivering, but I refuse to show that to him by wrapping my arms around my body to preserve heat.

Fuck. I hate the cold.

"It's interesting," he continues in a bored tone as he walks around the basement, studying every little nook. "There are no lingering spirits here despite their gruesome deaths." He stops in front of my furnace and places his hand atop it. His eyes go white for a second before they go back to normal.

"Hundreds of humans you have killed here. Yet not one of them was left behind. Odd."

"What the fuck are you saying?"

The blue aura around him shimmers and extends.

"No demons around, either."

"Why the hell would a demon be in my house?"

"To feed on souls, of course," he replies nonchalantly. "Do you know, twenty-five to thirty percent of souls refuse to cross over after death. They linger around, wallowing in their emotions. This room should be a beacon for them, yet it's not."

"So? Maybe I charmed them into the afterlife," I add drily.

He gives me a pointed look.

"Or someone else fed on them—something else."

"What are you talking about?"

In the blink of an eye, he's in front of me.

"Has Minerva been down here?"

"Yes. And if you're going to ask if she knows about my killings, she does." I roll my eyes.

His cheek twitches.

"So she knows about the death in this house, and she's been to this location..." he muses.

"Don't you dare," I grit out. "She's your fucking sister. Act like it! Instead of trying to find things to blame her for, maybe you could help her."

"Help her?" He releases a dry laugh. "I've done nothing *but* help her. And yet she does *this*. She gets embroiled with another human when it's a human who put her in this situation in the first place."

I frown.

"What do you mean?"

"Ah, so you don't know everything."

I raise a brow. I'm pretty sure he's talking about Lucien, and while it might piss me off to hear about him, it's only going to give me more reasons to desecrate his remains properly and violently.

"Our kind is not allowed to interfere in mortals' affairs, let alone get involved with them on a...personal level. That's the first rule she broke. The rest are just a consequence of that."

"When you say mortals, does that mean that you're—"

"Deities," he replies matter-of-factly. "Another thing you didn't seem to know."

I stare at him.

I gathered she was immortal, but not a fucking goddess! Though at this point, does it really matter? My fiancée is a demon slayer *and* a goddess? I whistle aloud. Damn, I'm a lucky guy.

"You're not...fazed." He frowns.

"Why would I be?" I shrug. "She's a goddess. That's seriously badass."

"Badass?" He narrows his eyes at me.

"You wouldn't understand," I say and dust the front of his shirt, uniform, whatever it is. "You're too starchy for that." I wink at him.

His lips flatten in annoyance.

Coldness spreads from the tips of my fingers up my hands and arms. I pull back, swearing under my breath.

"You should know your place, human."

"Right, I'm so sorry, oh my dear god, how could I ever put my puny hands on you?"

"Good that you recognize you *are* puny."

I raise a brow.

"Maybe. But certainly your sister doesn't think that. Did she tell you how quickly she took off her clothes for me?"

Now, I *am* being an asshole on purpose. Molokai doesn't deserve anything less considering how he's been speaking of *my* Minnie. Of course, perhaps I'm alluding to some salacious actions, but it's his fault if he misinterprets my words. Minnie did take her clothes off within a day of meeting me. Unfortunately, nothing else happened—something I still bemoan late at night when my arousal becomes too painful.

Molokai tenses and the blue aura surrounding his body intensifies.

He takes a step forward, and ice forms where his foot touches the ground. From his hand, an icicle in the form of a spear appears.

Oh, shit!

Is there something like a god shield? I look around my basement for a weapon, not that I stand much of a chance seeing he's holding my kryptonite—coldness.

"Kai!" Minnie calls out in outrage. "What are you doing here?"

"Trying to intimidate your human," I quip and walk to her, grabbing her by the waist and pulling her close to me. "You will not allow him to do that, right, Minnie?" I ask and pout at her. "You'll take care of your human like the good girl that you are."

She blinks, my tone taking her aback.

I never thought I'd end up the boy toy of a goddess, but seeing how she has those awesome powers and I have...well, only my murderous skills that don't work on gods, I should start taking my role seriously.

After all, she might be a proper goddess, but it's *me* she'll call her god in bed.

But I suppose her brother is not ready to hear that.

"Of course not. He knows better than to come here to stir up problems," Minnie says as she folds her arms over her chest.

"You're the one always stirring up problems, Minerva. I cannot believe I leave you alone for a short time and you're back to the same *bad* habits. You said he's your human guard, not your lover," he adds in a slow but intense tone.

"So? It's my business who I take as my lover. In fact, you might benefit from it yourself," she fires back. "Maybe if you had a bit more fun, you wouldn't be so quick to ruin mine."

Her brother glares at her.

"Keep your tone in check, little sister," he warns lightly.

"Why? It's the truth. You're so picky with all the females back home. Maybe you can find yourself your own human and stop bothering me about mine."

"Yes, tell him, Minnie," I whisper proudly in her ear.

She gives me a warning glance and I promptly shut up.

"And become a fugitive like you? Not only did you take up with a *human*," he spits the word as if it's the most disgusting thing, "but you also gave away your chastity. Both offenses punishable by death."

"Now wait a minute, why would her chastity have anything to do with this?" I interject.

"Did you tell him?" Her brother raises a brow.

Minnie bites her lip as she looks from him to me.

"Tell me what?" I frown.

It seems I'm finding a great deal of things about Minnie in this conversation—most of which she forgot to mention herself.

"She is not *just* a deity. She's the daughter of the King of Cryos. And in our world, highborn ladies are forbidden from being with a male without being officially bonded. Her betrothed found out about her affair with that human and publicly repudiated her."

Her lips flatten and her right eye twitches.

"Betrothed? You had *another* fiancé?" I ask in outrage.

She doesn't answer, merely staring belligerently at her brother.

"What fiancé?" I demand harshly.

Her brother smirks.

"Another deity, of course. We do *not* intermingle," he adds snobbishly.

"You mean I'm your *third* fiancé?"

"Not now, Marlowe," she murmurs in distress.

"Oh, yes now, Minnie. Didn't you think that might be something worth mentioning?"

"Why? It was an arranged union, and my betrothed was not of my choosing."

"It doesn't matter. How could you not tell me I'm your *third* fiancé? This is preposterous. Who is this deity?"

"Theron of the House of Pyros. He's a mighty warrior, soon-to-be a general in Commander Azerius's army. She could not have done better," Molokai comments.

"Well, she's *done* better," I shoot back, tightening my hold on her waist. "Don't worry, Minnie, that Theron dude is the next one of my list as soon as I figure out how to kill a god," I tell her.

She rolls her eyes.

"Are you done with your lecture, Molokai? Why did you even come here? Sentinels could be tracking you."

"I always cover my tracks," he replies.

"Then please cover them on your way *back*."

"Not until I get what I came here for."

"If you're trying to convince me to leave Marlowe, it won't work."

"It might not work now, but you *will* leave." He laughs drily. "If you care about your human, sooner or later, you'll realize that your presence only puts him in danger."

Minnie stiffens.

"I can handle myself," I say.

Molokai doesn't even look at me.

"I came here for an answer, Minerva."

She frowns. "What answer?"

"Have you been feeding on souls?" he asks directly.

"W-what?"

"Have you, or have you not fed on the souls from this house?"

"What's wrong with you, Kai? How can you even ask me that? You know it's forbidden."

"And we've already established you don't care whether something is forbidden or not."

"But not that." She shakes her head, her expression distressed. "Never that."

"Then how do you explain the lack of souls in here?" he asks as he motions his arm to the room. "I thought it odd the first time I came here after you told me of his killing habit. There was no whisper of a soul around. There's nothing now, either. Surely you must have wondered about it."

"I find it insulting that you'd think *I* consumed those souls, Molokai. You should know me better than that."

"I know you're cornered. And when someone is cornered, they do things they would not usually do."

"Then you have your answer. I didn't feed on souls. You can check my energy signature if you'd like," she says as she steps forward. Her aura turns blue, small shimmery particles floating in the air around her body.

Molokai narrows his eyes suspiciously. But he doesn't move.

"I believe you," he eventually says.

Minnie pulls back her energy and sighs deeply.

"I have wondered about it, but it's not all that odd. Sometimes it happens," she adds.

"Does it?" He raises a brow. "I have yet to encounter a place where so many mortals have perished and none of them lingered."

Minnie shrugs.

"You have your answer. Now please go."

He doesn't leave. He stands rooted to the spot, staring at her.

"There's another reason as to why I'm here," he mentions as he takes a deep breath. "They know you're hiding on Anthropa. They don't have your exact location, but the soldiers have been dispatched."

Minnie swallows.

"I see... How long before they find me?"

"A few human months if you're lucky. Less if they sent an efficient squad."

"Thank you for telling me. I'll plan accordingly."

He inclines his head at her. Then he's gone.

Left alone with Minnie, I can only stare at her as I try to make sense of everything.

She turns to me and gives me a shy smile. Whereas before I would have been taken by that mere sight, now I'm only left with suspicion.

"What else are you not telling me?"

TWENTY-SIX

SHE PURSES her lips and looks away.

I grab her chin and turn it so she can face me. "Look me in the eye and tell me the truth, Minnie."

"I don't know what you want me to say," she replies with a sigh.

"How about the fact that you had another fiancé? Or that apparently you're a goddess?"

"I—"

"No more lies."

"I never lied. I just...didn't tell you everything."

"Why?"

"Because I knew you'd react like this." She takes a deep breath. "You reacted so badly to Lucien. How could I tell you that I was engaged before?"

"I would not have reacted badly if you'd told me it was an arranged marriage and you didn't care for him. Sure, I'd probably research ways to kill him for the future, but that's besides the point."

"Marlowe, do you hear yourself? You're talking about killing a god. That's... That's not how it works."

"What do you mean?"

"We might get injured and we might lose our physical bodies, but our essence remains intact. Unless..." She closes her eyes briefly. "There's only one being in the entire universe who has the power to vanquish a god's essence—Commander Azerius." She gives me a sad smile. "He is known as the God Killer."

"Azerius... The one who's after you?" I frown.

"Technically, he's not *yet* personally after me. But he's the one in charge of the hunt. He exterminates the deities who break the heavenly law," she explains.

"I don't get what it is that you did so badly. You got involved with a human, so what?"

"You don't understand my world. We're supposed to be paragons of perfection. Once we step out of line, it's game over. So you see, gods might be immortal, but we're certainly not eternal. In fact, we're quite replaceable."

"I see. And you risked it all *knowing* you'd get punished for it? You put your life on the line just to be with that Lucien of yours?"

"Marlowe, please. Let's not talk about him again."

"How can we not when it's clear how much you loved him— enough to sacrifice your life for him."

"Please..." she whispers.

I shake my head and pace around the room. There are so many questions going through my mind—even more than before, when I had no idea *what* she was.

"Explain something to me, Minnie," I start.

She nods.

"You've already committed a crime. You're already hunted for it. So why can't we fuck?"

A small gasp leaves her lips.

"Marlowe—"

"What does one more broken rule matter when you've already been condemned? Your brother and everyone else think you've already broken that chastity rule or whatever. What difference would it make if you do it now?"

"It makes a difference for *me*," she replies.

"Why? You'd be doing something everyone else expects you've already done before."

"But I'd know."

"Again, why is this so important to you? I want to understand you and so far, everything I learn about you makes me more and more confused."

She stares at me for a moment before she goes around to the table resting against the wall. Her hands are enveloped in a blue shimmer that soon materializes into a book.

"What's that?" I ask as I join her by the table.

I glance at the book, but it's in a foreign language that I can't decipher. But there's a picture on the right page depicting a cave with an altar.

"What am I looking at?" I ask again.

"I stole this from the House of Moirai—that's the house that controls fate. It's an ancient text about the Primordial Goddess of Fate. This," she says as she points to the illustration, "is purported to be her hidden sanctuary."

"So? I don't follow."

"I suppose I should start from the beginning." She gives me a brief look before averting her gaze. "The origins of the universe are somewhat similar to what you've been taught. It all began with chaos. And from that chaos, the Primordial Gods were born. There were twenty-one of them. Seven of light. Seven of darkness. And seven nether that served as the link in-between.

"Bored and with immense powers, they decided to create toys to entertain them—mortals. But soon it became clear that their creation far exceeded their expectations. Mortals might have limited lifespans, but their souls are immortal.

"Since mortal souls are the product of the combined forces of the twenty-one Primordials, they're also the purest source of energy in the universe. Nothing has ever, or will ever compare. But soon, the Primordials realized that these souls had gained a free will of their own. Unable to control them anymore, they combined their forces again to infuse each soul with a thread of fate. Its master was to be the Primordial Goddess of Fate."

"Okay..."

"The Primordials then created their successors, the current Deities of Aperion and the Sons of Tenebreis who became the new keepers of the balance in the universe. I won't get into too much detail of what happened after, but there was a war between the three factions of Primordials and fourteen of them turned against the Seven and locked them in a mystical prison called Tartarstasis." She pauses. "As a side note, this is why the Sons of Tenebreis seek to corrupt as many souls as possible. They need the energy of the souls to unlock Tartarstasis and free the dark Seven."

I slowly nod as I try to keep up with all this new information.

"After they got rid of the dark Seven, the other Primordials disappeared without a trace. No one knows where they are or what happened to them. The Houses of Aperion are merely their successors and they bear the same designation—as in, they fulfill the same role."

"I still don't understand what any of that has to do with the fact that you won't let me fuck you."

"Patience, Marlowe, I'm getting there." She rolls her eyes at me.

What can I say, when it comes to getting in her pants, patience is the least of my virtues. Although... I must say, until now, I've certainly behaved like a saint.

"Though the House of Moirai currently controls the fate of all beings, the one who has precedence above them all is the Primordial Goddess of Fate. But as I said, all the Primordials disappeared eons ago and no one knows where they are."

"Right. And?"

"This, right here, is supposed to be the Primordial Goddess's sanctuary." She points once more to the illustration. "And the legend says that if a pair of lovers consummate their bond for the first time in the Primordial Goddess's oasis, they will be linked by a thread of fate no one will be able to unravel. Not even the House of Moirai."

I tilt my head and frown at her.

She releases a frustrated sigh.

"Don't you see? If we go to this place and consummate our bond there, we'll be granted a fated bond. Then, not even the other gods will be able to oppose our union."

"Does it even matter if they oppose it or not if you're still hunted?"

"Ugh, Marlowe! You're not listening! This could be my clean slate! If our bond is recognized by the Primordial Goddess of Fate herself, then no one will be able to go against it. I'd be free of my charges and well...free to be with you."

Now that sounds much better.

"Let's go then. The sooner, the better."

She grabs my shirt and fists it in her hand.

"There's just one issue..." she murmurs in a small voice.

"What is it?"

"It's a mythical place. No one knows where it is."

I stare at her.

Then stare again.

And then stare some more.

"You don't know where it is," I repeat numbly.

She nods apologetically.

"For fuck's sake, Minnie! Does that mean you're not going to sleep with me until we find this goddamn mythical place that might not even exist?"

"Well...yes."

"Minnie!" I groan aloud.

"But don't you see, Marlowe? If we can find it, then it would be the answer to all our problems. I'd be free from persecution and we'd be able to be together. Forever."

One word piques my interest.

"Forever? When you say forever you mean..."

"Once you're my bonded mate, you will have the same lifespan as me. We would never have to be apart. Never," she adds fervently.

That changes things.

I ruminate quietly over the issue at hand. Of course there's still the possibility that this mythical place doesn't exist. But what if it does?

We'd then be together forever—what I've wanted from the beginning.

Ah, but this is quite a dilemma, isn't it? Who knows *when* we'll find it if it does indeed exist?

"When you say consummation, does that refer only to the act itself, or can we...do other things?"

She presses her lips together.

"I don't know. But it's better we don't take any chances."

"That's why you've never kissed me on the lips?"

She nods.

"But... Why the hell would you appear naked in front of me then? Why tempt me like that?"

"Because at that time, I wasn't sure about the terms." She traces her fingers on the written part of the text. "This is written in Ancient Aperite. It's a dead language, so there aren't many people who would know how to translate it. It took me a long time to teach myself to finally make sense of what was written in the book."

I thread my fingers through my hair and sigh. How the fuck did everything turn so complicated?

I throw a glance at my ring-making equipment and realize I've been working so hard all day for nothing. She's not going to marry me until we find this goddamn mythical place.

"It's not that I don't want you, Marlowe. I very much do. But this is an unprecedented opportunity and we can't dismiss it," she continues.

The entire thing is absurd. But it's clear she believes in it.

"What about Lucien?" I suddenly ask.

"What about him?" she inquires tentatively.

"Why didn't you sleep with him then? When you didn't know about the terms?"

"That's..." She swallows and averts her gaze. "That was different," she mumbles.

"Different how?"

"He was a sick man, Marlowe," she explains weakly.

"So you would have slept with him if not for that," I state in a tight voice.

She doesn't reply, yet the answer lingers in the air.

"I see."

The rage bubbles beneath the surface, but I can't let it come out—not now. We have far more important things to discuss. And as much as I hate the situation we're in, I'd do anything to help her. Even remain a monk for the rest of my life.

Fucking hell.

I cannot believe I'm contemplating this. After weeks of intense sensual torture, I now find out I may never get to touch her like I want to. As long as she believes in that mythical place, there's no way she's going to want to engage in anything sexual. And I'm too much of a fucking fool for her to go against her wishes. I'd never force her if she doesn't want to.

The issue is that she clearly wants to as well.

We're both standing on the precipice, but she's waving a very clear stop sign so we don't fall.

Is it hard? Damn sure.

But if this place actually exists, if there's an actual opportunity for her to stop being hunted and for us to spend an eternity together... That's a gamble I'm willing to take.

I know what everyone must be thinking. Who is this Marlowe and what happened to the selfish bastard from before?

The answer is rather simple.

Minnie happened.

"We need to talk about those soldiers coming for you. What's the plan?" I change the topic. I'm going to save my Lucien rage for when his remains get delivered to me. Then it's game on.

"We'll need to leave this world soon," she answers slowly.

"Okay." I nod.

"You're...fine with that?" She blinks.

"Of course. We're in this together. Where you go, I go and all that."

"Except it's not that easy." She sighs as she manifests the book away. She turns to face me and crosses her arms over her chest. "Mortals cannot stay in a foreign world for more than a few days. And even those days are torture as the new world slowly depletes your body of its strength."

"Great to be mortal," I mumble drily.

"There's a way, though. There are certain potions that would allow you to live in another world without issue. For that, we must find a number of special plants. The only ones who might have these plants in Anthropa are witches."

"Then that's what we'll do," I tell her.

She stares at me. Her chin is lowered into her chest, her big eyes looking at me strangely.

"What?" I frown.

"I'm trying to understand you," she mentions slowly.

"You're not the only one," I fire back.

She scowls.

"I just told you we cannot be together physically for the fore-seeable future and that we must leave your world, and you agreed just like that?"

"Why do you find it so hard to believe? You're mine. Whether I've fucked you or not."

She blinks.

"I just... I didn't expect this, that's all."

"And what did you expect?" I raise a brow.

Her cheeks redden and she looks away.

"For you to be tired of waiting and take me anyway."

"What?" I ask, taken aback by her answer.

She bites her lip as she all but avoids to look at me.

"You thought I'd what? Rape you?" My voice becomes harsh as outrage slowly fills me to the brim. She thought what of me?

Yet it's not just outrage that overwhelms me, it's also disbelief. She slowly nods.

"You thought I'd *rape* you?" I repeat, still unable to process this.

Have I ever given her any indication that I might do something like that? For fuck's sake, I've behaved like a goddamn saint even when my blue balls were killing me. I could have easily kissed her on the lips, many times. Many, many times. I didn't lack opportunity. Yet I never crossed that line. So how the hell would she think I'd do something like that?

To say I'm insulted is an understatement.

"Maybe I even hoped you would," she adds in a soft, barely audible voice.

My eyes widen as I stare at her in shock.

"You what?" I croak.

Her lips tremble as she struggles to speak.

"Maybe if the choice was taken away from me, then I wouldn't continue hoping for a miracle," she confesses. "I know I'm chasing a myth, and while I'm skeptical about the existence of that Sanctuary, I'm also equally optimistic about it. Two warring emotions inside me with no resolution in sight. But you *could* have given me that resolution."

"By raping you? By taking you by force?"

Another nod.

"I know it sounds bad. I'm sorry. I just... I'm tired of running away, Marlowe. I'm tired of waiting for something that may never come. But this stupid heart won't let me stop hoping," she cries out, banging her hand over her chest. Tears rim her eyes as she finally raises them to meet mine. "I'm just so tired…"

"Minnie…" I swallow.

"But you never did. I waited, tested the grounds, planted the seeds in your mind. But you never once pushed me too far."

I'm rendered speechless, so she just continues. Her voice is soft, but hurt. There's a grittiness to it that's imbued with pain and frustration.

"You proved me time and again that you *were* the man I knew you were, even when I hoped you wouldn't. Sounds rather paradoxical, doesn't it?" She gives a dry laugh. "I both hate and admire you for that, you know…"

"Minnie, do you think me capable of something like that?" I ask, trying to choose my words carefully.

"No," she says as she shakes her head. "Which is ironic considering you kill people." She laughs. "Would I have *wanted* you to force me? I can't say for sure. Would I have hated you for it? Perhaps. But all I know is that sometimes I wish I didn't have to make any decision at all. I'd love to live for once, you know. Without the burden of fighting for my life; of one wrong choice that can condemn me to death…"

Her lips tip up in a sad smile. So sad it damn well pierces my heart.

"I'm sorry if my words upset you. Maybe I didn't phrase it as well as I should have," she continues. "It's just something I've been struggling with."

This is the first time I've heard the word struggle on Minnie's lips.

Although I've only recently found out about her past and the fact that she's being hunted, I've never once seen her down or pessimistic about her situation. In fact, ever since I first met her on the highway, with barely any clothes on her back and starving, she's been nothing but cheery and bubbly about life, finding joy in everything around her.

I've been so wrapped up in her brightness that I failed to see the lurking shadows.

She's been shouldering such a weight for so long... I can't begin to imagine how hard it must have been for her.

I take a step forward. Then another until I stand before her, my arms wide open. She eyes me warily, but slowly, she reaches for me, nestling within my arms and letting me be the brightness to her shadows for once.

"You don't need to make all the decisions anymore, Minnie. That's why I'm here. But I will *not* take away your choice from you. I'll merely share half the burden."

A tremor goes down her body and a sob echoes in the stillness of the room.

I hold her tighter.

Her cries are soft at first, but slowly, they intensify until she's bawling.

She cries and cries. I don't interrupt her, not wanting to intrude on her grief. But I hold her throughout it all so that she knows that even when her feelings are out of control, I'll be there to share her burden. I might not be able to take those emotions away, but I can be there for her as she slowly processes them.

How magnanimous of me.

For once, my instinct isn't to kill, but to protect.

"How do you manage to surprise me at every turn?" she asks as she pulls back, her eyes clouded with tears.

I smirk.

"That's my specialty," I say and wink at her.

The ghost of a smile appears on her lips.

I've never been good at consoling people—not that I've tried before. But it seems I didn't do such a poor job, and pride suffuses me at the thought that I can at least do this for her—put the smile back on her face.

"I was afraid you'd hate me for leading you on," she whispers. "And you would have been within your rights to do so since I've hidden so much from you."

"I could never hate you, Minnie. I might have wanted to kill you on occasion, though," I joke.

She hits me playfully in the chest.

"Well, now you know I can't die," she fires back.

"Wouldn't have stopped me from trying." I shrug.

She blinks, then laughs. Tears are still rolling down her cheeks, but the sound of her laughter makes me sigh in relief.

"There you go again with your morbid thoughts." She shakes her head in amusement.

"What's wrong with them? In fact, since you can't die, I could technically kill you and you'd come back to life. Think of it as foreplay." I wiggle my brows suggestively at her.

"Marlowe!" she exclaims, scandalized.

"What? We can't fuck, but we can play around with murder. Isn't that a great idea?"

"I'm not sure killing me would qualify as a great idea," she mumbles.

"Why not? I'd cut you here," I say as I trace my fingers down her neck. "Then here," I continue as I reach her chest. Going lower, I touch her lightly between her legs.

She draws in a sudden breath.

"I could cut you up until the pain becomes pleasure. Would that count as consummation? If I bring you to orgasm using a knife instead of my cock?"

She blushes furiously, and as she opens her mouth to speak, she stumbles over her words.

"I... That..."

"I'm joking, Minnie," I add. She stares at me for a moment before she exhales in relief.

Or maybe I'm not joking.

I have to admit, I've never considered mixing murder and sex, but as the images flash inside my head, I can't help the rush of arousal that flows to my cock.

Seeing Minnie naked, sprawled on the floor in a pool of blood while she's writhing in pleasure might not be such a bad idea.

If only she thought so too...

My phone rings in my pocket. Taking it out, I note it's Giles.

"Yes?"

"I have secured the remains. We are loading them on the jet as we speak. They should reach you sometime in the morning," he states, cutting straight to the chase.

"Perfect. Good job, Giles."

"You owe me one, Marlowe." He chuckles.

"I'm letting you fuck my mother. I'd say we're even," I add drily and hang up.

Minnie is watching me with a perplexed expression on her face.

"What was that about?"

"A surprise." I wink at her. "I have a very special surprise planned for you tomorrow."

Her face lights up just like her former fiancé's remains are going to light up in my furnace—after I desecrate them a bit more.

I might be *a little* mad at her for hiding so much from me, especially concerning her amorous past. But I'll take my anger out on Lucien's remains.

Ah, but the anticipation is killing me.

I just hope Minnie will be a good sport about it.

TWENTY-SEVEN

WHEN I ASKED for Lucien's remains to be brought to me, I expected some scattered bones, maybe a few textile scraps.

I didn't expect a mummified body!

I stare in shock at the large box Giles brought over.

His skin is a brownish color, and though a little desiccated, his face retains most of its features.

High cheekbones, a defined jaw, and a strong nose. His eyes are closed, lending him a peaceful image in his death—almost as if he were asleep.

He's still wearing his military uniform, though some of the material is worn and torn.

"What's this, Giles?" I ask as I raise my gaze to meet the nonchalant one of my secretary.

"Lucien de Vitry," he answers in a bored tone.

"That I know. But how the hell does an old corpse look like this? Shouldn't he be a mass of bones right now?"

Giles purses his lips.

"His burial place was on a plot of land in Southern France. Incidentally, that happens to be one of the only peat bog locations in France."

I frown.

"Peat bog? What's that?"

He rolls his eyes.

"It's a type of wetland that accumulates large deposits of dead plants. It's known to be a good environment for natural mummification." He pauses. "I should let you know that I had a very hard time finding the body, especially considering your deadline. The area is a national reservation and access is prohibited to the public. You have no idea the ropes I had to pull to even find the burial place, let alone find someone willing to go dig for it."

"Yet you found it," I remark.

"I'm good at my job." He inclines his head.

"But a mummy?" I repeat. "This is unbelievable."

More unbelievable is the fact that I'm staring Minnie's dead fiancé right in the face. Sure, he's a bit dry and well...dead, but this is remarkable nonetheless.

But now another thought plagues me. If he's so well preserved, what if Minnie decides to keep him and find a way to revive him? She's a goddess. I'm sure that wouldn't be too hard for her.

For fuck's sake. I'm already competing with a dead man's memory. I don't need to compete with a fucking *undead* man. Just thinking about losing to a fucking mummy is unacceptable, and frankly, humiliating.

Seeing as how Lucien is far more whole than I expected, perhaps my plan to build a bonfire out of him and present it to Minnie might not be the best idea.

Or...

"Help me get him out of the box," I tell Giles.

"Marlowe..." He groans. "He died of tuberculosis, and he's mummified. Are you sure it's a good idea to handle the body?"

I wave my hand dismissively. Grabbing two pairs of surgical gloves and two masks, I hand them to Giles to put them on while I do the same.

With some equipment in place, I grab onto Lucien's shoulders while Giles handles the feet.

"On my count," I say. "One. Two. Three."

We raise him up at the same time and move him toward the table.

Yet despite the—quite impressive—mummification, Lucien's limbs are not held together as well as I would have expected. The weight of the bones and dried muscle presses on the thin layer of skin and one of his arms gets detached from his shoulder.

It falls to the ground with a resounding thud.

Giles and I share a look. He shakes his head at me but continues to help me move the mummy onto the table.

"It's fine," I mention as I pick up the fallen arm. "I wasn't going to leave him whole anyway."

Because leaving him whole might mean Minnie can resurrect him—of course I don't know if that's even possible, but I'm not taking any chances. If I want to ensure my candlelight dinner with the complementary bonfire is a success, Lucien cannot be whole.

He'll need to be hacked to pieces.

My nose wrinkles in disgust as I realize that with so much skin and dry muscle still attached to the bones, the bonfire will smell rather like...smoked meat.

Ah, the lengths I go to in order to ensure my competition is extinct.

Especially as it appears that the concept of *dead and buried* might not hold the same power as before since he's already been dead and buried. And somehow still managed to keep his damn handsome face.

I swear under my breath.

"Giles," I call out suddenly.

"Yes?" He raises a brow.

"Who's more handsome? Me or the mummy?"

He blinks. "What?"

"I require an answer. Who's more handsome? Me or the

mummy?" I ask again as I position myself next to the dead man. I crouch lower to put my face next to his so Giles can assess it better.

"Uh…"

"The truth, Giles. I need the truth."

Being this close to the mummy, I note there's a musky smell coming off it.

Ew.

"He's a mummy, Marlowe. Dead. Why would you compare yourself with a dead man?"

"Tell me, Giles!"

He takes a deep breath.

"You," he mutters under his breath.

"Me, right?" I nod pensively as I once more look at Lucien's face. "He does have nice cheekbones, though. Are they nicer than mine?" I ask as I pat my cheekbones.

"No, Marlowe," Giles says automatically.

"And his jaw. It's very sharp, don't you think?"

"Not sharper than yours," he immediately adds.

I nod, satisfied.

"He might have been handsome, but I'm more so," I muse to myself.

"He's a *mummy*, Marlowe," Giles interjects with a groan. "Have you finally lost it? What's this obsession you have with a goddamn dead man?"

I ignore him. There's something else I must check.

I pull up the jacket of his uniform, tearing a good chunk of it in the process. Buttons fly to the floor, accompanied by scraps of fabric.

Damn it.

His stomach is sunken in, the entire abdomen dried out.

I push against my disgust and pull on the hem of his pants.

"Marlowe! What the hell are you doing?" Giles asks me in an outraged voice.

"Making sure I'm bigger than him," I mutter, focused on getting the pants off.

"Marlowe! Have you completely lost your mind?"

"Perhaps, Giles. Since he's already here, I might as well check so I don't have intrusive thoughts later on."

"Sweet Lord," Giles whispers, shaking his head. "You've gone mad."

Oh, yes. I've gone mad. Mad with jealousy.

I manage to pull the pants down to his knees, though the material is too sensitive to remain intact. It tears in a myriad of pieces that fall to the ground. Underneath, he's wearing a pair of drawers that are stuck to his skin. Still, there's an outline there—a *very* big outline, even in his mummified state.

I raise my gaze to Giles.

"No. You're not making me compare your dick size to a fucking mummy!"

"Don't worry, Giles. I won't ask you that. I'll compare it myself."

Before I can let the disgust overwhelm me—this is quite unsanitary, though I try not to think about it—I go to a drawer and remove a measuring tape from inside.

"Goodness gracious, you've gone mad! Absolutely mad!" Giles continues to mumble while I focus on getting the white material of his drawers out of the way.

I'm not sure what I expected to find, but I'm quite shocked to realize that his dick is quite intact. It's flaccid, of course, but well mummified. Perhaps the layers of material have protected his flesh even better than the rest of his body.

It's a dark brown, the same shade as his face. That bog surely did a number on him.

I spend a few moments analyzing it—from a purely scientific viewpoint, of course. There's nothing gay about it, I swear, nor necrophiliac. I'm simply gathering data.

For a flaccid mummified dick, it hasn't shrunk too much, retaining much of its fullness and size.

He is, of course, uncircumcised.

Got you there, buddy, I think to myself in satisfaction.

But the visual estimation is not enough.

I unravel the tape and measure it from the base of his pelvis to the tip.

"I can't believe I'm taking part in this," Giles continues to mutter, at some point crossing himself and saying a prayer. "This is beyond criminal, Marlowe."

"It's research, Giles. If you're so against it, you can see yourself out. I'm busy."

"No, no, no. I'm not leaving you with a naked mummy. Your mother would have my hide."

"Then stay." I shrug.

The measuring tape says a little over five inches.

I scowl. That's a lot for flaccid. Perhaps he was a shower not a grower. Although...

Mine is about the same flaccid and a little over nine erect.

I swear under my breath.

"Giles?"

"What now, Marlowe?" He rolls his eyes.

"Could we, theoretically, pump liquid into his dick to see how much it distends?"

He gawks at me in shock, then crosses himself again.

"No. Leave the poor man alone. He's already dead."

"But I need to know," I mutter to myself.

"It's going to damage the corpse more than it already is. You're taking this too far." He pauses. "Are you still seeing your therapist?"

"As a matter of fact," I start and then suddenly pause. "Not anymore."

Giles sighs. "Does your mother know about this?"

"She must, seeing that *you* know," I fire back. "And what you know, she automatically knows, too."

"Damn it, Marlowe. Do you want to send her into an early grave? She's always worrying about you, and you go and dig up a century-old corpse and start desecrating it. You've done a lot of fucked-up shit, but this—"

"Why would she worry about me? I do perfectly well for myself. I have a job, a house, a steady income, and I'm not in jail. If this isn't the standard for leading a good life, I don't know what is."

I put the ruler back in its drawer and pull back the pants on the mummy—or what's left of the fraying material. Although I'm reluctant to admit it, Giles has a point. I'm behaving erratically.

Once upon a time, I would have never touched an old and dried-up corpse, especially one that likely still has the tuberculosis bacterium inside it. But I've come to terms with the fact that I've left the old me behind, erratic as that person was, and I've embraced a new type of insanity.

The Minnie kind.

Just thinking about her and this Lucien makes my blood boil. How dare she have *other* fiancés? Two others, too.

I don't like being the third.

I don't like the fact that she's been in this dude's proximity, let alone that there's another man out there who had a relationship with her in the past—whether it was arranged or not.

Worse? These thoughts have become so poisonous that I can barely close my eyes at night. And if that's not enough, every other waking moment of the day, I'm even more consumed by jealous thoughts.

"Your mother has always worried about you," he continues. "Ever since that incident..." He flattens his lips as he trails off.

"We don't *talk* about that incident," I growl.

Giles shakes his head.

"The incident is the only reason why she's overlooked your

crimes for this long, you know that. But this is a new type of fucked up. You need help."

"And what do you suggest?" I ask mockingly.

He clears his throat.

"For starters, I'm going to stop enabling you. This is the last time I'm helping you with a request."

I narrow my eyes at him. Sure. I wonder how long that's going to last, since he always says the same thing but ends up cleaning up my messes anyway.

"Fine. You can see yourself out." I turn my back to him as I fetch my surgical instruments to get down to work.

He stares at me for a few moments before he finally leaves. But not before he adds something else.

"Your mother's birthday is at the end of the week. I hope you haven't forgotten."

"I haven't," I snap. I totally have.

"Good. I'll see you there."

Then he's gone.

And I'm alone with fucking Lucien.

I sigh as I study him anew. Grabbing a chair, I place it next to the table and take a seat.

There's something off about him—and I'm not talking about his mummified state.

From the moment Giles brought over the box and revealed Lucien's corpse, I've been on edge. It's as if a myriad of anxious ants made their way under my skin and pace around my body from head to toe, making me restless and even more erratic than usual.

"Good thing you died, old chap," I tell the mummy as if he could hear me. "Now I have her all to myself. And she'll never think about you again. Never."

By getting rid of his remains, I'll be getting rid of him from this world once and for all, and naturally, he'll fade from her memory too.

Nodding to myself, I grab a chainsaw and start to work. Luckily, an arm has already fallen off his body, so I merely have to repeat the action with the other one. Next are his legs. I cut each leg in two—the tibia with the foot and the thigh.

As I cut through the dried-up flesh, a noxious smell threatens to make me ill. Still, I persevere. I'm a man on a mission, and I'll be damned if I stop before this mummy is cut up.

But as I continue my work, a chuckle escapes me as I think about the nineteenth century practice of grinding up Egyptian mummies to dust and consuming them as medicine. Of course those were intentional mummies while Lucien over here was merely lucky to find himself in suitable environmental conditions that led to his mummifications.

Maybe I should grind him up?

Ah, decisions, decisions.

Should I turn him into fine dust, or should I throw him in the furnace?

In the end, I decide to go for the latter. It will be a great show, too. But since he still retains a lot of his body mass, I'll have to start the fire in advance.

I ponder on that issue for a few moments.

I suppose I could burn his body beforehand and keep his head for the grand gesture. Wouldn't that be the most romantic gesture?

I'd save the best for Minnie and *she* can throw it in the furnace to signify the fact that she's moved on from him. Then we could watch him burn together, perhaps even have a glass of champagne and some cookies.

The idea sounds nice. In fact, I'll only get *one* glass. That way, since we'd share a glass, it would be like an indirect kiss. Alas, in the absence of the real deal, I'll have to make do.

After all the parts have been hacked off, I throw the body in the furnace and set the temperature to high. For the head, I grab a tray and place him carefully on it, covering the entire thing with a cap. Then I place it in my freezer. Since it still has so much soft tissue, it will likely start to stink soon, and I still need to plan the details of the dinner.

Satisfied with my plan, I leave the basement and go greet Minnie, who, oblivious to my genius plan, is currently cooking lunch.

The delicious smell of steak and potatoes hits me the moment I enter the kitchen—a vast improvement from the smell of dried corpse.

Ah, life is certainly good—and about to be better once I remove my competition from this plane of existence.

RED-AND-WHITE CANDLES FORM a heart on the ground, and in the middle of it, I placed a table and two chairs. I'd cleaned up the basement a while ago and started on the arrangements for our dinner. Rose petals are scattered all around the room. Of course I can't take all the credit since I got most of the advice from the internet.

I have a full course meal prepared, together with a variety of chocolate desserts for my chocolate-loving girl.

The furnace is still going strong, and most of the body has already been burned to ashes. But the head looks surprisingly better after a few hours in the freezer. It still looks...human.

I scowl.

I hope she won't look at it and fall for him again. That's not the plan.

No, the plan is for her to willingly throw his head to the flames so to speak and close that chapter of her life. Then we'll have our glass of champagne and indirect kiss and I'll feed her expensive chocolates while she tells me how much better I am than Lucien.

After being tortured for so long by Lucien's nefarious shadow hanging between me and Minnie, I'll finally be able to move on. Of course, there's still that Theron fiancé god or whatever, but I'm willing to take it one day at a time. Perhaps after Minnie and I succeed in clearing her name, I can befriend that God Killer and ask him for a *tiny* favor. But that's neither here nor there. I'm getting ahead of myself.

For now, I need to ensure that my candlelight dinner is a success.

In between hacking off Lucien's body, I managed to finish the ring, too. The package with the custom jewels arrived early this morning, and I filled one stone with a few drops of my blood and another with a few drops of my cum.

Red and white.

Perfect for my girl.

It took some tinkering to figure out how to set them on the silver band, but I think I did a good job.

I can already picture her swooning when she sees the result.

It is truly unique *and* handmade—exactly what she wanted.

I go about setting the table with the food I'd prepared. Well, prepared might be an overstatement since I ordered it from a Michelin restaurant. And since I've recently found out she cannot properly digest meat and other animal byproducts, I made sure everything is vegan.

It's nine and a half in the evening when I'm done.

I take out a special red paper and write a few words on it: *Come to the basement at ten.* Then I seal it in a pretty envelope and take it up to her room. Since she cannot withstand strong smells, I decided to forgo the perfume on paper. Instead, I bit my lip until a few drops of blood reached the surface and I pressed them against the envelope—I'm sure she'll appreciate the extra touches.

Leaving it at her door, I knock a few times before running away so she doesn't catch me.

God, I sound like a goddamn lovestruck teenager—yet only one of those statements is true.

Back in the basement, I take big, long breaths to calm my

nerves as I watch the hands of the clock slowly move into position for her arrival.

All the while, I repeat my lines in my head to make sure I'm not going to blunder this.

First the dinner. Then the ring. Then the head. Then the champagne and the indirect kiss.

Good Lord, I cannot believe the lengths I'm going for only an *indirect kiss*. But it's better than nothing, no?

I hear the door to the basement slowly opening and turn.

Another big breath.

The time has arrived.

"Marlowe?" She frowns. "What's this?"

TWENTY-EIGHT

"I HAVE A SURPRISE FOR YOU. COME," I say as I take her hand and lead her to the table. Pulling the chair for her, I make sure she's seated comfortably before joining her on the other side of the table.

She's looking around with wonder in her eyes and my heart thuds furiously in my chest as I await her reaction.

"You did this for me?" she asks in a small voice.

I nod.

"You wanted something unique, so I prepared something unique for you." I give her my signature smile.

She blushes.

Ah, my charm is working.

"You put a lot of thought into this. I don't know what to say."

"You like it?"

"Very much."

"Then that's enough for me. I have more surprises for you, too." I wink.

"Wow... I should have put on something nicer," she says as she looks down at her clothes.

She's wearing one of my shirts that looks like a dress on her and a pair of black leggings. The mere fact that she's wearing *my* shirt makes this so much better. She already looks stunning on a daily basis, but like this she's absolutely breathtaking. So much so I have to remind myself *not* to forget to breathe.

"You look perfect, Minnie. You're always perfect to me."

She flutters her lashes as she averts her gaze, her entire face red.

"What's gotten into you, Marlowe? The candles, the flowers, the compliments... Are you quite all right?" she asks with a wicked gleam in her eyes.

"I'm more than all right, my little heathen. I realized that I have not taken my fiancé duties seriously until now and I aim to remedy that."

She narrows her eyes at me.

"Is this still about Lucien and Theron? I thought we moved past that."

"Of course not," I mumble.

She stares at me.

"We should eat. I got you something special," I quickly mention as I reveal the first item on the menu, a creamy vegan risotto with truffles.

Her eyes widen and she nods in appreciation.

She takes a bite.

"Oh, this is fantastic," she exclaims.

I smile to myself.

Food, check.

We eat the first course and then I unveil the dessert. A variety of chocolates and chocolate cakes that delight her even further. She eats almost all of them—which is just as I intended.

Once we're done with the food, I take away the dishes and clear the table.

Minnie watches me closely, her lips drawn up in a smile.

She looks...happy.

Because of me.

I fucking did that.

I put a smile on her face.

I mentally high-five myself. This is how it's done, ladies and gentlemen.

"Would you mind checking under the table? I think you dropped something."

Her brows go up in question. She leans to look under the table and for a few moments, she doesn't speak. She doesn't move. She doesn't react.

I wait with bated breath for her to say something.

Slowly, she gets up, holding between her tiny fingers the ring I'd worked so damn hard to make.

She looks at it and swallows hard.

Then she looks at me, and her eyes glisten with unshed tears.

"What's this, Marlowe?" she asks on a whisper.

"What do you think it is, Minnie?" I smile as I walk toward her. Dropping to one knee, I take the ring from her and slide it on her ring finger.

It fits perfectly. Good.

She's speechless for what seems like forever. Her eyes flitter from me to the ring and back to me. Her mouth opens a few times, but no sound comes out.

"I can smell your blood on it. Your blood and..." She presses her lips together as another blush stains her cheeks.

"Yes, my blood and my seed. All for you."

She squeezes her eyes shut, but her mouth tips up at the corners.

"You made this?"

"Of course. The band, too. I learned how to forge a ring just for you," I boast confidently.

She opens her eyes and stares at the ring, turning her hand around to study it better.

"It's beautiful, Marlowe. This is the best surprise," she murmurs, her voice breaking with emotion.

"I'm not even going to ask the obvious question, since the answer is yes," I tell her.

She raises a brow at me.

"Is that so?"

"Of course. You already agreed. You can't take it back. I won't let you," I warn her. "The ring is for you to know my devotion and for others to see that you're taken—not that they're going to see much of you anyway since I plan to keep you for my eyes only."

"You're such a romantic, Marlowe," she adds dryly.

"Really? Thank you. I try." I nod in satisfaction.

She shakes her head at me, but the smile on her lips tells me I did a damn good job.

"You're impossible."

"I aim to please." I wink at her.

Getting up, I go to the furnace and turn it back on. The fire inside further illuminates the basement, creating an even more ethereal atmosphere. Gazing inside, I note that there's little left of the body—a few scraps of bones. Not to worry, they'll be destroyed on the second round.

"What are you doing?" she asks as she rises from her seat. "What's that smell?" She wrinkles her nose in disgust.

"What do you think it is?"

"I don't know, it smells odd. Did you kill someone else, Marlowe? Is that it?" She rolls her eyes at me. "Who was it this time?"

"I didn't *technically* kill anyone," I reply smoothly. "I merely took care of the already dead."

Her brows are knitted in confusion.

"I don't follow."

"I have another surprise for you," I mention and go to the freezer.

Opening the door, I go inside and grab the platter containing Lucien's head. I can't wait to see Minnie's reaction. But more than anything else, I can't wait to see her denounce Lucien and willingly throw him in the flames. I want her to pick up his head, tell me I'm the only one for her, now and forever, and simply dump that son of a bitch in the furnace where he belongs.

Then I'll be able to rest assured that she's fully mine. I don't even mind waiting as long as it takes for us to consummate our relationship if I'll have the certainty that she's mine—body and soul.

But that's my issue. I know I'll have her body—though it might take some time and I might die from blue balls, but it is what it is—but do I have her soul? She has yet to tell me she loves me. Not that I said it either, but I want *her* to be the one to say it first since I reckon my feelings for her are pretty clear. I mean, I let her blow her nose on my shirt—multiple times too. That in itself means I fucking love her since no one would even be able to get close enough to me to do that, let alone to leave behind their gross bodily fluids. Yet because it's her, I even find it cute.

Insane, no?

But that's how I know she's *it* for me. I don't care if she's a goddess, a demon slayer, or whatever else. I don't even care if she used to eat dumpster food, though I'll never let her live that down. I only care that she's mine and only mine.

And this moment is about to solidify that for me.

Finally, Lucien will be a thing of the past (granted, there's still Theron, but I'll worry about him later since he never engaged her affections like this bloke).

I go back to the main room of the basement where Minnie is waiting for me with her arms crossed over her chest. One brow raised, she watches me with suspicion in her eyes.

"I'm almost afraid to ask what's inside," she mutters when I join her in front of the furnace.

"It's something I've prepared for you. For us. This is the mark of our beginning, Minnie, and I want you to do the honors."

She frowns.

"What honors?"

"Ta-da!" I pull the lid to reveal Lucien's mummified head.

Her eyes grow wide with shock.

"That..." She swallows. "That..."

"I want you to throw this into the furnace with the rest of the body. Put the past behind us," I murmur.

She slowly turns to stare at the fire burning inside the furnace.

"You mean... The body... The rest of the body is there? Burning?"

I nod, smiling. "The perfect idea, no? Letting the fire metaphorically cleanse all past connections. This is *our* start, Minnie."

She shakes her head, her expression petrified.

"What have you done, Marlowe?" she whispers.

My brows pull together in confusion.

"I got rid of my competition," I answer matter-of-factly.

She continues to shake her head as she takes a step toward the furnace, leaning in to watch the flames lick the remaining bones and turn them into ash.

"You..." she croaks. "You burned him..."

"Not entirely." I smile. "See, I kept one piece for you so you could burn him yourself," I add proudly. The whole purpose of this is to do it together.

She turns sharply to me and before I know it, her palm connects with my cheek. The sting of the slap takes me by surprise, as does the sudden pain in my chest.

"What the hell is wrong with you?" she demands in a ragged voice.

I'm too stunned to react.

She grabs the detached head and holds it between her hands as she stares at it.

"You..." she whispers, but she's not looking at me.

She's looking at *him*.

And she's looking at him like she's never looked at me.

With... Love.

My fists clench by my sides.

"How could you?" she rasps out, tears rolling out her cheeks. "How the hell could you?" she yells.

Blue mist surrounds her body and her eyes become a lighter blue shade as she glares at me. Pure hatred emanates from her and before I can say anything, a strong gust of cold wind hits me in the chest, throwing me backward.

"Minnie—"

"Don't you say another word, Marlowe!" she cuts me off.

She cradles the head to her chest lovingly as she turns to look at the furnace again. The blue mist that surrounds her spirals into the furnace, turning everything to ice.

"You said you didn't care about him anymore," I say in a slow, tense voice.

The tension inside me is like a tightly wound coil that's about to snap and the last thing I want is to add more fuel to the fire— ironically. I hold myself still, though a storm rages inside of me the more I see her interact with that fucking head.

It's against her chest. His fucking face is next to her chest, a place I never got to touch.

Yet he's doing it. Even dead he's fucking doing it.

As if my hatred for that dead man wasn't potent enough, I find that with each passing second, it festers into something more. Something ugly. Something destructive.

I take a deep breath.

Her lip twitches and she holds on tighter to the detached head as if to guard it from me.

A blow reverberates against my ribs, and I wince at the physical pain.

"I said I loved him and he died. You didn't have to...desecrate his body. How did you even find him?" She takes a deep breath. "How could you even think to do this?"

"Because he's *dead*!" I grind out. "He's dead and I cannot kill him again. This is the only way."

"The only way to what?" She narrows her eyes at me.

"The only way to make sure there's nothing holding you back."

She gives a dry laugh.

"Nothing holding me back?" She raises a brow. "Are you sure it's not the other way around? Nothing holding *you* back?"

"He's already dead. Of course there's nothing holding me back," I reply, frowning.

"Really? Because you had to dig up a dead man and disturb his resting place. And for what? For some deranged show of force? To stroke your fragile ego?"

"My what?" My eyes flash at her.

"You heard what I said. You have a fragile ego," she repeats. "But that's not all, is it? You also don't trust me enough since you had to do *this* to convince yourself I've moved on when I've repeatedly told you I have."

"Minnie—"

"Don't interrupt me, Marlowe!" she snaps. "You went too far this time." She shakes her head. "When I first told you about Lucien, I was upset about your reaction, but I thought it was normal. You were jealous that I had another fiancé. Fair enough. But I told you he died. He is *gone*."

"He's still here," I mutter under my breath.

She scoffs at my words.

"See what I mean? You don't trust me, do you? If you did, you wouldn't have done this. You would have listened to my words and trusted that he is my past and you're my present. But no, you had to go and ruin everything." She swallows hard as she chokes on the last words. "But to desecrate an innocent man's body for your messed up purposes? That's low. Even for you."

"You don't understand, Minnie. I did this for us," I try to explain. But she doesn't let me.

"Us? You did it for *you*. You did it to satisfy some weird hang-up you have about my past when I've told you repeatedly exactly what it was."

"But that's exactly it! He's still here, in your memories. He's still present."

"He will *always* be in my memories."

My features harden.

"And since I cannot erase those memories, the least I can do is erase him from this world. He might be dead, Minnie, but he's not dead enough for me," I growl.

"Dead enough? Do you hear yourself, Marlowe?"

"I thought you'd understand." I sigh.

"Understand what? That you don't trust me? Oh, don't worry, I fully understand that."

"It's not about trust!" I exclaim.

"It's all about trust," she counters.

"No, it's not. It's about the fact that you're holding on so tightly to him at this very moment while arguing with me. It's the fact that you're choosing *him* and not me."

"What the hell, Marlowe? How many times do I have to tell you he's dead?"

"But he's still here," I grit out, throwing my hands in the air.

She shakes her head at me and takes a step back. Disappointment mars her features, but the only thing I see is the way she's holding that goddamn head as if it were more precious than gold.

She's holding it like she should be holding *me*.

A rage unlike I've ever experienced bubbles up inside of me, rapidly seeking to get to the surface.

I reach forward and snatch the head from her arms, and with all the strength I can muster, I slam it to the ground.

The skin cracks. Pieces of hair and skull scatter around.

But it's not enough.

Before Minnie can stop me, I stomp on it with my foot, placing my entire weight on it until it breaks into a myriad of unrecognizable pieces.

She doesn't move.

She's simply staring at me, stunned.

She opens her mouth to speak, then closes it.

"*Now* he's gone," I declare, yet there's a hollowness inside of me even as I glance at the mess on the floor. She should have been the one to destroy it, not me. She should have been the one to *want* to see him gone.

Instead, she's shedding tears for him.

Her eyes are on the broken pieces of her ex-fiancé, tears staining her cheeks, shivers claiming her body. She's reacting to it not as if he were her past but as if he's still her present.

And I hate that more than anything in the world.

Because I can see it. It's there, in the depths of those dark eyes.

She's not mine.

She's never been fully mine.

And now? She might never be.

No! I refuse to believe that.

I ball my hands into fists as I turn to her.

"Why are you crying?" I ask her in a brusque tone. "Why are you shedding tears for him?"

"You... How could you... I don't..." she murmurs incoherently.

She cannot bring herself to face me, her attention still on the last pieces of Lucien.

"How can you say you're mine when you're crying for him?" I grind out, slowly becoming more and more erratic. My body vibrates with unreleased tension as emotions I never thought myself capable of fill me to the brim.

She doesn't hear me—or she doesn't want to.

Dropping to her knees, she reaches out for one of the bigger pieces of his head, then for another. She slowly gathers them in one place, her hands trembling as she tries and fails to put him back together.

I kick at the pieces, scattering them around the basement.

Stunned, she falls on her ass. Finally, she brings her teary eyes to mine.

"How could you?" she asks again.

My nostrils flare as I crouch next to her. Grabbing her chin between two fingers, I stare into her eyes and ask, "You still love him, don't you?"

She doesn't answer.

"You do. I can see it in your eyes."

Again, she doesn't answer.

She looks at me with a mutinous expression, her lips pressed together in animosity.

"Do you love me, Minnie?"

Something flickers in her eyes.

"Do you love me?" I repeat.

"Do you think you deserve it after what you've done?" she retorts, her voice dripping with disgust.

"Ah, but you see, you've just proven me right. You're *not* over him. And you can't even bring yourself to tell me you love me."

Her lips pull back and she bares her teeth at me.

"You don't *deserve* my love," she spits out.

"Really?" I raise a mocking brow. "And he does? And he fucking does?" I yell as I grab a piece of his scalp and crumble it in my fist.

Her expression slowly morphs from one of disgust to one of determination as she pushes me back.

She's strong, I'll give her that.

The power of her blow sends me back reeling, and I fall on my back.

Before I can gather my bearings to react, she's on top of me, straddling my hips. She scratches and bites me as she screeches like a fucking banshee.

"Fuck you, Marlowe! Fuck you!" she cries out, even going so far to use that word she doesn't approve of.

She drags her nails across my neck. They're sharp enough to break the skin, and blood flows to the surface.

"Fuck you!" She continues to yell, hitting and slapping me.

It hurts. But it hurts fucking good. And in spite of her anger, I know she could put more force into her blows. With her powers, she could punch a fucking hole through me, yet she doesn't.

And that gives me *some* hope.

Her squirming on top of me also gives me a boner, which, all things considered, it's quite fucked up. Then again, I *am* a fucked-up bastard.

Oh, I'm still angry as fuck about her reaction to Lucien, but I'm also getting turned on by this savage side of her.

"Fuck you, Marlowe! Fuck you! Fuck you! Fuck you!"

I grab her hands.

"Yes, fuck me, Minnie. At least then I'll have the one thing you didn't give to saint Lucien," I yell at her.

Her eyes widen, and I take advantage of her momentary distraction to reverse our position. I turn her on her back and loom over her.

She gasps as she feels my hardness rubbing between her legs and she involuntarily pushes herself against me.

I freeze as a frisson of pleasure spears through me.

She stops moving, too.

We're both breathing hard as we stare into each other's eyes.

"I'm risking everything to be with you, Marlowe," she whispers. "Why is it not enough for you?"

"I'm a greedy bastard, Minnie. I want it all or nothing."

She gulps down.

"Can you give me that? Can you give me *everything?*"

"Everything?" she whispers.

"Everything you gave him and everything you *didn't*. Everything you don't even know you have to give. I want everything," I rasp out, my voice hoarse.

She stares at me.

"You don't realize, do you?"

"Realize what?" I frown.

She opens her mouth to speak, but before she can say anything, a loud sound permeates the air.

My ringtone.

I swear under my breath.

"Realize what, Minnie?" I repeat.

She shakes her head. "You should answer that."

I let the phone ring until it stops. But then it rings again. And again.

With a tired sigh, I get off her and reach in my pocket for my phone.

"Yes," I snap.

"That's no way to talk to your mother, Marlowe," she chides.

"What do you want that could not wait, Mother?" I ask as I continue to watch Minnie.

She slowly gets to her feet and dusts her clothes. She glances at the floor where Lucien's remains are and I expect her to try to put him back together—again.

She surprises me when she doesn't. Instead, she just takes off the ring I'd so painstakingly made her and throws it in the furnace before turning it on again.

Giving me one last disappointed look, she walks out of the basement.

"My birthday party, of course. It's in two days. I hope you haven't forgotten about that."

"Of course not," I grit out.

"Good. I'll see you and Minnie then," she adds in a chirpy voice before she hangs up.

I'm left staring at what's left of my perfectly planned dinner—or not so perfect as it seems.

I sigh.

I don't think Minnie wants anything to do with me now, let alone accompany me to a goddamn party.

TWENTY-NINE

I STARE in the mirror at the marks on my skin. That savage cat did a number on my face and neck. I look like I got attacked by a wild animal, and it will undoubtedly raise some brows. My mother in particular will likely badger me for an answer as to how I got these injuries.

Since the debacle in the basement, I've had time to reflect on my actions. And I've come to the conclusion that I did nothing wrong. So why the hell is she so mad at me? If anything, I should be the one who's mad considering she blatantly chose that saint Lucien over me.

She cried over his detached head.

She tried to put him back together.

What about me?

What about my heart that was crumbling with each tear she shed for that bastard? Why didn't she try to put *that* back together?

I scowl.

This is not going well. She should have been fucking impressed with my surprise, not incensed. We didn't even get to the champagne, and that means I didn't get my indirect kiss.

Now *that*, I'm even more mad about.

How dare she think I did something wrong when she's the one who cares more about Lucien's scattered body parts than my own whole ones?

I'm not asking for much, am I? I just want to be the only one in her affections: past, present, future.

But it's rather clear that while I may have owned the present, the past and the future are now under question mark.

Fucking hell.

Why are women so difficult?

I would have been better off on my own, like before. Solitude means there would be no one to disappoint or to anger.

Yet as soon as that thought arises in my mind, I mentally berate myself.

The me before Minnie was merely existing, not living. I cannot imagine ever going back to a period in time where she wasn't in my life.

It was a sad and hollow existence, just like I was a sorry excuse of a man.

There's no point in thinking about my life before her since it ceased to exist the moment she got into my car on that cold, snowy night.

If only I knew how to get her to see my perspective, though... Or maybe, understand hers better—though I'm sure it's erroneous. But as it stands, she refuses to talk to me now.

With an annoyed sigh, I leave my room and spot Minnie in the hallway.

She's dressed in a black dress and black tights, together with a black lace veil that covers her face, hiding her features.

Satisfaction blooms inside of me.

Even mad, she still covers herself.

She wouldn't have agreed to come if my mother hadn't called again yesterday and asked to speak with Minnie specifically. I don't know what they talked about, but as she hung up, Minnie told me she was going to join me at the party.

She didn't say anything else. She glared at me and then went to her room. And she's been there ever since.

Until now.

"You look good," I tell her as I let my eyes roam down her body. She looks ready for a funeral, not a birthday party, but I'm not mad. Minnie makes death look hot.

She scoffs at me.

"Don't think this is anything but a favor to your mother. I'm not talking to you," she fires back.

"You're talking to me right now," I note drily.

"Because I'm *forced* to do so. Not because I want to." She crosses her arms over her chest. "You're still an asshole, Marlowe."

"But I'm *your* asshole. Doesn't that count for anything?" I murmur as I step closer to her.

She takes a step back.

"You're getting ahead of yourself. I'm still waiting for an apology," she says as she straightens her shoulders.

"You'll have to wait an eternity," I joke. "I'm not about to apologize for making sure you're *mine*. Just mine."

She half-turns. I can't see her expression to know what she's thinking.

"Good thing I have an eternity to wait," she adds saucily. Then she turns with her back to me and starts down the stairs. Her hips sway from side to side in a maddening display of sensuality that literally has me by the balls.

I mutter a string of curses under my breath and go after her.

The car ride to my mother's home is quiet.

She doesn't speak. Not even when I ask her a simple question like how's the weather. She thoroughly ignores me.

I grumble under my breath.

How the hell do I fix this rift with her? Without compromising on the fact that I want her only for myself, with nothing and no one standing between us—not even a dead dude.

As we reach my mother's house, I park the car in the driveway and we get out. I open the trunk and get the present I'd prepared for my mother, and we head to the door.

Minnie gives me a side-eye as I move closer to her, but I ignore it and put my arm around her. At the same time, the door opens and my mother greets us with a wide smile on her face.

"Marlowe! Minnie! Welcome!" she exclaims as she rushes toward us to give us each a hug.

I clench my teeth as I let her hug me. It's her birthday after all. I suppose it's the least I could do.

She presses her lips against one cheek, then the other.

"I'm so happy you're here," she murmurs, her entire face lit up with happiness.

I nod tightly.

She moves on to Minnie, giving her a tight hug as well.

Minnie's attitude transforms under my eyes. Where she was icy with me, with my mother, it's like watching a flower bloom in spring.

I curse under my breath.

My mother gives me a harsh look. Then her eyes widen.

"Whatever happened to your face, Marlowe?" she shrieks.

Of course, here it comes.

Minnie gives me a pointed look.

"A wild animal encounter," I tell my mother.

"A wild animal?" she repeats, shocked. "Oh my, Marlowe! Did you get a rabies shot? Please tell me you went to the hospital immediately and got a shot. Those things are so dangerous. A few hours and you can drop dead."

"You could say so, Mother." I give her my signature smile.

She narrows her eyes at me.

"Did you or did you not get it?" Before I can answer, she turns to Minnie. "Did he get it, dear?"

Minnie blinks, taken aback.

I look at her, a smile on my lips. Yes, dear, please answer.

"Uhm, he did?"

"Good." Mother sighs. "That's good to know. Although I don't even know how a wild animal got near you to do that, Marlowe. You're so averse to anything unclean," she murmurs worriedly.

"Indeed," I drawl. "But it seems that a little wild cat snuck inside my house and did quite a number on me."

"I hope you called the authorities, dear. Rabid animals are no joke," mother continues.

My eyes are still on Minnie.

"She got away. What can I say, Mother, I have a soft spot for strays."

Minnie blushes and looks away.

"You do? I never knew that," Mother adds pensively. "Although I suppose there are a lot of things I don't know about you, though not for lack of trying. At least now that Minnie is in your life, I hope you'll visit more. I do so miss you sometimes..."

I purse my lips. This conversation is becoming uncomfortable.

Clearing my throat, I take out my perfectly wrapped present and dump it in her arms.

"Happy birthday, Mother," I mutter uncomfortably.

Her lashes flutter in surprise as she takes the gift from me. I expect her to put it aside and open it later on—that's the way she's always done it.

But this time, she tears at the packaging to reveal a pearl necklace and an envelope. She barely glances at the necklace—I'm sure she has plenty of them already—but as she opens the envelope, her eyes grow wide with wonder.

"Two tickets for an all-paid cruise on the Mediterranean," she whispers. "One in my name and one in Giles's name." Glancing up at me, her eyes are moist with tears. "Oh, Marlowe!" she exclaims. "This is truly wonderful, thank you."

"It's nothing," I mumble.

"How can it be nothing when it's everything? I've been praying for the day you'd accept my relationship with Giles and this... Thank you."

"He's a good man," I add rather awkwardly.

She smiles, the lines on her face becoming more accentuated. Still, she looks more beautiful than I remember her looking in her youth.

"He is. He's the best man I could ever ask for."

They've been together for two decades—officially. In that time, I've had plenty of opportunities to asses Giles and his influence on my mother. And though I might not show it, I do care for her happiness.

Giles makes her happy.

He helped her cope after my father's—extremely fortunate—death.

He put the smile back on her face.

And for that, he'll forever have my gratitude.

Of course I also can't fault his work ethic. He's professional to a fault, but he's also an ally. Considering the things he's done for our family and the amount of shit he's swept under the rug for me... Yeah, the man is a force to be reckoned with, even with that starchy exterior of his.

"I have something for you, too," Minnie adds as my mother puts away my present.

My brows go up in surprise. She never said anything about another present—not that she's talking to me much these days. But I informed her that this gift would be from the both of us and she didn't have to worry about anything else.

Clearly, she didn't listen (probably because she currently hates my guts).

She opens her bag and removes a small glass figurine depicting my mother and Giles. It's masterfully done and something that no one would be able to pull off overnight.

Unless...

"Oh, Minnie. This is gorgeous. Where did you get this from?"

"Secret." Minnie winks.

It dawns on me then that she didn't buy it.

She made it.

Using her powers.

"Secret, huh?" I raise a brow at her.

She releases a soft humph and ignores me.

"Come, the others are already here. You must meet Marlowe's siblings, Minnie. I don't think you've had the chance to do it yet."

"I'd love to." She nods with a smile. One that dies on her lips the moment I grab her arm.

She scowls and mutters something under her breath.

"We're a couple. We must behave like one," I whisper in her ear.

"You mean we must *pretend* to be one. Last I remember, I threw away your ring," she says through gritted teeth.

I SHRUG. "Do I look like I care?"

I feel her eyes on me from behind her dark veil.

"I told you, Minnie. You're mine whether you like it or not. You wanted me to take your choice away from you? There you go. I will not allow you to leave me. Ever."

She digs her nails into my arm.

"Does it cost you that much to offer me an apology?" she whispers in a tight voice.

"No. I could offer you an unlimited number of apologies, but none of them would be genuine. Would you like that? Would you like me to lie to you?"

"No..." she murmurs.

"Then you will not get an apology because I'm not apologetic at all."

She shakes her head.

"And that's the issue, Marlowe. If you understood *my* side, you would understand what you did wrong. But you don't." Her voice trembles as she trails off, and I sense the vulnerability in those words.

"Minnie—"

"Everyone, here comes Marlowe and his girlfriend, Minnie," my mother cuts me off as she announces our arrival to everyone.

"Fiancée," I correct her automatically.

Minnie elbows me in the ribs.

The drawing room is filled with people. Giles is standing by the window, a glass of scotch in his hand. Around the piano are my little sister Irene and my younger brother Cristopher, both fooling around with a cacophonous tune. Irene is twenty, home from college, while Cristopher is six years younger than me and still living with my mother.

Ah, yes, if you're wondering about the math, you would be right to be suspicious. I'm pretty sure Irene is Giles's daughter. I have my suspicions about Cristopher too. My mother never admitted to it publicly, but he looks far too much like Giles did in his youth for it not to be the case.

A few close friends of my mother's are sitting at a table, chatting. They only look up as they see us enter, and their expressions immediately turn sour.

They don't like me. They never did.

They assume I'm the black sheep of the family, when in fact, a better contender for that role would be Cristopher. He doesn't even have his own place, for fuck's sake. And aside from his trust fund, he has no other income. He's jobless, useless, and a whole slew of other words ending in -less.

But the actual black sheep of the family is none other than my older brother, Julien. Whereas I have a rather amicable relationship with Irene and Cristopher—as in, we exchange a few words once in a blue moon—I haven't spoken with Julien in years.

Speaking of the devil. Didn't Mother say he'd bring over his fiancée to the party?

A smile pulls at my lips as I realize I might have stolen his thunder by announcing Minnie as my fiancée. Ah, brotherly feuds. How I missed them.

I scan the room until I find him. He's talking with two of our uncles from Mother's side while a timid woman stands a few feet behind him, her body language orientated entirely toward him. He's wearing a slick tuxedo, his dark hair combed back. In his hand, he has a pipe that he keeps puffing with gusto, the pretentious bastard.

He's supposedly a renowned surgeon, but Giles and I know the amount of malpraxis lawsuits he's managed to get out of over the years—all due to good legal representation, not a lack of guilt.

"Fiancée? And you didn't tell anyone?" My mother turns to me, her eyes wide.

At that moment, everyone stops what they're doing and becomes focused on us too.

Minnie digs her nails further into my arm to express her dissatisfaction with my proclamation, but I ignore her.

"Yes, Mother. Minnie is my fiancée. We'll be wed soon," I declare and plaster a smile on my face.

She clasps her hands together in happiness as she hurries to hug us both again.

"This is the best birthday present, Marlowe. You have no idea how much it pleases me to know you've found such a lovely girl." She smiles at Minnie.

"Thank you," Minnie murmurs abashedly. "Your warm welcome to the family means so much to me."

She's so diplomatic even though five moments ago she was ready to have another go at me.

"Of course, darling. Oh my, I have to go tell Giles about this," Mother exclaims as she rushes to the other end of the room.

Warmth spreads through me at seeing her so happy. She might

be annoying as fuck, but she's a sweet lady. After what she's been through, she deserves nothing but happiness.

Mother is gesturing excitedly at Giles, and as he meets my gaze from across the room, he gives me a nod of approval.

I wink at him.

But as we step farther into the room, whispers abound around us as everyone speculates on Minnie's appearance, her face covering, and her status as my fiancée.

Julien notes my arrival and he turns to us, his eyes narrowed. Grabbing the woman behind him, he makes a beeline for us.

"Marlowe. I didn't think you'd come," he mentions in a faux cultured voice.

"Mother's birthday is the one occasion I would not miss."

"And this is..." His eyes go to Minnie as he studies her from head to toe.

I get the urge to push her behind me, even covered up as she is, so this idiot doesn't ogle her.

"My fiancée, Minnie."

"Minnie." He clicks his tongue against his teeth. "What an odd name."

"Short for Minerva," Minnie interjects in a cold voice. She's holding tightly onto my arm, her body tense. I glance at her and raise a brow in question.

She doesn't react, merely maintaining a tight grip on my arm.

"Is it?" Julien murmurs. "And who's your family?"

Leave it to Julien to bring up pedigree, since that's all he cares about.

"Why don't you introduce us to *your* partner, Julien," I say pointedly as I change the subject.

The girl is still one step behind him even though he's got a good grip on her arm.

He pulls her forward, so hard she almost trips.

Blond hair, blue eyes. Julien's type. Every year, he brings the same type of woman to mother's birthday party, but this time, she's not just some random fling. She's his fiancée—if Mother's words are to be believed. Considering how much of a manwhoring pig Julien is, it's quite surprising anyone would want to settle down with him.

"Are you all right?" I ask politely, since her fiancé clearly doesn't care.

But the moment the words are out of my mouth, Minnie's fingers dig into my skin harder than before. She looks up at me, and up close, I can see her expression through her veil.

She's...fuming.

I smile.

Ah, my little heathen. You might be mad at me, but you can still get jealous.

"I-I'm fine," the girl mutters in a soft, unassuming voice.

Julien pulls her roughly to his side, and the sleeve of her dress rises up to reveal some discoloration on her arm.

Bruises.

Minnie notices that too, and her alarmed eyes find mine.

"Who allowed you to speak?" Julien grits out in her ear, his expression changing to one of pure malice.

"I-I'm sorry," the girl whispers.

His hold on her arm tightens and she releases a small yelp of pain.

"Marlowe..." Minnie whispers.

Julien stares down at the girl and when he's sufficiently satisfied with her cowering demeanor, he turns to us once more.

"This is Cara," Julien says in a bored voice, his expression now neutral. "We are getting married in the spring."

The excitement in his tone at such a declaration is nonexistent. He says it as if he's speaking of a grocery list.

"Congratulations," Minnie adds in a tight voice. She stares at the girl, and I feel the tension in her body. "Would you like to come with me, Cara, and leave the men alone to talk?"

I see what Minnie's trying to do and pride fills me at her initiative. I give her a nod of approval.

"I—" Cara starts to speak, but Julien cuts her off.

"There's no need as there will not be much talking to be done."

"But surely you'd like to catch up with your brother?" Minnie probes further.

Julien narrows his eyes at her.

"I said no. Cara will not go anywhere with you," he states in a rough, almost menacing voice.

"Watch your tone, Julien. Minnie didn't mean anything by it. She was just excited to know her future sister-in-law," I add in an attempt to defuse the situation.

No matter how much I'd like to punch that smug expression off Julien's face, this is still Mother's birthday party and I wouldn't want to cause her any distress.

"It's fine, Julien," Cara murmurs, forcing a smile. "I'm sure she meant well."

He turns sharply to her.

"What did I just tell you?" he asks through gritted teeth. "Shut the fuck up when I'm talking."

Her lips part on a small O. "I'm sorry," she whispers, averting her gaze. She takes a step back behind Julien, using him to shield herself from view.

Both Minnie and I stare at them. Their interactions are... unsettling.

"You don't have to apologize for anything, Cara. You did nothing wrong," Minnie interjects. "If anything, a certain asshole should shut the fuck up," she says in a sweet voice.

My lips pull up in a smile.

That's my girl.

"I believe the saying is *ladies first*, isn't that right, Marlowe?" Minnie asks.

"You're right as always, love," I murmur. "No real man would talk like that to a lady," I say as I give Julien a pointed look.

He's always been a prick, but goddamn, I never took him for an abusive bastard.

As Julien redirects his attention to us, I note a twitch in his cheek. His body is tense, and he appears on the verge of losing it. His nostrils flare and he's visibly seething.

Cara tries to pull him away, but he slaps her hand aside and pushes her back. Taking a step forward, he attempts to get in Minnie's personal space—an intimidation tactic, I'm sure. But I'm not about to let that happen.

Just as he moves, I slide in front of Minnie, blocking him.

"Who the fuck are you to talk to me like that?" Julien snarls. His shoulders are so tense, the seams of his expensive tuxedo are about to pop.

I narrow my eyes at him. Is he really doing this in front of everyone? Julien's always been concerned with his reputation, and an outburst like this goes against everything he cares about.

"Careful with that tone, Julien," I warn again. "If you'd like, I'm more than happy to recommend some anger management classes. It's clear you need them."

He bares his teeth at me.

"Fuck you, Marlowe. You fucking freak," he grinds out.

I shrug. "Alas, I'd rather be a freak than a fucking abusive twat."

His eyes flare up, and a shadow of worry crosses his face.

But as soon as it appears, it's gone. He snorts as he leers at Minnie.

"At least I got myself a looker." He laughs derisively. "Is she disfigured?" He nods at Minnie. "Is that why she's covered? Or is she too ugly?"

"What did you say?" I grit out, grabbing him by the lapels of his tux.

I flex my arm, ready to punch him, but Minnie stops me. She quietly shakes her head.

"*She* is none of your business. Don't you fucking address her if you don't want to get your ass kicked in front of the entire family," I tell him in a low voice.

"I'm so scared, Marlowe," he says in a high-pitched voice, mocking me.

I tighten my hold over his tux. For now, our conflict seems to have gone unnoticed. But if this continues, everyone will undoubtedly be able to tell something's not right.

Fucking asshole. I can't believe he's doing this at Mother's birthday party no less.

"Julien, I'm warning you."

"With what, little brother?" He raises a brow. "Perhaps I might be the one to kick your ass this time," he fires back. The venom in his voice takes me aback.

Fucking hell. He's really testing my patience, isn't he?

We've never gotten to blows before, but I suppose there's a first time for everything.

I've never liked him anyway.

"You forget"—he leans in to whisper—"that I'm the perfect son while you're just a fucking weirdo. Why, I bet you had to pay her to come with you, didn't you? We all know you're secretly gay."

"What the fuck is wrong with you?" I grit out.

Yes, there's always been animosity between us, but it usually translated in passive-aggressive comments or simply not talking to each other. This is the first time he's been so vile to my face.

He draws back, his lips pulled up in a malefic smile.

Grabbing Cara in a bruising hold, he drags her away from us.

"Talk to you later, brother," he says and winks.

He leaves the drawing room, going up the stairs to the first floor of the house. Cara follows behind dutifully, more like a servant than a goddamn fiancée.

"I'm sorry about that," I whisper to Minnie. "He's never been this vile before. And for all his faults, I never thought he'd get physical with a woman."

After what we witnessed our mother go through in our childhood, the last thing I would have imagined was for him to repeat what my father did. I may have never liked Julien, but I never thought he'd stoop so low. I wonder if Mother knows, though it's unlikely. If she did, she'd have his hide for raising his voice at a woman, let alone beating one up.

Minnie's watching Julian and Cara closely as they depart.

"This is not typical of him, you say?" she asks in an odd voice.

"He's a pompous prick. He's always been one. But I never knew him to be aggressive. Or straight up vulgar. He cares too much about his reputation to do that."

"I see," Minnie murmurs. "So this is a recent behavior?"

"Can't speak about that since I haven't seen him in a year." I shrug. "But I can't remember him being like this."

She bites her lip.

She opens her mouth to say something, but Irene and Cristopher make their way to us.

"Marlowe and a fiancée. If this isn't the event of the year." Cristopher whistles as he pats me on my back. I tense. He knows I hate it when he does that, but he keeps doing it every time.

Every single fucking time.

I glare at him.

Irene, on the other hand, is at Minnie's side, complimenting her on her outfit.

"You're pretty," my little sister gushes. "Now I see how you got Marlowe to propose. You're so put together, and he's a freak about cleanliness. The best match!"

"Your brother is not a freak," Minnie suddenly says, her tone harsher than I expected from her.

"Come on, you don't have to hide it," Irene continues, chuckling. "We all know how bad he can get. I don't even know how you can stand him, to be honest."

"We've all been wondering," Christopher adds. "Ever since Mom said he was bringing home a girl, we've been making bets." He wiggles his brows suggestively. "Although... Why are you wearing a veil? This isn't a funeral." He reaches with his hand to touch her veil, but I stop him.

"I believe you'll need this hand if you're to ever find a job. Careful so you don't lose it," I say in a strained voice.

"Easy, bro. I was just kidding."

"He was, Marlowe! You're no fun!" Irene whines. "See, this is what I mean. He wouldn't know the meaning of a joke if it hit him in the face," she says to Minnie.

"You're being too harsh with your brother. He has a wicked sense of humor," Minnie replies.

"Marlowe? Are we talking about the same Marlowe?" Both Irene and Cristopher laugh.

"Nah," Cristopher adds. "Even when we were kids, every time we'd play, he'd just sit in his room and watch us from his window like a creep. There was this one time we played a prank on him and replaced his liquid soap with water. Harmless, no? Wrong. He threw a fit about it and then he got revenge."

"By replacing our soap with glue! How are those two even equal?" Irene chimes in. "Ours was a harmless little prank, but his went too far."

"It was antibacterial soap," I mumble drily. "I spent two whole sleepless nights until Giles bought me another bottle."

"See? Freak." Cristopher laughs. "He can't take a joke."

Minnie looks between my two siblings, her lips pursed.

"I don't see how that's harmless if you know your brother's concern about cleanliness. In fact, I find it rather cruel that you'd do that," Minnie points out in a stern voice.

My brows go up in surprise at her words.

"No... That..." Irene stammers.

"Marlowe? Could I have a tour of the house? I find the current company rather lacking," she says in a haughty voice.

My heart pounds in my chest as I realize this is her way of defending me.

Me.

After I fucked up.

She's still taking my side.

"Indeed," I say with a smile. "If you'll excuse us..."

As we turn to leave, Minnie grabs a glass of champagne from one of the waiters and dips one finger inside. She swirls it around the liquid, muttering something in a low, barely audible voice.

"What are you doing?" I frown.

"Come with me," she says, her voice tinged with worry.

THIRTY

"WHERE ARE YOU GOING?" I ask as I trail after her.

She leaves the drawing room and goes into the foyer. She stops, looking right and left before proceeding to the stairs.

"Minnie?" I call out.

She doesn't answer me.

She keeps walking, stopping every now and then to reorient herself.

"Do you even know where you're going?"

"Don't talk," she mutters. "You're messing with my focus."

My brows draw up in confusion. But as she continues walking along the east wing of the first floor, I simply follow behind, curious to see what she's up to.

Maybe she's trying to find a more secluded place for us to talk. My heart beats faster in my chest as I let my imagination run wild.

She defended me in front of my siblings—something no one's ever done before. That has to mean something, no? Maybe she's decided to forgive me and she needs a quiet place to tell me that. Perhaps it's because she needs to remove her veil so I can see her features clearly as she says those long-awaited words.

If I'm lucky, I might even get a hug. Or another kiss on the cheek.

The possibilities are endless, and my blood pounds mercilessly in my veins, flowing heavily to a certain region of my body.

Fuck.

It doesn't help that I'm getting an exclusive view of her delectable backside as she moves her hips from side to side.

Minnie in heels is a force to be reckoned with—and one that has the potential to do permanent damage to my cock. But Minnie in black with frilly lacy details?

My heart cannot take that.

How she manages to look both sexy and cute at the same time is a wonder. But I'm not one to complain since she's mine. My woman. My fucking girl.

She heads toward a room at the end of the hallway, and my excitement gets the best of me.

Anticipation boils in my veins as I get ready for this conversation.

I'll even admit I was a *tiny* bit wrong. Anything to get those pretty eyes of hers to look at me as they did before—with quiet admiration instead of vehement disapproval.

"You don't need to go that far, Minnie. I think we can talk here, too," I tell her as I clear my throat.

She turns sharply toward me and presses a finger to her lips.

I frown.

Grabbing my hand, she leads me to the end of the hallway where she stops in front of a door. But she doesn't open it.

I'm about to ask her what she wants to do when a loud voice echoes from inside the room.

"How many times do I have to fucking tell you, Cara? Don't fucking disrespect me in front of other people!" Julien rages at his fiancée.

My eyes widen.

"What are you doing?" I mouth to Minnie.

She shakes her head and presses her finger to my lips.

"Listen," she whispers.

"You know better than to fucking speak without my permission, don't you?" He continues, his voice becoming increasingly more aggressive.

"I'm sorry." Cara's voice is barely audible. Submissive. Hurt.

I glance at Minnie.

Is this why she wanted to come here? Because she thought Cara might be in danger?

Minnie must read the question on my face because she nods.

"On your knees," Julien rasps.

Minnie's eyes flare up in concern.

Before she can say anything, I bypass her and kick the door open.

"What the fuck?" Julien shouts.

Cara is on her knees in front of him, her neck red. Julien's trousers are half open and his fingers are wrapped up in her hair, tugging painfully.

"I should be the one asking that. What the fuck do you think you're doing, Julien?" I grit out.

"This is a private matter," he mutters as he pulls his zipper up.

Cara wobbly gets to her feet. She sways from side to side before Julien grabs her arm and pulls her to his side.

"Is he hurting you, Cara?" I ask.

"Am I hurting you?" Julien echoes, his eyes narrowed as he watches her.

"O-of course n-not," she mumbles as she averts her gaze.

"I don't know what your fucking deal is, Marlowe, but stay out of my business," he grits out as he walks by me and pulls Cara behind him.

Minnie comes in at the same time as he's trying to exit. She trips on the threshold and spills her glass of champagne all over Julien.

A loud, howl-like sound erupts from him the moment the

liquid makes contact with his skin. He shrinks back, his entire body racked by pain. But it only lasts a few seconds as he quickly gets his bearings together.

He wipes himself, but as I reach Minnie's side, I note redness on his hands where the champagne had spilled on him. It's almost as if the liquid burned his skin.

"Fucking freaks, both of you," he curses. He glares at Minnie, pure malice dripping from his gaze.

"You..." He grinds his jaw as he takes a step toward her.

I pull her to my side and meet his gaze, daring him to do something.

His lip twitches. His light brown eyes are now eerily black, as if his pupils had melted into his irises. There are black ink blots around the white of his eyes. A protruding vein throbs at his temple, and I sense the anger radiating from him.

"Me?" Minnie asks in an innocent voice. "It was just an accident."

He gives her a harsh stare before he hurries out of the room, muttering a string of curses under his breath. Cara looks back at us, her expression horrified. But she helplessly follows along as Julien drags her back to the party.

Minnie and I stare after them.

My instinct is to act and demand an explanation from Julien.

This isn't right. He's clearly hurting her.

"I think we need to call the police," I add in a tense voice.

God, I never imagined I'd call the cops on my own family. Yet here we are.

Damn it all to hell. I still cannot believe that Julien would behave like this, our conflict aside. He knows how much our mother suffered under father's autocratic rule; how she'd try to hide her bruises from us until it wasn't feasible to do so anymore—until she was almost left for dead because of that bastard.

"No," Minnie says, pressing her lips together. "This isn't a police matter."

"What do you mean?"

She appears deep in thought for a moment before she says, "I need to speak to your mother."

"What? What do you think my mother is going to do, Minnie? That idiot needs to be held accountable for what he's done and Cara needs a restraining order against him," I tell her.

She shakes her head.

"Did you see how he reacted when I spilled the champagne on him?" she asks absentmindedly.

"I don't see what that has to do with—"

"It burned him. It burned his skin," she adds.

"What?"

"We need to find your mother. I need to know something."

She takes my hand and leads me back to the party.

Scanning the area, she spots my mother and Giles.

"There. Come."

"What's this about?" I keep asking, but she doesn't answer.

"Oh, there you are, dear," my mother says with a smile as we reach her.

"How long has Julien been with Cara?" Minnie asks directly.

My mother blinks and raises her brows in question.

"Let me think... Six months? Around that time. But why are you curious about that? You can ask him yourself."

"And how long has he been abusing her for?"

"Minnie," I hiss.

Mother's eyes widen in shock. "W-what?"

"How long has he been abusing her for?" she repeats.

"I don't... That is... What?" Mother stammers, her expression filled with shock.

Minnie then turns to Giles. "Do *you* know?"

Giles presses his lips together and sighs.

"I met Julien four months ago at an event. Things were strenuous between him and Cara, but I didn't see any evidence of abuse."

Minnie nods slowly.

"Abuse? But how could you even think of that? My Julien would never," my mother exclaims.

"Cara's arm is full of bruises, Mother. It's bad," I add with a sigh. "We just came across Julien being rough with Clara upstairs too. Her neck was red."

"No. Maybe they had an argument or something. You can't think Julien would do that. Not after what happened with your father..."

"I would have thought so too, but that girl is traumatized, Mother. Surely you noticed," I add.

Now that Pandora's box has been opened, the least I can do is try to make my mother see that Cara could be in danger. Julien might be her son, but she would never allow him to endanger another woman.

Her expression morphs to one of shock, then disappointment before she finally whispers, "Are you sure?"

"Yes," Minnie replies. "Cara is terrified of him and with good reason."

I pinch Minnie. She really has no tact, does she? I still don't understand why she had to break it to my mother so directly. She should have let me do it, and not at her birthday party, for God's sake.

"Minnie. Perhaps we should let my mother talk to him first," I murmur in a low voice.

She shakes her head.

"There's no time. We need to act fast."

"What are you talking about?"

She takes a deep breath as she pulls me aside so Giles and Mother don't hear as.

"Your brother is possessed by a demon, Marlowe."

"What?"

She nods grimly.

"I could sense something was off at first, but I couldn't tell exactly what since I'm trying not to use my powers too much. But once you said this was odd for him, I decided to try something."

"The champagne?" I ask. She did something to it, didn't she?

"Yes. I chanted a mantra to bless the champagne so it acts as a demon repellent. You could say it works the same way as holy water works for the church. They're essentially results of the same process."

"So you dumped holy champagne on him?" I chuckle.

"It's not a laughing matter, Marlowe. This is serious. You saw how it burned him. That's a telltale of a demon. And if this has been going on for more than four months, it's very possible the demon has already consumed his soul and is looking for the next victim."

"Back up a little and make me understand how this works," I say, still not convinced.

"Remember there are two types of demons. This is the second type. Originally, it was a corrupt soul that's now controlled by the Sons of Tenebreis for the sole reason of harvesting the power of more souls. He's likely a low-level demon since only those can possess bodies while they consume the original soul. But that doesn't make him any less dangerous. In fact..." She trails off as she glances back at Julien.

He turns to us at the exact time, an odd glint in his eyes. Somehow, Cara is not with him, and immediately, red flags go off in my head.

"If he's already consumed your brother's soul, then he's already looking to harvest more souls. He can do it slowly, by possessing another body. Or he can do it fast." A troubled expression crosses her face. "And the fast way is murder."

"What are you saying? That he's going to kill Cara?"

"Cara and anyone else who stands in its way. A low-level demon needs around one hundred souls to advance to the next level. And who knows how many other souls he's consumed in the past. He could be close to ascending."

She seems genuinely troubled by this notion, but I still cannot wrap my mind around Julien being possessed by a demon. I mean, sure, he's an asshole. But maybe he just takes after our father instead.

"Really, Minnie?" I raise a brow. "Are you sure it wasn't a fluke? Or I don't know... Maybe my brother is just an abusive bastard."

"The mantra always works," she adds with a shake of her head.

"You only got a few drops on his skin. You can't be sure it was the holy champagne that hurt him or if he was already hurt," I point out. "Maybe Cara fought back."

"But—"

"It's not that I don't trust you. But we have to be sure."

"So what do we do then? We can't just let him be, regardless if he's a demon or just an abusive piece of shit." She sighs.

"Do it again. But this time, have him drink it," I tell her. "Here." I stop a waiter and grab a couple of glasses of champagne.

She takes a glass from me and, turning with her back to the crowd, she swirls her finger inside it while chanting her mantra. Then she gives me the glass and takes the other one, repeating the process.

"Done."

I nod.

"Good. Let me handle this."

Taking both glasses, I head toward Julien. Minnie remains behind, her eyes on me.

His eyes are narrowed with suspicion when he sees me approach him.

"I'm sorry about upstairs," I start. "I shouldn't have barged in like that."

He watches me closely.

"You shouldn't have," he says in a low voice.

"Here," I say and hand him a glass. "Why don't we agree to get along for Mother's sake? It's her birthday party after all."

He doesn't seem convinced. He eyes the glass, but as he reaches for it, he changes his mind last minute and grabs the other glass. Alas, Minnie had the foresight to do her mantra on both.

But he's not drinking. Not yet anyway. It seems he needs more persuasion.

"Really?" He raises a brow at me. "And am I to presume you didn't already tell Mother everything?"

"And what would I tell her?"

He clicks his tongue against his teeth as he stares at me. He brings the glass to his lips, but then decides against it.

He takes a step closer so only I can hear what he has to say.

"Cara is not the innocent victim you think she is, Marlowe. So stay the fuck out of it."

I release a dry laugh.

"Is that what you're going with?"

"I don't have to go with anything." He shrugs. "And I don't need to prove shit to you. Now Mother, on the other hand." He shakes his head. "You just couldn't keep your mouth shut and let me deal with it."

"Deal how? Beat her up until one day she ends up dead?"

"You're the one to speak about killing people?" he fires back.

"I don't. Kill. Women," I grit out.

"How virtuous of you, Marlowe. As it happens, I don't either," he spits out. "Stay the fuck out of my business and let me deal with Cara."

He brings the glass of champagne to his lips and gulps it down in one go. He slams the glass on the nearest table, all the while staring at me.

There's no sign of distress. No pain. Nothing.

Minnie said the holy champagne would burn if he was a demon. But nothing happens to Julien.

He wipes the sides of his mouth with a napkin.

"Stay out of it," he repeats as he backs away.

When he's out of sight, Minnie joins me.

"I don't understand..." she murmurs. "I was so sure..."

"You saw him. He drank the entire thing and nothing happened."

"Maybe my mantra was wrong. Maybe I did something..." she continues.

"Minnie. Not everything needs to have a supernatural explanation. My brother is simply an asshole. That's it."

"But—"

"What I think we should do is find Cara and get her to file a report against Julien," I tell her.

She purses her lips. Finally, she sighs.

"I suppose so. But I've never been wrong before..."

"You're not using your powers to the fullest. Perhaps that's why."

She sighs.

"Maybe. Fine. Let's find Cara."

I still have the other glass of champagne in my hand, and though I'm not the biggest drinker, I find myself quite thirsty. I take a big swig of champagne and put the glass on the table, following after Minnie as she tries to find Cara.

The moment I swallow the liquid, though, I feel a slight discomfort in my gut.

I cough and sputter.

Minnie turns and frowns.

"Marlowe?"

"I'm fine. Must have gone down the wrong way," I croak.

She looks at me for a moment then nods.

"Come on," I say and fall back into step with her.

My throat is a little sore but nothing too bad. I guess this is what I get for not being a habitual drinker.

The party is in full swing as we leave the drawing room. Mother is a little concerned about what we told her about Julien, but Giles is doing his best to comfort her. Then again, she still has to put on a fake smile for the sake of her guests.

Minnie and I look around the ground floor of the house with no success. There's no trace of either Julien or Cara.

"Can you sense anything?" I ask her as we go back to the first floor.

She shakes her head.

"There's a small buzz, but I can't pinpoint the location."

As we reach the second floor, I suggest we split up.

"You take this floor and I'll search for them on the third floor."

"If you find them, call my name, okay?" Minnie says.

I nod and proceed to go up the stairs.

Even though Julien is not a demon, he's certainly pretty demonic. I'm still struggling to reconcile the fact that he might be abusing his fiancée with the man I grew up with. Sure, he could be a pompous ass, but I never knew him to be aggressive. I also can't begin to imagine what must be going through Mother's head right now.

Realizing her son might be taking after our father must gut her to the core.

As I reach the third floor, I check the east wing first.

Stepping onto the hallway, memories of my childhood assault me—none of them too pleasant. Flashes of blood and screams invade my mind.

I swallow.

The noise had woken me up one night. I must have been around five or six. I walked slowly out of my room, following the harsh sounds, only to find my mother in the middle of the hallway in a pool of blood with my father looming over her. She was half naked, writhing in pain, while my father grunted on top of her.

Unfortunately, that's only *one* of such memories. My entire childhood is filled with the image of my father in the throes of anger and my mother bleeding helplessly as she tried to protect her children.

I was helpless to help her back then—would be helpless for years to come.

But one day, I wasn't anymore.

One day, I set her free.

I close my eyes.

I suppose that's why the situation with Julien hits so close to home. No matter how much I might dislike my brother, I can't help but be disappointed that he'd do the same shit we suffered in our childhood.

The east wing is clear.

I see my old room, but I don't want to step inside it. It's been years since I last went inside and every time it puts me in a foul mood.

Cursing under my breath, I pivot and head to the west wing.

I only take a few steps before I hear a creaking sound coming from the game room from the fourth floor.

Frowning, I go up the stairs to check. It might be nothing, but it could also be something.

What I didn't expect, however, is to open the door and be greeted by the same sight that's been replaying in my head for years.

Blood.

There's blood on the floor.

So much blood it's flowing in all directions.

And in the middle of the room, there's a mountain of corpses. Four, to be precise.

The two at the bottom are my uncles. Their insides have been shredded, their entire chest cavity seemingly removed. Blank eyes meet my shocked ones.

On top of them is Marie, one of my mother's friends.

But the last one... The last one is Julien.

His eyes are open and unblinking. Blood is pouring from his mouth, still trickling down his face and neck—a sign he must have been slain recently.

"What the..."

Behind the corpses is a figure swathed in darkness. It slowly turns. Dark, savage eyes flicker with interest. A dark, shimmery mist surrounds the figure, growing in size with every passing second.

Its lips slowly curve up in an unnatural smile before dark tentacles reach for me.

Cara.

Cara was the demon, not my brother.

THIRTY-ONE

"FUCKING HELL!" I grunt as I dodge the incoming tentacle.

Why didn't Minnie warn me demons were so disgusting? It's like black tar is oozing from every single one of Cara's orifices, and the mere thought that I might get a drop of that substance on me has me queasy. Even more so than being the target of a hungry demon.

In my attempt to run from the tentacle, I slip on the bloody floor and barely keep myself from falling. Leaning back, I avoid the tentacle aimed at my face by the width of a strand of hair—which, admittedly, is not much.

I can't even exhale in relief because demon Cara retracts her tentacle, only to send it flying again toward me.

"You," she calls out, her voice thick and raspy and well, quite frankly demonic.

"Me?" I give a nervous laugh. "I think I just got the wrong room. If you'll excuse me," I say as I make a run for the door.

But as I'm one step away from it, the demon slams it shut.

Ah, for fuck's sake. Of course this demon *has* to have some telekinetic powers.

Cara's body appears to be decaying as the dark mist gets

stronger and stronger. Her cheek is melting until only a black viscous substance covering the bones remains. Just as I'm about to point out the fact that she/it is losing their face, she jumps up on the ceiling and crawls toward me.

It crawls!

I suddenly feel like I'm in the *Exorcist* but without the priest to will this demon away.

"Minnie? A little help here?" I call out as I run from the demon.

More bodily parts melt away from what was formerly Cara until what's left behind is a monstrous mass of mangled flesh and oozing tar.

Yuck.

Okay, I've made up my mind. I don't want to become a demon —ever. Not when it means looking like *that*. I mean, personal hygiene? I don't think demons have heard of it. Or if they have, they probably don't even care about it because they can harvest souls while being dirty too. And that won't work for me.

Nope.

I'm out.

Unfortunately, I'm not out of the room yet. And as I run around from this disgusting demon, all I can do is think of ways to buy myself some time until Minnie comes here and displays her demon slaying things—now that's going to be hot. Of course I'll indulge in the hotness of the event only after I ensure I don't die. I'm not about to pull a fucking Lucien and leave my Minnie behind for another fucker to come along and sweep her off her feet.

No, I'll be doing all the sweeping—just not with this demon. Although, I might have to inquire if there's a demon slaying academy for humans since I do have the killer skills—pun intended —and though I may like to be the boy toy of a goddess five days a week, I'd also like to be her protector for the remaining two. Or even the reverse. I'm not picky.

Minnie might be badass, which is admittedly quite hot, but I want to be even more badass. At least then she might find it in her heart to forgive me for my past—and let's face it, future—transgressions.

"I smell good," the demon growls, probably meaning that it smells something appetizing—aka me.

"Oh no, you smell *bad*," I retort, almost out of breath. "And I'd appreciate it if you continued to smell bad from a distance."

A howl-like sound erupts from its makeshift mouth—all the skin and muscle has fallen away at this point—and I suppose this is not the time for humor. I mean, if it lost its human appendages, then I'm pretty sure my humor will be lost on it too.

Another tentacle reaches for me, and this time, I'm not able to evade it and it strikes me in the chest, throwing me against the wall on the far side of the room.

Fuck.

That hurt like a bitch.

"Minnie?" I call out again, my voice cracking from the pain.

The demon crawls toward me, now only a few steps away.

How the hell is no one hearing the noise? But then I remember the loud music playing on the ground floor and realize likely everyone is oblivious to what's happening here.

The demon has almost entirely shed its human appearance, now taking the shape of a monster with no face. It has no eyes, no nose, only a large mouth with rotten teeth that it opens on a growl as it stops in front of me.

Oh, fuck. That shit stinks.

A smell of rotten flesh and sulfur hits me right in the face.

I turn my head to the side as I attempt to breathe some clean air.

This is so foul, I think I'm going to have nightmares about it for the rest of my life. Not the monster. Sure, it's ugly as fuck, but not that scary. The smell, though? That shit is the most disgusting thing I've ever smelled in my life.

I take big gulps of air as I assess my surroundings to try to get out of this situation.

The monster is slower now. It's in front of me, but it's not moving. It's simply...staring at me—though I don't know how that's possible with no eyes.

How does someone go about killing a demon? Do I recite a prayer? Make the sign of the cross?

Do I even *know* a prayer?

Damn it! I should have paid more attention in Sunday school.

As I'm racking my brain for some type of prayer that might keep this putrid thing away from me, it advances even more toward me.

"Smells good..." the same guttural voice from before speaks.

Just when I expect the demon to open that big and smelly mouth and swallow me up, I'm shocked to see it drop before me, lowering its head in front of me.

What the...

Its tentacles are now wrapped around me like a cocoon. They're not touching me, but noxious dark smoke emanates from them, seeping into my skin.

I stand there, confused about the turn of events.

Is he not going to kill me? Not that I'd want that, but it would be more normal than the weird-ass kneeling thing this demon's doing right now.

"Marlowe!" Minnie calls my name as she pushes the door open.

Detecting the motion, the monster shifts from its position, this time moving in front of me. Its tentacles are spread out around me like a shield.

"I'm fine," I shout. "But if you could hurry and exorcize this demon or whatever it is that you do, that would be appreciated. It smells fucking foul here, Minnie."

"Don't move, Marlowe," she grits out, coming farther into the room.

"Oh, trust me, I'm *not* moving," I grumble.

If I shift my face even one inch, I'll get another whiff of that pungent smell.

Blue shimmery light surrounds Minnie's body. A long ice sword protrudes from her hand, her eyes focused on the demon.

It releases another loud howl.

Keeping some tentacles still around me, the demon uses the rest to launch an attack against Minnie.

She slashes at the tentacles, and as they fall to the ground, they transform into liquid tar. But it's in vain, as others grow in their place.

"Your brother's dead, Marlowe," she points out as she continues slashing the tentacles.

"Right, as if I didn't notice." I roll my eyes. "Cara was the demon."

"Cara?" Minnie's veil slips off her head as she rapidly moves around the room. "But how?"

"Don't demons trick people and all that?" I call out, still trying to hold my breath so I don't inhale the toxic fumes.

"They do but..."

"There you have it. My brother wasn't possessed. He was just an asshole."

She slashes some more tentacles as she reaches the middle of the room. One step closer to me.

"Oh, I'm sorry he died," she says suddenly.

"It is what it is. He was an asshole."

"Still, he was your brother," she mentions.

"Estranged brother. Shouldn't you focus on slaying this demon? I'd really like to breathe normally again."

"It's not as easy as you make it sound, Marlowe. I'm trying to keep my powers under the radar," she says in an annoyed voice. "Instead of criticizing my fighting, why don't you thank me for saving you?"

"You haven't saved me yet," I point out.

"That's just a technicality," she adds, breathing hard as she spins around and cuts a tentacle trying to hit her from behind. "It should be done soon."

"How soon? Please say within the next few minutes because it's really getting stinky in here."

"You and your obsession with cleanliness," she scoffs. "If you only knew about the conditions in which I had to fight demons before..."

"I don't think I want to know," I mumble. "It's enough that I know you ate from dumpsters, Minnie. I still haven't forgotten that."

"It was just a few times, okay? And the food was sealed."

"Still from a dumpster."

"Ugh, Marlowe. Can you just shut up? You're messing with my focus," she says right before a tentacle catches her in the chest, throwing her against the wall.

Ouch.

I know how that feels.

But unlike Minnie, I don't have her fancy healing powers.

She grinds her teeth as she gets up.

"Damn it, why did this demon have to be close to ascension?" she mutters, annoyed.

"Ascension? What do you mean by that?" I frown.

"It's at the cusp of becoming a mid-level demon. Hence the monstrous appearance," she explains while fending off more attacks from the demon.

Oddly enough, it hasn't moved from its position in front of me. All the attacks are remote, using its tentacles.

"Well, can't you call your brother or something?" I ask, bringing my hand to my nose.

Goddamn it. I'm definitely going to have stinky nightmares for the foreseeable future.

"No. I will not call my brother for a low-level demon. Do you think I'm that weak?" she asks, clearly offended.

"Since you can't use your full powers..."

"Marlowe, you're not helping!"

"Right," I say as I realize. "I should be cheering you on instead. Go, Minnie!"

Her eyes connect with mine and she gives me a deadly stare. In her empty hand, she materializes another ice sword and launches herself at the demon. She cuts some of the tentacles while evading others and in a matter of seconds, she's in front of the demon, slashing at its midriff.

It's a clean cut. The monstrous creature splits in two, the upper half falling to the floor and turning into a puddle of black ooze.

Disgusting.

"I think the words you're looking for are *thank you, Minnie.*"

I smile at her as I finally inhale properly. There's still some lingering smell but much more doable.

Minnie's still holding on to her ice swords, and since her hands are busy and she can't push me away, I grab onto the front of her dress and pull her toward me.

"Thank you," I whisper.

My lips connect with her cheek, awfully close to her mouth. God, the temptation is debilitating—even in such a grimy environment and after almost being killed by a demon.

I press my lips harder against her skin, and a small sigh escapes her.

Her lips part, and I trace my tongue along the edge of her mouth, tasting her.

"Marlowe..." she whimpers. "This... It's not right... We shouldn't..."

She can't bring herself to tell me to stop, so I don't.

I keep my mouth on her cheek. Her sweet scent drifts to my nose and I inhale greedily. She's a literal breath of fresh air in this fucking putrid world, and I cannot help but become intoxicated on her.

As I slowly draw back, I note the stunned expression on her face.

Her sword disappears from her right hand and she brings it to the place where I just kissed, touching it reverently.

"You're welcome," she murmurs, her face flushed.

I smirk at her.

"It's not so bad to be a damsel in distress if I get *that*," I add with a wink. In fact, being the boy toy of a goddess has never sounded better. I get to watch her slay shit—hot. I also get to reap the benefits—also hot. It's a win-win situation.

Goddamn it, I'm a lucky bastard.

But no sooner are the words out of my mouth than the black tar that's staining every corner of the room pools together in the center. Every drop gathers around, forming a big black pond. It swallows the corpses, almost like a black hole that's absorbing everything in its proximity.

And when it's done pulling all the organic matter inside of it, it starts growing vertically. The black tar swirls around, building blocks that resemble something slightly humanoid, but with misshapen features.

"What the fuck is that?" I exclaim.

Minnie swivels, her eyes growing wide.

"I was too late. It's ascended," she whispers.

The demon releases a mighty roar that shakes the entire house, sending a wave of energy straight at us. Minnie puts her shield up just in time to evade the brunt of the attack, but the surrounding area doesn't stand a chance.

Two holes appear in the wall behind us, one on each side. The cold air of the night seeps inside. As I look back, I note the fallen debris has now blanketed the backyard.

Fuck.

"We need to evacuate everyone. Now," Minnie says in a tight voice.

"There's a fire alarm in the hallway. Cover for me," I tell her and run toward the door.

"Marlowe!" Minnie calls out for me, but I ignore her. I run at full speed, avoiding the monster in the middle of the room. Surprisingly, though, it doesn't even mind me. Its attention is fully on Minnie—almost as if I didn't exist.

Her eyes widen when the demon doesn't make an attempt to hurt me, but she follows after me all the same, enlarging her shield to cover me, too.

When she moves, the demon moves too. It releases another roar, this time louder, more powerful.

The entire foundation of the house shakes, mimicking an earthquake of at least seven on the Richter scale.

This demon version might be stronger, but it's slower, too. Sure, the house quakes with every step it takes, but it's almost as if watching everything unfold in slow motion.

I reach the hallway and pull on the fire alarm. The sound immediately blasts through the house, and in a matter of seconds, the music from downstairs stops. Cries of panic and confusion reverberate through the hallway as the guests filter out of the room.

Minnie stops in the doorway, turns toward the monster, and creates a blue energy blast that hits it in the chest. Even though the blow makes a dent in its body, the injury quickly closes.

"What now?" I ask, since it doesn't seem as though anything can harm the demon.

"We need to draw it out in the open so I can summon it out."

"Summon what?"

"I need to draw out the essence of the demon to the surface to kill it. Until then, he's going to use the souls he consumed as a shield. So if I attack him now, I'm only going to harm the souls inside of it," Minnie explains rapidly.

"Use the backyard. I'll go down and make sure everyone is safely out."

By that, I mean my mother and Giles. I couldn't care less about anyone else. Although, for my mother's sake, I'll include Cristopher and Irene, too. She's already lost a child. I don't want to add more grief on her plate.

Minnie turns to me, her features tight.

"All right. But first," she says as she backs away toward me, still holding her shield in place. The demon, too, advances.

When she reaches my side, she manifests her ice sword and cuts horizontally across her wrist.

"Drink this," she says, thrusting her arm in my face.

I frown.

"It will protect you in case you need to heal from an injury."

Since time is limited, I refrain from commenting or making a joke along the lines of how hot this is. I grab her arm and bring it to my lips, sucking in her blood before the wound closes.

It's warm. Sweet. Surprisingly tasty. So much so, I wouldn't mind drinking more of it, and as I greedily suck on the wound, I'm disappointed to realize it's already closed.

I'll ask for more later.

Maybe we can make it a game too, and she'll let me do the cuts then drink her up.

Ah, damn it. Now's not the time to think of kinky scenarios that I doubt she'll let me enact without that fucking bond in place.

"Go!" she exclaims as she tries to keep the demon busy so I can make my escape.

I give her a worried glance, somehow unable to move from the spot.

"I can handle myself, Marlowe. Go and take care of the guests."

"I know you can but—"

"Go! Now!"

Pressing my lips together, I reluctantly leave her to deal with the demon while I dash down the stairs.

The fire alarm is still blaring, and the closer I get to the ground floor, the more panicked voices I hear.

"Mother?" I call out, scanning the area for her and Giles.

The main door of the house is wide open, and I note a gathering of people on the front lawn. I rush there, combing through the terrified faces until I find my mother.

She's in the driveway, standing next to Giles. His arms are tightly wrapped around her. Cristopher and Irene are pacing around, both on the phone.

"Oh, Marlowe," she exclaims when she sees me. "What's happening? We felt the earthquake, then the fire alarm..."

"You need to leave here, Mother. Now." Turning to Giles, I hand him my keys. "Go to my house and keep everyone there for the time being."

"But, Marlowe..." My mother touches my arm. "What's going on? There's no smoke, no fire..."

"You need to leave. I'll handle the rest."

"What about your brother? I can't find Julien and Cara anywhere," she murmurs, her brows pinched together in worry.

I take a deep breath.

Fuck. I'm not good at this.

What do I tell her? That her son's dead and that his fiancée was a fucking demon who's now trying to kill everyone? As if she'd believe me—hell, no one would.

"I'll take care of it, all right?"

Giles looks at me with an odd glint in his eye. Then he turns to my mother.

"If Marlowe says we need to leave, I'd listen to him," he finally speaks.

"Tell everyone else to leave too. No one should go inside the house. Is that clear?"

Another rumble echoes in the stillness of the night. I slowly turn, my eyes widening as I see the entire structure of the house quaking and ready to collapse.

"No. I'm not leaving without my Julien," Mother argues.

"I told you I'll deal with it. You need to leave," I rasp.

The other guests are moving frantically about, trying to get to their cars.

"Giles, please," I address him, my tone serious.

"Come, Simone. We must leave."

"But Julien..." she continues.

I'm about to lie to her and tell her Julien got out with Cara before. But before I can do that, another thundering sound erupts from the house.

The entire facade of the house collapses, the wall crumbling to the ground. Without stability, the next floors follow suit.

Minnie...

She might be powerful, but as she said, even gods are not indomitable.

"Giles, I'm leaving them to you," I say as I turn and run back to the house.

I only take a few steps when Minnie is thrown in the air by the demon, who is now even bigger in size.

My eyes widen. It must be around ten feet tall at this point.

Its bulky, misshapen frame rises from the fallen debris of the fall.

Minnie gets up, but she's wobbly on her feet.

Her dress is in tatters, and blood stains every visible inch of her skin.

She's breathing hard as she looks back, her features tense when she sees that most of the guests are still in the driveway.

Everyone is screaming bloody murder now.

If they'd been scared at the sign of an earthquake and a potential fire, now they're absolutely terrified as they come face to face with the ugly mess of mangled flesh that's this demon.

"Marlowe..." my mother whimpers.

I don't have time to console her, though.

Giles is already dragging her and my siblings away to the car, so I focus my attention on Minnie.

Reaching her side, I let her lean on me as she recovers from the blow.

Her skin is healing, but she looks out of breath. Tired.

"Minnie, maybe you should—"

She shakes her head.

"I have things under control," she murmurs, her voice ragged.

I raise a brow.

"The demon is almost double the size it was before," I point out in a dry voice.

"That's the point," she wheezes. "That's its demonic essence. Now I just need to end it. Stay back." She pushes me out of the way, but I don't think she realizes her strength because I'm thrown back a few feet. I barely keep myself from falling. But at the same time, the demon releases a loud, earth-shattering growl and advances forward.

It's nimbler on its feet than before.

And as it rushes toward Minnie, dark smoke surrounds its body, almost as if it's seeping into the atmosphere, infecting it.

A bright blue light erupts from Minnie's chest.

She becomes covered in a translucent blue armor. It molds to her body until there's not an inch left uncovered. Her hair, too, flows down her back, lengthening until it reaches her ankles. Around her face appears an ice-like face mask that covers her cheeks, forehead, and nose. Only her eyes and lips are still visible.

The armor appears to come from deep within her, and I soon realize that it's made of ice.

She manifests her ice swords in each hand, and before I can blink, she's out of sight.

She moves with the speed of light as she strikes against the demon.

I can only make out some flashes of blue and the horrible cries of pain of the demon as she slashes at him, time after time.

But whereas before it could immediately mend its body, this time, the ice blade cuts deep within its essence, fast and strong so that the demon cannot heal.

With each blow, she chips away at its body.

It tries to strike back, both with its crooked arms and with his energy blasts, but she's too fast for him.

She flashes herself from his back to his front, then to the side and back to the front, cutting away at him.

Within moments, the demon is back to its previous size, shrinking an inch every second.

When he's about four feet tall, Minnie stops in front of it. She aims both swords toward his chest, angling them at an angle so the blades meet at his core.

She pushes both swords inside the demon at the same time.

Blue shimmery particles—Minnie's energy—soon overtake the black mist surrounding the demon. The blue swallows up the black until the body of the demon disappears.

But I don't think it's over.

From within that mist, something else comes out. It's barely visible to the naked eye. It's almost a translucent light that swirls around in the air. In fact, as I squint to get a better look at it, I notice there's more than one such lights. They move around in the air, as if seeking something.

The skin on the bottom of my palm vibrates. It's an unusual hum, one that's both painful and exciting at the same time.

I grab my wrist to stop myself from shaking, but it doesn't seem to work.

What the...

The lights from before rush toward me.

Eyes wide, I step back and cross my arms over my face in a defensive stance.

There's no attack.

Nothing.

I look around, not seeing the lights anymore. My palm has stopped itching, too.

I frown.

Minnie is breathing hard as she retracts her ice blades. She slowly turns to me.

Her eyes are no longer black but a translucent blue shade.

She walks toward me.

The armor is still on her body, and up close, I note that it's pure ice.

The armor *is* her—her power. And it molds so fucking well to her body, there's almost nothing left to the imagination.

Damn, that's hot.

All I want to do is grab her by the waist and pull her in for a kiss—even though that fucking ice might freeze me to death. But who cares at this point?

I might hate the cold, but I like Minnie more.

"Marlowe?" My mother's voice filters through my primitive brain.

Both Minnie and I look around and realize my mother still hasn't left. She's on the other side of the street, with Giles barely holding on to her.

"Shit," I mutter.

"Don't worry about it," Minnie says as she touches my arm lightly.

Yep, I was right. Fucking cold. But she's also fucking hot, so I think they cancel each other out?

Her eyes flash a deep blue and in a matter of seconds, everyone still around collapses.

"They will not remember anything when they wake up," she mentions. Turning her attention to one of the cars in the driveway, she uses her powers to move it at full speed toward what's left of the house. Once close to the debris, she sends a couple of long, icy spikes toward the car reservoir.

Realizing her intent, I go to one of the guests and pat his pockets, finding a lighter.

She gives me a knowing smile.

Flicking the lighter on, I throw it toward the car.

The explosion is immediate.

"They'll think reckless driving caused the fire. Your brother and his fiancée died as a result of it and his body could not be recovered," Minnie adds.

Unable to help myself, I grab the hand currently on my arm and pull her to me.

It's cold but damn hot, too.

Her eyes widen and she looks at me in surprise.

The mask around her face recedes, the ice seemingly melting in her face.

Her hair, too, becomes shorter while her eyes return to their original dark color.

She swallows hard.

"You were amazing," I murmur as I press a kiss on the tip of her nose.

She sighs and leans into my touch, letting herself react.

Her armor melts into her skin, too, until she's almost naked in my arms. The scraps of clothes barely cover anything, so I take off my blazer and cover her with it.

Sweeping her in my arms, I head toward my car. She must be exhausted after defeating that demon.

Once more—hot.

Perhaps I should feel sorry for my brother's death, but at this point, I can't seem to muster feelings toward any other person.

"Marlowe?" Minnie whispers, her face buried in the crook of my neck.

"Huh?"

"I used my full powers." She pauses, then gulps down. "I need to run away... Again..."

I open the car door and place her on the seat. Kneeling in front of her, I lay a kiss on one knee. Then the other.

Then I simply place my head on her lap for a few moments.

"No. *We* need to run away. Where you're going, I'm going, Minnie."

THIRTY-TWO

RUNNING AWAY with a wanted goddess might not have been on my bingo card for the new year, but I can't complain. I get to keep Minnie all to myself, and that in itself is a win.

I leave a voice message to Giles to take care of my mother and then I direct my focus to the most important part.

The actual running away.

Since we'll be leaving together, we need to find those plants Minnie mentioned that will allow me to go to other worlds. That means we must first find a witch who *has* those plants—though seeing how my last meeting with a witch went, I don't think they'll easily hand over the plants.

Alas, we'll just have to apply a little force.

"And this is..." Minnie blinks as she assesses our new vehicle.

"A van. It's fully equipped too," I add, proud of myself.

Perhaps I got ahead of myself when she told me she'd have to leave eventually, but I've been scouring the internet for the perfect car for a while now, and as it happens, it got delivered to my place a few days ago.

"I can see that. But when did you get it?"

I shrug.

"It's always good to be prepared for the worst," I say. "You have to look inside. There's a tiny kitchen and a bed!" I exclaim as I open the door and invite her in.

I might have had an ulterior motive in choosing this minivan. Since we'll be traveling in it for a while, we'll be forced to share these close quarters. That also means sharing that tiny bed. Sure, it might be uncomfortable for my frame, but at least Minnie's body will be plastered against mine.

I might even get another kiss. Maybe somewhere other than my cheek...

A man can only dream.

"That's... Impressive?" She mentions with a strained smile. She's tired. I can tell.

Tired and hopeless, going by the way her smile doesn't even reach her eyes.

She's wearing a long hoodie and a pair of leggings that she's changed into a few moments ago. Over her shoulder is a bag full of clothes and shoes for the road. I have a similar one at my feet that I prepared in advance for such emergencies.

"I also stocked the drawers with canned food and protein bars. They should last us a while."

She's skeptical as she gets inside, dumps her bag on the small bed, and looks around the van. She opens the drawers to inspect the contents, nodding at my choice of food and snacks. Of course I had to stock up on the chocolate cookies, though I expected a more enthusiastic response from her part.

"This is fine. We should leave now."

I stare at her.

No praise for my foresight? For my effort? Nothing?

"Right," I mutter.

I place my own bag inside the van, then go around to the driver's seat and put on my seat belt. Minnie joins me in the passenger seat, and I start the car.

She's awfully quiet as I head onto the freeway, and no matter how much I'd like to have a serious conversation with her—aka find out if she's forgiven me yet—we have other pressing matters to tend to.

I mean surely she can't still hold a grudge after I was so close to being killed by a demon, no? Danger should make the heart grow fonder not colder. Though since she's a goddess of ice, perhaps hers is perpetually cold.

I scowl.

It wasn't cold for fucking Lucien.

I still haven't forgotten her proclamations of love when she couldn't be bothered to say the same words to me. Granted, I haven't said them to her either, but isn't it obvious how I feel about her? Perhaps it's not love in the traditional sense since what do I know about that type of love? But it's something far deeper, far more obsessive, and far more potent than that.

"Where are we going?" I ask her once we cross the state lines.

"I don't know," she mentions with a shrug.

I slowly turn to her.

"You don't know?" I raise a brow. "We need to find those plants, don't we?"

Another shrug.

"Yes. We need to find a witch who has them first."

"Well, shouldn't you know where to go then?"

She presses her lips together.

"Witches aren't particularly fond of gods," she says with a sigh. "My kind tried to exterminate them a long time ago, so I'm not sure how we're going to find a witch amenable enough to part with precious plants."

"And you're telling me this *now?*" I grit out. "Minnie!"

"What?" she grumbles.

"You've known about the fact that we might leave sooner or later. I prepared everything in advance. The least you could have done was to research who might have those plants."

She mutters something inaudible under her breath, and I'm struck by a sudden realization.

She might not have *wanted* me to come with her. If she did, surely she would have already had a plan in place.

My nostrils flare at the thought that her plan might have just been sneaking out in the middle of the night and leaving me behind.

Fucking hell.

"Then think about it now. Where might we find someone with those plants?" I ask, making an effort to keep myself under control.

But I'm not pleased. Oh, I'm far from pleased. But this is not the time to get into another argument.

"Can't you look them up on that internet of yours?"

"I've looked enough into witches on the internet to know that ninety percent of them are fake. It's not going to help. Why would they hate gods anyway? Shouldn't they worship you or whatever?"

She shakes her head. Looking out the window, she takes a deep breath before she speaks.

"Witches are the offspring of minor deities and humans, something that's forbidden in my world. In fact, interspecies mating is not only prohibited, but most often than not impossible. Witches and a few other hybrids are the exception to the rule."

"How so?"

"It all comes down to energy levels. Each being is born with a certain energy level. In my world, the higher deities have the most advanced energy levels, while minor deities are at the bottom. To ensure a viable offspring, the energy levels of the parents must be similar. So even within my society, a higher deity can never procreate with a minor deity. It's the same with other species, too, especially mortals. But as I said, there are exceptions to the rule. Some mortals are born with exceptional energy levels. It's rare, but it happens. If one such mortal mates with a minor deity with slightly more elevated energy level, the offspring may be viable."

"So we could never have children?" I frown.

I'd never given much thought to my own offspring, but then again, before Minnie, I'd never given any thought at all to women.

She tilts her head to glance at me, her smile tremulous.

"Chances are that we won't," she admits. "I'm not sure if a true bonding might change that, since there's never been one between a deity and a human."

"I see." I nod tightly.

"It's why most marriages are arranged in my world. A powerful deity must have an equally powerful mate. It's both political but also driven by our biology."

"What about demons? Could you, theoretically, have children with a demon?"

"Marlowe! Don't even think about it!" she exclaims in outrage.

"I'm just curious, Minnie. Trust me, after that encounter with demon Cara, the last thing I want to do is turn into a smelly ugly thing. No, thank you."

She stares at me for a few seconds before she scoffs.

"With made demons, no. Even a twelfth level demon, which is the highest, only has similar energy levels to a minor deity. They could, of course, have offspring with other minor deities or even some extraordinary mortals. But it's unlikely since they're always controlled." She shrugs. "The Sons of Tenebreis are a different matter, though. Since we're both directly descended from the Primordials, we're technically the same species. It's just that they feed on souls for nefarious reasons and we don't."

"Is that why your brother was so concerned with you consuming those souls?"

She nods.

"An Aperite deity can turn into a demon too. If I consume even one soul, my energy signature would change forever."

A shudder goes down her body.

"But I'd never do that. Never…"

"You'd never do what?"

Both Minnie and I jump in our seats at hearing Molokai's voice coming from behind.

"What the fuck?" I exclaim, my heart pounding from the jump scare.

"Kai!" Minnie appears to be equally rattled.

"A heads-up might have been nice, dude," I mutter under my breath, adjusting my mirror so I can see him better.

He's leaning against the back of the seats, resting his elbows on the top of the chairs behind us.

"The soldiers have been dispatched," he says, giving his sister a long, hard look. "They're probably at your last known location as we speak."

"There was a demon situation," Minnie mumbles.

"You should have called me."

"There was no time for that, Kai."

He releases a loud humph.

"I hope you're going toward a portal to leave this world," he then adds.

"Not yet. Marlowe won't survive it unless he gets the *aqü* tincture."

"He doesn't have to survive," Kai mutters.

"Thanks for the vote of confidence," I say with a roll of my eyes.

Who even invited him here? I don't like the dude. Now, I know, I know, when you're marrying someone, you're marrying their family, too. But perhaps I can find a way to kill two gods...

Hmm, the idea is rather appealing.

"He's coming with me, Kai. That's not negotiable."

He glares at Minnie, then turns and glares more violently at me.

I lean back and flutter my lashes at him since we've already decided his only language is *non*-language.

He scowls at me.

I scowl back.

"Stop it, you two," Minnie grits out.

"I didn't say anything," I say innocently.

She raises a skeptical brow at me.

"We need to find the plants for the *aqü* tincture, Kai. Do you have any idea where we might get them on Anthropa?"

"Witches," he replies, his tone dripping with disgust.

It seems no one is a fan of witches around here.

"Yes, I know that too. But how do we *find* a witch that has those plants? Anthropa isn't exactly a small world."

His lips flatten. Before I can blink, he's gone. And before I can blink again, he's back, now holding an old book in his hands.

"There are a few clans that are purported to be the most powerful," Molokai muses as he flips the book open. "But there's only one of them currently in the US and A."

He passes the book to Minnie, pointing to an open page.

"Stuart," she reads. Glancing at me, she shows me a genealogical tree. "There's only one living Stuart witch listed here. Katrina Hale."

"I don't suppose you could work your magic and find out where she is?" I ask Molokai.

"Don't push your luck, human."

"And here I thought we were becoming best buds." I sigh dramatically. "We'll be family soon, Kai. This is no way to treat your brother-in-law."

His eye twitches. A vein protrudes around his temple as the temperature suddenly drops in the van.

"Kai. Stop it!"

"You are not marrying a *human*, Minerva," he growls. "I'll never allow it."

"You don't have to allow it," Minnie grumbles.

"Oh, come on, Kai! Imagine all the good times we'd have

together. We can go fishing and demon killing. Of course you do the demon killing and I do the fish killing—and occasional human killing. Bro bonding style." I wink at him.

"You will not marry *this* human," he amends.

He's as starchy as Minnie suggested. No sense of humor.

I shake my head in disappointment.

"Both of you. End it. We need to find this Katrina Hale of the Stuart clan."

Molokai and I glare at each other some more. His nostrils flare. So do mine.

A few moments pass, and once we're both satisfied with the amount of glaring that has occurred, we finally break eye contact.

"Hand me my phone," I tell Minnie.

She rummages through one of the drawers and gives me my phone.

"At least use your mighty powers to ensure we don't crash," I tell Molokai since Minnie shouldn't use any more of her powers.

He looks about to argue, but as I take my hand off the wheel, the car remains on a steady course.

I quickly do an advanced search for the name Katrina Hale. It's useful that the genealogical tree has a date of birth as well, so I'm quite confident I have the right person.

Damn, she's in her eighties but looking decades younger.

"New Orleans," I state. "She has a shop in the French Quarters."

Minnie bites her lip.

"How far is that from here?"

I plug in the coordinates in the GPS and show her.

"Twenty hours of driving?" Her eyes widen. "That's so far, Marlowe..."

"We'll drive for another five to six hours until it gets dark. Once we find a good place to park, we'll sleep the night and be back on the road in the morning. As long as I get a good sleep, I'll be able to drive nonstop tomorrow."

Minnie purses her lips.

"Can't you teleport us, Kai? With the car? Pretty please?" she asks in a sugary sweet voice. But as she turns to look at her brother, her mouth drops open in shock when she realizes he's no longer there.

I tsk at her.

"Your brother is an odd one."

"Tell me about it." She shakes her head. "He might be willing to help me, but that doesn't mean he'll make things easy for me."

"At least we have a name. It's a start. So what if it's twenty hours away? Think of this as a road trip. Me, you, one bed." I wiggle my eyebrows suggestively at her.

She gives me a pointed look as if she just remembered she's still supposed to be mad at me.

"I'm not talking to you," she suddenly says and turns with her back to me.

"But you've been talking to me until now," I protest.

She shrugs. "It was necessary. Now it's no longer necessary."

"Minnie," I groan. "What the hell..."

"But if you're going to apologize... Maybe I can find it in my heart to forgive you," she murmurs, though she's not looking at me. She's gazing out the window. "Then I'll be more amenable to me, you, and one bed."

Goddamn it. She's playing a tough, tough game.

How the hell am I supposed to resist the temptation of *me, you, one bed* when it's all I've been dreaming about? Even so, I cannot bring myself to ask for forgiveness for something I'm categorically not sorry.

Fuck you, Lucien! If I could stomp on you again, I would.

I clear my throat.

"I'm sorry I was insensitive," I say, choosing my words carefully. "I didn't think about your feelings, and for that I apologize."

She turns briskly to me, her eyes narrowed.

"Are you really sorry?"

I swallow.

Nope. Not sorry. I'd kill, desecrate, kill again, and desecrate again that fucker.

"I'm sorry I made you sad. It wasn't my intention. I hope you know that," I speak in a low voice. That much is true. The mere fact that she shed tears because of something I did tore me up on the inside, and for that I can't even forgive myself.

"I don't like to see you cry, Minnie," I reluctantly add. "It physically hurts me when you cry."

She blinks, probably surprised to hear that.

"Then why did you do it?" she asks in a small voice.

"Because I'm a fucking jealous bastard who wants to be the sole object of your affections," I grit out roughly. "I want to be the only one for you, Minnie. Past, present, future. Hell, an eternity to come. The mere fact that you were in love with someone else before... It guts me," I admit.

A frisson goes down my back as I feel myself more vulnerable than I've ever been. I don't even dare look at her, keeping my eyes on the road for fear I might see pity in her eyes—pity that she's never going to feel the same about me as she did about Lucien.

Fuck that. I don't want the same. I want more.

I want her to love me more, want me more, need me more. I want her to only draw her next breath because *I* am by her side. And yes, I want her to choke if I'm not there.

I'm sick, aren't I?

I sigh.

"Marlowe... You have to know some—"

"You know what? Why don't we make a pact," I suddenly state.

Her brows bunch together in confusion. "A pact?"

"We won't talk about Lucien ever again. I won't bring him up. You won't bring him up. It will be like he never existed."

Yes, that's a mighty idea. This way I can pretend she's never looked at another man before—that I'm the only one for her.

"But—"

"We shouldn't let him cause a rift between us, Minnie," I continue.

"You're right." She sighs. "I'm not going to bring up the past anymore as long as you don't."

"Deal," I say and give her my best smile.

She rolls her eyes at me, but slowly, she returns my smile.

We look at each other for a few seconds before we both burst into laughter.

"That doesn't mean I don't get to be jealous of *other* men," I feel compelled to add. "That's the fun type."

"The *fun* type?" she repeats. "What does that even mean?"

"Well…" I give her a sheepish smile. "You're the most beautiful woman all those men will ever see in their lives. But you're mine. So it gives me pleasure to see them realize that you're taken. It gives me even more pleasure to beat the shit out of them to make sure they *understand* that you're taken."

Her expression sobers up.

"When are you not thinking of murder?" she mumbles under her breath.

"It's murder for *you*, darling. That's what I call a special type of murder." I wink at her.

"And not too long ago you wanted to murder *me*," she fires back.

"I'm still considering that," I murmur seductively as I lean into her.

"W-what?" she sputters. "You still want to murder me?"

I smile. "Because I know you'll come back."

I cup her cheek, stroking her lips with my thumb.

"Because you'll always come back to me, right, Minnie?"

Her eyes flash at me, her features tense.

She gulps down hard.

"Right, Minnie?" I repeat.

"Right…" she whispers, suddenly averting her gaze.

"Good girl." I chuckle.

She flushes a deep red and turns to look out the window.

She hasn't said she's forgiven me yet.

But even as her eyes stray from me, her hand seeks out mine, wishing to be held. Even as her words might be absent, her body tells me everything I need to know.

THIRTY-THREE

I'VE BEEN DRIVING NONSTOP for the past six hours.

Now that we know our destination, could we simply take a flight there and arrive in a matter of two short hours? Yes. But that wouldn't serve my current purpose, which is to spend as much time in Minnie's proximity as possible.

I'm awful, I know.

But you know I have it bad when I'd eschew comfort for hours of torture behind the wheel. Alas, having her by my side throughout it all is worth it.

If only she didn't sleep for hours at a time.

Damn it!

I wanted to take this opportunity to charm her with my wit, not listen to her snore blissfully away. Granted, it's a cute snore. Everything she does is cute. But that's beside the point.

She should be awake and keep me company.

I pull up to a gas station to fill up the tank and clear my throat.

She doesn't stir.

I clear my throat louder.

Her lids move slowly.

She yawns loudly, stretching like a cat.

"Are we there yet?"

I stare at her.

"We're not even halfway there," I point out drily.

"Oh."

She blinks a few times and scrubs her eyes before she takes in her surroundings.

"I need to get more gas. Do you want something from the convenience store?"

She considers my words for a moment.

"I'll come with you," she finally says.

As we get out of the car, I stop her. She raises her brows at me, but I simply get a scarf from the back and place it over her head and face.

"Good call." She smiles as she wraps the scarf properly around her face.

I pump the gas into the car and we both head inside the store to pay. Minnie scans the shelves while I go to the checkout to pay.

"Find anything?" I call out.

"Are these good?" Minnie asks as she waves around a bag of chips.

"Grab them and let's find out," I say. I don't eat junk food. Before Minnie, I barely ate any sweets. Of course her arrival in my life meant that I've now developed a sweet tooth just as much as I've developed a Minnie tooth.

She grabs the bag of chips and a bunch of other snacks and joins me at the register.

The cashier rings them up, every now and then glancing at Minnie with an odd expression on his face.

I narrow my eyes.

He can't see her, not with her scarf wrapped around her features. But the fact that he studies her like that bothers me nonetheless.

"Eyes here," I grit out when I note he's staring at her for more than a second.

He startles at my tone and mutters a barely audible apology.

Minnie rolls her eyes at me.

Once we've paid for everything, we head back to the car.

While I arrange the items carefully inside the back of the van —we don't have much space as it is and we have to be mindful of it—Minnie stretches by the car, breathing in the fresh air of the night.

"You didn't mention it," I start as I close the door to the back of the van. "But do you have a specific world you want to visit after we get that tincture?"

"Hmm. That's a good question. There are so many worlds out there, that we can simply take our chances."

Take our chances? That sounds like a recipe for disaster.

"Surely you have something in mind," I probe.

I get anxious at the mere thought that we might not have an actual plan in place.

"Nope." She shrugs. "Once we get the tincture, we'll have to find the closest portal since I can't use my powers to teleport us anywhere. Portals are tricky, though. Without a clear direction, we could end up anywhere. But that's the fun part, no? We get to explore new things," she adds excitedly. "And in the process, maybe figure out where that sanctuary might be."

I raise a brow at her.

"You do realize I'll get old while you will not. By the time we find that sanctuary, if we ever do, I might be heading to the grave."

"Nah," she says with a wave of her hand. "Yeah, you'll get old, but if I give you some of my blood regularly, it should slow down the aging process."

That piques my interest.

"More blood you say?"

I've never thought of myself as a blood guy, but Minnie's blood is so damn delicious. It must be all those cookies she eats on a daily basis because goddamn. I've never tasted anything so sweet and addictive. Now I not only have a Minnie tooth but also a

Minnie blood tooth. Just another addition to add to my newly formed collection of all things Minnie.

There's also the matter of drinking the blood. The act of wrapping my lips over her skin, licking and sucking.

Ah, fuck. Too many tantalizing images dance before my eyes, and I have to awkwardly adjust my erection.

"If it can heal you, it can also heal your decaying cells. Now I'm not entirely sure for how long that will work, but we should be fine."

"So you're not sure?"

Of course she's not sure. At this point, I don't think she's sure of anything. And because I'm a lovestruck idiot, I don't even mind it.

She could lead me into a fucking hell pit and I'd gladly follow her.

"We'll be fine, Marlowe," she mentions with a smile.

I don't believe her, but she could sell me the most outrageous lie and I'd buy it without questions asked.

I open the door for her to hop in when a bunch of loud noises make me stop.

"Yo, girl, drop the scarf and let me see your pretty face," a man's voice calls out.

My body tenses.

"If it's as pretty as the back, we're screwed, man," another speaks, after which laughter ensues.

My lip twitches as I look around for the source of the noise.

For fuck's sake. Even covered, she's still getting too much attention. Granted, her backside is rather delectable-looking, but that's only for me to observe.

A group of three youths emerges from behind a truck. One of them is smoking a cigarette, which I'm pretty sure is illegal at a gas station, especially so close to the fuel. Another has a can of beer in his hand, while the third one went the hardcore route and is holding a half-empty bottle of Smirnoff.

I instinctively pull Minnie by my side, shielding her with my body while I glare at the strangers.

"Marlowe. Don't," she whispers. "Let's just go."

She can sense the tension in my body especially as they continue to leer at her.

She fists my shirt as she holds on to me, stopping me from advancing toward them.

"Move along, fellows. There's nothing here for you," I say in a tight voice.

"Move along, fellows," one of them repeats in a mocking voice as he tries to imitate my accent. "That all you got, posh boy?" He laughs.

"We're not looking for trouble," Minnie says.

"And the lady speaks. You got a nice voice on you, cutie." One of the men whistles as his eyes roam over her body.

This is it. Fuck.

I take a step forward, but Minnie is still holding on to me and shaking her head.

"We shouldn't," she whispers. "Let's just leave."

I ball my hands into fists.

"It's not worth it, Marlowe. We'll just draw more unnecessary attention to ourselves," she continues.

They leer at Minnie, continuing to say foul things about what they'd do to her, and the moment they insinuate they'd lay a finger on her, all bets are off.

The dude smoking the cigarette is especially cocky, grabbing his crotch and thrusting his hips.

I push Minnie behind me, disentangling her fingers from my shirt.

"Marlowe, no..."

"It could have been your lucky day," I say with a smile. "If only you'd have walked away."

They laugh at me, and as I get closer, one of the guys pulls out a gun on me.

I roll my eyes. Of course. It's three to one and they still need a gun to protect their nasty asses.

He aims it at me.

"Not so brave now?" The guy chuckles.

I shrug.

His finger is on the trigger and he levels the barrel at me, probably thinking it will intimidate me.

"We'll have a turn with the girl and you get away with your life. Sounds like a bargain?"

I press my lips together, feigning terror.

I glance back at Minnie and she's watching me closely.

"That sounds like a bargain," I start. They smirk and laugh, practically patting each other on the back for their show of strength. "But I'll have to refuse."

Taking advantage of their inattention, I tackle the guy with the gun, pushing the back of my palm against his wrist and aiming the gun upward. He squeezes the trigger and a shot goes up in the air.

Hmm. I wonder how long it will take for someone to call the police after that noise. Or, seeing the state of the area, perhaps this is a normal occurrence and no one will care. I truly hope for the latter so I can take my time with these *brave* lads.

Moving to the side, I slam my forearm against the boy's shoulder while holding on to his arm.

He cries out in pain when his shoulder pops out of its socket. His arm goes limp, and it's easy enough to grab the gun from his hand.

Unfortunately, he wasn't the only one carrying a gun.

What is it with youths and guns anyway? They can't be more than eighteen.

One of the other guys points his own gun at me, his finger itching on the trigger as he tries to get a good aim. His hand is shaking, and I bet his clothes are already soaked with nervous sweat.

"I'll kill you," he cries out. Even his voice is trembling. "I'll fucking kill you."

"Do it, Drew," the guy in my hold wiggles anxiously as he tries to escape. "Shoot him!"

"Fuck, man!" He squeezes his eyes shut and pulls the trigger.

Ah, newbies.

He doesn't even make sure where his target is. And as I note his finger pressing against that little mechanism, I merely grab the dude next to me and push him in front of me to act like a shield.

He gasps.

The shooter gasps too.

"You shot Mickey, dude. What the hell!"

Mickey cries out in pain as he crumbles to the floor. Drew's eyes bulge in his head, sweat already dripping down his face. He aims the gun toward me again, but his hand is trembling so much, the barrel of the gun moves haphazardly and he misses again.

I'm not a fan of guns—never been. It's just a coward's weapon. Can you even feel you're killing someone if you're not up close and personal? Can you actually feel the life slipping from your victim's body if you're a distance away, averting your gaze and hoping you hit a mark?

No.

I prefer barehanded fighting to guns. And I prefer knives to fighting. But at the moment, I can't be picky since I don't have any knives at hand. Pity. I could have carved a pretty image on their faces—something along the lines of loser, rapist, coward. Or a combination of the three. Of course they didn't rape anyone *yet*, but seeing their bravado, I have no doubt they have in the past or they will in the future.

Youths these days, man.

They're more dangerous than the ordinary criminal. And it's not because they might be strong or particularly smart. But because they're reckless. Their frontal cortex isn't developed enough yet to realize what they're doing, and just like Drew, they aim recklessly everywhere, hoping something sticks.

"Minnie, hold this," I call out and throw her the gun I nabbed from Mickey.

She uses a small fraction of her power to telekinetically bring the gun in her hands. She then aims it at the other man.

"Uhm, Marlowe?"

"Yes?" I ask while I maneuver Mickey around to keep him as my shield. Blood is already pooling on the ground, and some of it gets on my clothes too.

Fuck.

I'll need a shower. And disinfectant. Who knows what these dudes might be carrying? As a precaution, I grab Mickey's arm and check for needle marks. Okay, good, he's not a junkie. But that doesn't mean he didn't dip his prick into something disease infested, and I don't want that blood anywhere near me.

I screw up my face in disgust, but then Minnie speaks again.

"I'm not allowed to kill mortals," she mutters, still holding the gun.

I stare at her.

She gives me a tight smile.

Fucking great.

While Drew aims his gun at Minnie, then back at me, then back at Minnie, the third dude decides to play the valiant and runs toward Minnie to tackle her.

Her eyes widen, but she easily sidesteps him and uses her powers to keep him immobile.

"What the fuck!" Drew mutters in disbelief. "Crew, what the fuck is going on?"

"I can't move, dude. I can't move!" Crew cries out.

I shake my head.

Discarding the bleeding Mickey, I rush to Drew while his attention is on Crew. I punch him in the gut, right below his ribcage to cut his airflow. Once he's gasping for air, I grab his gun and empty his bullets. He doesn't have many left—lucky him.

One ends up in his foot, the second in his other foot and the last one in his knee.

He collapses to the floor, writhing in pain.

"You can let him go," I tell Minnie as I make my way to the third lad.

She withdraws her powers, and he falls to the ground with a thud.

He scrambles quickly to his feet, glancing at his mates and wondering whether he should run away.

Coward.

Before he can make a run for it, I grab his hoodie and hold him. His feet move, but he's not covering any distance. Looking back, his eyes meet mine and they widen in terror.

"I'm sorry," he mumbles. "I'm so sorry about this. Please let me go."

I roll my eyes.

"Maybe we should let him go…" Minnie starts, but I stop her.

"You may not be able to kill humans, Minnie, but I can," I tell her with a smile.

Dragging Crew in front of her, I make him kneel before her.

"Now, what did you say about my woman? Care to repeat?"

"N-no. I didn't… I…"

"What was it? That you wanted to take turns with her?"

"That was Drew! I didn't. I—"

"So you wouldn't have joined in? You wouldn't have done the same thing as your pals?"

He blanches at my words. "Please… I'm sorry."

"Watch out," Minnie whispers.

I look sideways and note that Mickey's dragged himself off the ground and is trying to take a swing at me with the bottle of Smirnoff.

I wrap one hand around Crew's neck, holding him on his knees, and use the other to stop the incoming blow.

The bottle breaks against my fist, and a few shards of glass cut through the skin.

Double fuck. I hate people.

Mickey's eyes flare up in shock when he sees his blow doesn't bother me. But he's too slow to run away with a gunshot in his gut.

I grab the front of his shirt, pull him closer, and bring my knee to his stomach, hitting him where he'd been shot.

An agonized cry erupts through the stillness of the night, and he falls next to his buddy.

More sorrys and pleases ensue as now both Mickey and Crew are begging for their lives.

Keeping my hand on Crew and my foot on Mickey, I ask Minnie to hand me the gun.

She rolls her eyes at me but does as told.

Drew tries to move, so this bullet is for him. And lucky me, it lands between his eyes.

Damn, I whistle. For someone who's not the best at handling guns, that's certainly a feat.

But I cannot even rejoice at my small James Bond moment because I still have to deal with these two fuckers.

"Minnie, drop your scarf."

"W-what?" She blinks in shock.

"Do as I say."

She's confused about my request, but she slowly unravels the scarf to reveal her face.

Leaning down, I force both Crew and Mickey to look at her.

The effect is immediate.

Their pupils dilate—though that could also be from the pain —and their expressions shift from pain to enthrallment.

"What do we think, lads? She's beautiful, isn't she?" I ask them.

"So beautiful," Crew whispers.

"The most beautiful," Mickey agrees.

Their injuries are forgotten. Their predicament, too. All they care about now is the picture of perfection in front of them.

"But see, that's the catch," I whisper. "She's mine. And you dared to look at her."

I doubt they understand my words since they're too busy ogling Minnie. But that in itself requires a punishment.

I grab each of the men by their napes and smash their faces against the pavement.

There's a faint sound of pain but not much else. They're still trying to get a look at Minnie.

I smash their faces again. And again.

I smash them until I hear the bones crack, until their faces are bloody and disfigured. And when that's still not enough to get them to stop looking at her, I grab one of the larger shards of glass off the floor.

The first is Mickey. He did say the nastiest things, didn't he? So as he's looking at my Minnie, all battered and bloodied but still conscious enough to be enamored by her, I dig the glass into his eye socket and carve out his left eye.

I dump it to the ground before I do the same to the other.

Only when his sight is gone does the spell break and his cries of pain begin anew. But while he's writhing on the floor, I apply the same treatment to Crew.

Left eye first, right eye second.

Their chorus of agonized screams are like a symphony to my ears.

Minnie is rooted on the spot, staring at me.

I wink and smile at her.

Grabbing the almost limp-from-pain bodies, I dump them atop dead Drew.

"Get in the car," I tell Minnie.

Digging through their pockets, I find a lighter. Given the

alcohol on the ground and the fuel nearby, this should do the trick. I flick it open and throw it next to the bodies.

A small flame erupts, slowly growing bigger as it encounters other things to consume in its path.

Before the fire gets out of control, I get behind the wheel and drive the van out of the gas station.

Minnie's quiet.

She's not looking at me.

"Was all that necessary?" she finally asks, half an hour into the drive.

She bites her lips in uncertainty as she fidgets with her hands in her lap.

"What? You'll have to be more specific."

"I get that you beat them up. They were rude. I also get that you defended yourself when they pulled a gun. But did you have to..." She swallows. "Did you have to mutilate them, too?"

We drive by a forest, and I pull the car off the highway, seeking cover among the thick foliage.

I stop next to a gathering of tall trees. There's no beaten bath in the forest, which means it should be a safe area to stop for the night—with no other unwelcome surprises. I need to replace the number plates too since I have no doubt that sooner or later someone will put a BOLO on the van. Since we're leaving this world—if everything goes as planned—I don't have to be as careful with the coverup as before. But I also can't let us get caught while we still have work to do.

As I stop the engine, I turn to look at Minnie.

"Was it necessary to smash their faces?" I ask in a bored voice.

She nods.

"No. But I wanted to." I shrug. "Was it necessary to dig out their eyes? No. But I wanted to."

"But—"

"We agreed on something, didn't we, Minnie?" I let my lips curve up in a smile.

She frowns.

"I still get to have fun beating the living shit out of anyone who looks at you."

"Yes, but—"

"No buts. They wanted to have a look, and I let them have a look. But that comes with a price. It will *always* come with a price."

She tilts her head to the side, studying me. Her brows are furrowed, her eyes troubled.

"I've known for a long time who you are, Marlowe—*what* type of man you are. But I've never really understood why." She licks her lips. "How are you so violent? So bloodthirsty? You're a kind man. I know you are. But this side of you..."

"This side of me?" I raise a brow.

"Sometimes it scares me," she admits. "It fascinates me, but it scares me all the same."

Now that's the right praise. Giddiness explodes in my chest to the point that I forget I'm dirty, sticky, and covered in blood. She finds me scary and fascinating.

Ah, that must be the most romantic thing she's ever said to me.

"When did you become like this?" she asks, her voice soft but firm.

THIRTY-FOUR

I DON'T ANSWER HER. Getting out of the driver's seat, I open the back door of the van and head inside. Rummaging through the drawers, I get the first aid kit and disinfectant, as well as a towel, a small bowl with water and some clean clothes to change into.

Minnie follows after me and closes the door to the van.

The space is small and seems even smaller from the thick tension clogging the air.

She wants an answer. I'm still formulating one—a more cosmeticized version of the truth that will keep that fascination there and will not turn it into terror. Or worse, contempt.

"Let me," she murmurs as she grabs the first aid kit from me.

She takes a seat on the bed next to me and opens the kit. Dousing a bandage in disinfectant, she then wipes it all over my hand and knuckles, cleaning the injury and the residual blood around the area. Then she surprises me when she brings her lips to my flesh, her pink tongue peeking out to trace the hard ridges of the cuts from the glass.

My skin hums alive as her hot mouth opens over my flesh. The spot where her saliva touches, the wound slowly closes up.

I stare at her in shock.

"What..."

She smiles sheepishly.

"My saliva has a healing agent, too," she murmurs. "It's not as potent as my blood, but it can heal superficial wounds."

She continues to lick my wounds slowly, methodically, until they all heal.

"Take off your shirt," she says.

Not one to refuse such a command, I quickly divest of my shirt and throw it on the floor.

She grabs the same bandage, adds more disinfectant to it, and wipes the blood on my chest, neck, and face. Her touch is light but firm. She's done this before, hasn't she?

She worked for the Red Cross in 1918.

I quickly push that thought away because it will inevitably lead to Lucien again, and we promised not to speak about that anymore.

Even though I want to.

I want to ask her if she did the same for him. If she cleansed his wounds and put her lips on his skin to heal his injuries.

Did she?

Did those precious lips of hers touch that bastard's skin, too?

I recall the picture I'd seen of them, and he'd had bad scarring on his face and hand. Perhaps more on his body.

A smile pulls at my lips.

It seems she wasn't as generous with Lucien as she is with me, letting me feel the warmth of her mouth on me. Though I must admit I'd rather have her mouth on *other* parts of my body.

When the first bandage is too soaked in blood, she takes another, repeating the process with the disinfectant and continuing to wash me.

Maybe I should tell her that she doesn't need to pour that much disinfectant on my skin—it will dry it out. But at this point, I can't bring myself to say anything that might ruin the moment.

I just watch her, keeping this interaction close to my heart.

A strand of hair gets in her face and she blows it away. Her brows are drawn together in concentration.

Every little movement of hers is mesmerizing. There's a certain grace to the way she glides her small hands down my chest, almost as if this was the prelude to a seduction.

From this view, I can study her at leisure. The way her cheeks flush ever so slightly. The way her lips tremble with a mix of desire and uncertainty. The way her eyes glint so powerfully in the dim lighting of the van.

Fuck. Me.

She's…stunning.

Absolutely stunning.

As she brings the piece of material to my face, her eyes meet mine.

She stops.

Her chest rises and falls with every labored breath.

Mine does too.

A loud thudding echoes in my ear.

My lungs feel constricted. Every gulp of air is like a poison that seeks to infiltrate my body. But every blink of my eyes that brings her into focus miraculously presents me with an antidote.

She bites her lip.

My lips ache, too.

She leans in.

I meet her halfway.

"Marlowe…" she whispers, her voice holding me hostage.

I stare into her eyes and she stares back. Heat radiates from her body, transferring onto mine and banishing the cold away.

There's something in her gaze. Something that eludes me, but something that pulls me in all the same. There's longing, but there's also fear and regret.

"You're killing me, Minnie," I whisper.

A smile pries at her lips and she shakes her head.

"I told you I don't kill humans," she adds jokingly.

"I might be the exception to the rule."

"You're the exception to everything," she whispers. "Everything but that. Not when I've sacrificed so much to..." She trails off, squeezing her eyes shut.

"Why did you come here, Minnie? To my world?" I pause. "To me?"

Her eyes snap open.

"You know why."

"You could have escaped to any world. Why this one?"

She licks her lips.

"Because you're here," she whispers.

An answer that shoots straight to my heart.

"Minnie... You need to pull away. I'm too weak to resist you."

"I don't think I can resist you either," she murmurs.

"Then we have a problem, don't we?" I smile as I cup her cheek.

She leans into my touch, closing her eyes and releasing a deep sigh.

"I want you," I tell her honestly. "I want to kiss you so badly, I'm fucking drowning in want."

She grabs my hand and lays a kiss in the center of my palm.

"But we can't do that, can we? We can't even do that..." I curse under my breath as I take my hand away and move back, putting some distance between us.

She gulps down, her expression troubled.

She opens her mouth to speak, then closes it.

Her eyes sparkle with unshed tears.

She looks away and a tear slips down her cheek.

"No, darling. Don't," I whisper. The mere sight of her like this breaks my heart.

She gets up and looks around the van. She opens cupboard after cupboard until she finds what she's looking for.

A knife.

I frown.

She slowly comes to me, a determined expression on her face.

I don't get to ask her what she wants to do because as she gets back on the bed, she comes straight for me.

She straddles me, wiggling her bottom as she settles right against the ridge of my erection.

Fuck.

Before I know it, a searing pain erupts from my chest as she brandishes the blade around. She starts from my neck and goes lower, cutting my pectorals, my abs, until she reaches the band of my pants. Right above my belt, she makes a horizontal cut.

"Minnie..." I groan when she leans in and opens her mouth to lick the blood from the last cut. She traces her tongue against the gash, tantalizingly close to my groin.

A shudder goes down my body.

The pain now has a sweet edge to it. And as she continues to swipe her tongue all over that cut until it heals, I want to slash myself from head to toe so I could have her mouth all over me.

My back hits the mattress from the onslaught of sensation.

She slowly moves up my body, licking and kissing the cuts she'd made on my abdomen, then the ones on my pectorals.

When she reaches my neck, she takes her time. She sucks in the blood, healing the cut before making a new one with her teeth.

I wrap my fingers in her hair as I hold her. With every lick, I thrust my hips against her. It starts slow, but as she continues her ministrations, my cock becomes rock hard.

"Fuck, Minnie," I rasp.

She's on top of me, her pussy cushioning my erection as I pump against her.

It barely registers that there are multiple layers of clothing between us. There's only the pure sensation of having her so close to me.

Her scent invades my nostrils, sweet, musky, and needy.

And with the way she gyrates her hips, I know she wants to be fucked.

She needs it as badly as I do.

A low moan erupts from her throat as she punctures the flesh just below my jaw with her sharp teeth. Blood flows into her mouth and she laps greedily at it, making out with my wound the way I'd like to make out with her cunt.

Grabbing the knife from her hands, I roll her over and loom over her.

She regards me with hooded eyes as I cut through the material of her shirt with the sharp blade. The fabric falls to the side to reveal her naked torso. Her tits are full and plump, her nipples puckered and begging for attention.

She bites her lip invitingly, not knowing what that gesture does to me or how it challenges the little control I have left.

"My turn," I whisper.

I cut a straight line from her sternum to her belly button. Blood pools to the surface, staining her skin. The red is a stark contrast to her milky flesh, and I lean in to catch those errant droplets.

The taste hits my tongue, making me groan in appreciation.

So fucking sweet.

It's like a nectar from the gods, which is quite fitting considering she *is* a goddess. But she's *my* goddess.

I lick a path from her stomach to her chest, letting my tongue rest between the valley of her breasts.

She's looking down at me, her pupils dilated with desire.

Her wounds quickly close, but I'm quick to make more incisions so I can feast on more of her delicious blood.

I've always been prone to addictions. But I've never imagined my most debilitating one would be her.

Her blood.

Her body.

Her soul.

Her goddamn big eyes that look at me as if I were the only thing who matters to her.

This is not *just* an addiction. It's gone far beyond that.

It's become a necessity to my survival.

In the beginning, she was just a breath of fresh air in an otherwise putrid world. Now, she's the only air I want to breathe—the only air that can keep me alive.

I bite and suckle her flesh, committing the taste of her to mind.

What we're doing is wrong. Forbidden. But why does it feel so damn right?

Why does it feel like this is what we should have been doing from the beginning?

And it's not just about sex.

It's about nearness. Touching. Connection.

She arches her back against me as I trail my tongue up her neck until I reach her face.

I pepper kisses along her delicate jaw.

And in a moment of madness—of needing more than I was given leave for—I bring the knife to my own mouth, wrapping my lips around it and sucking it in until the blade cuts through my flesh. Until my mouth fills with the bitter, metallic taste of my blood—a contrast to the sweetness of hers.

But that's not enough.

I swirl my tongue around the blade, cutting it in a myriad of places.

The pain is immediate, but the need for her is much greater than any physical discomfort.

Her eyes widen as she sees the blood drip from my mouth.

But before she can say anything—before she can admonish me for doing something so ludicrous—I grab her nape and pull her toward me.

She opens her mouth against mine with a moan. The touch of our lips is not delicate—it's not what I would have envisioned a first kiss to be like. It's wild and needy. It's primal and possessive.

Her arms are wrapped around my neck, her legs holding me in place against her.

She tastes my blood. She steals my blood.

Just like she stole my heart.

I push my tongue inside her mouth and press tighter on her nape so she's closer to me—so our mouths become a point of fusion until we're not just two people but one.

One mess of tangled limbs, of tangled mouths, of tangled tongues.

One mesh of blood and eternal longing.

She sucks on my tongue before reaching out with her own, touching it, stroking it.

She whimpers against my mouth and I swallow the sounds, coaxing her into letting me in deeper.

She mimics my previous movement and grabs onto my hair. I do the same.

We both pull and tug, eliciting both pain and pleasure. We wrestle around the small bed, never once tearing our lips from one another.

My body hums everywhere she's touching me. Heat, hot, scorching heat envelops me.

I'm in heaven, but with the temperature of hell.

I bite her lip. She bites mine.

I suck her tongue. She sucks mine.

I swallow her sighs. She swallows mine.

Her every move matches my own. It's so natural, so instinctive.

For the first time in my life, there's no overthinking. There are no crowding thoughts in my brain threatening to drown me. Because the only thing I'm drowning in is her.

She's the first to draw back.

Her hair is mussed, her lips swollen from the kiss.

She swallows hard and licks her lips, staring at me with a mix of shock and desire.

I stare back at her as I fight my own bodily urges to keep going, to claim her, own her.

"We shouldn't have done that," she whispers, though I don't detect any regret in her voice.

"We shouldn't have," I murmur with a smile.

She fights against returning the smile, but it's a lost battle as she starts giggling.

I let myself crash down onto the bed next to her, linking my fingers through hers.

"I doubt a bit of kissing will change anything," I say.

"You call that a bit?" she asks, her cheeks scarlet red.

"For my liking? Yes. A bit."

She laughs.

Turning onto her side, she trails her fingers on my chest.

"I wanted to be good for once," she whispers. "Resist temptation and show I can be virtuous. I wanted..."

I turn to face her.

"You didn't want it, Minnie. You *wanted* to want it. It's different."

"Perhaps. But it seems I cannot control myself."

I raise a brow at her.

"That makes two of us. And I doubt that Primordial Goddess or whatever is going to hold it against us." I lean in to kiss her naked shoulder. It's sheer willpower on my part not to look at her tits and get overly excited again.

She takes a deep breath.

"I hope so, Marlowe. Because I want this to work. I've banked everything on it working."

"Even if it might turn out to be just a myth?"

"Even then," she admits with a sigh. "Because this is the only way we could be together forever. It's the only way no one could ever break us apart."

"So it's not just about you getting absolved for your mistakes?"

She scoffs.

"If I had been that worried about those mistakes, as you call them, do you really think I would have committed them in the first place?" she asks, her expression suddenly serious. "Sure, it might be nice for once not to be chased around by an army of soldiers sent to capture me and ultimately execute me. But no matter how much it might seem like I was naive, or that I didn't know what I was getting myself into, I promise you that I always knew. I was as prepared to face the consequences back then as I am now."

I frown at her words.

"Then..."

"The only variable is *you*," she states unequivocally. "So what if I get caught and killed? I've never been worried about my own death, though it seems quite daunting. But I'm afraid of losing you. That's my biggest fear, Marlowe."

"Minnie," I murmur as I squeeze her hand.

"So you see"—she pauses as she gives me a sad smile—"it might seem ludicrous that I'm holding out for a myth, but I'm willing to bet everything on the infinitesimal chance that it might be real than not try at all, and eventually, lose you."

"It's not ludicrous at all. I'd do the same if I were you."

Her lips tip up.

"But isn't sharing blood just as intimate as sex?" I raise a brow.

Her eyes flare up in surprise. I suppose she hasn't considered *that*.

"It is... Oh damn, why didn't I think of that too?"

She hides her face in her hands.

I chuckle at her reaction.

"Holding hands like this, too, can be incredibly intimate," I continue. "Being in the same bed, sleeping together. All of these are intimacies too. Depending on the person, they might be even more intimate than sex."

She drops her hands, her brows knitted together.

"What do you mean?"

"Twenty-first century, remember?" I laugh. "For some, sex is just an activity, whereas actually sleeping next to someone might be more intimate. It's all about the perspective."

She blinks, then purses her lips.

"Not in my world," she mutters with a sigh. "I told you, there's little contact between the sexes before marriage. And because all the unions are arranged, feelings don't exactly factor in."

"So no kissing? Nothing?"

"Well... I suppose some engaged couples could get away with that. But no female would let herself be seduced *before* marriage. A female's firstborn is the most powerful. So males who take a female as their mate want to ensure that the firstborn will be theirs, which is why the chastity clause is so important. There have been a lot of cases where the male found out his mate had carried another child before and accused her of deception. Some were even executed for it." A shudder goes down her body.

"That's...fucked up," I add, shocked.

"Right? It is! Unmarried males have a lot more freedom, and a lot of highborn males frequent bawdy houses."

"What about your brother?" I wiggle my brows. "I'd be shocked to learn he goes to bawdy houses."

Minnie laughs.

"Molokai? Never. He's dedicated to his job. He'd never do anything to jeopardize his position. My other brother, though..." She trails off, screwing her face in disgust.

"You have another brother?"

That's news to me.

She nods.

"His name is Maledo. He's the oldest and the heir to the King of Cryos. He's been married for"—she uses her fingers to count—"six thousand years? Maybe seven. It's been a long time, anyway. They have two kids, so they're done procreating. They've mostly gone their separate ways now. Maledo is a w-whore. I don't think there's a maid in the palace he hasn't slept with."

She shakes her head in disapproval.

"And his wife knows?"

"She probably has a lover too, so she doesn't care. The children are grown up as well. I believe the eldest is about to get married too?"

"Your world sounds insane."

"It is." She laughs. "You know, I used to be in the demon-hunting branch of our military under my brother. Even though we often traveled to other worlds to vanquish demons, we were never allowed to linger or interact with the native population. So to me, everything in Aperion was completely normal until I learned that it can be different."

"In 1945?"

She nods tightly, her lips pressed together.

Her eyes find mine, and she's probably wondering if I'm going to break my word and bring Lucien up again.

But I won't. I have no desire to mar this precious moment between us with the memory of that fucker. Let him rot in hell.

I clear my throat.

"You asked me when I became like this," I start uncertainly.

If we're going to lay the cards on the table, I might as well come clean with everything too, no matter how shameful the past might be.

She raises her brows in surprise.

I look away and inhale deeply.

"I don't know if I told you much about my father."

"You never said anything about him."

I give her a tight smile.

"He was not a good man. He was an addict with a temper. When he was sober, he would only beat my mother *lightly*—and by that I mean that he would make sure the bruises could be hidden under her clothes. When he was drunk or high, he didn't care about that anymore. He beat and beat and beat her, and some-times he raped her too."

Minnie gasps.

"And sometimes he beat us, too. Julien took the brunt of it

until he went to boarding school when he was twelve. After that, I was next."

"Marlowe..."

"She had ten, twelve miscarriages? I lost count. She'd get pregnant after he raped her, but then she'd miscarry when he beat her to a pulp. My earliest memory is of coming out of my room and finding my mother in a pool of blood, barely able to move."

"Did she try to leave him?"

"She did. A few times. But my mother's family was perhaps worse in that their only response to her cries for help was to *bear it*. They told her to fucking bear it, otherwise it would look bad on the family name."

"What?" Minnie's eyes widen.

"I remember at least two distinct occasions in which we ended up at the police station. But because my father had money and influence, the police never investigated."

"What about Giles? Didn't you say he's been with the family for years?"

"He started working for the family a couple of years after that. But he was only a driver. He was twenty-three, fresh out of college, and looking for a summer gig before applying for big boy jobs." I smile as I remember the way Giles had told the story.

"Twenty-three?" Minnie frowns. "And your mother was..."

"Thirty."

"She's older than him? Wow! I wouldn't have thought so."

"She's actually the reason why Giles never went on to apply for his big boy job. I think he must have fallen for her around that time. But he didn't know about the abuse, or how bad it was, until later on."

"But how? Surely he'd be able to see the injuries and..."

I shake my head.

"We were isolated. Giles was Father's driver. My mother and I weren't allowed to leave the house without a good excuse. She homeschooled me, and we spent most of my childhood inside the house."

"That's..."

"Bad, I know." I chuckle. "My mother was pregnant with Irene around that time, and I think my father knew the baby wasn't his. I remember that night perfectly. Mother had just started showing when my father confronted her about Giles. He'd installed cameras in the house, you see, and he'd caught them in the act."

"Your mother had an affair with Giles?" Minnie asks.

I nod.

"I think in those years, Giles was the only one who kept her alive. I was becoming more and more withdrawn, and I think she felt...alone. I can't blame her for it since I could have been a better son. I could have spent more time with her, helped her more—"

"How old were you?" Minnie interrupts me.

"Eight."

"Eight? You were a kid, Marlowe!"

"Was I ever?" I muse. "Even as a kid I knew more than a child should ever know—had seen more than most adults, too. I could have done better."

Minnie shakes her head at me.

"Even in my world children are children. We might age differently than you. But a child is a child."

I shrug.

"I heard them arguing that night, and I knew what was going to follow. He was going to beat her and she would have another miscarriage. I don't know what I was thinking, or if I was thinking at all. But when their voices became louder, I went there. I usually went there when they'd fight, which wasn't to my benefit since his blows didn't really discriminate." I give a dry laugh. "But this time it was different. They were in the hallway by the kitchen, and I remember grabbing a knife as I passed through the kitchen. I grabbed it and I snuck up on him."

I close my eyes as I visualize that moment.

"He was too busy yelling to hear me approach. The first stab was at the back of his knee. I was quite short for an eight-year-old." I chuckle. "But he quickly fell to his knees, and I administered the second stab. Then the third. And the fourth. Quite frankly, I lost count of the number of times I stabbed him."

"You...killed him?"

"I did. Although it didn't really register as such at that time. I only wanted to make him stop. I didn't want my mother to hurt again."

"Marlowe, that's horrible. I'm so sorry," Minnie whispers.

I hold her closer to me.

"I didn't speak for four years afterward. Trauma and all that." I chuckle. "It didn't register what I'd done for a very long time. Until I was seventeen, and I did it again. And then again at eighteen. And since then, I haven't stopped."

"Your mother and Giles helped to cover it up, didn't they?"

"Yes. They tried to help in their own way, but ultimately, they realized that I'm just...not quite right in the head." I smile.

Minnie's eyes flare in shock and she pinches me.

"Don't say that!" she exclaims.

"It's the truth. I don't know whether I was born like this or I slowly became like this. Either way, there you have it. I killed my own father." I pause. "And then went on to kill a hundred and sixty-something people. I think I've lost count now, especially after that demon attack." I chuckle.

"That's not funny, Marlowe." Minnie frowns. "Your father was a monster and he deserved what he got. I just can't imagine you... An eight-year-old stabbing a grown man. You poor thing," she murmurs, stroking my cheek.

"I didn't tell you this so you can pity me," I say between my teeth. "You've shared so much of yourself and your past, and I... Well, I wanted you to know me better." I attempt a smile.

"Truthfully? I suspected something like this might have happened in your past," she admits shyly.

My brows go up.

"Your kills are very specific. They're all abusers in some way, aren't they?"

I slowly nod.

"And *only* men," she continues.

Another nod.

"You're still killing him, aren't you? Every man you kill is a stand-in for your father."

I freeze. My blood runs cold.

I'm about to deny it. But as I open my mouth to speak, I realize there might be some truth to that.

"You're quite the psychotherapist, aren't you?" I fire back in a playful manner.

Frankly, the last thing I want right now is for my lover to psychoanalyze me and tell me I have daddy issues. Perhaps I do, but that's not something I want to think about now.

I'd rather think about Minnie and her delectable little body. Especially since her tits are still out in the open, begging to be touched—and licked, sucked, and kissed.

I lean in and lay a kiss on her brow. Trailing my lips down her face, I stop when I reach her mouth.

Using my thumb to part her lips, I kiss her.

This time without blood. This time without an excuse.

This is a kiss for the sake of a kiss.

She melts into me, returning the kiss and joining her tongue to mine, stroking, probing, exploring.

She doesn't protest that we shouldn't do this anymore, that we should both be virtuous, chaste, and abstinent. No, she meets my passion with her own fiery one.

We kiss for moments on end, for hours on end. All we do is kiss.

WE REACH New Orleans the following day, a little before 10:00 p.m. I've been driving almost nonstop since dawn. But despite my exhaustion, there's a bright side to all of this.

Finally, there's no more snow and cold.

The weather is in the high sixties, and I'm ready to burn my winter coat and go bask in the sun.

"Let's find a world that isn't very cold," I mention as we enter the busy city.

"You forget I'm an ice deity," Minnie mumbles drily.

"You might manipulate ice, but your body's hot all the time."

"Pervert," she whispers.

She's dressed in a pair of yoga pants and an oversized black T-shirt with a skull illustration on the front. Ah, how I miss her maid uniform. It was the best thing that's ever happened to me—without including the kiss, of course. Even better, I could kiss her from now on when she's also dressed in the maid uniform.

Fuck. That's hot.

But also concerning.

Do I have a maid fetish?

I think so. I don't know where that comes from, though, since we never had any maids growing up—at least none I personally knew.

Maybe I just have a Minnie Maid fetish. Yeah, that sounds about right.

"You know what I mean." I chuckle. "Your body temperature is off the charts—which by the way, is amazing. You're so warm and cute and cuddly," I murmur as I glance at her.

"That's how you'd describe a pet," she mumbles, giving me a death stare.

"Well…"

"Don't say it, Marlowe," she threatens. "Don't you dare call me your pet again."

"I wasn't." I pout. "Well, not a pet exactly. You're my cuddly companion," I say with a wink. "That I also kiss." I sneak in a kiss on her cheek. "And whom I also hug to my chest when I sleep. Actually…" I stop when it dawns on me. "You're more like my own teddy bear."

She narrows her eyes at me.

Did I say anything wrong?

"Teddy bears are cute. Although you don't look exactly like a bear. Maybe a little cat? A cute, tiny, cuddly cat?"

"As in a pet?" She raises a brow.

"Minnie! You're not listening. It's a plushie not a pet."

She glares at me.

"Warm, cute, tiny, and cuddly," she repeats. "That's how you see me?"

"Don't forget beautiful and smart and sometimes annoying, but that's only when you don't wash your clothes or shower regularly. And you've improved a lot since you moved in with me, so it's not very often that I find myself annoyed with you anymore. Although… You left your clothes from yesterday on the floor of the van and I had to put them in the laundry basket. You must be careful," I drone on, becoming very excited about getting a hotel room and doing laundry.

"Weirdo," Minnie mutters, but her lips are curved up in a smile.

I wink at her.

The traffic is intense as we enter downtown. There's a procession of cars that won't end, and loud music blares from speakers all over the block.

I frown and poke my head out the window to look.

Despite it being so late and dark, there are lights everywhere. A hundred or so feet away, the traffic is only allowed to proceed right or left. The road up ahead is blocked, with police cars and officers monitoring everything.

"What is it?" Minnie asks as she strains to see.

"I think it's some festival," I say.

Behind the police barricade, I note a crowd in costumes, dancing around and moving up the restricted block.

"A festival?" Her eyes sparkle. "I've never been to a festival before."

"Not even in your own world?"

She shakes her head.

"We have some formal parties where everyone important gathers, but I wouldn't call it a festival. It's more like...a business meeting."

"Business meeting for what?"

She bites her lip.

"Marriage. I had my debut a few hundred years ago, and that was to introduce me into society and for me to meet eligible males. Since I didn't receive an offer at that event, I was forced to attend a few others until my parents agreed on a match," she explains. "But other than that, I never went to any fun parties, let alone a festival."

The urge to be snarky about her first engagement is overwhelming. But I hold my tongue. I'm finally in her good graces. I don't want to mess this up, no matter how I'd like nothing more than to ask what those parties included. How much did that first fiancé of her see or touch? Did she dance with him? Talk to him? Flirt with him? Laugh with him? All of the above?

It doesn't matter that it was an arranged marriage. All those things should never have happened. They're reserved exclusively for me.

I grumble something under my breath and pinch my leg.

Don't screw this up, Marlowe...

"Oh, really?" I force myself to say. "Then what did you usually do for fun over there?"

"Fun?" She frowns. "Not much. I worked under my brother, and we killed demons. I suppose that was fun."

I stare at her. Then shake my head and smile.

Of course I'd get the only girl in the entire universe whose idea of fun is to slay demons.

Not that I mind it.

Seeing her in action was on a whole other level.

She could slay me all day long if she wanted and I'd merely thank her. Especially if she does it in that sexy ice costume of hers. I'll even forgive the cold.

"Why don't we check out the festival then? I've never been to one either."

She turns to me, her face lit up with excitement.

"Can we?"

"Why not?" I shrug. "We can park around the corner and go."

"Oh, yes, Marlowe. Please," she says as she clasps her hands together. "I'm so excited."

I smile at her. How could I ever say no to her?

We slowly get out of the traffic and I pull up on an adjacent street where, to my luck, a car is just leaving the parking lot.

I take off my seat belt, but Minnie suddenly stops me.

"Wait. I want to change my clothes." She pauses as she scans me. I'm wearing a rather comfortable fleece shirt and pants combo. Not something very fashionable. "You should, too."

"All right," I say.

We get in the back of the van and Minnie quickly takes off her shirt and leggings and dumps them on the bed. I, of course, grab them and fold them nicely to the side.

She remains in her bra and panties, and I do my best not to stare too much, otherwise I'll get overly excited.

"What about this?" she asks as she pulls a black dress from her bag. It's a bit wrinkly, but I note it's not too short, so no one would be able to ogle her legs—that's only for me to do.

"That's perfect," I tell her as I put on a pair of dark jeans and a white button-down shirt.

And since we're going out in public, she dons her black lace veil to cover her face.

Once we're both ready, we get out of the van and head toward the source of the noise.

The music is blaring loudly in the air, together with excited screams from the crowd.

As we get there, it's pretty clear this is some sort of masquerade party. Everyone is wearing costumes, some more outrageous than others. Like that Snow White and the seven dwarves surrounding her.

Ah, well, at least Minnie won't stick out too much with her mask.

I grab her hand and pull her in front of me so I can hold on to her midriff as we make our way through the crowd. The edge of the street is full of people watching a dance performance, and we stop for a moment, too. But soon we see there are a lot of other things to do.

There are stalls with food and games littered on every side of the street, and they're all full.

"Marlowe..." Minnie whispers in awe. "This is like in the movies!"

"Movies?" I chuckle. "What movies?"

"Well." She licks her lips. "We used to watch a lot of movies in the forties. It helped the morale of the troops for when they had time off from the war. And one in particular had a scene with a fair. It looked so fun," she explains excitedly.

"In the forties, huh?" I raise a brow at her. "Is that where you picked up that accent?"

Her eyes widen.

"How did you know?"

I laugh.

My mother was onto something for sure. It is an Old Hollywood accent that Minnie has going on, but it's only because she tried to mimic those movie stars. I suppose that's how she learned some of the language too.

"It's cute," I simply say.

She blushes and looks away.

We walk around the different attractions and stop at a cotton candy stall.

Minnie regards the pink cotton candy curiously and I buy her one.

"Come on. Try it."

She licks her lips and grabs a small piece of the cotton candy. Placing it in her mouth, she frowns as she slowly chews it. Her eyes grow wide and she gives me a pointed look.

"Marlowe! This is so good!" she exclaims, grabbing a bigger piece and shoving it into her mouth. "Have some, too."

With how much gusto she's eating, I don't dare take a piece. Instead, I sneak my arm around her waist and pull her into me. Lowering my mouth to hers, I kiss her and taste the sweetness on her lips.

"Good indeed," I murmur against her lips.

She freezes. But then she surprises me when she shoves another piece of cotton candy in her mouth and raises herself on the tips of her toes to give me another taste.

She does this repeatedly.

Every time she takes a mouthful, she kisses me and shares it with me.

By the time she's done, I'm at my sugar limit but not at my Minnie limit.

But she's too excited about the rest of the attractions to think about kissing me some more.

I'll forgive her this time.

We walk around, and she can't stop marveling at the atmosphere and the way people are having fun. She's basically skipping with happiness. Now, I may not be the skipping type, but I follow stoically behind her, keeping her close to me so no one can get any ideas.

Her face might be covered, but in that dress, she's a bombshell anyway.

I scowl just thinking about anyone ogling her and I scan the area to see if I need to beat the shit out of anyone.

"I want to try that," she says as she points to one of the booths where people are shooting balloons for the chance to win a prize.

I nod at her and go to the booth. After I pay, Minnie takes her position behind the rifle and points it at the balloons. She shoots the first one and hits the target.

She repeats the process until there are no balloons left.

The booth keeper gives her a harsh stare—he probably hadn't anticipated that a tidbit of a girl would have such a good aim.

"Good girl," I whisper in her ear as she goes to choose her prize.

There are a lot of plushies on display. Since she got all the balloons, she gets to choose one of the bigger ones. To my surprise, she opts for a tiny red teddy bear with a rather wretched expression on his face but with a heart in the middle of his chest.

She grabs it with both hands, her eyes wide with wonder as she stares at it.

"Why didn't you pick a bigger one?" I ask as we leave the stall.

"Because this reminded me of you," she mentions.

"Of me?" I frown.

"Yes! See." She points at his scowling face. "This is you most of the time."

"Now, Minnie, I'll have you know that's a certified condition called resting brooding face. You wouldn't understand," I mumble.

"You didn't let me finish." She pouts. "You might scowl a lot, but you also have a big heart," she says and points at the heart in the middle of the bear's chest.

"Oh."

I can't argue with that. Especially since that heart of mine that I didn't even know I possessed before her beats only for her.

Heat travels up my neck and I feel myself flush awkwardly.

Oh, Lord. This is worse than I thought. Not only do I suffer from resting brooding face, but also from the lovestruck flush.

Who would have thought that I, one of the most prolific uncaught killers in the history of the country, would become a fool for a slip of a girl?

I glance at her from the corner of my eye and my heart skips a beat. She's even more beautiful when she smiles with joy. I gulp down.

My chest is tight and uncomfortable. I grab her shoulder and pull her flush against my body.

That's better.

I might be sick with love, but I have my cure right here, next to me.

We keep walking, and Minnie buys a few more sweet treats before we reach a crowded area.

There's a live band playing in the corner, and people are dancing right and left. The fact that they're doing this in costume makes it even more hilarious. You can spot some Marvel villains twerking—which isn't exactly an image I want in my mind. There are also all sorts of horror halloweenesque types of costumes, with blood and gore and open wounds.

While I'm silently judging people for their costume choices,

Minnie finishes her caramel apple and with sticky fingers, grabs my hand and pulls me toward the middle of the crowd.

She could have at least wiped her fingers on a napkin.

But instead of grumbling about it as usual, I do something better. I grab her hand and lick it clean.

Her eyes widen in surprise, but then she giggles as she helps me clean her up with my tongue.

That sounded way dirtier in my mind.

"I'm not exactly a dancer," I say and clear my throat.

"I'm not either, but we can try. Come! The music is so nice!" she exclaims as she pulls me deeper into the crowd.

I can't say no to her, of course.

Instead, I try to find a roomier spot so no one accidentally touches her. But that's rather hard when everyone bumps into each other.

I grind my jaw in annoyance.

But then I spot her hopeful expression and sigh.

I won't ruin it for her.

So I swoop her into my arms. She wraps her legs around my waist while hugging my neck with her arms.

Her face is so close to mine, I can smell the particles of sugar still on her lips.

"We can dance like this," I murmur softly.

Her lips curve up, and she threads her fingers through my hair.

I sway from side to side with her in my arms. I'm sure I'm not doing justice to the rhythm, but I don't care about that when my attention is wholly focused on her.

I sweep her veil to the side so I can see her face better, and not for the first time, I beat myself for not realizing what a beauty she was from the start.

Gazing into her big black eyes, I can't help myself from telling her, "You're the most beautiful thing I've ever seen."

She smiles at me indulgently.

"That's nice of you to say, but I know there are other women far more beautiful than me."

"There are?" My brows go up. "Where? I don't see anyone else."

She shakes her head at me.

"You're such a flatterer."

"You know I'm not. I'd never tell you falsehoods, Minnie. You're the only woman I see."

Her cheeks are tinged with red, and her lashes flutter in embarrassment.

I cup her jaw, tracing my thumb over her lips before I lean in to kiss her.

Her lips are pump and soft, and oh so inviting. I nibble on her lower lip before I dive deeper, exploring her mouth and tasting all the sweetness she has to offer.

We sway to the music and kiss.

The world fades away until nothing else matters but me, her, and this kiss.

She's the first to pull back, her eyes glistening with unfulfilled desire. But there's also restraint. Her body is trembling with want, but she keeps herself still, putting an invisible barrier between us.

"I hope you're not going to regret every kiss we share from now on."

She swallows, then musters up a smile.

"We can kiss. As long as kissing is all we'll do," she whispers. "I just pray the Primordial Goddess will understand."

"If she won't, then we'll make her. I'm not going to let anyone stand in our way, Minnie," I tell her firmly.

"I appreciate the thought but—"

"No buts." I press my finger against her lips. "You're stuck with me forever now, Minnie."

She rolls her eyes at me.

She doesn't seem to understand how serious I am about this. I made a promise to myself and I'm going to keep it no matter what —I'm not going to die like that bastard Lucien and leave her alone.

No. Minnie is mine. I don't care what I have to do to ensure we'll always be together.

The song changes to a slower one and she places her head on my shoulder.

We move to the beat of the song just as our hearts beat in sync with one another.

Her body suddenly tenses, and she pulls back.

She frowns and looks right and left.

"What?"

She tilts her head to the side, her eyes narrowed.

"I sense something."

"Sentinels? Soldiers?" I ask, already getting ready to make a run for it.

She shakes her head.

"Demons. Tens of them..." She trails off as she focuses on a point behind me. "They're getting close."

"Tens of them? Is that normal?"

"No. It's entirely abnormal. Demons have their own hunting grounds and they don't share. For this many to be in the same area, it can only mean one thing. Their master sent them here."

I quickly sober up.

"They're after you, aren't they?"

She purses her lips.

"I don't know. This has never happened before. And they don't usually go after deities, unless..."

"Unless what?"

"Their master got wind that Aperite deities are hunting me and decided to hunt me first. A deity's soul is an enormous source of energy. There's no telling what a demon could do with that much energy. And if it were to get to a Son of Tenebreis..." She gulps down hard, her features shrouded in worry.

"How many demons can you fight at once?" I ask as I wade through the crowd, making my way back to where we left the van.

"If I use my full powers, I could take on maybe four, five depending on their level. But that would give away my location again."

"Four or five? Didn't you say you felt tens of them?"

Her lips flatten.

"High level too, from what I can tell." She pauses. "They're getting closer," she whispers.

"We'll get to the van in no time," I add as I increase my pace.

We bump into people in our hurry, and some are not pleased about it, shouting curses at us as we try to make our way out of the crowd.

Minnie continues to look over my shoulder and study the crowd for any potential danger.

"Four are less than a hundred feet away. A couple behind them, too. And..." She pauses to concentrate. "Marlowe," she whispers, her voice trembling. "There are three of them at the end of the block too. We're surrounded."

"No. We're not. We just have to get to the van and get the hell out of here."

"If only it were that easy." She takes a deep breath. "With this many demons in one place, Aperite soldiers are bound to show up too. It's just a matter of time before—"

"It's either the demons or the gods," I complete her sentence.

She nods.

"What about your brother?"

"I don't want to put him in danger. They'd dispatch more than one soldier to deal with the demons and I don't want anyone to suspect that he's been helping me. That would brand him a traitor and he'd be arrested too."

"Damn it," I mutter.

As we reach the edge of the crowd, Minnie jumps out of my

arms and scans the area for demons. Sure enough, three of them are heading toward us from the direction of the traffic.

Minnie's eyes flash a light blue before a loud bang erupts from the direction of the demons. The police in charge of traffic safety step in, giving us enough time to make a run for the van.

Except...

We both stop in front of the empty parking lot.

There's no van. At least not anymore. Either someone purposefully stole it, or we somehow got on the wrong side of the law. Of course I no longer believe in coincidences, so the former explanation makes more sense.

Either way, we're trapped.

THIRTY-SIX

"THEY'RE COMING." Minnie squeezes my hand. "They're everywhere, Marlowe…"

"Fuck," I mutter. "Any other ideas?"

The demons stopped by the police are once more advancing toward us. From the end of the boulevard, a few other demons approach, just in time for the ones who'd followed us through the crowd to emerge.

"Only one. A church. Doesn't matter what denomination. As long as it's hallowed ground, it should keep out the low levels and significantly weaken the higher ones."

"A church it is then."

I quickly take out my phone and search for the nearest church on the map.

"This way," I say and grab Minnie's hand, crossing the street haphazardly and heading down a narrow alleyway.

I take the most convoluted way to the church in hopes we can lose them.

"They're following us," she murmurs as she glances back. "How much farther is it?"

"There." I point out to the church's tower in the distance.

It's about two or three minutes away.

We increase our pace.

The demons are not far behind. The possessed people all walk slowly behind us, which is odd.

I've seen firsthand what a demon can do. So why aren't they striking? Why are they just following us? More importantly, why are they waiting for us to reach the church when they can attack beforehand.

We soon reach the church. It's a 19th century Catholic building but also a historical landmark of the city.

The gates are vaulted and imposing. But also locked.

Minnie uses her powers to unlock the doors and we barricade ourselves inside.

"Get any holy items you can find," she mentions as she looks around the cathedral.

The colored glass filters the light from the outside, lighting up a path for us to find our way in the darkness. I use the flash on my phone, but it doesn't do much considering the sheer size of this construction. The ceiling is tens of feet high, and if this wasn't such a precarious situation, I might have taken the time to appreciate the beauty of the building.

As it stands, we're in a crisis.

Minnie heads to the altar and grabs all the crosses and other religious paraphernalia she can find.

"If they come inside, I'll use my powers. But there are so many of them." She sighs. "You hold onto these. If they come near you, use them to defend yourself," she says as she hands me some crucifixes and a container with holy water. "It might not do much, but it's better than using your fists."

"Will they turn into monsters, too?"

She turns to me, her expression grave.

"We'd be lucky if they did. That means they're low to mid-level demons. But if they maintain their humanoid form..." She trails off, and for the first time I note the fear entering her gaze. "Those are high-level demons and they're much, much more vicious. And powerful."

"You're strong. I saw you in action," I mention.

She chuckles.

"I may be strong, but I'm not that strong. Four to five high-level demons? Sure, I could handle those and a slew of low to medium. But I have a feeling those are not low or medium."

"But who the hell would organize this attack? And how would they be able to track you if your gods couldn't?"

She bites her lip and shakes her head.

"That's what I'm wondering, too. If they were, indeed, sent by a Son of Tenebreis, then how the hell could they track me? The Sons of Tenebreis have been locked inside Tartareia for thousands of years."

"Didn't you say they can control demons?"

"Yes, remotely. But as you said. If Aperite deities cannot find me when we're physically in the same realm, how could a demon from Tartareia manage that?"

"Has this happened before?" I ask. "Have those Sons of Tenebreis sent demons after a god before?"

She shakes her head.

"Maybe it has and I don't know. But as far as I'm aware, demons do everything in their power not to be found by our soldiers. This is all so weird." She takes a deep breath. "Hopefully, they won't be able to enter the holy grounds and—"

No sooner Minnie spoke than the doors of the church begin to rattle.

Her wide eyes meet mine.

"Take shelter behind the altar and keep the holy items next to you."

"I'm not about to—"

"Do as I say, Marlowe," she cuts me off.

In the blink of an eye, a thin strip of ice covers her entire body, forming a suit similar to the one she'd had on at my mother's house.

Kneeling on the ground, she presses her open palms on the floor and murmurs something.

Ice forms from her palms and covers the entire floor of the church, enveloping the walls and the furniture.

She continues whispering the same chant as the rattle of the door becomes louder. But before she can finish her chant, one of the ceiling high windows shatters, and a figure jumps inside.

What the...

Another window shatters, then another. The demons flock inside the church one by one, slowly, methodically, as if they were taking their time.

Immediately, I notice a difference between these demons and the one that had possessed Cara. That one had been volatile, hungry. These ones are sentient.

At last, the door breaks too, and some twelve, fifteen more demons step inside the church.

Their expressions tighten with pain as they step on the ice-coated floor, but it doesn't seem to deter them. It's just an inconvenience, but they remain focused on their objective.

"Oh, no," Minnie mutters, taking a step back.

"What?"

"Take cover, Marlowe! These are all high level. Damn it! I infused the ice with the same blessing chant as the holy water, and it barely tickles them."

Fuck.

That's bad.

Especially since I count more than twenty in total.

Twenty fucking high-level demons.

"Marlowe, go!" Minnie yells at me.

I shake my head. I'm not about to let her deal with twenty high-level demons when she just confessed she can only take on four or five at a time.

Clutching onto the crucifix and the holy water, I grab my pocketknife and get ready for those fuckers to strike.

"I'm not going anywhere, Minnie," I grit out. "If it's our fate to die here today, then we're going to face death together."

"But—"

"I'm not running," I repeat.

She glances at me, worry reflected in her features.

"You still have my blood in your system, so you should be good for now," she says. "But please take care."

I give her a hard nod.

The demons are slowly approaching. It's almost like watching a zombie parade with the way they're moving. There's no urgency, no hurry.

Minnie manifests her ice swords and she gets into a position to fight.

The holy ice she'd created is slowly dissipating now, absorbed by the demons as they congregate in the front of the church.

Minnie frowns.

Instead of striking, they gather in a formation—somewhat similar to the one the sentinels had assumed. But there doesn't seem to be a leader among them.

They extend their arms, almost touching each other, but not quite. From the first demon's fingertips, a black smoke erupts, winding out like a thread. It reaches the second demon's fingers, and he shudders. Black smoke envelops its entire body and he passes on the black smoke current to the next demon. They do this until the first is connected to the last through that black smoke.

Slowly, they raise their gazes toward us, their eyes fully black. And in that blackness, a small, red spot appears, almost like a laser beam.

They move in sync as they come toward us.

Minnie summons her energy shield, and a blue shimmery light envelops her from head to toe. She's ready to strike as they come closer.

But to both our surprises, the demons don't pay her any attention.

They pass by her as if she were invisible.

A look of pure astonishment crosses her face and she swivels to follow their movements.

Their attention is focused on the back of the church.

On me.

Minnie's eyes widen in disbelief.

"Run, Marlowe!"

I throw the container with holy water toward them and back away.

The liquid splashes onto the floor, touching their feet. But it barely makes them wince.

Minnie throws back her arm, a spear of ice growing in her hands, which she throws at the demon leading the formation.

But just as it's about to strike it, a shield forms over the demon formation, repelling the spear.

Minnie repeats the action a couple more times from a few different angles, but the result is the same. When she realizes they will not stop their advance toward me, she flashes herself in front of me.

"What's going on?" I ask.

"I don't know," she mutters in a strained voice. "I've never seen high-level demons behave like this before. By all accounts, they should be sentient and have a fully developed personality at this level. But this... This is more like a hive mind mentality."

"They're linked through that smoke," I point out.

"Not only. They're linked through whoever is controlling them." She takes a deep breath. "I've been in countless battles over the centuries, Marlowe, but I've never encountered a Son of Tenebreis who could control so many high-level demons at once, and remotely."

"Do you think he might be near?"

"I don't know. I truly don't know what's going on anymore. They're not after me, that much is clear."

The march of the demons continues. They're not belligerent, nor do they initiate an offensive. Their actions so far have been only defensive, which makes this all the more confusing.

"Then what the hell do they want?"

"I don't know," she repeats on a whisper. "But whoever is controlling them must be extraordinarily strong to make these demons immune to my blessings chants."

"What do we do then?"

She purses her lips. Reaching for my hand, she gives me a quick squeeze.

"If we can't hurt them, then the only thing left to do is protect ourselves."

Cold seeps into my skin, transferring from her body onto mine.

The shimmery energy surrounding Minnie extends to me, slowly materializing until it becomes a sphere of pure ice, and we are both encased in it.

The demons don't react.

They move forward until they reach the sphere, and that's when they break formation. They create a circle around the sphere, keeping their dark smoke tether in place.

From my vantage point, it looks as if they're holding hands in a circle around us, ready to start dancing. If this hadn't been a life-and-death situation, I would have perhaps laughed at that mental image.

"What are they doing?" I ask Minnie, who's watching them with apprehension. She anxiously nibbles on her lower lip.

"I don't know," she whispers.

The black smoke amplifies until it fiercely bursts to the surface. The demons lean back, and a hole opens in their chests that funnels the black smoke and aims it straight at the ice sphere.

Loud bangs reverberate through the domed church, the echo of the blows deafening.

The smoke hits our shield like a myriad of cannon balls, shot in rapid succession.

Minnie wobbles on her feet, her eyes wide. She grasps onto me for balance as the blows become more incessant and more powerful.

Her eyes turn a light shade of blue as she forces more of her energy to the surface, reinforcing the shield with another layer of magical ice.

Her entire body is tense as she focuses her powers to keep the demons out, but I fear even that's not enough. Not with the way the entire foundation of the cathedral is trembling. Not with the way I can see nothing at all but black smoke devouring our shield.

With the combined strength of twenty high-level demons, I doubt Minnie can last much longer.

"Minnie…"

"I'm trying to reach my brother," she says in a strangled voice. "But I can't even make a connection. Something is blocking it. Something…" She gasps for air. "This isn't right. They shouldn't be this powerful…"

Oh fuck. If she's trying to call her brother here despite the danger, that means this is getting out of control. Worry fills me to the brim as I glance from the black balls of smoke that keep hitting our shield to Minnie's pale features that are marred by pain.

"What do they want?" I ask. "Maybe we can give it to them."

"What? Are you insane? We can't give them anything. You can't reason with demons, Marlowe."

"They were coming toward me," I mention. "What if I just surrendered and—"

"No," she states categorically. "That's out of the question."

Another loud bang rattles the shield. More balls of smoke hit it from all sides, and the first layer is already cracking.

Minnie is almost out of breath.

I hold on to her tightly, but I can tell she's hanging on by a thread.

Icicles hit the ground as the first layer of the shield collapses.

The demons step forward, increasing their attack.

Minnie's eyes flicker between a light and dark blue. Her fingers are wrapped tightly around my upper arm as she struggles to keep herself upright.

Her chest rises and falls rapidly as she focuses to maintain the shield, but I can tell this is draining her.

"Tell me how to help," I whisper. It pains me to see her like this. Not only is she weakening with every passing moment, but it seems the attack on her shield is physically hurting her.

She shakes her head.

"There's nothing you can do," she replies, grinding her teeth. "This is as far as my powers go. I'm only a fledgling deity." She lets out a dry laugh.

"You're four thousand five hundred and fifty-eight years old," I remark.

"But my kind is only considered mature at three thousand years old. I'm the youngest in my regimen—was the youngest." She winces and closes her eyes to take a deep breath. "My brother would have been able to handle this. Anyone would have been able to handle this better than me..." She trails off, her voice filled with hopelessness. "Why do I always mess things up?" She lets out a soft cry as tears roll down her face.

"Minnie," I start as I shake her.

She slowly opens her eyes to look at me at the same time another loud bang erupts in the air, more ice falling to the ground.

Suddenly, she looks so young and uncertain, and it breaks my heart that she's doubting herself.

"I destroy everything I touch, Marlowe," she whispers. "I shouldn't have come back to Anthropa. I shouldn't have put you in danger. This is all my fault."

Panic takes hold of her as her words become more and more erratic.

"I'm so sorry," she continues to whisper, tears rolling down her face.

I cup her cheeks and wipe her tears with my thumbs.

"You're the most badass person I've ever met," I tell her sincerely. "And this is not meant to flatter you. It's the truth. You're stronger than you think, so don't you dare give up. We're not dying here tonight."

She shakes her head. Tension lines mar her face from the effort of keeping the shield up and running. Her eyes continue to shift color, never settling on one for more than a minute.

"Say it with me. We're not dying here tonight," I demand.

She squeezes her eyes shut and hesitates.

"Say it, Minnie!"

"We're not dying here tonight," she finally whispers.

"Good. Now let's think. There has the be a way to separate these demons. They're this strong because they're acting as one entity. Individually, they should be more manageable."

She bites her lip as she turns her attention to the demons and our surroundings.

"Talk to me. How do you usually fight against demons?"

"We draw their essence out and then we slay it. Easy for one demon, hard for twenty," she adds drily.

"What else?"

She rubs her temples, deep in thought.

"There's a chant that might work to separate them. I've never used it myself, but I've seen it done before. It's used by our High Priestess to cleanse demonic energy from an object, or a deity that has been infected with demonic essence. I'm not sure if it will work, though," she mentions.

"Let's do it. What do you need?"

"Water. An offering. And the chant."

I look around us.

"Can you melt the ice?"

She shakes her head.

"It would require too much concentration and I can't afford to be distracted."

"Okay, fine." I think for a moment. "What about blood? It's liquid."

She licks her lips.

"It might work."

"Good. Next for an offering..."

"It has to be something that you genuinely value for the ritual to work," she adds.

"What about this?" I ask as I take out the ring I'd made for her from my back pocket.

Her eyes grow wide with surprise.

"How do you still have that? I threw it in the furnace."

"And I salvaged it."

"You..." She swallows. "You went into the furnace after it?"

I wink at her. Of course I wasn't about to let my hard work go to waste.

"Would it work?"

She takes it from my hand, handling it with great care.

A smile pulls at her lips.

"You valued it enough to save it," she murmurs softly. "I should have valued it more, too."

"So it works?"

She nods.

The demons blast the shield and another crack appears in the ice.

Sweat beads over Minnie's forehead as she gets to her knees and places the ring on the floor. Next is the blood. She's about to cut her own flesh when I stop her.

I take out my retractable blade and cut a straight line across my palm, letting the blood pour over the ring.

"Marlowe." She gasps.

"Another offering." I smile at her.

She wants to argue—I can tell. But there's no time for it.

She's getting paler by the minute. Hell, if she lost even a bit of blood, I'm sure it would have had an adverse effect on her physique with how weak she's becoming.

She gives me a tight nod and gets to work.

Splaying her open palms over the blood-covered ring, she starts chanting in a foreign language.

Another blow to the shield creates an even larger crack. One that leads to a myriad of tiny fissures across the entire sphere. From my left, some pieces of ice are already starting to chip off.

Fuck.

It's only a matter of seconds before they'll poke a hole in the shield.

I rush to the area that's about to rupture, and I place the crucifix against the inner part of the ice. When the next ball of smoke hits the weakened area, it's diverted by the holiness of the crucifix.

Sweet.

I'll have to ask Minnie later what the deal with holy objects is, especially since she mentioned it doesn't matter what religion they come from—they're all hallowed all the same.

That crack is safe for now.

Minnie continues chanting.

But the smoke balls concentrate on the upper part of the sphere now. The sides clear out, the demons becoming visible again.

The holes in their chests have enlarged as they channel that dark energy from within. It spills out of their bodies and spirals out in the air, going up five, six feet before descending with full force over our icy dome.

Bang. Bang. Bang.

With their concentrated efforts on one particular spot, the ice shield is quickly weakening. First, it's the fissures. Then the small chips on the outer side. Then comes the first crack.

"Minnie..." I call out, my voice hoarse. "Hurry up."

Her voice picks up the pace as she speeds through the lines of the chant.

The smoke plunges up in the air again and hits once more, this time breaking the shield and flooding the inside of the sphere with the noxious demonic energy.

Minnie coughs and splutters before finally saying the last words of her chant. A bright light flashes out from her palms, enveloping the entire cathedral.

I squeeze my eyes shut, unable to look at it.

My ears ring as a sharp, screechy sound erupts in the air. I wobble on my feet, falling backward.

"Marlowe?" Minnie whispers as she comes to my side, shaking me.

I dare to open my eyes and note that the shield has entirely collapsed now. But the demon formation has been broken as well.

The demons are scattered throughout the cathedral, their chests fully healed up. There's no more black smoke. Only a lingering bright light that still burns my eyes.

"Are you all right?"

"I think so." I nod as I get to my feet.

Though the ritual managed to separate the demons, the hardships are far from over. They're slowly advancing toward us again, with the closest one a mere foot away.

Minnie summons up her swords, and placing herself in front of me, she assumes a fighting stance.

The first demon steps onto the remnants of the ritual, and the moment his foot touches it, he collapses to his knee, his mouth opening on a shrilly scream. Not even a few seconds later, his entire body is pulverized, turning from physical matter to a gray, amorphous smoke that ultimately dissipates in the air.

What the...

Minnie is equally surprised.

"I've never seen something like that in my entire life," she murmurs, stunned.

"It must be the ritual. He stepped on it."

She nods. "But how do we draw the others to step on it, too?"

No sooner is the question out of her mouth than the other demons begin their attack too. They charge at us from all sides, and Minnie brandishes her swords around, cutting at them.

But these demons... Now I see why they're high level. They mimic her weapons, though theirs are made out of that dark smoke.

While Minnie fights with a couple of demons to my right, I note a fast approaching one to my left.

I only have my retractable blade, so I block the demon's sword with it—what a fine David and Goliath moment. Of course the sword cuts right through my tiny blade, so close to my hand that I jerk away. The handle of the knife slips from me and falls to the floor.

Minnie shoots me a worried look, but she can't do anything since she's surrounded by more demons now, all going at her with full force.

I suppose the only thing left to do is some bareknuckle fighting.

My palm stings. Even though the wound is healing faster than normal, it's still not as fast as before when I had Minnie's blood right away.

The demon charges at me with his sword, and I dodge to the side and push my palm against his shoulder while trying to take his weapon with my other hand.

I only manage to touch the dark sword before the demon's mouth opens wide, the same shrilly sound from before coming out. He starts shaking violently and crashes to the floor. His body, too, dissolves into a gray dust that's swept away by the night breeze.

Minnie glances at me in confusion.

This demon didn't step into the ritual. If anything, he just...

I don't have the time to think things through as another demon comes toward me. A middle-aged guy with a balding head and flaring nostrils grabs me by my shirt and throws me to the ground.

The breath is knocked out of me. Taking advantage of my position, the demon grabs my hands, pulling them together to secure them with cuffs.

"Marlowe!" Minnie cries out. She tries to come to me, but more demons swarm around her, blocking her path.

"Goddamn it," I mutter under my breath as I push against the middle-aged demon. He presses my hands close together to tie them up, but as I struggle against him, my wounded palm makes contact with his skin.

Only a few drops of blood are still left on my palm, the wound mostly closed now. But as those drops make contact with the demon's skin, the same thing happens. He screams in pain before he disintegrates.

I stare in shock at my palm.

It wasn't the ritual, was it?

It was my blood...

THIRTY-SEVEN

THIS MIGHT BE A GAMBLE, but I roll on the floor to the place my broken blade had landed and I use it to cut my hand again. And just as a demon makes to grab me, I press my bloodied palm onto his face.

He screams, falls, and disintegrates.

It...worked?

I don't have the time to wonder why my blood might act as poison to those demons. Clutching onto the blade, I make more cuts along both of my palms and run to where Minnie is currently fighting six demons.

Six demons at once.

Damn.

"Marlowe, stand back," she grits out as she parries a blow, then another. With her attention on me, she fails to dodge one of the blades and it cuts her across the chest.

A faint gasp leaves her lips, but she keeps fighting, not letting the pain slow her down.

I reach her side and despite her continuous protests, I place myself in front of her.

"Are you mad?" she asks.

"Perhaps," I answer noncommittally

The demons stop fighting, too. They share a look and speak a few words in a language I cannot decipher.

"Alive," Minnie echoes. "They're saying they need you alive."

"Me?" I blink.

She nods numbly.

"We can worry about that later. First—" I grab her swords, one in each hand, and I smear my blood all over the blades. "Hit them now."

She frowns at me, but the moment she's no longer behind me, the demons try to attack again.

Not me. They don't swing their swords at me. Only her.

Minnie parries a couple of blows before she manages to cut a demon across his back.

I hold my breath as I wait for the process to repeat itself, and sure enough, it does.

Scream, fall, disintegrate.

Her brows bunch together in confusion. But she knows time is of the essence, so she quickly recovers from her shock and swings her swords again.

More demons fall after they make contact with my blood. But with how many of them there are, it's still not enough.

I press my lips together as I think of something that might help.

Then an idea comes to mind.

"You can freeze anything, can't you?"

She nods.

"Here," I cut a fresh wound in my palm, "use my blood as bullets."

"I don't under—"

"Trust me, all right?"

There are nine more demons still inside the church.

Minnie gives me a nod, and swiping my blood on her fingers,

she blows onto it until the drops become solid. She shoots them at the demons.

A few manage to do avoid them, but half are not so fortunate. Scream, fall, disintegrate.

Minnie's eyes widen, but she grabs my hand and swipes more blood that she turns into bullets.

The remaining demons, having seen the effects of the ice bullets, summon energy shields to block the blows. But it seems even those are useless as the bullets pass straight through, reaching the intended target.

One by one, they fall. One by one, they're all gone.

We're both breathing hard as the last demon disintegrates. The wind sweeps away the last remainder of that grayish dust.

We're alone.

Minnie slowly turns to me, her expression indecipherable.

"What was that?"

"What do you mean?"

"The blood. How did you do that? How did you know how to do that?" she asks in a tight voice.

"I didn't. I just saw it worked and—"

My words are cut off as she slams me against the wall of the church. The sharp icy blade digs into my neck as she stares at me intently.

"What are you?" she grits out.

"What? What are you talking about?"

"That's not normal. I've never seen anything like that before. So tell me. What are you?"

"Human," I answer drily. What else does she want me to say?

She shakes her head.

"Impossible. If you were just a human, that would have never happened."

"I don't know what you want me to say, Minnie. I'm as confused as you are."

She narrows her eyes at me.

"They sent you to mess with me, didn't they?" she asks, her cheek twitching. "They knew I was coming here to find you and they sent you to mess with me."

"What the hell are you talking about, Minnie?"

"Not even a Supreme can destroy a demon like that—a high demon, too. This doesn't make any sense," she murmurs to herself.

Her blade is still against my throat, and while the pricking of the sharp edge is uncomfortable, I can't deny that this is rather hot.

Damn it, Marlowe! Stop being a horndog at the most inappropriate times!

Yet the images come unbidden. It doesn't help that her dress has ridden up her ass and I get a tantalizing peek of creamy flesh through her ripped tights.

I swallow hard, and the blade digs deeper into my skin.

The pain is a welcome distraction, but it does little to relieve the ache in my balls. My cock hardens the more I watch her determined stance and the way she tries to be all serious and intimidating. Too bad that it does the opposite.

God, I have it bad.

We've barely escaped a demon attack with our lives intact and all I can think of is Minnie, barely clothed and ready for murder. It doesn't even matter that it's my murder she's preparing for. That makes it even hotter.

My fingers itch to pull my zipper down and ask her to move her blade to my cock; press it against my shaft until it becomes bloody and messy. Then, maybe she'll take pity on me and heal me up with her tongue again. Maybe spit on it and make it even more messy so then she'll have to clean it up with her mouth.

Don't do this, Marlowe! Don't think about her mouth on your cock. It's only going to make things worse.

"What are you, Marlowe? Answer me," Minnie repeats.

"Human, Minnie. I'm very much human," I reply, clearing my throat in an attempt to dispel all those dirty images going through my mind.

Her nostrils flare at my answer.

"The demons... They were after you, too, weren't they? They didn't even bother with me until I was in your way. What are you hiding, Marlowe?"

She has a point with that. The demons barely looked at her when they entered the cathedral and only wanted to get to me.

"I'm not hiding anything. Come on, Minnie. You know better than that."

"Do I?" She raises a brow. "Because everything has been rather fortuitous until now. You killed those sentinels. Now the demons. There are also no wandering souls in your house..." she muses. "And you..."

"Me?" My lips curve up.

"Stop smiling at me!" She jabs her knife deeper into my flesh. "You're messing with my focus."

"I don't know what you want me to say, Minnie. I had no idea my blood could do that. I'm just as confused as you are."

"Are you?" she asks skeptically. "Why offer to use your blood in the ritual? We could have easily used mine. But it wouldn't have had the same effect now, would it? Because you're not human."

"I offered because you were already weak. I didn't have any ulterior motives," I explain with a sigh. "How would I know that it would have that effect on the demons?"

"I don't know. You tell me. How did you know?"

"Minnie, this is absurd—"

"It's not. I've never heard of someone's blood acting as poison to demons before. Never. How do you explain that?"

"Maybe it's something I ate?" I offer.

She kicks my leg.

"It's not the time to be funny, Marlowe."

"I'm telling you I don't know. What more do you want?"

"To know what you are," she says. "And who sent you."

"No one sent me." I roll my eyes. "We're getting into conspiracy theory territory here and I don't like it."

"Because it is a conspiracy," she cries out. "Of course it is. They probably knew I'd come here, after you, and they laid me a trap," she continues, not making much sense.

"Who is they, Minnie?"

"The House of Moirai. They control everything. They must have..." She closes her eyes to think. "They must have done something. I know it."

"Minnie, this is getting out of hand. I'm the same person as before. And I'm human."

She tilts her head to the side.

Taking the sword from my neck, she swipes her hand over the flat surface of the blade and chants something in a low voice. Then she presses it against my skin again.

I wince at the sudden searing sensation.

Her eyes widen. "No, it can't be..."

"What are you talking about?" I ask, more confused than ever.

"I don't know," she whispers. "I don't know anymore. But this... Whatever this is..." She takes a deep breath.

I cover her hand with mine, lowering the blade.

"Trust me that I don't know anything about this. I swear it to you."

She presses her lips together as she regards me.

"Those demons were sent to capture you. Alive. The question is why."

"Hey, maybe I have some funky mutation that makes my blood poisonous to demons and they wanted to study me?" I add jokingly. Although that doesn't seem too farfetched considering what transpired.

She stares at me. Then she brings the blood-stained blade to her lips. She licks the blood off it, smacking her lips together as if trying to determine if there's something wrong with it.

Taking advantage of her momentary distraction, I grab her by the neck and switch our positions. Pushing the back of my palm against her hand, I kick the sword to the side. It falls to the ground with a thud and disintegrates.

Minnie's eyes widen as she gazes up at me.

"You know fully well who I am, Minnie," I murmur. "Does it really matter what's in my blood?"

She licks her lips.

"Aren't you the least curious?"

I shrug. "Maybe. But I'm more concerned with you believing me rather than knowing what's wrong with my blood. And frankly, I don't appreciate your lack of confidence in me."

She shakes her head. "No. You don't understand. They're not to be trusted."

"Fuck them and fuck everyone else," I grind out. "Does it look like there's anyone here beside you and me?"

Her lashes flutter.

"I don't care about your gods or your demons or whatever fucking else. I only care about you and our relationship. I care about the fact that you fucking doubt me."

"But, Marlowe—"

"Shh," I whisper and press my finger against her lips. "No more words, Minnie." I lean in and press my forehead against her. "You can think anything of me, but the fact that you would doubt my loyalty to you guts me."

She inhales sharply.

"Do you think I'd hurt you?" I ask her softly.

"No."

"Do you think I'd betray you?"

"No."

"Do you think I'd ever keep secrets from you?"

She gulps down and hesitates.

"No," she finally answers.

"Good. Then that's settled." I nod and pull back. "As far as whatever the fuck happened here, we'll have plenty of time to figure that out while we're away from this world. You used your powers, so I assume they already have your location."

"You're right," she murmurs. "I'm sorry."

I step away from her and take a deep, calming breath.

She's right that this is all strange, but I don't like that her first thought is to suspect me of having lied to her about my identity.

I don't know why the fuck those demons were after me, but we don't have the time to dwell on this. Not when the soldiers after her are probably heading to our location as we speak.

I pat my pockets for my phone. Pulling it out, I note that the screen's cracked.

Great.

I mutter a string of curses under my breath and squint to make out the address of Katrina Hale.

"Let's go," I tell Minnie and head toward the exit.

She follows after me, her head bent down.

As we get out of the church, she quietly slips her hand in mine.

"Are you mad at me?" she whispers.

"I'm not," I start. "Perhaps a little disappointed."

"Oh."

"We'll talk more about this later."

She appears as if she wants to say more but eventually nods and follows me in silence.

We get to the Main Street and hail a cab.

Since she doesn't have her veil anymore, Minnie buries her head in my shoulder.

The driver regards us suspiciously. Especially since our clothes are torn and bloody.

"Costume for the festival," I mention with a fake smile.

He narrows his eyes but doesn't comment.

It takes us some twenty minutes to reach the designated address. I pay and we get out of the car.

"This is it?" Minnie asks as we identify the house number.

It's an old gothic manor with vines intertwined all over the facade. Three stories with an attic that has seen better days and with windows covered with pieces of wood.

A crow caws from the yard. Perched on a tree branch, the bird stares at us.

A shiver runs down my back.

Eerie.

But I suppose after everything that has already happened, a crow stalking us is the last of our worries.

I push the gate open. It releases a loud screech, making the crow caw again. But this time, when I look at it, I note it's flown on the top of the fence.

It's watching us, tilting its head from side to side.

As we step into the yard, the crow flies off the fence, perilously close to our heads.

"What the fuck?" I curse, swatting the bird away.

Its caws become more insistent as it surrounds us before finally flying away just as the front door of the house opens.

"I don't like this," Minnie whispers as she huddles closer to my side.

I grunt and hold on to her tighter.

I may have been a bit annoyed with her for her accusations, but I find that I cannot ignore her for too long. Already I have an insane urge to hug her and kiss her and just feel the warmth of her skin against mine, which is odd considering the fact that she should be the one consoling me.

Alas, after we leave this world, we'll have more time for that.

I'm already thinking of the different pouts or cute expressions I can make to prompt her to console me, perhaps with a few kisses. And preferably a little lower down my body.

Now I know she said we can only kiss, but she didn't specifically say kisses on the lips.

Already, my mind is conjuring up other types of kisses, with me on my back, her cunt in my mouth while she's on top of me sucking on my cock—erm, kissing.

Goddamn it. Why did those Primordials have to create males with such a primitive brain concerned only with mating?

I groan the moment I think about the word mating because that invokes a whole other slew of images that go far beyond kissing.

Fuck! Those demons don't even need to try to hurt me since I'll likely die of blue balls if we don't find that sanctuary.

"Marlowe?" Minnie whispers, gazing up at me.

Her eyes are once more a dark color, but there's something awfully vulnerable and frail about her expression that tugs at my heartstrings. Funny, until a few months ago, I would have sworn up and down I didn't have a heart. Now? It fucking sings.

"What?" I ask, sharper than intended.

She presses her lips together and flutters her lashes.

"Before we go in," she starts hesitantly.

I raise a brow at her to continue.

"Promise you're not mad at me?"

She peers at me from beneath her lashes as she huddles closer, pressing her entire body against mine.

"I'm not mad at you," I murmur.

She gives me a tentative smile.

And to show her the truth of my words, I cup her cheeks and lean in to press a kiss on her forehead, then her nose before finally reaching her mouth.

I let my lips linger on hers for a few seconds before drawing back.

She puckers her lips, waiting for more, and I chuckle.

"Later," I whisper and tap her nose.

She lets out a disappointed sigh but graces me with a dazzling smile.

Not even the crow cawing in the distance can ruin the fuzzy feelings that smile gives me.

We step inside the house.

The foyer is fully lit, leading into an antique but well-maintained living room. There are two couches in the middle of the room facing a fireplace. Bookshelves are built into the walls, and they're all littered with books.

Witches and books. Seems to be a common theme.

As we step deeper into the room, the entrance door suddenly closes.

Minnie startles and clutches my arm tighter.

"Don't tell me you're scared," I tell her.

She licks her lips. "Not...scared."

"But?"

"I watched a lot of horror movies while I was living at the cinema. They all had creepy houses like this."

"Minnie, you hunt demons. I'm sure there's nothing that can scare you."

"Well...not exactly."

I frown. "And what's that supposed to mean?"

"Zombies," she squeaks. "I mean, have you seen them? They're so ugly and decomposed and they want to eat your brains and—"

"Zombies are real?"

"They could be," she points out. "I haven't been to every realm out there. There are thousands upon thousands of species. Zombies could be one." She shrugs.

I chuckle.

The sound of the floor creaking has both of us abandoning the mirth and focusing on our surroundings.

"Hello?" I call out.

The house echoes a hello back.

Right. Not creepy at all.

The floor creaks again.

We both turn to look at the staircase. But just as we head back to the foyer, a voice speaks from behind us.

"Welcome."

Turning, we come face to face with a middle-aged lady—based on looks alone, since her age would put her in the old category.

There are very few lines on her face, and the only indication that she's past her youth is the gray hair she keeps tightly in a bun at the back of her head.

She's wearing a long cream dress belted at the waist. She's a little taller than Minnie, but she's still a small lady.

"Hello. We are—"

"I know who you are," she interrupts me.

"You...do?" Minnie blinks.

Katrina smiles.

"I've been waiting for you."

"What? How?" I ask.

"Come with me. Let us have some tea and we'll talk."

"We don't really have the time to linger, I'm afraid," I add politely.

She waves her hand.

"The house has wards. No one will find you here."

Both Minnie and I share a look.

"Let's go," Minnie whispers.

Katrina winks at her. "Good choice."

She leads us to the back of the house, into a spacious kitchen with a long, wooden table in the middle.

"Take a seat, please," she mentions.

We do, and that's when I notice that the water is already on the stove, boiling. Katrina busies herself around the kitchen, placing three tea cups on the table, milk, and sugar. She pours tea in each of our cups before taking a seat.

"You must be Marlowe." She nods to me. "And you Minerva."

"Do you have the sight?" Minnie suddenly asks.

When she sees my confused expression, she explains, "The ability to see the future."

"No." Katrina smiles. "Unfortunately, I don't have that gift. My great-grandmother did, though. She was one of the most accurate seers to ever walk this earth."

"Is that how you know who we are?" Minnie probes.

"No. I never met my great-grandmother, though I'm told she was a fine lady."

"Then how?" Minnie frowns.

"Please, drink your tea. I'll be right back." She rises from her seat and leaves the room.

I take a sip.

"This isn't bad," I mutter. It's hot, pepperminty, and with a hint of spice. After the demon debacle, I find myself rather thirsty, so I quickly empty the cup and help myself to a second one.

Barely a few minutes pass and she's back, holding a couple of letters in her hands.

"I moved to New Orleans in nineteen sixty-five, after my grandmother died. She was the one who taught me everything about witchcraft. Back then, I didn't want anything to do with witches and demons and all those things anymore. Not after my brother's death anyway."

She places the letters on the table, resting her palms on top of them.

"No one knew who I was or what I was. I wanted to start fresh." She smiles. "But one day, a lady knocked on my door and handed me these." She points to the papers. "She said one is for me to read, and one is for me to keep for its intended recipient."

Katrina separates the letters. One is opened. The other is still sealed.

"Who was this lady you speak of?" Minnie asks.

"I truly don't know. She didn't introduce herself. She only told me that I'd know what to do once I read the first letter."

"And? What was inside it?"

Katrina takes out a sheet of paper from the envelope.

"The first part of the letter is dedicated to me. It has some... private information, all meant to ensure I believe in the contents of the letter and the intentions of the sender." She pauses. "The second has instructions."

"Instructions?" I frown. "For us?"

"Indeed." Katrina turns to look at Minnie. "I know what you seek, Minerva, and I have spent the last fifty years gathering all the necessary ingredients." She glances at the tea cups. "You've had a taste now. Did I do a good job?" she asks with a mischievous smile.

Minnie's eyes meet mine as it dawns on us what she means.

The tincture. She's talking about the tincture.

"I don't understand. Why? Why would someone care about this? About us?"

"Because everyone plays an important role in the big scheme of things."

Minnie tenses.

"Was it the House of Moirai?" she asks on a whisper.

"No. It was not. The person who penned these letters is not your foe, Minerva. On the contrary, she wants the best for you. I have followed every single instruction in the letter. The house has strong wards that prevent both gods and demons from peeking inside. The tincture is made from the best ingredients in the entire universe. And then there's this."

She pushes the unopened letter toward us. Minnie grabs it, about to open it when Katrina stops her.

"You are not to open it now."

"What? But when?"

"When a mark appears on your chest. Right here." Katrina points to the area right above Minnie's heart. "When that happens, you will open this letter and find the answer to everything."

Minnie frowns. I squeeze her hand under the table in comfort.

"Is this about the sanctuary of the Primordial Goddess of Fate? Is the location inside?"

Katrina shakes her head.

"I'm only allowed to tell you this. Inside, you will find the way to vanquish the being named Azerius. But only if you follow the instructions and open it when that mark appears upon your chest."

"W-what? Vanquish Azerius?" Minnie utters in shock.

"I gather you know who that is?" Katrina asks.

Minnie nods numbly.

"The most powerful being in the universe," she whispers.

Katrina doesn't seem fazed. She simply smiles at Minnie and pats her hand.

"You vow to open the letter only when that mark appears on your chest?"

"I-I vow." Minnie nods.

"Good. Then my duty here is done. You may eat, sleep, and replenish your strength. There's a portal not far from here that will take you to your desired destination."

Katrina rises from the table.

"Wait! How do you know our desired destination?" I ask.

Even we don't know our destination. It was supposed to be random, no? Somewhere to blend in and lose ourselves in the crowd.

Katrina slowly looks up.

Both Minnie and I follow her gaze, where a large painting covers the entire ceiling. It's a portrait of a couple, their faces painted with a myriad of colors. The man has long, white hair, a stark contrast to the paints on his face. His eyes are a light shade of blue. The dark-haired woman next to him is smiling brightly at the artist, some of the paint cracking around the corners of her mouth.

Minnie releases a loud gasp as she grasps onto my sleeve to keep herself upright. She squeezes my arm, her mouth opening and closing.

"What? I don't get it?" I whisper.

"But you do, don't you?" Katrina addresses Minnie.

"That's it, Marlowe. The sanctuary," she says as she points at the painting.

I frown, unable to understand what she's talking about.

"Behind the couple. Look. It's the same as the drawing," she continues as she materializes her book in front of us and points to the page with the illustration of the sanctuary.

I look at the painting on the ceiling, then at the illustration.

There's the same stone formation in the back, down to the discoloration of the wall and the placement of the stalactites.

"Where is it? Where do we need to go to find that place?" Minnie asks excitedly.

Hope shines in her eyes, and she's barely keeping herself from jumping up and down. Her cheeks are red with joy and optimism, and it slowly dawns on me that this is it.

We can finally be together.

I grab her hand, squeezing it tightly.

Katrina glances from Minnie to me, her lips tipped up in a pleasant smile.

"Arkgor. The place you're looking for is in a realm called Arkgor."

THIRTY-EIGHT

"WE SHOULD BE RESTING," I tell Minnie, who's currently jumping on the bed, squeaking with happiness. Which, granted, is pretty justified. She's been holding onto this hope for so long, that she deserves to express her joy however she wants.

Katrina insisted that we spend the night at her house so we can recoup our strength and prepare for what is to come. She let us use the attic to have more privacy, which includes a bedroom and a bathroom. She was a sweet lady, giving us food and everything else we needed for the night.

But while Minnie is happily rolling around on the mattress, I can't help but think that everything was...too fortuitous.

How the hell did we get so lucky that some random person dropped two letters some fifty years ago that held the key to solving all our problems. Not only do we now know where the sanctuary is, but we also have the potential weapon to destroy that Azerius dude.

It's all too...neat.

And I can't help but feel that we're missing something.

Who wrote those letters and what was their goal? We don't even know that.

But I can't say anything to Minnie now since I don't want to ruin her moment of happiness. I'll have to find a later time to broach the subject and suggest we tread carefully—that this might be a trap.

I dry my hair with a towel after a long-awaited shower and place my clothes on a chair to dry for tomorrow.

As I take off the towel from around my waist to climb into bed, Minnie suddenly stops me.

Her eyes flare with shock as she slowly takes in my body.

She releases another squeak, but this one imbued with her maidenly outrage.

"Yo-you aren't wearing clothes."

"Fine of you to notice," I reply drily.

I'm still wearing my underwear, though it's only semi-dry. Her maidenly sensibilities should thank me for that since I didn't want to make her uncomfortable by sleeping in the nude.

"Uhm..." she murmurs as she stares at my dick. She wiggles to the edge of the bed, rolling on her belly until her face is almost at the same level with my crotch.

Fucking hell.

"Soon. I'll see you soon," she whispers to my dick as she gives it a small poke. Then she giggles.

"What the—" I startle.

She smiles lazily, her attention still fixed on my dick.

"Look, Marlowe. It knows we're going to mate soon, too," she exclaims as she points to my rapidly hardening cock. "It's so big, too." She gasps. "You're going to break me in two, aren't you?" she coos at it.

Of all the things she could have said...

Jesus Christ, this woman is going to be the death of me. Now I won't be able to stop thinking about shoving my cock into her cunt so hard, she'll scream in both pain and pleasure as she stains my shaft with her virgin blood.

"Minnie." I take a deep breath. "Go shower."

"But I'm too happy. And this is exciting," she says as she tries to touch my dick again.

Oh yes, something is excited all right. Perhaps overly excited might be the term.

It's official. I require sainthood. I'm performing a miracle right here and now by not spreading her legs and breaking her in half just as she wanted. Hell, with how close her mouth is to my crotch, I'm surprised my dick isn't already down her throat.

See? Saint material.

Saint Marlowe of the Hard Cock.

I berate myself for my stupid thoughts as I grab her wrist before she touches me. I suppose it's the exhaustion. It must have gotten to my brain.

"No, it's not fun." Oh, it's way too much fun, but my control is too strenuous as it is. "You need to shower. Wash your hair too."

She blinks, then looks at me with puppy eyes.

"Now?"

"Now."

She pouts.

"But I was talking to—"

"Don't fucking say you were talking to my dick or I'm going to lose it."

"But I was," she protests, her expression the picture of innocence.

Goddamn it all to hell. This is too much, even for my herculean restraint.

"Minnie, you need to wash the demon grime off you."

"Can't I do it a bit later?" She gives me a smile.

I shake my head.

"Now."

"But your—"

That's it.

I give up.

Swooping her in my arms, I carry her to the bathroom. I rip

the dress off her body—it's torn anyway. She's left in her bra and underwear, and I step into the shower with her. I turn on the cold water—the only remedy for me at this point, no matter how much I might hate it—and I start washing Minnie's body.

Minnie whines and pouts and wiggles to get out, but eventually, I get her to stay still so I can carefully scrub her clean.

"Calm down, you dirty little girl," I say with a chuckle when she struggles to leave while I soap her body.

"Why are you doing this to me?" she cries out.

"Because you need to be clean. Remember our deal?"

"But, Marlowe—"

"No. This is out of the question. Now sit down so I can wash your hair."

She looks as if she's about to argue, but eventually, sits down on the shower floor so I can shampoo her hair.

It's grimy and dirty and a little tangled. I take my time lathering it in shampoo, then slowly detangling it as I rinse that off.

All the while, she has a pout on her face as she mutters something under her breath.

"What is it with you and water? You're a goddess princess. Shouldn't royals wash more often?"

She shrugs.

"It's wet," she mumbles.

"It's water, Minnie. Of course it's wet."

She screws up her face in disgust but stops trying to run away.

I rinse her hair thoroughly before washing her body again.

This time, she holds her hands up and stands still, letting me do the work.

To say it's torture to have her semi-naked and at my mercy like this is an understatement. Especially since I get to touch all parts of her body.

Ah, the sacrifices I make for my little heathen.

When I'm satisfied with how clean she is, I step out of the shower.

She's watching me intently but doesn't make to move.

"You should…erm, wash your private parts," I mutter.

Her cheeks redden.

"Oh."

"You will wash, all right?"

She takes a moment to think about it then says, "Can't you do it for me?"

I BLINK. My own body heats up.

"That would not be wise, Minnie."

"But it would be nice," she whispers.

"I'm sure it would be. But I don't trust myself with you completely naked." I take a deep breath. "Wash up and I'll meet you back in the room."

She eventually nods, and I leave, although that might actually be the hardest thing I've ever done.

While she's finishing up, I tidy up the bed and make sure everything is in order.

Minnie comes out with a towel wrapped around her body. She's suddenly shy as she surveys the room.

"Come. We need to rest. We'll be waking up early in the morning," I tell her as I slide between the clean sheets. Ah, I missed the smell of fresh laundry.

She nods and gets into bed too, a distance away from me.

I turn off the light, but neither of us goes to sleep immediately.

"Uhm, Marlowe?"

"Yes?"

"I'm sorry about my outburst from earlier today. You're right. I shouldn't have suspected you."

"It's fine."

"No. It's not fine. I…" She turns to her side to look at me. "I've been so suspicious of everything and everyone for so long that it's become second nature. But I want to clear something up."

"You really don't have to, Minnie," I tell her.

It happened in the aftermath of a trying event. Adrenaline ran high, and for a moment, we actually feared for our lives. Not to mention the little surprise of what my blood can do. All things considered, I understand why she said what she said.

"It wasn't you directly that I was suspicious of," she mentions, sliding closer to me. "It's the House of Moirai. They're all sneaky bastards, and I wouldn't put it past them to do this to you to get back to me."

"You keep mentioning the House of Moirai. But why would they want to do anything to you?"

"Because I messed with the natural order of things," she adds slowly.

"By getting involved with a human?"

She hesitates.

"You could say so," she murmurs.

The sheets rustle as she moves closer until she's stuck to my side. I put an arm around her shoulders, and she rests her head on my chest.

"Soon we'll be together," she whispers.

I press a kiss on her forehead.

Soon cannot come soon enough.

KATRINA SURPRISES us with breakfast and a small bag full of food for our travels. She also gives Minnie a dress to wear since hers was destroyed.

"Thank you so much for everything. You have no idea how much it means to us," Minnie murmurs after we finish eating and get ready to leave.

"There's one more thing," Katrina mentions. "You said demons were after you," she says as she turns to me.

I nod.

"We don't know why. But it seems they were sent there to capture me."

She nods thoughtfully.

"I might have something to help."

Going to one of her cabinets, she takes out a feathered pen.

"There's a rune that might help keep you hidden from the demons," she explains. "If you'll allow me." She points to my arm.

I look at Minnie.

"What rune?" she asks.

"It's a protective rune that keeps one safe from demons. It's been in my family for generations."

Minnie appears skeptical about it, but I shrug.

"Okay. If that's going to help, then please."

I shrug my sleeve up and present her my arm.

She presses the tip of the pen into my skin, digging it inside. A yellow light emanates from it as she traces a small symbol on my forearm.

Minnie comes closer to have a peek, her brows knitted together in confusion.

"I've seen that before," she mentions. "Our priestesses use it."

"It is an ancient symbol." Katrina smiles.

"As far as I know, it means release not protection," Minnie continues as she places her hand on my arm, stopping Katrina from finishing it.

"Yes. It is a release of the energy the demons might be using to track him."

I glance between the two of them. Minnie doesn't seem particularly impressed with the explanation.

"Why would your family have something like this?" She probes.

Katrina doesn't seem rattled by the question.

"We've been exorcising demons for as long as I can remember. We've also been hunted for that very reason. This symbol has offered protection to countless of people in my family."

"Maybe you remember it wrong?" I say to Minnie.

She frowns. "I don't know…"

"YOU SAID you're only marginally familiar with the work of the priestesses. Perhaps they use it for defense too."

"I'd never do anything to harm either of you," Katrina interjects. "It is my duty to make sure you get where you're meant to be."

"I suppose so," Minnie relents. "Fine. Go ahead."

Katrina finishes the design, and once she lifts the tip of the pen off my skin, the etching sears itself into my flesh. There's a pricking sensation followed by a light hum before the symbol disappears as it gets absorbed into my skin.

"Thank you." I incline my head.

Minnie grabs my arm and inspects it thoroughly, her eyes narrowed. She traces her fingers along the area where Katrina tattooed the design onto my skin.

"Does it meet your approval?" I ask jokingly.

She makes a deep sound in her throat, but her attention is still on my arm.

"It's similar to what I saw at the Temple, but there's something different. I cannot tell," she adds in annoyance.

Katrina brings out a map of the area and hands it to us.

"I've marked the spot where the portal is as well as the path you should take to avoid detection. It's in the marshes, so the environment isn't the most welcoming. But I trust that you'll manage just fine."

"Thank you," Minnie says absentmindedly as she takes the map to study it.

There's an X where the portal is located, and a red line that leads from our current location to the portal.

"This is very helpful."

We take the food bag and the map, and we head to the exit.

Katrina follows behind, a gentle smile on her face.

"May you find what you seek," she says as she waves goodbye.

We wave back and set out on our journey.

It's early in the morning. The air is humid and the temperature is in the high fifties. Not bad.

We take a cab to the marshes after which we rent out a boat to follow on the path Katrina outlined.

All the while, though, Minnie has a troubled expression on her face.

"What's wrong?" I ask after I pay for our boat rental and we get inside.

She purses her lips.

"I don't know. I should be happy we got all this information but—"

"You can't help but feel it's too fortuitous?"

SHE NODS. "Last night I got too excited when I heard about the location of the sanctuary. But the more I think about it, the more I question it. Who could have written these letters?" She muses as she takes out the sealed envelope from her pocket. "And who would have known we'd come here? That we'd be looking for the sanctuary or the tincture? It all seems too...convenient."

"You think it's a trap?"

"I don't know. I'm itching to open this, but there's also a part of me that wants to wait and see—the part of me that still hopes this is all real and not a ruse. I mean, vanquishing Azerius? That's just hard to imagine."

"How come he's so powerful?"

"His identity is a mystery. But for thousands of years, he has served as the Commander of the Aperite forces." She pauses. "And the executioner for all deities that misbehave. He's not called the God Killer for nothing. Every single deity in Aperion fears him. The demons too. When the Sons of Tenebreis will break out of

Tartareia—they're bound to do so at some point—he's the one everyone is counting on to lead the war against them. And from what I hear, he's also set to become the new Polemos Supreme."

So he's the most feared guy in the universe. Damn. Now I'm curious about the contents of the letter too. How does one manage to defeat someone so strong?

"You mentioned that term before—supreme. What does it mean?" I ask.

Minnie purses her lips.

"It's difficult to explain since most mythologies in the universe that have a pantheon consider their deities to be absolute. In reality, no deity is absolute. As I told you before, we might be immortal, but we are not eternal. The position itself, however, is eternal. A Supreme is the representation of a god for a certain designation." Her brows pinch in concentration. "Take the gods in Anthropa's mythologies. Like the god of water. Or the god of earth."

"Right." I nod.

"In reality, those are just designation. There's no one god of water, or god of earth. There's the Supreme position that is the equivalent. But the people who fill that position come and go. Of course they usually hold onto their positions for thousands or tens of thousands of years," she explains.

"It's strange to hear that even gods can be replaced."

"Yes. The strongest deities in a House are nominated for the Supreme position when it becomes vacant. It's why the entire Aperite society operates on power and prestige. And every clan within a House competes to have as many Supremes from their families as possible. It's not at all that different from your world, actually."

"Who is the Ice Supreme?"

"Krisaides. He's not from my branch of the family. I know of him, but I've never met him. He's been a Supreme for far longer than I've been alive."

"And your first fiancé?" I ask in a sharp tone.

She rolls her eyes at me.

"I'll have you know I only met him a few times and always in the presence of a chaperone. He's the heir to the King of Pyros, but from what I hear, he's not as strong as the current king. I don't know how he's going to be received when he takes the throne. Although, after he repudiated me—very publicly I might add—he gained some sort of a reputation for being an honorable and upstanding Aperite."

"Honorable and upstanding because he abandoned you?"

She sighs and nods. "It is what it is. No one in my world would accept a female who's had an affair, let alone an affair with a mortal," she adds flippantly.

"Still, it must have hurt to have everyone turn against you."

"I was hurting about other things at that time to care much about what others thought of me."

I grind my teeth to stop myself from asking if she was hurting about Lucien. But I have no doubt she was hurting about his death. Jealousy bubbles inside of me and I do my best to keep a leash on it. The last thing we need is another argument—especially after I promised her we would not broach that subject again.

I take a deep breath and look at the map instead.

Inhale. Exhale.

It appears that not even desecrating that fucker's corpse was enough to curb my rage.

I pretend to look around to orient myself. There's a strip of land not too far from us, and I try to cross reference it with the map.

"I think that's where we need to get off," I mention.

Minnie nods.

She's sitting primly in the boat. The dress Katrina gave her gives her a sophisticated look. It's a navy blue with frilly lace around the collar and four pearl buttons on the chest.

She looks damn good, but that's something else I try not to notice.

Just sleeping in the same bed with her last night was torture enough. Her almost naked body was flush against mine, and I'd be lying if I said I got a proper sleep.

All I could do was take a trip to the bathroom every few hours to get some relief, but at this point that doesn't even work.

Soon—I tell myself. Soon, we'll be able to be with each other in every way imaginable, and perhaps some that I can't quite imagine—yet.

I smile at the thought.

We reach the shore and I get out first, then help Minnie too.

"That way," I tell Minnie as I spot a sign that matches the one on the map.

We only take a few steps, though, when I'm hit by a debilitating headache. I groan aloud as I rest my arm against a tree to get my bearings together.

"Marlowe?" Minnie frowns. "What's wrong?"

"I don't know," I mumble.

I try to look at her, but my vision is clouded. I reach for her, blinking repeatedly.

"You don't look well," she says, worried.

"I don't feel w-well," I barely get the words out when my knees buckle and I fall to the ground.

THIRTY-NINE

"MARLOWE?" Minnie's asks in a panicked voice.

I force my eyes open.

"What happened?" I croak.

"I don't know. You passed out," she murmurs, gently touching my face. "You're warm to the touch too."

"I feel warm," I mention and try to get up.

My head still hurts, and I feel a debilitating weakness in my limbs. But I manage to get to my feet without falling again.

Minnie regards me with a worried look.

"Here," she says, cutting her wrist. "Drink some of my blood. Maybe you caught one of your human colds."

"Maybe."

I grab her wrist and bring it to my lips, then suck on her blood.

Before, this had an immediate effect on my body. Now? Not so much.

"Are you good to continue walking? We could rest a bit longer until you feel better."

"No. I'm good," I lie. "We need to go now before those soldiers track you. With our luck, they're probably not far behind."

"Are you sure? You're a little pale," she whispers.

I nod tightly. "I'm fine. Let's go."

She grabs my arm, almost as if she's suspecting I might topple over if I don't have any support.

I force my legs to keep moving, but it's a struggle.

What the fuck is happening to me?

I was completely fine just moments ago.

We walk for a few more minutes before we're forced to stop again. I'm breathing hard, and my chest feels constricted.

Finding a tree, I sit down and lay my back against the trunk, taking in big gulps of air.

Minnie paces around in front of me, fidgeting with her hands.

"You're not well, Marlowe. And my blood didn't help you at all. How is that possible?"

"I don't know." I close my eyes briefly. "I don't know," I repeat numbly, unable to even articulate my thoughts.

"There was nothing wrong with you before. Nothing," she continues. "So what—"

She suddenly stops. Her eyes grow wide as she hurries to my side. She pulls up my sleeve and inspects my arm.

"Oh, Marlowe," she mutters in disbelief.

I look down and I don't even have the strength to be shocked at the sight.

The place where Katrina tattooed the rune onto my skin is covered in dark spots, and they're spreading. Already half my arm has turned black.

"I should have never allowed her to do this. I should have trusted my instinct," she whispers.

"I don't understand." I frown.

"Me neither. Unless..." She trails off. "This was a release rune. I'm certain of it. It wasn't a protective one."

"What does that mean?"

Her lips flatten as she touches my arm softly.

"It's not a rune that's used by itself. It's a pair. For a release rune to work, something must be contained first."

"A disease?" I ask weakly. "Is this a sickness?"

"Your phone. Give me your phone," she says.

Since I don't have the strength to look for it myself, she pats my pockets in search of it. Once she retrieves it, she scowls at the shattered screen.

"What are you doing?"

"Your mother. Call your mother."

"Press two and hold," I tell her. "She's on speed dial."

Minnie nods and presses the number two, though it takes her a few tries to get it right due to the damage to the screen.

Eventually, she manages to start the call and put it on speaker.

"Marlowe? Is that you, darling? Where are you?" My mother immediately picks up.

Minnie shakes her head at me. If I speak, she's going to know something's wrong and she'll worry.

"Simone? This is Minnie."

"Minnie? Good God. Is Marlowe with you?"

"Yes, yes. He's sleeping. We've decided to elope. I hope you're not too mad about this."

"Of course not, darling. But... Has he heard about Julien?"

"We have. I'm so sorry for your loss, Simone," Minnie says.

My mother goes into a long monologue about how much Julien meant to her and how hard she's taking his death. Minnie does her best to console her, hurrying through the conversation since I'm getting more feverish by the second.

"And then I couldn't get in touch with Marlowe and I feared the worst. Oh, Minnie, thank you so much for calling."

"Actually, I called because I wanted to ask you something," Minnie says.

"Yes, go ahead, dear."

"This might sound strange, but when Marlowe was a baby, or anytime during his childhood, did you take him to see a"—she pauses as she searches for the right words—"a mystic of some sort."

"A mystic?" My mother echoes. "Of course not. We don't believe in that sort of thing."

"Then was he ever sick as a child? Something that the doctors couldn't treat?"

There's a pause on the other line.

"Now that you mention it, he was. I think he was around three. He got this awful fever that wouldn't go down with any medication. The doctors didn't know how to treat it. They even claimed he was not going to survive it. But why do you ask?"

"And how did he get better?" Minnie asks.

"It was such a lucky thing. There was a doctor from Boston who came all the way up to New York to see him. She'd been working on a new treatment for pediatric fevers, and she wanted to see if she could help him. The treatment was successful from the first try. That dear woman didn't even want to accept any payment. She said she was just doing her duty. The funny thing is that after that illness, whatever it was, Marlowe was never sick again. Not even a common cold. It was a miracle."

Minnie freezes. She meets my gaze and I know what she's thinking.

The word duty is awfully familiar, is it not?

"And this doctor. Who was she? What was her name?"

"I don't remember. It was twenty-five years ago," Mother answers.

"Can you tell me anything about her? How did she look? Anything that you thought was out of the ordinary?"

"Why are you asking about this, Minnie? Is my son all right? Did something happen?"

"I'm fine, Mother," I call out, struggling to keep the tremor out of my voice. "Please answer Minnie. This is important."

"She was in her forties, I think. Lovely lady. But she only stayed in town for a few days. When Marlowe got better, she left."

"Nothing strange at all?"

My mother takes a moment to think.

"Not really. I suppose it was a bit odd that she used a quill to write down her notes. I mean, who does that anymore?" She laughs. "Even twenty-five years ago, that seemed rather ancient to me."

"A quill? I see. That was everything I needed to know. Thank you, Simone."

"Thank you, Mom," I say. Then, before I can lose my courage —or before this strange illness overtakes me, I say something I don't ever remember saying before. "I love you."

"Marlowe! Ah, my darling. I love you too, baby! Please come back to visit soon, all right?"

"All right," I croak.

"We'll talk to you later, Simone. Thank you for this, and I'm sorry about Julien. Please take care of yourself."

Minnie hangs up and the phone falls from her hands.

"A quill," she repeats. "As in a feathered pen."

"You don't think that..."

"Whatever she did when you were young stopped this illness. Now? It's back. But I don't know what it is, Marlowe. Or how to fix it."

"We should try to go. The portal should be an hour away."

"You're not fit to walk an hour!" she cries out.

"I must try."

"No." She shakes her head. "We need to go back and ask Katrina what she did to you—ask her to reverse it."

"Minnie... We'll get caught."

"I don't care," she adds, her lashes filling up with tears. "I don't care about any of that. She just needs to fix you."

She presses her palm against my forehead and gasps. Tears roll down her cheeks.

"You're burning up, Marlowe. Even for my elevated body temperature, this is hot. Do you understand what I'm saying?"

I grab her hand and hold it to my face. Leaning into her touch, I take a deep breath.

"We need to go."

"Where do you think we're going? Look at yourself, Marlowe!" Minnie grits out as she unbuttons my shirt.

The dark spots have already extended toward my chest and neck.

Is this...necrosis?

It's almost as if whatever this illness is, it's eating all of my healthy cells.

I grasp onto the trunk of the tree and force myself to my feet.

"Marlowe, please," Minnie whispers.

"Let's go," I strain out.

She places my arm over her shoulder and we slowly start walking.

"I can teleport to Katrina's house and ask her—"

"No. You will get caught. You can't do that."

"But, Marlowe. You're getting worse," she murmurs.

"We need to get to the portal, Minnie. That's all that matters."

She grumbles under her breath, but with enough coaxing, she acquiesces to my wishes and we go on.

The way to the portal is grueling, but I do my damn hardest not to show it. I can tell she's one second away from teleporting both of us back to Katrina's house, consequences be damned.

But I'm not about to allow her to place herself in danger.

This...illness, whatever it might be, will pass. If she gets caught, that's the end for her.

She shoulders half my weight as we walk, and every ten-fifteen minutes, we take a small break.

"Here," she says as she hands me some water.

Taking out some food from the bag, she unwraps a sandwich and brings it to my lips for a bite.

I force a smile.

"Have I told you how beautiful you are today?" I whisper as I stare at her. "You're so beautiful. And I'm so lucky to be with you."

"It's the delirium speaking," she mumbles.

I shake my head as I slowly munch on the sandwich. I don't have much of an appetite, but this might help me regain some strength.

"It's not. I'm serious. You're the best thing that's ever happened to me," I tell her sincerely.

"Am I?" She bites her lip. "Because if it hadn't been for me, we wouldn't be here in the first place."

"You heard my mother. I was sick long before I ever met you. This isn't your fault."

"But if we hadn't come here, Katrina wouldn't have made you sick again," she whispers.

I squeeze her hand.

"The more important question is why she cured me in the first place? Why contain the illness only to release it twenty-five years later."

"It must have something to do with your blood and what happened to those demons. But for the life of me, I cannot figure out what might be the cause. You're not a deity. You're not a demon. So what are you?"

"If you don't know, then how could I know?"

"Can I... Can I try something?" she asks in a small voice.

I nod.

Creating a small pin out of ice, she grabs my black arm and sticks the sharp tip into my skin.

"Does this hurt?"

I shake my head.

"What about this?"

She pulls the pin downward, creating a small gash.

I shake my head again.

Blood pools to the surface, but it's not red.

It's black. Tar black.

Minnie's eyes widen.

"Marlowe..." Her voice trembles.

"What is it? Why is it like that?"

She gently swipes her finger over my wound, gathering some of the blood and bringing it to her lips for a taste.

She chokes and bends over, heaving as she tries to spit it out.

"Minnie?"

"I... Give me a moment..."

She takes big gulps of air. Tears coat her lashes as she wipes her mouth with the back of her hand.

"What is it?"

"It's foul. Noxious," she mutters, wincing as she spits the remainder of the blood.

"But it was fine yesterday."

"It's this..." She points to my rapidly expanding dark spots. "It's poisoning your blood."

"Poison?" I croak.

Fucking hell.

I curse under my breath and lay my back against the tree. The gravity of the situation is slowly dawning on me. My body is becoming increasingly weak, and as the dark spots expand, pain echoes in my limbs. I can feel this spreading all through my body. My chest is almost fully covered by dark, painful spots. Probably my legs, too.

"I don't know what type of poison. But it's..." She squeezes her eyes shut. "It hurts."

"Here." I hand her the water.

She gulps it down, trying to wash the taste of the blood.

"What the hell did she do to you, Marlowe?" she asks, her expression terrified. "It's unlike anything I've ever seen."

"I'm dying, aren't I?"

"No, no. Don't even say that. Don't even think about that. We'll figure it out somehow."

She stands up, pacing around. She scrubs her hands over her face.

"Minnie..."

"Don't speak. I'm trying to think."

"Don't do anything stupid on my account, Minnie," I grind out.

She doesn't listen.

A blue mist surrounds her body, and within seconds, another person appears.

Molokai.

He narrows his eyes at Minnie, but as he slides his gaze toward me, surprise flares in his features.

"Kai. I need your help," Minnie says as she rushes to her brother.

"What's this?" he asks as he studies me intently.

"We don't know. But it's spreading fast. I fear that..."

Kai steps toward me. Crouching next to me, he takes my arm to inspect the dark spots.

"Walk me through what happened," he says.

Minnie recounts everything that happened in the last few days, including the conversation with my mother and the fact that we suspect Katrina may have contained my illness as a child, only to release it now.

Molokai grunts, his expression pensive.

"Witches are not allowed to harm humans," he notes.

"Would it be considered harming if she cured me when I was young?" I ask, taking big gulps of air in between words.

"If she did it with the intention of making you ill, yes."

"But why? Why would she do that?"

His eye twitches. He uses his dagger to cut my arm, seemingly thinking to do as Minnie had done and test my blood.

Minnie stops him.

"I already did that. It's noxious. The mere taste of it made me retch."

Molokai frowns, but he doesn't stop. He cuts through my afflicted flesh, coating his blade in my black blood and dripping it onto the ground.

With a different blade, he cuts his own palm and squeezes a few drops of blood on top of my own.

The effect is instantaneous.

My blood acts like an acid, burning off the cells in his blood. Fumes erupt from the chemical reaction until the black blood has swallowed his red blood fully.

"This is what it did to the demons, too," Minnie whispers in shock. "When his blood touched them, they dissolved."

Molokai brings his attention back to my arm.

The cut he'd made has already healed, an oddity in itself.

"It's a poison, isn't it?" Minnie asks.

"If it is, I have never seen the likes of it before," he adds in a rough voice. "And if it dissolves my blood, too, then it means it can kill deities and demons alike."

"I don't care about that. It's killing him!" Minnie exclaims.

Molokai clicks his tongue against his teeth. With his blade, he cuts through my shirt, throwing it to the side until I'm naked from the torso up.

The dark spots have now reached my neck and are quickly spreading to my face.

Molokai studies my torso. His expression is blank and I find it hard to read what's going through his mind. Does he think I'm going to die? The bastard is probably rejoicing at that little fact.

Fuck.

He's probably going to kill me himself now that I'm so pitifully weak I can barely move. That way, he can protect his precious sister from a puny human like me.

I groan in pain as I try to shift, but my body doesn't want to obey me.

"I wonder about that," Molokai muses. "Look." He points with his blade to my chest. "Going by the visible pattern on his skin, the poison must have already reached his heart. He should have been dead already. Yet he is not."

"What are you saying?"

"Whatever this is—whatever he is." He pauses, his lip twitching. "Those demons must have known something, which is why they tried to capture him. And in the hands of the Son of Tenebreis, his blood could be the end of us."

"What can we do to help him? How do we get rid of the poison?" Minnie asks.

"We don't," Molokai replies, standing up. "Surely you see how dangerous and advantageous something like this could be, Minerva. It can help us get rid of all the demons in this universe," Kai says in a cold voice. "I must report it at once."

Her eyes widen in fear.

"You will do no such thing," she cries out and pushes him out of the way. Placing herself in front of me, she covers me with her body. "Don't you dare, Kai!"

"Stop the theatrics, Minerva. You're doing yourself and him a disservice."

"You... You want to use him? To use his blood?"

"If not us, then the demons will. He is a liability. At least with us, he'll serve a greater purpose."

"What's wrong with you?" she spits out.

"Nothing." He shrugs. "I'm just laying out the facts. Demons will keep coming after him, and when they do capture him, it will prove deadly for Aperion."

"I'm not letting you take him or do anything to him."

He stares at her, his mouth set in a grim line. His eyes flash a deep blue in a code-like pattern.

Moments pass before he utters, "You don't have to let me do anything. It's already done."

Minnie frowns. "What are you talking about?"

Just as the words are out of her mouth, three figures appear in the distance.

Minnie steps back, her entire body trembling.

"You... You betrayed me?" she whispers, her voice breaking with pain.

"On the contrary. I negotiated with Commander Azerius on your behalf. Aperion will get the human, and you will not be executed."

Steps thud onto the ground as a huge man strides toward Molokai. He's wearing a dark bulky iron armor, and at his waist is a bright white sword that gleams in the sun. Half of his face is covered in a myriad of tattoos resembling runes. His eyes are dark and unfeeling, his expression entirely blank.

The atmosphere immediately grows heavy, the air harder to breathe.

A chill runs down my spine. With each step the man takes, a piercing pain reverberates in my chest, making me gasp for air.

Behind the newcomer trail two men of similar height and build, both armed. Their armors are different than the first man's. One of them is wearing a burgundy armor while the other has a dark green one. They're both half a step behind the first man, suggesting the power hierarchy.

Minnie gasps as she steps back, falling next to me as she loses her footing. She reaches for my hand, holding it tightly as her entire body is racked by tremors.

"Commander Azerius." Molokai inclines his head.

FORTY

MINNIE FREEZES. All the color drains from her face.

"What have you done, Kai?" she whispers.

"What's best for you," he replies flippantly.

Azerius stops in front of us, his shrewd dark eyes studying us.

"This is the human you mentioned?" he asks in a haughty tone.

"Yes, Commander. His blood displays an unusual poisonous agent that's deadly to both demons and deities alike."

Azerius tilts his head to the side.

"Get the female out of the way," he commands.

Molokai inclines his head and reaches for Minnie. She kicks and fights, but he easily immobilizes her.

"Minnie," I grit out, though I'm powerless to help her.

Her terrified gaze meets mine as she struggles in Molokai's hold, and she shakes her head at me.

Her brother takes her to the side, and one of the soldiers steps forward to help keep her still.

"Don't touch her," I call out with all the strength I can muster. "Don't fucking touch her!"

Azerius glares at me. With a wave of his hand, my voice is gone.

I try to scream, but no sound comes out.

What the fuck?

"That's better," he comments in a bored tone. "You didn't mention the human was obnoxious, too, Molokai."

"Apologies, Commander."

"Mortals," Azerius mutters. "Obnoxious lot, all of them."

Rage bubbles inside of me. Wait until this mortal can move and disintegrate you with his poisoned blood. At least then something good will come out of this dreadful situation.

"They are, indeed, quite bothersome," the man in the red uniform agrees.

"Detail your findings, soldier," Azerius says.

"Permission to show you?" Molokai asks.

"Permission granted." Azerius nods and steps back.

Molokai leaves Minnie in the care of the two other soldiers and he makes his way toward me. He takes out his knife, but instead of cutting my arm as he'd done before, he brings the blade to my chest, cutting a straight line from my sternum to my abdomen.

Fuck. That hurts. And I can't even make a sound.

Black blood oozes to the surface, dripping down my chest.

Molokai is careful not to touch it as he swipes some of it and repeats the experiment with his blood, showing Azerius how mine destroys his.

Azerius watches intently, his expression inscrutable.

"And you say this happened to the demons as well?" he asks.

"That's what my sister said."

"I see," Azerius replies.

The soldier in blue shares a look with their commander, and it appears that an unspoken conversation passes between the two.

"You will honor our deal, Commander?" Molokai asks.

Azerius turns to him.

"Minerva An'yan committed a grave sin, soldier. She'll be tried accordingly."

"But you will not execute her, right?" Molokai continues, doing his best to temper his hopeful tone.

Azerius narrows his eyes.

"What do you think this is, soldier?" he asks as he points toward me.

"A poison. I have never seen its kind before," Molokai replies.

"A poison?" Azerius raises a brow. Then he smirks. "This is no poison. It is the result of a crime against nature."

Molokai frowns. "What do you mean?"

"He is not sick. He is an abomination," Azerius continues. "Something that should have never existed, yet still walks this earth."

"I don't understand."

"What are you talking about, Ze?" the soldier in the blue uniform asks.

"You know fully well what this is, Cerenios. You have seen it before, though not in a mortal."

The soldier named Cerenios freezes.

"You don't mean..."

"That's exactly what I mean."

"What the hell is this? What's happening to Marlowe?" Minnie asks, her alarmed gaze flittering from Cerenios to Azerius.

"I didn't give you leave to speak, female," Azerius thunders, purple tendrils of energy floating around his body.

"I apologize for my sister, Commander. She's a foolish female," Molokai intervenes.

"Foolish, indeed." Azerius lets out a dry laugh. "Because this is all her fault."

Everyone frowns.

"What do you mean?" Molokai inquires in a measured tone.

Azerius pivots. Hands behind his back, he strides casually to Minnie's side.

He gazes down at her with disdain, his nostrils flaring.

"There's a reason why no one outside of the House of Moirai

can intervene in a mortal's fate, Minerva. And this"—he nods to me—"is precisely why."

"I don't un—"

"You don't understand. Of course. Your little undeveloped brain could not understand the enormity of what you have caused."

"Ze, tone it down," Cerenios mutters.

Azerius's gaze snaps to Cerenios.

He shuts up and straightens his back.

"Cerenios, explain to this ignorant lot how Minerva's actions have caused this."

Cerenios clears his throat, anxious to be put on the spot. But out of everyone, he seems to have the closest relationship with Azerius since he even calls him by a nickname.

"When Minerva broke into the House of Moirai and tampered with the threads of fate, she created a rippling effect. That effect was further amplified when she interfered with the designated reincarnation times at the House of Psyche."

I meet her gaze and note the turmoil residing in her eyes.

She looks at me and mouths, "I'm sorry."

She didn't tell me that. She didn't say anything about breaking those laws.

Why would she not trust me with it?

Unless...

She knew.

From the beginning, she must have known something was wrong with me, that her actions had an effect over me. That's why she was following me, isn't it?

The pain in my chest intensifies.

How many more things did she hide from me?

"His soul reincarnated in the mortal plane at the wrong time, which caused a chain reaction that resulted in him being born the offspring of a mortal," Cerenios pauses, glancing at Azerius for approval. "And a Son of Tenebreis."

"No, that's impossible," Minnie mutters in shock.

"Is it?" Azerius chuckles. "You're the one who created this monster, Minerva. He is an abomination who by all accounts should have never existed. But because you interfered with fate, here he is. A hybrid."

No. This cannot be right. I know who my mother and my father are. And though my father was a piece of shit, and downright demonic at times, he was not a demon. I'm certain of it.

"But the Sons of Tenebreis are trapped in Tartareia," Minnie whispers.

"Most of them, yes. But there are those that were not in Tartareia when the realm was sealed. They still roam free," Azerius continues. Looking at me, he adds, "According to the laws of nature, a Son of Tenebreis should never be able to successfully mate with a mortal and produce offspring. Not only has it never happened before, but it is forbidden."

"He's not evil. Please. Just... Let him go, please," Minnie pleads with him.

I try to speak once more to tell her that she needs to be safe, not me, but my voice is still muted.

"He might not be evil. Frankly, I don't give a damn about him. But because such a hybrid is an abomination, we are now faced with a rather peculiar situation. His blood is, indeed, poisonous. It can kill a god, just as it can kill a demon," Azerius says, staring at me with an odd glint in his eyes.

He takes a step forward, but Molokai blocks his path.

"Our agreement, Commander?" he asks through gritted teeth.

Azerius gives him a bored look.

"I didn't agree to anything, soldier. Your sister is guilty. She'll be executed. This mortal is guilty for merely existing, so he, too, shall be executed."

He draws his sword and he continues toward me.

Molokai grabs the handle of the sword.

"You agreed," he says roughly.

Azerius stares him down.

"Stand down, soldier," he commands.

"Not until you give me your word that my sister will be spared."

"Your sister is the reason why we find ourselves in this situation in the first place. If I am to kill this mortal, then she too deserves death. It is only right."

"I don't care," Molokai grits out. "I only care about my sister. You must spare her. Please."

Azerius takes a moment to consider the request.

"No," he answers, and right as Molokai gets ready to strike, a purple mist sends him flying in the distance.

"Kai!" Minnie cries out.

"You should advise that brother of yours to behave, Minerva. Otherwise, I'll end up one general short, and I would not like that. It is bothersome to sort through applications to find a replacement."

This guy...

Azerius redirects his attention to me. His white sword gleams in the sunlight as he wields it in front of me.

I meet his gaze and see nothing in it. There's no emotion, nothing.

Only emptiness.

"Please don't. I'll do anything," Minnie begs and cries.

"There's nothing you can do, female. You have both broken the law. You're both going to die."

He raises his sword and aims it toward my neck.

My eyes widen in shock that this is how everything is going to end. After everything we've been through together, this cannot be the end.

She might have lied to me, and she might have hidden a lot of things. But she's still mine. My Minnie. And I can't let her go without a fight. I can't die and let her meet the same fate.

No. I refuse to do so.

Mustering all the strength I'm able to, I fill my lungs with air and shout as loud as I can.

"M-Minnie!"

The sound of my voice takes on a life of its own as it pushes the sword away.

A brief look of surprise crosses Azerius's face.

Something uncoils inside of me, something dark and vicious. A taste for blood unlike I've ever felt before.

My limbs are still weak, but through sheer willpower, I force them to move.

I get on my hands and knees and crawl toward her.

Tears roll down her cheeks as she looks at me. She's struggling against the hold of the two soldiers—the next ones to die at my hands. She says something, but I cannot make it out.

I only know that I need to reach her. I need to tell her how much I love her—that nothing in the entire universe could change my feelings for her.

Protect!

The instinct to protect her and keep her safe roars to life inside of me, spurring me further even when I think I cannot take another step.

Ah, the pitiful image I must strike like this, on my knees, moving like a snail. But with every step, the invisible chains around my body rattle.

"Minnie," I croak. "I'll...save...you."

I'm almost there.

I extend my arm, grabbing a fistful of her dress as I force myself to stand on my knees.

"You're mine," I whisper. "I won't let you...go."

"Marlowe." Her cries of pain are more potent than the poison currently running through my bloodstream. Yet it's because of that poison that I know what to do.

I look up at her, hoping my eyes can convey my thoughts.

She looks at me, teary and inconsolable as she fights to get her arms free.

But as our eyes connect, she knows.

I know she knows.

The ground is damp. Wet.

Her eyes turn a light blue as the dampness forms to ice, and with it, the small blades of grass turn into sharp blades—sharp enough to break the skin.

With shaky fingers, I rip one of them and dig it in my arm, letting the blood flow.

If my blood kills, then let it kill them.

Let it...

My mouth drops open. A soundless moan escapes me as I feel more liquid trickle down my chest. I dare to gaze down, only to see a large hole in my chest and a fist protruding from the other side.

I gasp for air.

"Nooooo!" Minnie's cry envelops the entire marsh.

In my last few moments of awareness, I'm sure of two things.

My blood kills, but it didn't kill him. It bathed his skin, but it didn't burn it; it didn't dissolve it.

Then there's Minnie's wail that touches my bleeding heart, making it bleed even more.

The ground shakes.

I sway from side to side, but I'm still conscious enough to see her eyes turn to white.

"Noooooo!" she screams, and the power of this scream sends me flying.

FORTY-ONE

I OPEN MY EYES.

There's water all around me, floating through me.

There's still a hole in my chest, but it's slowly mending.

All around, I'm surrounded by water.

Miles and miles of water. And I'm floating in the middle of it.

There's no one around. Only me and some fish swimming around my body—probably hoping to get a bite. Too bad they'll likely get indigestion. Hell, I'm hoping they'll get indigestion. I hope everyone fucking dies. Starting with that fucking Azerius and his soldiers, and then Minnie's traitor of a brother. He deserves a slow, painful death for betraying her like that.

But as that thought arises, I frown.

I look right and left.

Where the hell am I?

The other question being, am I still on Earth?

The sky is a beautiful navy blue and filled with stars, a contrast to the wretchedness I feel inside. In the distance, I can make out the sound of seagulls and the horn blasts of a ship.

I don't know how I ended up here, in the middle of a goddamn sea, but she saved me. Somehow, Minnie saved me.

But that means she's still there, with them; captured.

Soon, she's going to be executed.

The hell she is!

If I have to destroy the entirety of Aperion, I'll do it—especially since I now know I possess the weapon to do so.

A sense of urgency blooms inside of me, and my skin starts healing with increased rapidity.

I must find a way to get back to her. Fast.

I bring my hand to my face, wiping the saltiness of the water from my eyes. But that's when I note the strangest thing of all.

The rune is gone.

The dark spots are gone.

What...?

I don't get to dwell on my new condition or to make a plan to get to Minnie because I hear a loud, piercing call.

"Intruder!" Followed by, "Capture!"

Well, shit.

TO BE CONTINUED

BONUS CONTENT

ALSO BY VERONICA LANCET

Standalones

Fairydale

Frivolous

Morally Corrupt

Morally Ambiguous Duet

The Cute Psycho

His Hell Girl

War of Sins Series

The Taste of Revenge

The Foiled Plan

The Counterfeit Lover

The Sins of Noelle

The Moral Dilemma